WARRIOR DRAGON

DRAGON RISING SERIES, BOOK 5

TRUDI JAYE

WWW.TRUDIJAYEWRITES.COM

Hi! My name is Trudi Jaye, and I've got a secret.

A secret society, that is.

Especially designed for people like you who love reading my books, the Trudi Jaye Secret Society is a place filled with magic and laughter, and most of all... free stories.

Everyone who joins the society is given access to an ancient tome full of the stories, novellas, bonus epilogues, and deleted scenes from all the different Trudi Jaye series.

Called **The Shadow Archives,** you can access it by heading to my website and joining the secret society...

Join my Secret Society today... if you dare!

www.trudijayewrites.com/shadow-archives

Warrior Dragon (Dragon Rising Series, book 5)

Published 28 May 2024 by Star Media Ltd

Copyright © 2024 by Star Media

Cover design: PCTC Design

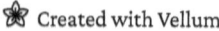 Created with Vellum

For my Dad, who believed in me.

PROLOGUE

It's been a long time since they dumped me in this small, padded room.

I don't know how long.

Days maybe.

Weeks.

It could be years, I don't even know. My brain feels fuzzy, and time seems to have no meaning in this blank white space. I don't know how long I spent swimming in a sea of agony from using the spell web after they kidnapped me. I don't know how long it's been since I first arrived here. All I know is that it's been long enough for the director and his minions to get me away from my family and friends without a fight. For them to hide me away inside this blank cell where I'm being kept like an animal, weak and totally at their mercy.

I've been served more meals than I can count, but there's no regularity between them. Sometimes they seem to forget I'm here and don't bring food until my stomach is crawling with hunger. I don't even know if it's some kind of torture technique, or if they genuinely just forget. The small toilet in the far corner of the room makes everything smell bad, and I have to lie turned away from it to sleep.

The only reason I'm still alive is that the director wants the spell web, and he'll do anything to get it. At least I know they don't have another spell web yet, otherwise I'd be dead.

I curl up on the metal bed, the hard mattress scratching at my skin. I bring my knees up to my chest, and wrap my one good arm around my knees. The arm that was broken lies next to me, pain radiating out in prickling waves, but I don't care. It seems the least of my problems right now.

I don't know how much longer I can take this.

The room is holding my powers in check, muffling the spell web, making my dragon abilities disappear. It's like one of the Earthbound boxes, except all around me. They've somehow managed to take the original technology and expand on it. I haven't felt this weak in years—if ever.

It's affecting my senses. There's fluffy cotton inside my head instead of brains. I don't know how they're doing this to me, but I really wish they'd stop. My whole body feels like it's been used as a punching bag at a boxing gym. This is everything I thought they might do to me, but amped up by ten.

Even worse, I don't know if the others managed to defeat the demons. Are they all alive? My father. Hazel. Blade. Carrick. My stomach gives a tiny somersault. And where's Seth? Is he okay? What about his stupid wife? Did she get brutally torn apart by the demons? Is it wrong that part of me hopes she did? *Has he forgotten me already?*

I shake my head, pissed off at the maudlin thoughts. I just have to assume they're all fine, and they're trying to find me. The other option is... not acceptable. I refuse to let

Director Holden and his minions get to me. I'm going to survive this.

The lock in the door on the other side of the room clicks. The big metal doors slowly open, and two men walk in.

The first one is Connor McKenzie. He's just as attractive as Hazel had described to me, all blond hair and striking blue eyes. But his good looks are somehow chilling. I can tell instinctively that they're just a mask, and underneath, he's anything but beautiful. He's been visiting me regularly to both gloat, and then in the same breath cajole me to turn the spell web over to him. Hazel always told me he wasn't entirely stable, but since being here, I've realized exactly what she meant.

The second man steps out from behind Connor, and everything inside me freezes. His pitiless dark eyes pierce mine. The Man in Black stands beside Connor, a smirk on his face as he stares down at me.

This is my worst nightmare.

I don't know how I'm going to survive.

CHAPTER
ONE

I wake slowly, my brain still hazy. I keep my eyelids closed against the outside world. Pain envelops me.

Needles of agony suddenly spike their way up my body and I scrunch my eyes shut even tighter, concentrating on breathing in and out, long and slow, just like Si taught me. It eases my panic, and some of the pain, but it doesn't magically give me back my dragon strength.

Even before I became a dragon, I never felt this weak.

This useless.

They only partially knocked me out when they moved me, and I had the vague impression—as I drifted in and out of consciousness—of being lifted, pushed in a gurney and travelling by either plane or train. Even at one point Lakas' face peering down at me like I was an insect in a microscope. Nothing concrete, nothing specific. But I know I've been moved to a new facility, to a new cell, and I have a new jailer. I'm now in the hands of the one man who hates me more than Director Holden.

Lakas.

The Man in Black.

Killer. Monster. *Dragon-hater.*

Director Holden told me once that he blames me for his daughter Liling's death, and that's why he dislikes me so much. I've never been sure if he realizes it was actually Lakas's bullet that killed his adopted daughter—surely he knows?—but he doesn't hate Lakas like he does me.

I've never mentioned it because, honestly, I agree with him. It *was* my fault. The bullet that killed Liling was meant for me, and while it was the Man in Black who pulled the trigger, she leaped in front of the bullet for *me.* To save me.

It's definitely my fault she's dead.

Thus the logic of Director's Holden's motives makes sense to me, because they're my thoughts too.

But Lakas, the Man in Black, he hates me for an entirely different reason. He hates my *species.* He hates all dragons, and hates me most of all because I've somehow come to represent dragon kind to him.

To be clear, I've never personally done anything to him.

He, on the other hand, killed my friend Liling, was part of the attack on the rebel outpost that killed more than a hundred of my friends and colleagues, attacked and almost killed Seth, and kidnapped Hazel and tortured her. If anyone should be hating anyone, it's *me* that should hate *him.*

And don't get me wrong. *I do hate him.*

He's fucked up, twisted and brutal. He thinks he's on some kind of God-given mission to save the planet from the evil dragons.

Except his methods make him worse than anything the original dragons could ever have done.

So as I lie here, broken and scared, I know a couple of things for sure. I know I don't want to die here at the hands of the Man in Black, and I don't want Director Holden to end up with the power of the spell web as his to use however he likes.

I'm going to do everything in my power to get myself out of this situation.

I just don't know how the fuck I'm going to do that yet.

I'm lying on a hard, cold surface, my eyes still closed, my attention focused on holding myself motionless, breathing, and ignoring the gradually decreasing pain.

There's a rumbling vibration underneath me that's strangely soothing, and the smell of cleaning products, which makes my nose twitch unpleasantly. I'm fairly certain there's no one else in the room with me, but knowing the director, he's probably got some kind of camera trained on me, waiting for me to wake.

There's something hard around my wrists, holding me in place, like an animal chained to a fence. I try to move my feet, but they're tied together as well. My arm is mostly healed, but I don't know who did it or how. It makes me aware that I've been unconscious for a significant amount of time. The powerlessness of it sends a shiver along my skin, and I try not to think too much about what else they could have been doing to me while I was unconscious.

I try to use my dragon senses to see if there's any kind of a heat signature near me, but I can't access anything. It's like there's another of the Earthbound's magical boxes—the ones that keep dragons from being able to access their powers—somewhere nearby. Except it's not just that there's a box next to me... it feels like I'm still *inside* an Earthbound box.

I know I'm not in the same place I started out. This Earthbound machine is next level compared to the one holding me in check at the previous facility. It feels all-encompassing, holding tighter to my powers, binding me in a way that's inflexible and rigid.

Now that I've noticed it, I realize the buzzing of the box is coming from everywhere. I hold still, trying to see if there are any gaps inside the bubble of sensation, but I'm totally surrounded. Its discordant vibration is setting my nerves on edge, and I shudder.

How am I supposed to escape if they've got me locked in some kind of giant dragon-proof box?

Eventually, curiosity gets the better of me and I open one eye. I peer around the room. It's long and narrow, with a bed on one side that I'm lying on, and a small open area next to it. On the other side of the room, there's a bench with a small sink, and cupboards. Everything is made from stainless steel and shined up so brightly it hurts my eyes. There's nothing else in the room aside from me. No chairs, tables, cups, random pens. Not a window or even carpet. Everything is basic, metal, and very, very clean.

Where the hell am I? What day is it? Is everyone okay? Did they make it out of the battle with the demons? Is that why no one has come to help me?

Is it because they're all dead?

I close my eyes against the questions. I can't think like that. I have to assume they're all safe.

That Seth's powers as a phoenix made him invincible against the demons.

That my father's wily smarts and his newfound ability to shift into his chameleon shape kept him safe.

That Carrick's strength was enough to destroy the demons that came at him.

I have to believe that they're looking for me right now, even as I lie here. Maybe they'll burst in at any moment and set me free. I can almost see Seth's face—with a mixture of strength of purpose and anger for whoever did this—as he stands over me, untying my bonds, helping me to stand and stumble out of this place. I turn my face to the door, waiting for him to arrive.

Nothing happens.

I let out a strangled sob. I lift my hand to my mouth, to cover my weakness. Except my wrists are cuffed to the side of the bed, and all I can do is pull against the hard metal and make a rattling sound that does nothing except grate on my already frayed nerves. If I was full strength, the cuffs wouldn't hold me. If I could turn into my dragon form, *none* of this would hold me.

But I can't do anything.

Inside I'm angry. Burning with fiery dragon rage. I'm powerful and strong. Things like this don't happen to me. I'm the protector, the one who rescues others.

But I'm not that person right now. I'm a lifeless shell of my former self. I don't understand how they're keeping me this weak and still allowing the spell web to cover everyone. I can feel it inside me, pulsing and pumping alongside the blood in my veins. But I can't see the grid, and I can't access its power. Nothing is sharp and defined and *extra* like it was when I was properly bound to it, even when it was killing me slowly—and sometimes not so slowly.

It's still killing me, and I feel the pain as it sizzles along my veins. But I can't connect to it, there's nothing I can do. This disconnected feeling scares me.

It's like I'm trapped behind a glass wall. I can see it, but I can't touch anything.

Can't do anything. Can't be anything.

Can't *help* anything—or any*one*, including myself.

Except I must be in control somehow, or they wouldn't

need me here. I must be blocking their ability to create a new spell web, or they'd have killed me already.

That much I know for sure.

The only problem with this is that my thoughts keep slipping in and out of my head, too silky to catch. I can't plan. I can't figure out what to do. Whatever they're giving me is affecting my ability to do anything.

So I lie here.

Waiting.

Waiting for someone to save me.

Waiting for my brain to click into gear.

Waiting for an escape plan to fall into place.

Waiting.

CHAPTER
TWO

Hours—or maybe days or weeks—later, the lock on the door on the other side of the room clicks.

The big metal door opens slowly, and two men walk in. I hold my breath.

Is it Lakas?

The first one is Connor McKenzie. He's dressed in an expensive suit and a smirk.

The second man is Director Holden, his suit all shiny and neat as a pin—another man who looks one way on the surface, and has a darker soul underneath. His expression is gleeful, his eyes bright with the victory of finally having me here under his control. He tried to capture us when we visited him at the SIG headquarters, but we had Hazel on our side. It must have hurt to have us escape when we were on his home turf.

I let out my breath.

I'm at Director Holden's mercy with no one to help me. I know he hates me, and can't wait to punish me for all my supposed crimes.

This isn't going to end well. But at least it's not Lakas.

This is what it feels like to have no powers, and no way of defending myself.

I don't like it.

"Mei, so lovely of you to join us here," says the director, barely managing to hold in his excitement.

"Fuck off," I say, unable to act the part of scared prisoner, even if that's what I am.

"Now, now. I wouldn't be too aggressive. If you ask nicely, I might tell Lakas to spare you the worst of what's coming." Director Holden's voice is silky-smooth, his eyes glittering. I know he's not planning to spare me anything.

Just keep your wits about you and look for the right opportunity. It'll come to you, if you're patient.

As always, Jeff's advice pops into my head at just the right time. I spent so many years being taught to survive by Jeff and Si that I know what their advice would be without asking.

I take a breath to calm myself down. I just need to stay focused and outsmart the director. He thinks he's won already, which means he'll do something sloppy and stupid. I just need to bide my time.

"Nothing more to say? No rude words or gestures?" Director Holden moves closer, and peers down at me. "You don't look so dangerous," he murmurs. "I always thought you looked kind of scrawny."

I manage to resist the urge to spit in his face—except I think there might be fire in my eyes, because the director moves back quickly like he's been stung. "Inject her, see if your serum works," he says sharply to Connor.

Connor moves forward, and I watch him closely. Hazel told me all about his skills as a siren, how he can get human women to do anything he wants, and how he was obsessed by her. Now that they've suppressed my dragon abilities, will he be able to do the same to me?

When he pulls out a syringe with a needle that looks way too big, I struggle backwards.

"Don't move, it'll only make it hurt more," says Connor. There's something in his eyes that tells me he'd love it if I kept struggling. He likes to cause pain.

I hold myself still. "What's in the needle?"

"Something to make sure you're a little more amenable to our requests," says Director Holden.

"You haven't even asked me for anything." I push myself as far up against the edge of the back wall as I can. "Shouldn't you check to see how amenable I am, before injecting me with stuff?" The rumbling vibration of the metal wall beneath my shoulder distracts me for a moment.

Director Holden leans closer. "Mei, I want you to use the spell web to kill any of the supernatural population who won't cooperate with me. Will you do that for me?"

I frown. "That's what you want to do? Kill off a whole bunch of supers who don't agree with you?"

"Yes. Now will you help us?"

"Of course not!" I say, indignantly.

"See? And now we try the large needle." Director Holden smirks down at me.

Connor grabs my arm, shoves in the needle and presses down on the syringe. While the director had been distracting me with his idiotic requests, Connor had been sneaking closer and he caught me by surprise. I didn't even get to struggle.

Immediately, I feel a terrifying surge of magic flooding through my body, reaching and grasping at me, trying to control my senses. It's an invasion, but it also feels somehow soothing and persuasive, and I just want to give in to it. Some kind of distillation of a siren's abilities, perhaps? I give a ragged scream, then try to curl in tight, an immediate physical rejection of whatever he's shoved inside me. Except I can't move, I'm cuffed to the edge of the bed.

Instead, I manage to pull all my magic and power into my core, and lock myself down inside a fortress in my mind. They can't get to me here, can't force me to do anything I don't want to do.

"Is it working?" asks Director Holden.

"Can't tell. She seems to be resisting, but it might be a reaction to the magic."

"This better not kill her," growls the director. "We need her alive until we sort out your new spell web. Don't mess this up, McKenzie, or you'll be the one wishing you were dead. You're already on thin ice."

I listen to his words and scream, but this time it's safely locked inside my head. I'm fighting whatever magic they put inside me, and it's a desperate battle, one that I'm not entirely sure I'm going to win.

The door closes, and I open my eyes to see if they're gone. But it was just Director Holden leaving.

Connor is standing next to the bed, watching me with fascination. He has a notepad, and he's writing something down, presumably how I'm reacting to his ridiculous experiment.

Fire is burning inside my body, and while I can't stop whatever alien magic is swirling through my veins, I can protect my inner core, my dragon essence, and the spell web.

The only problem is that I don't know how long I'll be able to protect myself like this.

I open my eyes, and look at Connor. I manage a smile. "Is that all you've got?" I say.

"It's just the first attempt, Mei," says Connor, smiling back down at me. "I've got so many other things I could use on a dragon. And I'm excited to try them all. I'm *pleased* that this first one isn't working as well as Director Holden might wish it had." He glances toward the door and makes a sour face.

I can't help struggling against the metal bindings one last time, even though know it's a waste of my energy. Connor wants to test me like I'm some kind of rat in a lab.

"Nothing will work," I snarl, my vision turning red. "Nothing you do will convince me to help you."

Connor grins. "That's fantastic news, Mei. You're going to be a worthy adversary."

THREE

I t's been a while since Connor left. I think I've slept, but I'm not sure. The second lot of drugs he tried made me sleepy, and as much as I fought it, I eventually gave in. But I don't think those ones worked either. The spell web is lying dormant inside me, and my dragon is lying in wait for the moment it can burst free. I wouldn't want to be whoever my dragon catches when that happens, that's for damn sure.

The door clicks open and I glance toward it. Will it be Connor or Director Holden? I don't know which one is worse. Connor walks in first, and I let out a tiny breath. It makes me realize he's the better option. I don't know what the director is likely to do, he's too unpredictable. Too smart.

At least I know what Connor will do. He just wants to hurt me.

Except, there's someone coming in behind Connor. I catch sight of a black coat and hat, and my breath lurches to a halt in my throat.

The Man in Black.

He's finally here in person. My worst nightmare, come to life.

And if we're going by the look in his eyes as he stares down at me, he's here to kill me.

My heart rate picks up to double speed, and I automatically start struggling against the bonds holding me in place. My brain locks into automatic, and all I can think is that I need to get out of here.

Except... didn't Director Holden say that Connor had to keep me alive? Surely that applies to the Man in Black too? It might be the one thing that saves me. I try to keep my breathing even, and not let either of them see how scared I really am.

"Remember what Holden said, Lakas. You're convincing her to help us, not killing her. We need her for our plans," says Connor, like he can read my thoughts.

Lakas sneers at Connor. "I don't want to kill her. Not yet. She has to pay first."

"Pay for what?" I ask, my voice cracking. "What did I ever do to you?"

Lakas turns back to me, his eyes are burning with such hatred, I can't help the shudder that rolls along my skin. "Your kind are evil. You deserve to pay for what dragons have done to my people." His eyes are black and pitiless.

"I haven't done anything," I say, unable to help myself. The fact that the desperate words were wrenched out of me proves that I'm much closer to the brink than I realize. Connor's injections have been taking a toll. Fear and anger are my constant companions.

"Your kind are all the same," spits Lakas. "What one of you does, the others will do soon enough. If you haven't killed someone who didn't deserve it, or laid waste to someone else's home... well, you will soon enough. I'm just protecting other people from your reckless actions."

Lakas steps forward, his smile revealing yellowed teeth and fetid breath. I'm so focused on his face, I don't see his fist until it's too late. It's only my iron will that keeps me from screaming as he punches me.

THE WORLD around me is blurry. Shapes are indistinct. Colors seem faded and wrong. I don't know if it's from the drugs they keep forcing on me, or because Lakas punched me one too many times last time he was in my cell.

Either way, I feel like shit. I have bruises on my bruises. Cuts all over my body that hurt every time I move too much. Blood stuck in hard little pieces to my clothes. Sweat and dirt over my body. Burn marks that don't heal like they should.

I'm a *dragon*, for fuck's sake. How can I be *burned*? They're using some kind of magic, or maybe an Earthbound machine. I know it. My physical body is as weak as a kitten's.

All I can do is lie here and wait.

Wait for Lakas to hurt me again.

Because that's become the one certainty in my life right now. That Lakas will return, and he will hurt me. He wants me to use the spell web for their gain. He wants me to use it to scare people. To kill people. To control them. To put the SIG in total domination over all supers in the world.

But I refuse.

That's the one thing I know to be true.

I refuse.

Despite my determined thoughts, a tear leaks its way out of my eye, and I can't even lift my arm to brush it away. I want to wipe it away, to erase the evidence of my weakness. And I want to be angry about the fact that I'm crying, angry that I'm scared about what will happen to me when Lakas comes back into the room.

And he'll be back.

It's like he can't stay away. Like he has so much anger to take out on me, that he has to keep returning. I represent all the wrongs that the dragons of old did to him and his family.

I've learned that Lakas hates all dragons with an equal burning passion. And I'm the symbol of every time someone he loved was killed or maimed. And it turns out the dragons of old killed *all* of his family.

In a weird, twisted way, I get it. He's angry, he lost everyone he loved, and now there's a dragon right here for him to punish. He's been holding onto this pain for *centuries*. And now that he's got me here, he's going to enjoy the process of tearing me apart, piece by piece. Inside and out.

Except why did it have to be *me*?

A shudder wracks my body, and I moan in pain. I hurt so bad. But I refuse to give in to him, or the director. I refuse to hurt anyone else but myself. If this is where my life ends, so be it. The spell web is killing me anyway.

I won't use it to hurt anyone else.

The door opens. A rush of cold air hits me, and I gasp for breath. Lakas swoops into the room like a dark monster from my dreams. For all my big thoughts, I'm suddenly filled with a gasping kind of fear that I can't control. He's dressed in black, the same as the day he killed Liling, same as every day. The thought makes me wish I was stronger. That I could make him pay for killing my friend.

But I'm not strong enough.

I can't think enough.

All I can do is lie here and take what comes, and not give in.

Lakas doesn't mind either way. That's the other thing I've learned.

He *wants* me to resist, so he can get his retribution. So it all lasts longer.

"Another delightful day, is it not, Mei?" he says with a smile, as if we're meeting at a cafe instead of this horrifying metal box.

I just stare at him, determined not to give him what he wants. No fear. No expression. I wish to hell and back that I didn't have a tear track running down the side of my face.

"Nothing to say?" He shrugs. "Then let us begin."

I close my eyes, and curl up inside my mind. I refuse to let him get to me. I focus on the humming vibrations that are a constant underneath me, and the metallic smell of everything around me. Even the stench of my own blood and stale sweat that clings to me. Everything to ignore Lakas and whatever else he might do to me.

Which is why when he roughly injects something into my thigh, making it feel like I've just been stabbed, I jerk back in surprise. My eyes open wide and I glare up into his hawk-like face. Shudders wrack my body, and I hold in a scream—just.

"That got your attention, didn't it? Connor's been working on another serum. He asked me to give it to you, see if it works." Lakas peers down at me like I'm a bug he wants to crush. "I'm not entirely sure what it's going to do to you."

I feel the serum filling my veins, but it doesn't feel harmful like some of the other things they've given me. This one feels... relaxing. It makes me feel like I'm floating, the wind blowing through my hair. It actually feels kind of good.

Part of my brain is flashing a warning that this is a trap, but most of me is too far gone to worry. I lean back and close my eyes. My muscles ease back and I melt into the hard foam mattress beneath me. I don't like being relaxed around Lakas, but I can't seem to keep my defenses up. If this is the purpose of Connor's latest serum, it's working. I feel like I'm hovering in the air, tethered to nothing and no-one.

I can't decide if it's a scary feeling or if it's good.

At least it's not painful.

The feeling of floating is so strong, that I open my eyes just to make sure I'm still lying on the mattress. For a moment, everything is blurry, and I blink a few times, trying to get my bearings.

And then I freak out—or at least as much as I can right now.

The reason? I'm floating several feet in the air. Not only that. When I look down, I see my body right there below me, still lying on the mattress.

What the hell kind of serum has Connor invented? A floating spell? A flying spell? People would pay millions for something like that.

Except... How can I be up here, and down there at the same time?

Did Connor's serum *kill me*? Is this my soul floating away from my body? Am I *dead*?

People would *not* pay millions for that.

Below me, Lakas is frowning over my body, and he picks up my wrist, apparently worried about the same thing. He mutters to himself as he finds a pulse. I let out a relieved breath. At least I'm not dead.

Except if I'm not dead, what *the hell* is happening?

CHAPTER

FOUR

And then suddenly, it gets worse.

Without permission, my translucent floating body starts moving away from my physical one.

I try to force it back, worried I might somehow become permanently separated, but I have no control over where it goes. It's like an echo of my usual form, a little fuzzy around the edges, and it's definitely not interested in listening to me, or doing what I want it to. I float up into the air, up to the top of the room, and then, when I'm half expecting to hit the ceiling and stop, I somehow melt *through* the roof, like I'm made of mist.

And then I'm outside, in a murky otherworld so dim I have to squint to see anything. Wind is rushing through my body, and for a moment I'm confused... until I realize it's because I'm on top of a speeding eighteen wheeler *truck*, my floating body somehow keeping pace with the enormous vehicle's movement. The wind is just rushing air. Instinct makes me grab on to the top edge of the truck with one hand, and something about my panic makes my transparent hand actually do what I tell it.

I look around, head and heart pounding, eyes wide. It's a few moments before I can even think a coherent sentence. And then I'm stunned. *I can move outside of my physical body. I'm free of the inside of that room.* It all seems like a dream. How can this be real?

Except I know it is. And I've solved the mystery of where I am.

I'm inside a moving truck. That's how they've been keeping me hidden.

Suddenly it makes complete sense why no one has found me yet. A tiny section of my brain is impressed at the organization this would have taken. And then I remember everything else they've been doing to me, and I vow I'm going to take them down if it's the last thing I do. I glance at the misty, blurred body that I'm currently inhabiting. It probably *will* be the last thing I do. Being separated from my physical body doesn't seem like an auspicious start to the day.

I look behind me. The big shipping container that hides my cell is locked onto the bed of a big black truck. There are large box-like chambers at each end which are crackling with energy along a force field over the outside of the container. That's definitely what's been holding my magic at bay. My dragon fire burns inside me, wanting to get out. But my magic doesn't seem to work in this ethereal form. It's back inside the truck with my physical body.

Everything looks like a shadow of what it would look like in the real world. Where am I? What has Connor managed to do? Am I dying?

I don't *feel* like I'm dying, but you never know.

"You're not dying." A delicious voice I can only describe as melted gold speaks inside my head.

I almost let go of the hold I have on the truck, and look

frantically around, trying to find where the voice came from. I don't see anyone.

"Who's there? What do you want?" Is this how they're going to do it? They're going to drive me crazy and take the spell web from me while I'm distracted?

"You're not going crazy. You're a dragon. You can leave your body and travel in the shadow realm." Again the voice is inside my head, with no visible person for me to latch onto. It's soothing and sweet, and I struggle to fight against the desire to just believe everything the voice is telling me. It could be another trick.

"The what?" I scrunch up my face, trying not to freak out too much.

"The shadow realm. A hidden plane of existence behind our physical world."

Shaking my head, I'm still trying to make sense of what she's telling me. "I hear the words you're saying, but they don't make sense."

"I haven't seen another dragon in here since... well, for a very long time."

It feels like the voice is speaking directly into my head, but I'm still searching around, trying to find the source of the words. "Why can't I see you? How are you speaking to me?"

"I no longer use a body in the shadow realm. It just gets in the way."

"In the way of what?"

"Traveling."

"Who are you?"

"My name is Aurelia." The name rolls off her tongue like silk over my skin.

"What kind of creature are you?"

"I am a dragon," the voice says patiently.

25

I take a deep breath and realize she'd already told me that she was a dragon. I just wasn't paying attention, I was too busy freaking out. "Is it only dragons who can travel in the shadow realm?"

"Mostly. It takes practice and patience to get here."

"Or drugs," I say caustically.

"Is that how you found the shadow realm? Drugs?"

"My kidnappers gave them to me. I didn't even know this place existed." I glare around me, wondering how they'll be able to use me being in the shadow realm to their benefit.

"Much dragon knowledge was lost in the Great Purge," says Aurelia, her voice sad.

Her words snatch my attention back to her. "You're from before the Earthbound...?"

There's silence for a long moment, before Aurelia answers: *"Yes. I have been trapped for a very long time."*

I shiver. Or at least my transparent non-body shivers. "Where are you?"

"I'm encased in lava inside a volcano, not far from here. I can't go too far from my physical body these days."

"And you're traveling in the... shadow realm? To get here with me?"

"I have nothing else to do with my time. Ever since I woke from my hibernation I have been alone."

Her voice is soft, the sadness leaking into every syllable.

"How long have you been alone?"

"I don't know, exactly. I went into hibernation, meaning to only sleep for a few months, then woke when the mountain erupted and lava began to flow. I tried to escape, but it was too late. I've been here ever since. I managed to hibernate again for a while, but I woke when the humans started making too much noise."

26

"Too much noise?"

"Don't you find that humans are noisy creatures?"

I think about it for a moment. "I guess they are." I look around at the landscape flashing past me. I'm in a city, a muted dark version of a city, with cars and trucks flashing past us, high rise buildings scraping at the sky. "Can you help me? Send someone to come find me? I've been kidnapped."

The voice sighs. *"I wish I could help. But you're the first person I've seen inside the shadow realm for many years. And those on the other side of the shadows don't tend to see or hear us."*

"They can't hear us at all?" I think of Seth and my father. "I'm sure I know some people who'd be able to hear me," I say confidently, despite a flutter of despair in my chest.

Aurelia makes a sad sound. *"I wish that were true. Then perhaps you could come rescue me, once you'd told your friends to rescue you."*

"Then what do you suggest I do?" I snap.

"Rescue yourself," she says simply. *"You have more chance of getting out of your predicament than I do of getting out of mine."*

"If I can't talk to anyone, can't touch anything, and can't control where I go, how on earth am I going to rescue myself?"

"Well, I can teach you to control where you go. And sometimes, in the beginning, I used to be able to touch things, so I can try to teach you that as well."

"But I still won't be able to talk to anyone?"

"I'm sorry."

"How do I—" Suddenly, before I can even finish my sentence, a swirling wind builds up around me and I'm

27

being dragged back inside the truck, back down into my body. It hurts like a motherfucker and I can't hold in this scream.

Agony burns over my whole body, all through my internal organs. It even feels like the blood in my veins is throbbing. I'm stiff as a board and my body is shaking involuntarily. I don't know how to make it stop. Am I having some kind of fit? It feels like someone has zapped me with electricity, and then beaten my body with a baseball bat.

Maybe a baseball bat that's been electrified?

I can barely think over the pain ricocheting through my body, and all I can do is breathe through it, trying to survive.

Eventually, it subsides. The shaking stops and my body softens. I open my eyes, trying to figure out if this is because of something Lakas has been doing to me. But Lakas has left the room, and there don't seem to be any gaping holes in my stomach or other injection needle sites on my visible skin. No doubt it was boring messing with someone who was completely unconscious.

The pain I just experienced must be a hazard of leaving the shadow realm and returning to my physical body. How does Aurelia handle it? She must be really bored if she's willing to put up with feeling like that every time she leaves her physical body.

Or maybe just desperate after being locked inside lava for hundreds of years.

I shudder, trying to imagine what it must be like to be stuck like that, unable to move for hundreds of years. I've been here for days, maybe a week or two and I'm about to crack. Locked in place with no way out, and no one to come save you; it must be hell. No wonder she's willing to put up with the agony, if that's what's happened to her.

But for me, I'm not that desperate. I'm still hopeful I can find a way out of this room. For a start, I now know I'm on a truck. Surely that information will help me? I could try to find a way out the door, and overcome the driver. Or maybe someone will figure it out and rescue me?

No need to put myself through the excruciating pain of returning to my body if I still have other options.

I lean back on the hard metal bed, and close my eyes, trying to breathe through the last of the pain, hounded by the secret fear that maybe I really am that desperate.

CHAPTER
FIVE

My body aches for a long time after I return to it, but I eventually manage to fall asleep. My dreams are strange swirling patterns in gold and silver. A dragon's eye is staring at me, and then a mountain explodes with lava. The boom of the lava exploding into the air jerks me awake—except I'm not in my physical body, I'm back up above the truck, floating in my see-through shadow form.

"You're back," says Aurelia's disembodied voice.

"You're still here." I grab a hold of the top of the truck, to keep from falling off the side.

"I thought I'd follow your truck, see where you were going."

"And?"

"They don't seem to be going anywhere. They're driving around in circles."

I look around, trying to spot some kind of landmark I recognize, but it's all unfamiliar. The shadows make it harder to see anything clearly. "Where are we?"

"I don't know the name of the city. In my time, such places did not exist."

"Is this area your home? Where you grew up?"

"Yes. It was a beautiful place when I was a dragonet." Her tone implies it is not beautiful now.

"How long can you stay in the shadow realm?" I ask, trying to figure out why I was pulled back, and why I'm here again.

"I can stay here all day. But that has taken me a long time."

"Why did it pull me back into my body? Was it the drugs wearing off?"

"I do not know about the drugs. But when you first start traveling in the shadow realm, your physical body tries to pull your shadow body back to it. It does not like being separated from its soul."

"My soul?" I don't like the sound of that either.

"It is eminently practical, your physical body. If something happens to you in the shadow realm, your body will die as well."

"I could die in here?" I squeak out the words in surprise, glancing around me as the scenery flashes by. My fingers tighten on the edge of the truck.

"Not in the same way you can die in the real world."

"Then how? How could I die in here?"

There's a sigh, and then a swishing noise. Suddenly a shadow appears beside me on the top of the truck. *"You can die if you stay too long away from your physical body. If you get too far away from it. If you accidentally merge with a shadow that's much larger than you. That kind of thing. No bullets or knives will kill you here."*

The shadow looks small and indistinct, like she can't quite remember how she looks any more. I can make out long hair, and that she's short, like me. She's in her human form, not in dragon form, which I find curious, because I'm pretty sure dragons can only hibernate in dragon form.

"How come you're in your human form?"

"I can choose between my shapes. I like to fly as a dragon. But if I'm to be stuck on top of a truck next to you, I choose to be in my smaller form."

Makes sense. I nod.

"What is your name, baby dragon?"

"Mei Walker."

"And why have they kidnapped you?"

"They want my power. I have the spell web inside me, and they want to control it."

Aurelia hisses like I said I was a baby killer, then disappears from beside me.

Too late, I remember how much the other older dragons hate the spell web. It's the reason the Earthbound were able to slaughter so many of them three hundred years ago. "Wait! Don't go. It's not like that."

"What it is like, Mei Walker? Are you planning to kill off the dragons a second time?"

"No, no! Of course not. I took over the spell web from some bad people. There was a time when I thought maybe we'd be better off without it... But I learned that the humans leave us alone if they forget about us. The spell web isn't so bad." I hesitate. "Well, except for the fact that it's killing me."

Aurelia comes closer again, the shadows shifting cautiously around her face. *"It's killing you? And still you keep it?"*

"I don't know how to get rid of it," I admit.

"You are a strange dragon, Mei Walker."

"So they tell me," I mutter.

"What is your plan to escape?"

I look around, trying to use the flashing landscape as inspiration. At least I know what kind of a room I'm in. "I don't know. But I need to do something soon. I don't think my friends will find me if I'm moving around like this."

"Perhaps I can teach you a few things to help?"

I glance at the strange blurred face beside me. "That would be great, Aurelia." I'm not sure if she can teach me anything useful, but any information has to help right now.

"First thing is to build up how much time you can spend here, and to control when you leave and when you go back."

I shake my head. "I fell asleep and just found myself back here."

"It is possible to control it. And it doesn't hurt as much going back in, if you're the one in control of the process, not your physical body."

"Yes, please, teach—" Suddenly the same swirling wind as yesterday starts to suck me back into my body. "No!" I yell, trying to hold onto the shadow realm.

"Don't fight it, it just makes it worse," says Aurelia. *"I'll see you again soon."*

And then I'm being sucked back into my physical body inside the truck, the pain as my soul clicks back into my body making me scream. The agonizing electrical currents run through me, and I'm shaking and shuddering just like I did last time.

Except this time, I know it's possible for it not to hurt like that, and I'm determined to get back to the shadow realm. I need to find a way to escape; the shadow realm and my new dragon friend seem to be the best possible way right now.

I take deep breaths, trying to ignore the pain pulsing through my nerve endings. It's not easy to relax through the throbbing spasms but at least now I know next time I go to the shadow realm, maybe it will be.

CHAPTER
SIX

"*All you have to do is concentrate, Mei.*" The frustration is clear in Aurelia's voice.

"It's not that easy! You've been doing this for a long time. How long did it take you to learn the basics?" I've been trying for the past hour or so to concentrate, but nothing is working. Not the way Aurelia seems to think it should.

"*We were taught to wander the shadow realm when we were children. It was a basic dragon skill in my clan.*"

"Well, maybe not everyone can do it," I mutter. "Because this doesn't feel like a basic skill."

"*You made it into the shadow realm, that's the hard part. Now all you need is to concentrate a little harder, and you'll be able to move wherever you want to go.*"

"I don't think it's that easy."

"*Something is blocking you then. You're maybe even blocking yourself. Why would you be scared to do this?*"

I take a breath, even though my misty transparent body in the shadow realm doesn't need to breathe. It's apparently a habit I can't break.

Why would I be blocking the ability to move?

"Could it be the spell web?" I ask suddenly. It's still pulsing inside my body, even though I'm blocked from using its power. "I can't access it because of the machine they've got inside the truck. I'm surprised I can even do this, usually those machines block all dragon powers. My physical body is as weak as a kitten."

Aurelia murmurs and mutters to herself. The indistinct, hazy body she's taken to using for my benefit paces the top of the truck like we aren't going sixty miles an hour on the highway. I prefer to lie down and hold on, like I did the first time, even though Aurelia keeps telling me it isn't necessary.

"I don't think it's the spell web. It could be the machines I suppose, but if anything, they should have blocked your ability to get into the shadow realm, and you're here anyway. No, I think you're doing it to yourself, for some reason."

She turns and stomps in my direction, then sits down next to me, crossing her legs. She leans forward, giving me a clearer view of her strange face with no distinguishable features except golden eyes that are boring into mine. "Why are you scared to move around, to go back to the people you love?"

Anger prickles along my spine. "I'm not *scared*. I just don't want them to get hurt trying to rescue me. Lakas is a bad man. He'd love to get his hands on Seth. He'd torture him to within an inch of his life, just to see what he could do to a phoenix."

"Ah, so you're protecting them? Is that something you do often? Protect people?"

I hesitate. "I don't like people to be hurt," I mutter. "And I really hate bullies."

"I'll take that as a yes." I can hear the amusement in

Aurelia's voice. *"This isn't about getting them to rescue you. They won't be able to see you. This is about extending your skills in the shadow realm so you can rescue yourself."*

"What if I could find someone who could hear—"

"You're not stronger than me. I've been here for centuries. And I've never been able to find anyone who can hear me."

I stare out at the billboards rushing past us on the highway. I'm starting to recognize a few of the signs. The truck is driving around and around whatever city we're in. The words on the billboards are dark and indistinct, like the shadow realm doesn't want us to know exactly where we are. But I recognize the giant tomato and the smiling face of a woman from an ad I've seen before on television. At least that's something. "I still don't know what city I'm in," I say quietly.

"You're somewhere near me, and I know where I am."

"Where are you?"

"Mt Hood, Oregon."

I blink. "That's not what I thought you were going to say. That's across the other side of the country from where they kidnapped me. How did I get here?"

"I don't know the answer to that. But I do know that I can't reach beyond a certain point. I can't reach New York, and believe me, I've tried."

"Why New York?"

"That's where my family moved after I disappeared. Before... you know."

I nod. I do know. Before the Earthbound killed all the dragons.

"But my point is that you won't be putting anyone in danger by connecting to them. You won't even be able to tell them you're there. But it might help you gather useful intelligence. It might help you escape."

I nod. She's right. I need to clear my mind of the fears I have for all my friends and family. They can't help me now, even if they wanted to. I have to help myself. And it starts with this.

Taking another breath—that I still don't need—I focus on a person, just like Aurelia told me to. Seth. I picture his face, his gold-flecked hazel eyes, the scar down his cheek, his strong jawline. The determination to do the right thing that's practically etched into the lines on his face. The smile he saves just for me on his otherwise serious face.

And then suddenly I'm moving, so fast, I can't see anything around me. There's a whooshing sound, and then it stops just as fast as it began. I'm in a dark, damp cave. It takes a moment to adjust to the darkness before I see a shape near me.

Seth is lying on the ground, curled up in his human form like a cat in front of the fire. My heart leaps. He survived the confrontation with the demons. Relief surges through me, and I realize I'd been afraid of what I might discover. What if Seth had been dead?

But he's not, he's alive, lying here below me, wrapped up in a tight little ball—

But something is very wrong. Muted flames surround Seth's body, like he got partway through shifting to his phoenix form and then lost momentum. He's making a keening sound that breaks my heart. His eyepatch is crooked, and I can see part of his scarred eye. What's the matter with him? He seems lost. Like he doesn't know which way to go.

I kneel next to him, and hold out one hand, wishing I could touch him, let him know I'm here. His pain is my pain, and tears start to run down my cheeks.

"Seth, what's the matter? What's happened?" I whisper.

He looks up. His one remaining flame-filled eye stares around the room, like he's looking for something. "Mei?" he whispers.

My floating body shudders. *Can he hear me?* "I'm here Seth. I'm here with you. It's okay, it's going to be okay." The words come bursting out of me. It feels like my heart is being torn in half. He looks so broken.

He peers around the cave, eyes wide and hopeful. And then it's like his whole body sinks in on itself. "She's not here," he growls in an angry undertone. "She's gone, you idiot, and you can't find her. She's probably *dead*. It's been so long, they probably killed her already." He gives off a keening moan, scrunching his eyes shut, and rocking back and forth in a tight ball. "I should've protected her better. I shouldn't have left her. She's *everything* to me. Why did I leave her?" His tone is angry and desperate and he slams into his head with one palm. The sound of the slap echoes around the cave. "I did this to her. It's my fault she's dead."

"No, no," I say, trying to calm him down. "Seth, it's not your fault. You had to fight the demons. It was Director Holden. And Lakas and Connor."

Seth puts both hands up to his head, and is cradling it now. "It's not real. She's not here." Silent tears are flowing down his face. "I miss her so much. I should have protected her."

He can really hear me. The thought blows my mind. That's definitely not what Aurelia said I'd be able to do. "I'm okay, Seth. I'm going to escape and get back to you, I promise," I whisper. Where are the others? Why is no one looking after Seth? How could they—

It suddenly occurs to me that maybe there's no one else to look after him. That maybe he was the only one who survived the battle with the demons in Newport News. The thought sends a chill down my spine.

I need to figure out what's happening.

I take a moment to look around, to work out where Seth is. I see a familiar section of the rocky wall and recognize the cave; it's the one we rested in after the attack on the revolution headquarters by Lakas and the Earthbound. That's strange as well. Aurelia said she couldn't go far from her volcano, and here I am, hundreds of miles away from where my body is being driven around.

I feel the spell web swell inside me, like it's trying to tell me something. I might not be able to use it, or access it like I used to be able to, but I think it's giving me extra abilities here in the shadow realm. A small leap of excitement goes through my chest. What else can I do here? And how can I use it to help me escape?

"I'm alive, Seth. I'm going to get free and I'm coming back to you, don't worry."

Seth moans and puts his hands to his head. I take a step back. I'm making him worse. He thinks he's hearing voices. I thought coming here to Seth would help, but it hasn't helped at all. I need to get out of here, and find a way to escape.

The faster I do, the faster I can help Seth.

CHAPTER
SEVEN

"*You can go across the country?*" says Aurelia incredulously.

I can't decide if her voice is more parts surprise or wishful.

"I think it's because I have the spell web inside me, even though they're blocking my abilities with their machine," I say.

"*So perhaps you can actually talk to people? And travel further?*"

"I think I can. But I need your help. I don't know enough about the shadow realm to do it consciously and under control. I was trying to find Seth, but it just took me where he was without..."

"*Asking?*"

"Well, kinda. It was completely uncontrolled. I want to be able to do things on purpose, not by accident." I've had enough of learning about my skills by accident. I want to *know*.

There's a hesitation and the silence has a hidden meaning that I don't understand.

"What?" I say.

"Well, you've already gone further than I ever have. And I'm not sure there's any more control to be taught than for you to tell the shadow realm where you want to go, and then it takes you there."

"So I just think of the person, and it'll take me there?"

"Yes. Time and distance isn't quite the same in this realm. I definitely have a radius I can't go past, but I can travel that circumference in seconds."

I take a breath, thinking it through. Who do I want to contact the most? Who is likely to understand me the best? Who is likely to not completely freak out if I turn up and talk to them from the shadow realm?

It comes down to Carrick and Damien, my birth father.

But Carrick has other responsibilities. I know he'd drop everything if I asked, but he's in charge of the Earthbound Compound now. He's the Mountain King.

That leaves dear old Dad.

"Okay, I'm going to try to find my father. Wish me luck," I say.

"Luck."

I picture him in my mind. My strongest image is of him when he came to visit me after I found out the spell web was slowly killing me. He came up to me and hugged me, and in a twisted way it was one of the nicest interactions we'd ever had.

He's a chameleon, which means he can change to suit his situation, especially in his human form. He's charismatic, strong willed and stubborn, but if you passed him on the street, you wouldn't know it. His brown hair doesn't stand out, his brown eyes are just like a hundred others. His expression is studiously neutral, and his clothes are always the same kind of clothes that a thousand other men might wear.

But he's my dad, and despite his dubious parenting, I can picture every line of his face, how his eyes crinkle when he smiles, the tiny cowlick he tries to hide, and the subtle but shifty way he flicks his gaze around him to assess every situation.

And then suddenly the same feeling as before pulls at me, and a rushing sound fills my ears. If I needed to breathe I'd be gasping at the speed of it all.

Then I'm in front of my father. I feel a huge sense of relief at seeing him—another person who made it through the battle against the demons.

He's in a dingy motel room, pacing up and down. He's clearly been pulling at his hair, because it's standing on end. He's unshaven, his clothes are rumpled, and he looks worse than I've ever seen him.

I'm surprised. It takes a lot to ruffle my dad. Is he upset... because of me? I watch him curiously for a while. My father wasn't always very... fatherly. He's gotten better since we met again in New York, but for most of my life, I'd have sworn I wasn't that important to him.

So to see him pacing around, and to have the thought that maybe it's because of me... I have the sense that I'm just being hopeful. I peer around the room, looking for a calendar or a phone that might tell me today's date. How long has it been since I was taken? How long have they been searching for me? I don't know the answer, and it kills me.

My father is only marginally more held together than Seth and it feels like they're both on the brink of giving up on me. Like they've tried everything and it's all failed.

Dad puts one hand to his head, and pulls his hair yet again. "Maybe we should do another sweep of the SIG

Headquarters. Maybe he has her hidden there somehow," he mutters to himself. Then he turns and punches the wall of the motel, making the weak plasterboard cave in. As he pulls back his hand, shaking it to remove the broken pieces of plaster, I see the chameleon scales on his skin. He's close to the edge. My heart leaps in my chest, and if I could, I think there'd be tears welling in my eyes. It's all because of me.

I hesitate. I don't want to do to him what I did to Seth. My words made Seth fall apart even more than he had already.

But this is my father. He's the agent who was feared by all other agents when he was at the SIG, who is considered a legend, a ghost, and an urban myth. He can cope with this. He's dealt with all sorts of weird shit over his career. Maybe he even knows about the shadow plane.

"Hey Dad," I say softly. My see-through body wavers.

He turns around, and paces back the other way. If he can hear me, he has a much better poker face than Seth.

"I need your help. I'm in the shadow realm."

He stops, and spins on his feet, looking around the room. His eyes narrow.

"If you can hear me, you're not imagining this. I'm really here."

"What kind of trick is this? Who's there?" He pulls his gun out of its holster on his side.

"Dad, it's me, Mei. I'm here. I don't know if you've heard of it, but I'm in the shadow realm."

He keeps looking around, his expression guarded. He stares straight through me, and I realize he can't actually see me, even though he can hear me.

And he also doesn't believe I'm me. How can I—

Oh, wait. I know...

"Ask me a question, one that only I would know," I say, trying to contain my impatience. "I can answer it, and prove it to you."

Dad narrows his eyes, and glares around the room. "How do I know you're not just forcing Mei to answer my questions?"

"Jeez, Dad, suspicious much?" I pause, watching conflicting emotions cross his face. "Come on, try it out. See if I know stuff."

"Okay, fine. Who was your final SIG mentor?"

"Come on, Dad, ask me something harder than that. Jeff wouldn't be impressed."

He peers behind the curtain at the window, and then stalks to the bathroom and checks behind the door. "Who is working with Carrick to decipher the Earthbound texts?"

"Elena and the two other nuns..." I scrunch up my face, trying to remember their names. I'm completely blank. "I don't remember their..." I shake my head with a huff. "They seemed mean and grumpy."

A tiny twitch at the corner of his mouth is the only sign that Dad is amused by what I just said. "What did I say to you when we were captured by the director at the SIG head-quarters?"

"That the director was dangerous. And you were right."

"What else?"

I let out another unneeded breath and try to remember the conversation. It's a little hazy. "That we'd escape with some help from our friends. You were incredibly cryptic."

"And what did you say about Hazel?"

"That I liked her, because she gave you grief."

My father lets out a long breath, and visibly relaxes. "Okay. So if it's really you, then what's happening? Where are you? Have you managed to escape?"

"No, I'm still being held by Lakas and Connor."

Pain flickers across his face.

"But if you help, maybe I can escape," I say. "I have a vague idea where I am. They're driving me around and around in a massive truck. It has one of the Earthbound machines attached to it, and I can't use any of my powers. I accidentally discovered the shadow realm when—" I stop talking, realizing that he probably doesn't want to hear about how I was being tortured. "Anyway, I discovered it, and now I'm learning how to get around in this realm. But I can't move my physical body."

"Where are you?" he says, already moving to pack his things into his bag. "I can be there asap."

"That's the problem. I'm not entirely sure where I am. I only know the general area. I've been talking to another dragon in the shadow realm who says she's stuck inside Mt Hood in Oregon. I think I'm near there somewhere, in a big city. It's a big white truck."

He stops packing for a moment. "You're not giving me much to go on, Mei," he says with a sigh.

"I can try to figure out some more identifying markers, now that I know you're coming." I can't believe this has worked. He can hear me, he isn't freaking out, and he's coming to find me. I keep talking as he packs his bag and jumps into his car, and speeds out of the carpark of the low rent motel where he was staying.

"I'll get to the airport and get a flight. I'll be there soon." His foot is pushed to the limit on the accelerator and his hands are clutching the steering wheel so hard, they've turned white. "I'm gonna get you out of there, Mei."

"Thanks Dad." I feel the now familiar whooshing sound. "I have to go. But I'll see you soon," I say, relief flowing through me like a stream in springtime.

When I land back inside my body, the pain is less now that I'm not struggling against it. I have more pain from the burns and cuts that Lakas has inflicted on me in our sessions together.

He likes to torture me. He likes to hit, and cut, and beat me. Often without even saying a word, not even requesting anything.

Like I said, he doesn't really want me to give up too soon.

But now I have hope. A reason to think I might actually manage to escape this hell.

And that's all I need to keep going.

CHAPTER
EIGHT

I open my eyes blearily after a night spent practicing in the shadow realm with Aurelia. She's trying to teach me everything she knows about the shadows as fast as possible. Being back in my physical body is a shock after the lightness of the shadows. My muscles feel heavy and sore. I can barely lift my head. I don't know if it's because of everything Lakas is doing to me, or if it's how much time I'm spending in the shadow realm that's weakening my physical body. But it doesn't matter. I'm determined to keep learning as much as I can from Aurelia. I'm scared they'll decide to change their driving schedule and move somewhere else, outside of the area Aurelia can move about in.

She's been trapped inside the volcano for a long time, gathering knowledge like a third skin. I've been able to ask her questions about the powers of dragons, and also what it was like to be a dragon in her time and what really happened before the Earthbound killed them all off.

"It wasn't a proud moment for dragons, that's for sure," she'd said sadly. *"We were fighting, that is correct. We'd grown*

too fast, there were too many of us, so there were battles, yes. But we hadn't always been like that, and it's not a set fixture of a dragon's temperament that we have to be violent and territorial."

I think back over her words, and something inside me eases. People like Director Holden, Vincent and Lakas always wanted me to believe—like they do—that it's just in my nature to be violent and destructive. That all dragons are like that. I'd internalized it, believed deep down that maybe they were right and I was a danger to the world. That perhaps my protective streak was just an excuse to be violent and get into fights.

But I'm not like that. I don't like to be violent for the sake of violence. I'm just determined to stand up for my friends and family who need me, who need the strength of a dragon shifter on their side.

I let out a sigh, but the pain in my ribs turns it into a moan. My body aches everywhere. But now I have something to keep me going. My father is on his way. Last time I checked in on him, he'd landed in Portland, which is the largest city near Mt. Hood. It seems the most likely place for him to find us. He's been working on locating the truck and recognizing the billboard images that I told him about.

I've allowed a tiny amount of hope to swish about in my chest. Maybe Dad will be able to save me, now that he knows what's happening. He's a smart guy, a legend among agents. Surely that's enough?

Noise at the door to my cell makes me cringe, and I have to take a couple of calming breaths to control my reactions. I'm determined to stay steady despite everything. I watch to see who it is, hoping that Connor's coming to gloat. He's by far the lesser of the two evils presented to me.

But it's Lakas who skulks through the door, his dark

eyes glittering in the bright light of my cell. His long sharp nose creates shadows over his face, and his all-black garb makes him look like an evil human version of a crow. But he's a million times worse than a crow, he's a minokawa, an enormous creature of prey with a bitter streak a mile wide and an uncontrollable desire to act out his revenge fantasies on me.

Lakas prowls toward me, and I can't help the shudder that goes over my body. Even though I'm telling myself I'm going to be strong, I know what's coming.

"I have a surprise for you today, Mei," he says, his voice silky smooth.

I blink, trying to focus. That's not his usual introduction to our sessions.

He holds up a tablet device, and on the screen is a camera feed of someone lying in a cell similar to mine.

I look up into his face, trying to understand the significance of this person, who looks like they've spent some time with Lakas and his sharp metallic feathers.

"You don't recognize him?" says Lakas softly.

I shake my head. I can't see well enough to recognize anyone right now.

"I would have thought you'd recognize him. He's your father, after all."

I let out a moan, and my eyes dart back to the image on the screen. Is it my father? I can't even tell. I look back up to Lakas, doubts running through me. Is he trying to trick me? Surely my father wouldn't be so easily caught?

"You're lying," I whisper.

"Rest assured, it's him. I can bring him in to see you, if you like, for confirmation. We caught him trying to sneak onto the truck about an hour ago. I don't know how, but he found you."

Lakas's eyes narrow on my face, as if he's trying to figure out if I had anything to do with it. But he doesn't seem to know about the shadow realm and I'm not about to tell him.

"He's not that easily caught," I say, my voice croaky and raw. Painful.

Lakas sneers. "He's not even a full super. You think he's all powerful, but really he's just a human, with a human's pathetic lack of power." He presses a button on the tablet he's holding, and speaks into it. "Show his face to the camera."

I watch on the screen as someone crouches down beside the bloodied man on the screen. They grab his face and twist it so that it can be clearly seen.

The man has an egg-shaped bruise beneath one eye and drool is dripping off his swollen lips. He's unconscious... and most definitely my father.

My stomach twists. "Let him go," I say, feeling like I can't breathe properly. I've never felt so vulnerable. Panic sizzles through me, followed by a flickering rage that sparks and burns.

"I'm afraid I can't do that, Mei. He was captured trying to break into this facility. He's a liability."

I close my eyes, my hope draining away. My father was my rescue mission.

And now Lakas has him.

"Don't hurt him," I whisper.

"That will be up to you. If you don't do what we say, I may have to use some of the techniques I've been using on you... on your father. He's a human, he won't be as... durable as you are."

"That's not fair," I say, my voice rising. "You can't take it out on my father. It's my decision, not his."

Lakas shakes his head slowly, making tsking noises at me. "Life isn't fair, *dragon*. If it was, my friends and family would all be alive right now." His voice drops to a stony chill that makes me shiver. "Instead, they're all dead and buried."

"I didn't kill them. It wasn't me." Despite my efforts to stay strong, tears leak out the corner of my eyes. I brought my father here. It's my fault they're torturing him.

"Your *kind* killed them. And you're just like they were. It's ingrained into you. You can't help it."

"I'm *not* like that. I've never—"

"You killed Vincent. An innocent man, just doing his job."

"Vincent was never innocent. And he was trying to kill *me*."

"So you understand the concept of an eye for an eye?" says Lakas, his voice still soft and silky.

I can't help it. A sob works its way up from my chest, bursting out of me, wet and desperate and uncontrolled.

He lifts his free hand, and presses a button on the tablet. "Begin by tying him up," he says clearly into the speaker. Then he holds up the screen so I can see what's happening. I watch, because I can't not watch. A guard on the other end pulls my father up off the floor, and forces him to stand. He already looks half dead. His head is hanging down, and his body is sagging. He's not even fully conscious.

"Leave him be," I say, my words shaky and throbbing with emotion.

Lakas just sneers down at me. "You have the power to stop this, Mei. Your father doesn't have to suffer this way. If you do what I ask, he doesn't need to be hurt... any more than he already is."

Tears are making it hard to see and I watch as the guard

attaches my father to wall cuffs. He's standing spread eagled against a metal wall, just like the one in my cell.

"Use the taser," says Lakas. "To start."

My body twitches in remembered pain. "No!" I scream, even as the guard holds a taser against my father's side. He jerks and his face contorts in pain. The guard stops, and my father's body goes slack.

"Again," says Lakas.

"Stop it," I say, sobbing freely now. My head is thrashing side to side on the bed, and the cuts on my shoulders are aching like they've had salt poured on them.

"The only way to make me stop this is to do what I want," says Lakas, his rasping voice crawling over me. "Will you do what I want, Mei?"

"I can't," I say, thinking of all the people they will hurt. "I can't."

"Then we continue." He holds up the tablet again, and presses a button. "This time, use the blow torch."

The burns down the side of my body quiver in reaction. Images of when Lakas used the blow torch on my skin are etched into my brain. I want to be strong, to be able to say that my father isn't worth all the people who will be hurt by whatever they make me do. But I can't. I can't watch.

"Wait," I rasp, my voice raw and painful. "Stop hurting him."

Lakas turns to look at me, his eyebrows raised in question. Behind him on the screen the blow torch is about to touch my father's skin.

"I'll do it," I cry out, lost to any sense. "I'll do it. Just don't hurt him anymore." Another sob works its way out of my throat, despite my efforts to keep it inside.

I sense rather than see Lakas's smile. "Good little dragon. I knew you'd see it my way."

I peer wearily at him, trying to work out what he's going to make me do. He places the tablet down on the table at the end of my bed and uses a small key to unlock my shackles.

"Stand up. You're coming with me." He holds out his hand as if it's just a simple matter of getting out of bed and going with him. They've been blocking my body's ability to heal. I can barely stand.

"Come now, or your father might feel the blow torch after all," he says, his scratchy voice rubbing my nerves raw.

Scrunching my eyes closed, I draw on every ounce of willpower I have left, and push myself to sitting in the bed. Several places on my body scream in pain. A cut on my arm. The burns down my side. The cuts on my collar bone. Bruises along my back. It's almost too much.

But this isn't over yet. Something inside me pushes me to stand, and I stumble as I put all my weight on legs that might possibly have a fractured bone. My bare feet are cold against the hard metal floor.

"Good girl," says Lakas, like he's a school teacher encouraging me to greater academic heights.

I manage a glare in his direction, but can do nothing when he grasps my arm in one of his long-fingered hands, and pulls me in the direction of the door.

I stumble, but he doesn't slow down. He opens the door of the cell, and the vibrations get stronger and louder. The feeling underfoot is jarring, almost painful. There's a strange little hallway, lit only by a temporary light stand. Everything around me sways suddenly, and I crash against Lakas. He keeps me steady, until everything evens out again. What was that? Am I having dizzy spells as well?

But my brain is a actually less fuzzy out here, confirmation that there's something working against me in the cell. I peer around, trying to memorize everything about the inside of this truck. Is this some kind of secret cell that only the director and his cronies know about? Where there is no law protecting me, and no repercussions for what they do to me?

My skin tingles in fear. If the director decides to kill me, I'm dead. I have no defenses right now. And Lakas isn't exactly reasonable when it comes to dragons. He'll happily kill me, once he's finished playing with blow torches. The hallway sways again, and I stumble. Lakas tightens his grip on my arm, no patience for my lack of agility.

I don't know what's happening to me, it's like I'm lost in a world where gravity no longer exists. I could float away into the air, and I wouldn't be surprised. Has Lakas given me something and I didn't notice?

Lakas drags me along the hall, and then bangs on the wall, which is also made of metal. Where is he taking me? What is he going to do to me now?

I'm so caught up in my nightmare scenario, I don't immediately notice that the underlying vibration that has been my constant companion for the last I-don't-know-how-many-days is gone. It's only when the double doors in front of us open wide, and painful, searing light bursts into the darkened space, that I understand what's happening. We've stopped.

I wince, the light like needles on my weakened eyes. I can't see anything for a few moments, but eventually the light stops being too bright, and forms itself into shapes. Through the doors, there's a concrete parking lot. We're high up from the ground, and there's a low building in the background that's presumably our destination.

And for the first time in a long time, the machine isn't blocking all my dragon powers.

CHAPTER
NINE

I look around, still blinking in the harsh daylight. The big shipping container that was my cell is attached to the back of the truck—a sleek-looking cab and trailer, all done in an ominous glossy black with no signage anywhere. I've seen it in the shadow realm, but it's much sharper here in the real world. There's another small box-like chamber at one end, and I'm sure that's where the Earthbound machine is located.

My dragon fire burns inside me, pushing at the barriers, tired of being useless and frustrated. My power is unfurling from its prison, even this small distance from my cell. I'm on the cusp of being able to use it all again, I can feel it. I'm buzzing with electricity, the magic is sparking inside me, my whole body shaking with anticipation.

Lakas pulls on my arm impatiently, and drags me to the edge of the truck. There's a step ladder going down, and a burly goon at the bottom. I look down at him speculatively. I've taken on bigger guys and won.

"Don't even think about escaping," says Lakas, like he can read my mind. "I have your father, and won't think twice about hurting him with that blowtorch if you do." His eyes narrow at me. "And don't even think about trying to take me out, because if they don't hear from me, they'll kill him. Painfully."

I glare at him, my anger burning inside me so hard I'll probably get indigestion. But I don't dare test him, not when my father's life is at stake. Not when I don't have a plan, or even know where the hell I am. Huffing out a frustrated breath, I turn and climb down the steps. My bare feet hurt against the metal, but it's the least of my worries right now. Where are they keeping my father? Is he close by? In another truck? How many trucks like this could they possibly have?

I stop at the bottom of the steps, my feet touching concrete and that's when I feel it, like a familiar old friend giving me a hug. The spell web is wrapping itself around me, wanting to protect me from this latest disaster. Except they have my father and until I can free him, I'm locked in place, stuck dealing with Lakas. The spell web starts to work on some of my wounds, and I feel them healing—albeit much slower than usual—but still closing the broken skin, and easing the burns.

We seem to be in the parking lot of some kind of medical research laboratory. It's a long, low building, with the blinds pulled down at every window, and concrete where other buildings might have had trees or plants and flowers. There's a small sign to one side of the entrance saying 'BioMed Industries: Research and Development Lab'.

I shudder to think what they're doing medical research on if they're involved with Lakas and Director Holden. Probably *me*, given time. Perhaps once I've outlived my usefulness.

I stand at the bottom of the truck and try to figure out

what city we're in. The weather is good, warm and sunny, which makes me think we might be back in California. I can see a sleeping section behind the cab of the truck, and not much else. The only people here are me, Lakas, the truck driver and a couple of extra goons with gormless expressions who seem to have been hired for their muscles rather than brain size.

I wonder how Connor got on and off the truck? I have a feeling they stopped a few times and I was so out of it, I didn't even notice. Lakas probably just flew in and out using his enormous metallic wings.

Lakas climbs down and grabs my arm again. He drags me across the parking lot and through the glass double doors of the medical lab. He nods at the older woman with graying hair in Reception as if he knows her. She doesn't even blink at me, despite the fact I'm covered in blood and open wounds, one eye only half open, and struggling to remain standing as Lakas drags me along.

He pulls me—stumbling the whole way—down a hallway, through some big metal doors and then into a room that has nothing more in it than a large metal table and some basic metal chairs. There's not even a window to the outside. As my strength gradually returns, the spell web lying over Lakas becomes more visible. It's bright and strong, the crisscrossing red grid lines burning with energy, and he's all the more terrifying now I can see exactly how powerful he really is.

"You will sit down and do what I tell you," says Lakas, gesturing to the closest chair. "And if you do it properly, you might get to see your father."

"He's here?" I ask croakily, heart beginning to thump in my chest. Perhaps if he's here—

"No, he's not at the lab. But we'll be traveling again soon, and you'll see him in a day or two."

I sit down hard on the metal chair, feeling sick. This is really going to happen. I'm going to do whatever he wants me to do. I try to imagine a scenario where I let them torture my father, where he makes me watch and listen via the tablet device. My hysteria is bubbling close to the surface, and it's only the sight of Lakas's soulless black eyes pinned to my face like he's waiting for me to fall apart, that allows me stay in—albeit tenuous—control.

"Can I have something to eat?" I ask. Maybe if I can get some time alone in this room, I'll be able to think of a plan. Or even just calm down enough to stop giving Lakas the reactions he's after. My stomach rumbles, as if on cue.

Lakas glares down at me.

"I need to get my strength up if you want me to use the spell web," I say. "You haven't exactly been giving me regular meals lately." More often than not, he gave me nothing.

He glares for a moment longer. His left eye twitches and then he shrugs one thin shoulder. "Fine. I'll feed you. Can't have your body wasting away before we're ready to kill you, can we? But don't try anything stupid, or your father will suffer." He turns to leave, and I hear the click of a lock at the door, then his voice as he calls for a guard. I'm not being left completely alone. My heart sinks.

I stand up and shuffle around the edges of the room. I'm healing and already way stronger thanks to the spell web, but I still feel like I'm an old aged pensioner rather than a twenty year old dragon shifter. I blink a couple of times and focus on the room around me, looking for something that might help. There's no window to see out of, and the only vent is one high in the ceiling. The chairs are all solid, and the table folds away, but is otherwise useless to me. Under the door I see the shadow of the guard. There's no escape from this box of a room. I take a breath, then another, trying to calm the pounding beat of my heart as I hunt for something that might help me in a room where there's nothing.

The temptation to leave my body and travel into the shadow realm is so strong I have to clamp down using the last vestiges of my will power.

They have my father. They'll hurt him if I don't at least attempt to cooperate.

I'll figure out a way to save both my father and myself, and keep the spell web away from them, I know I will. I just have to stay alive until then. I walk around the room one more time, pushing at the walls, trying to find a way out. Then I return to the chair, resigned. If I'm going to get out of this, it's not going to be by escaping this room.

CHAPTER
TEN

The door opens again with a rush—almost like Lakas is trying to catch me in the act—but I'm back in the seat, arms crossed, legs stretched out, trying to look relaxed. Anything to piss Lakas off. His eyes narrow, and I know he knows I've been looking around. But he also seems confident that I'm under his control. I guess he's right.

Even though I feel stronger and I'm thinking more clearly—the Earthbound machine has definitely been turned off—I can't do anything, not while he has my dad. I roll my shoulders experimentally. At least my body is feeling better. Maybe it'll help me figure out a way out of this situation. I can almost feel my wounds healing. The burns down one side are tingling, like they're finally disappearing. My eye is opening a bit wider, and everything is less blurry.

Including Lakas. That's the one downside of being able to see better. I can more clearly see the evil intent written on his face. It's disturbing to behold. He walks right up to me, and holds out something small and pink. A plastic container filled with wobbly pink jello and a small plastic spoon.

"Jello?" I ask. "That's the best you can do?"

"Just be glad that I chose to get you anything," he snarls, and dumps it into my lap. His hatred of me contorts his features so that he doesn't seem entirely rational. My heart thuds uncomfortably.

I'm completely at his mercy.

Unless I decide that getting myself out of here is more important, a little voice whispers in a corner of my mind. My magic burns. My father would just be collateral damage. *The one person I couldn't save.*

I could do it right now. I'm strong enough. The spell web is on my side. Power surges inside me, pushing, thrusting, *wanting.*

Is keeping the spell web away from Lakas and Director Holden more important than saving my father, the agent-extraordinaire, Damien Walker? For a second, I teeter on the precipice of that thought. The spell web is too powerful to be in their hands. There would be many people, my friends included, maybe even my father, who'd encourage me to leave now, kill Lakas and keep the spell web out of their hands.

But I just can't do it.

I refuse to let them hurt my dad. He isn't perfect, but he's still family. My only blood relation. And as soon as he learned where I was, he came to rescue *me*. It's my fault he's here, being tortured.

Everything in me resists the idea of leaving him to die. I let out a tortured breath, decision made, and glance up to find Lakas watching me with his beady eyes. I pull off the plastic cover of the jello container and dip the spoon in, trying not to wince at the overly sweet raspberry flavor as the wobbly jello hits my mouth. I keep eating until the container is empty and my stomach has stopped growling. It wasn't exactly satisfying, but it was better than nothing.

Lakas is still watching me like a demented bird of prey, his tall body somehow resting in the shape of a buzzard waiting for its meal.

I shudder, the jello suddenly feeling not so secure in my stomach.

Whatever I do, I have to stop Lakas and Director Holden, and disrupt their plans. Worse comes to worst, the spell web is going to implode soon. When it kills me, the spell web will cease to exist and the problem will be gone. The director won't have access to it anymore. Lakas won't be able to blackmail me.

I try not to think of whatever potential bad thing Lakas is going to force me to do right now. I just have to keep myself in the game for as long as possible, and do the least amount of damage. And I'm done waiting.

"Let's get this over with," I say. "What do you want me to do?"

"It's very simple, Mei. You just have to use the spell web and do what we tell you. If you don't, your father will suffer."

"What *exactly* do you want me to do?"

"You need to attack the supers in Pismo Beach. Take them out, immobilize them." He says the words carelessly, and waves one long, thin arm in the air like it's just a little thing. "We need them to be defenseless against our agents down there. Preferably for good. Whatever attack you create will exclude our people going into the Every Day is

Sunday record store in Pismo Beach. They need to be able to get in, retrieve an object and get out."

I nod my understanding, wondering what could possibly be in a record store in a tiny town like Pismo Beach. Nothing important, surely?

"Right now?" I raise my eye brows, trying not to show how much my stomach is swirling at the thought.

Lakas pulls out his phone and messages someone, his long, creepy fingers moving quickly over the screen. "Soon," he smirks.

"Where are we?" I ask, looking around like a map might appear on the walls. "I need to get a sense of where I am."

Lakas looks at me suspiciously, but I just glare back at him. It doesn't really matter if he tells me now, or when he lets me use the spell web. As soon as I can use my full powers again, I'll be able to stretch out on the spell web and figure out exactly where I am, and where everyone else is as well. Lakas is just delaying the inevitable by trying to keep me in the dark. I guess I'm just trying to get information that I'll have in five minutes anyway.

"We're in Portland," he says reluctantly.

"Who's at Pismo Beach?"

He gives me another look. I stare right back. "I'll find out who's at Pismo Beach as soon as I jump into the spell web," I say. The urge to use my powers, to feel the full energy of the spell web's magic, is rising up inside me, like a tsunami that I won't be able to hold in check for much longer. I never thought I'd be so eager to feel its magic running through me again.

"Director Holden."

The words are like a thunderclap inside my head. This is it. I have the opportunity to kill the director. The spell web swirls up, reacting to my thoughts. I think they've turned the machine off, because my power is surging uncontrolled inside me, a storm that has finally been set free. My heart pounds in my chest. I'm easily more powerful than Lakas when I'm not being hobbled by one of the Earthbound's machines.

"Don't even think about harming him. I have your father, and I won't hesitate to kill him," snarls Lakas like he can see the thoughts running across my face.

What would happen if I did it? *If I killed Director Holden.* My breath leaves me for a second and I swim in the possibilities.

Would Lakas kill me? Maybe not at first, but he'd make me pay. And he'd definitely kill my father. I wouldn't even be able to get away because straight after I use the spell web, it'll attack me, and I'll collapse.

Which means the spell web would still be in Lakas's power, and my father wouldn't be there to help shape the future. There'd be a power vacuum at the SIG. Would Lakas try to take over? If he was in charge, what would Lakas do? My mind swirls until I can't see anything but the bloodshed that Lakas would create. It would be carnage.

What's the use of being a powerful dragon if I can't even be the one who *wins*?

Lakas grabs my arm and shakes me. "I mean it. You do anything and your father is dead. Not an easy death either. A slow, painful death with you watching every minute."

I stare at him, trying to see any compassion or pity. Anything that might give me hope. There's nothing but sharp lines and evil intent.

I need to figure out a way to take both Lakas and Director Holden down at the same time.

And free my father.

And keep the spell web in place.

And survive the wave of pain that I'm definitely going to feel once I use the spell web again.

All of it needs to happen at the same time for this situation to be solved.

I don't know how I'm going to do it.

Even worse, I don't think it's possible.

CHAPTER
ELEVEN

"Do it. Do it now." Lakas's expression is one of anticipation. "I just told them to turn off the machine, your power should be back." He thinks it's going to be messy and he's looking forward to it.

I don't tell him they turned off the machine a while ago. He doesn't need to know that his minions aren't following his instructions to the letter. That information might come in handy later.

The hard edges of my chair are digging into my legs and back where my wounds haven't fully healed. I'm still holding the small jello container, and the overly sweet, fake raspberry flavor is making my nose twitch. It doesn't matter, none of it does. The glowing power of the spell web is flowing through me, interlaced with the burning intensity of my dragon self. For the first time since we entered the Raven Industries building and I carried the missile into the sky, I feel whole.

Strong.

I could shift right here if I wanted to. My enormous dragon form would fill the room, and I'd bite the head off

Lakas's thin, cadaverous body before he could blink one of his disgusting bloodshot eyes. The urge to shift, to overpower Lakas and to show him who's the supreme supernatural in the room overwhelms me for a moment. My magic surges, and everything teeters on an edge. I can barely think. It could go either way.

Then I let out my breath.

I'm not going to do it. I need to find a way to save my father first.

So I close my eyes and reach out along the spell web with my mind. Being part of the power grid again is like a drug and I'm an addict who's been kept from her obsession for too long. It's very different to being in the shadow realm. The lines of the spell web flood my senses and for a moment I just wallow in the abundance of energy surrounding me. It's like swimming in an ocean of shimmering magic, power lapping at my body from all sides, warming me from the inside. I feel like I'm glowing.

Inside the web, I move along the highways, down the coast, searching for someone—anyone—I recognize. Intuition leads me toward the big cliff-side house that was Hazel and Blade's hidden sanctuary, until Connor's men attacked us there. The coastline is close, and my heart soars. It feels like I'm flying as the roads and houses below me speed by. It feels like freedom, and for a moment, I forget that I'm still trapped.

Then suddenly I'm there, at Blade's hideaway house on the cliff. And somehow, against all logic, Blade is there too, with another man I don't recognize. They're inside the lab where Hazel tested my powers. They're both powerful supers, their glow on the power grid brighter than most. I swoop in. I have to be fast. Lakas is waiting, looming next to my physical body.

Using the spell web, I implant the location and the name of the place where Lakas is keeping me into Blade's head. I don't have time to linger, and I can't spend time making sure he understands. I just have to hope it's enough. I sweep on through, heading down the coast toward Pismo Beach, reaching out with the magic that is now available to me again.

Luckily, I know Director Holden and I'm able to lock onto him through the spell web. I would have struggled to find the little second hand record store down a side street in the tourist town. He's standing on the footpath, wearing his usual suit and tie, and looks completely out of place. He keeps glancing at his watch like he's expecting something to happen. Me, I guess. I'm what's happening.

I take a breath and concentrate on making everyone around him go stock-still. I want to hold them motionless between one movement and the next, without hurting them. I don't think specifically about how I'm going to do it, I just let my imagination take over.

Out of nowhere a strange idea pops into my mind. The jello I just ate, wobbly and yet somehow just solid enough to hold itself together.

What if...?

And just like that, an enormous wall of wobbly clear jello appears on the streets around the director. It stretches out over everyone—except Director Holden—but it only affects the supers. The humans walk through it like it's not even there. The supers are caught up inside the jello, trapped like mosquitos in amber, hidden from the humans somehow, while Director Holden strides into the record store.

I feel him along the spell web, going into the store, then into some kind of secret area. There's magic protecting it, but he gets inside, and descends a set of dark stairs to a hidden basement. There's only one other person there, a mountain super, who's locked in the wobbly mess I've created using the spell web. I wait, feeling proud of my solution. No one has to get hurt. Lakas gets his way, and I get mine.

It's only when I stop and pay attention to the lone super protecting the basement that I realize there's a problem. The jello isn't holding him in suspended animation like I thought, it's trapped him inside, with no way to escape—or breathe.

I check along the web, and it's the same for all the other supers around the area trapped in my jello-like substance. They're starting to choke, gasping for breath. I'm killing them.

"I'm letting it go," I say out loud in my body, panicking. "He needs to get out of there."

"No. Leave it in place until I tell you to remove it," replies Lakas's disembodied voice, sounding distant, like I'm listening to it through a pipe.

"They're going to die. They can't breathe."

"I don't care. If you take it off early, your father dies."

Thunder crashes along my veins and I try to stay the course. I can't let him kill my father, not after all this. I wait another few seconds, watching through the spell web, feeling the pain of the hundreds of supers attached to it, trying to help them. I push little pieces of energy into them, trying to help them breathe a little easier inside the deadly jello I created.

I try to push the Director along, make him want to leave faster.

A mobile phone pings inside my head, and somehow I know it's Lakas back in Portland. "The Director says to stop doing whatever you're doing to him," he says, his voice grim.

I hesitate for another few moments, hovering between fear of what they'll do to my father, and fear of killing all the supers in Pismo Beach.

The mountain super inside the hidden room passes out, his body held up inside the jello like he's being held in suspended animation, surrounded by my stupid jello.

"That's it. I can't do this anymore," I say. I won't kill all those people, just because Lakas tells me to.

I let it go. Supers all around the area collapse to the ground, gasping and dragging in breaths like they've never breathed before. The humans nearby look on in confusion. As always, I wonder what they're seeing because of the spell web.

It's usually something weird, something you wouldn't expect. A story you would think the humans would never believe in a thousand years, that they always seem to swallow whole.

Director Holden is still in the basement looking for whatever he's trying to find. The guard is unconscious next to him on the floor. I can feel faint life signs in the guard, and I secretly pump a little bit of energy from the spell web into him, to make sure he's okay. In fact I go around and start doing that to everyone who was a victim of my jello attack. Just a little to help them out, to make things easier on them. Maybe even to keep them alive.

Finally, Director Holden finds what he's after. It's a book of some kind, hidden in one of the locked boxes in the room. I hate to think what it's inside it. Probably instructions on how to create some other Earthbound nightmare they'll use to hurt dragons like me.

For a second I panic. What am I doing? My father's life

isn't worth the annihilation of dragons a second time. Guilt crackles inside me, and I wonder what fresh hell I've just helped them create.

I promise myself that I will undo whatever it is I've put into play here today. There must be a way to both save my father and keep everyone else safe.

I let go of everything else, and allow myself to flow back along the spell web grid, flying and soaring along the lines, the wind cool against my ethereal body.

For a very brief moment, I experience a kind of peace.

Then it's gone. I'm back in my body, the chair hard against my back and legs, my neck stiff and my head already pounding in reaction.

"He has it." Lakas's pipe-distant voice confirms what I already knew. "But he says you stopped it early."

I'd be more afraid, except the dizzying effects of using the spell web for something so enormous are starting to tumble down over me. Searing pain strikes my head like a dart, and I groan out loud. This is far worse than anything Lakas could do to me, because it's soaked with the idea that this could be it. This could be the moment that everything ends for me.

The spell web could die, and take me with it, and I'd have no control over it, no way to stop it happening. I helped them do something awful, and I might be unable to reverse it like I promised myself. The only positive is that they'd no longer have the spell web under their control.

My whole body starts convulsing, and I fall off the chair onto the floor. My vision, which moments ago was so clear, blurs down into almost nothing, only shapes and impressions. The pain is immense, bigger than the world, bigger than anything I've ever experienced before. I try to close it down, to use the spell web to help me. But I can't find my connection to the spell web. It's there, but it's also not. It's like I'm still on that same ocean of power, but now I'm surrounded by a turbulent mix of waves and breakers and I'm being thrown about like flotsam.

I try to push myself back up to my hands and knees, but the pain is too much. All I can do is lie here on the floor, shaking and convulsing, and hoping it won't last too long.

None of my friends are here. Carrick can't save me. Seth is hiding in a cave. My father is in a cell.

And this time it's much worse than before. There's a sizzling, electrified fog over me, blocking me from the rest of the world. I can barely see what's happening, and I don't care.

Lakas can torture me again, punish me for stopping early, but it won't achieve anything.

I won't even feel it over the searing pain of the spell web attacking me from the inside.

CHAPTER
TWELVE

Hours, days, weeks later.

It could be any of them. Time has collapsed in my head, and I'm floating in a vortex of nothing. My eyes are heavy and I can't keep them open for long. My body feels like it's made of concrete. Breathing is difficult, and there's a pressure on my chest that's holding me tight against a hospital bed. The spell web is throbbing impotently inside me, spent and weak. They haven't even bothered to turn the Earthbound machine on again to negate my powers. There's no point.

I don't know where I am, but there's an IV line attached to my arm, and I'm dressed in a white hospital robe. A scratchy white sheet is covering me up to my armpits. No one else is in the white-walled room, but there are a couple of empty hospital beds on the other side.

In my head, I rip out the IV line, and leap out of the bed. I run to the door, and escape.

In reality, I can't even keep my eyes open for more than a minute at a time.

I know I need to escape, but the reason alludes me, like

a wisp of cloud just out of my reach. I don't know why, but I'm scared.

Minutes, hours, days later, the door opens. I blink my eyes open, forcing myself to meet whatever is coming my way. A tall, cadaverous man with a large beak-like nose walks in. He's dressed all in black, and I know he's my enemy. I don't know why. Maybe it's his dark soulless eyes, or the long, claw-like fingers.

Behind him is an older woman, with her gray hair pulled back into an efficient bun, and black glasses sitting on the end of her nose. She's wearing a knee-length skirt and a matching knit sweater, and is carrying a glossy black handbag over one forearm. She looks deceptively benign.

They come to stand at the end of my bed, and I close my eyes again, unable to hold them open any longer. I don't feel like I need to have them open, there's nothing I can do that will stop whatever they plan to do.

"Is she awake? She just had her eyes open," says the woman, her voice high and nasal.

"She's been in and out of consciousness. She's being held under using powerful drugs," says the man in a deep rasping voice. It ricochets down into my bones, and I feel a shudder inside my core. He's familiar to me, but I just can't remember who he is. It's a terrifying feeling.

"So why did you need me?" The woman sounds peeved, like a child denied a toy.

"We need her conscious to finish the next phase. She disobeyed me in the test run. We know the threat of her father's death is not enough to force her to kill people through the spell web."

His furious words swirl around inside my head, and I try to make sense of what he's saying. It feels like I'm trying to understand a foreign language with only an outdated book of translations and wishful thinking.

"What about the other two? The ones you captured trying to get inside?"

Something lurches inside my chest and I know her words are important to me. Whoever they've captured is someone I know. I'm certain I should understand what she's talking about, but I can't. Nothing makes sense.

"If her father wasn't sufficient, they won't be either. We need your artifact."

There's a shuffling noise, which I can only assume is the old lady searching her handbag. "Here you go," she says triumphantly.

"You're sure this artifact will control her, Ms Adler?" asks the man.

"Yes. It's extremely powerful. It was hidden in the depths of the library. The cats tried to keep it from me, but I outsmarted them." The woman's voice is so smug, I worry for the sake of the cats she supposedly outsmarted.

"Did you put out some fish for them to feast on?" asks the man in a derisive voice.

"That comment just shows you don't truly understand how the SIG library works. Collectively, those cats have more power than most supernaturals in existence today, including the dragons."

"Then perhaps they should be put down, instead of pandered to?"

"I'd like to see you try. They follow only one master and it's the soul of the library. I was lucky to escape with the artifact and my life."

"That will change once we are in control."

For some reason, those words make me shiver, despite

the heat in the room. I hold my eyes closed, desperately trying to remember what's going on around me.

"The cats beat to their own drum. They won't care who's in control," says the woman.

I like those cats, wherever they are.

The man makes a sound somewhere between a growl and a screech. "Once the director has been unleashed from the chains of the SIG and supernaturals are allowed to take their rightful place instead of hiding in the shadows, we'll put those idiotic cats in their place."

She murmurs agreement. "Those cats have been the bane of my life for the last fifty years. I'll be glad to be rid of them."

"Shall we begin?" asks the man, his voice rich with expectation.

"Right now? Straight away?"

"The plans are in motion. We must move quickly to play our part."

"What of the other men?"

"They are useful only for their ability to blackmail Hazel. They have been punished for daring to attack us, and I have set one free, to scamper back to his rebellion and tell of their defeat. The other has been locked in his cell to await transport to the compound when we leave tomorrow."

"You left him alive?"

"Barely. But yes, he's useful to us. We need Hazel and her ability with the demons. He's a useful bargaining tool."

"What about—"

"Enough. I'm done talking. We must determine if this artifact does what you say it does, and then use it."

The woman humphs, but I hear the swish of material as she moves closer to me, until she's standing at the side of my bed, right next to my head. I wish I had the energy to move away, to do something to save myself, but I don't. I force my eyes open, determined to see what's coming for me.

The woman, Ms Adler, is holding a piece of a bone about the length of my hand from the bottom of my palm to the tip of my middle finger. It's long and narrow and clearly only a piece of a larger digit. It's wrapped in a thick black ribbon of leather at one end, almost like it's a handle for a bone wand. There's a shimmer to the white-brown surface of the visible bone, and it's clearly not human, thankfully.

"You sure you know what you're doing?" asks the man, still standing at the end of the bed. I feel certain he has a backup plan if this trick doesn't work.

"Stop asking me that," she snaps. "You're not the only one with powerful magic." She's staring down at my face, watching my eyes like she's looking for something. "You don't look much like a dragon."

My eye lids are starting to feel heavy again, and despite trying to force them open, they drift shut over my eyes, blocking out this strange woman standing next to me.

She leans in, and whispers in my ear, her breath warm against my skin. "This bone is from one of your ancestors. It's been turned into an artifact for controlling your kind. Do not fight me, you cannot win."

I want to argue, to prove her wrong. To defend myself. But I can't even open my eyes.

She starts to hum under her breath, and weaves the bone over my face, neck, and chest, the tiny brush of air as she passes over my skin the only way I can tell what she's doing. I try to protect myself against the onslaught of magic that I feel building up in the air above me.

But my magic is weak, still recovering from the repercussions of using the spell web. I can only lie in the bed as her humming gets louder, and then forms into words. It's not in a language I understand, even though I strain to decipher it.

The man in black joins the chanting, moving around to stand on the other side of the bed from the woman, his low voice adding depth to the words. The magic above me grows stronger, until I feel it pressing down on my chest. My breathing comes in gasps, and I'm struggling to draw in air.

Their voices become even louder and faster, the movements above my face and chest more frantic. Soon there's a hurricane of air circling over me, pulling at my hair and sending chills along my skin. It gets increasingly colder, until I'm shivering, my body's automatic reaction to the freezing winds. The noise and movement increases above me, the cold is almost burning my skin, the magic sending painful pin pricks across my body.

And then suddenly it stops. The magic dies away, and there's silence.

I let out a relieved breath. I survived whatever the woman was doing to me.

"Here," says the woman. "You must be the one to do it."

Do what? My brain doesn't quite follow. But before I can decipher the words, the man pulls the collar of my hospital gown down, and the sharp end of the dragon bone lightly touches me for the first time, grazing the front of my shoulder. Goose bumps appear over my skin and I shudder. What is he—?

Suddenly, the man shoves the bone deep into my shoulder, the jagged edge ripping through my flesh. Excruciating pain bursts out from my shoulder. It's so sudden and intense, I scream. And then scream some more. Blood pounds in my head, the blinding agony howling through my whole body like a desert wind across the sand.

Adrenaline floods my system, and suddenly I can open my eyes. The first thing I see is the bone fragment sticking out of my shoulder, right up to the leather handle. A slimy green glow is emanating from it, lighting the face of the man as he stands next to my bed, one hand still on the bone.

He's smiling, showing off his yellow pointed teeth, like he enjoyed every second of hurting me. I'm surprised he doesn't give it a twist to make it worse. The pain fades slightly, only to be replaced by a dark uncomfortable sensation that crawls across my skin, starting from the wound he's just made and spreading out. Soon it's coating me like a layer of slime, oozing everywhere.

"Raise your arm," says the man. He's so familiar, I know I should know him, but my brain just isn't working properly.

My arm lifts into the air next to me like it belongs to someone else's body. A moment ago, I couldn't move anything. Now he's commanding my body? I push against the compulsion to hold my arm in the air. It doesn't move.

"Lower your arm."

Again, my arm follows his instruction without consent from me.

"Turn your head to face me."

My head turns like I'm his puppet. Everything inside me is trembling at the thought. I'm no longer in control of my movements. Does that mean he's in control of my thoughts? Is he now in control of the spell web?

Beside me, the man starts to laugh. It's a sharp, crackling sound, and reminds me of razor blades and nails. My fear is a physical thing inside me, skittering about and making me shake. It was bad enough before, when I couldn't move. But now these people control my body, and that's so much worse.

"This is the best present you could ever have given me, Dorothy Adler. You are a much better librarian than I ever gave you credit for," he says with an evil smile.

And just like that, my memory returns. Lakas is the man beside me. The woman is Dorothy Adler, librarian at SIG Headquarters, and the bane of Hazel's life when she was living in New York.

The men they captured must be Blade and his friend. The ones I told where to find me. I led them straight into capture and now Lakas has Blade trapped in a cage. *Hazel will never forgive me if he dies.*

Even worse—for me—Lakas is going to use me for whatever terrible plans he's formed and I won't be able to stop him.

Lakas owns me now.

I shudder uncontrollably. I should've taken him out when I had the chance. Now it's too late, and I have a feeling I'm going to regret it for the rest of my—very short —life.

I close my eyes and fall restlessly into the darkness.

CHAPTER
THIRTEEN

When I wake again, Dorothy and Lakas are gone, and there's another patient in the room with me. I gaze across at the unconscious body of Blade. He's been heavily beaten, his face is swollen and there are cuts and bruises all over his face and arms. The rest of his body is hidden beneath a white sheet, but I'm sure it's the same. I guess he needed more medical attention than they thought.

The bone is still sticking out of my shoulder, throbbing in time to my heart beat, and the oozing coating of green curse magic is all over my body. If I could move, I'd throw up.

The door opens and Lakas enters the room. He smiles when he sees me watching him. "You're awake. Perfect. They said the meds would wear off soon."

The slime shifts and shimmers, reacting to his presence like a moth to the light. He's somehow connected to the magic of the dragon bone in my shoulder, probably because he was the one who shoved it into my flesh.

He doesn't seem to expect an answer from me, so I

don't attempt it. I haven't spoken since I passed out after using the spell web. I still don't know how long ago that was.

It could be years. Or hours.

"You're going to do something for me, and this time, you won't be able to disobey me," he says.

I shake my head, the movement nothing more than a millimeter of movement, but his sharp eyes catch it nonetheless.

"You don't believe me? That bone sticking out of your shoulder is a fragment of a rare golden dragon, one of the royal line. One so powerful, none could bring her down. She was arrogant and vain, and thought she was indestructible. But she was destroyed by the might of the Earthbound's machines three hundred years ago, just like the rest of your kind, and her bone turned into a weapon. It's poetic, don't you think?"

I flick my gaze to the bone, and then back to him.

"The leather handle? It's her skin, cut from her body as she died. Bound to her bone, like you are bound to me."

Painful bile rises up through my oesophagus, burning at the base of my throat, but I can't actually throw up. It just sits there like a reminder of all my failures, of everything that led to this moment, of me being completely in Lakas's power, unable to refuse his commands.

Lakas smiles, his thin lips stretched unpleasantly across his face. "This is better than being the one who gets to kill you. It's so much more impactful. This way, you will be punished for the crimes that your kind perpetrated against my people. My *family*."

He's in full passionate-outrage mode, and even if I could speak, there'd be no point telling him that I wasn't the one who killed his family. I represent everything bad about dragon kind to him, and there's no way he's going to change his mind. I have a feeling that even when I'm dead, he'll still want more revenge on my kind. He'll find another unsuspecting dragon to focus his revenge plots on.

"You will do what I tell you. You won't be able to pull back or change your mind. You will do it, and carry it through to the bitter end. And it will be your fault when the people die."

I feel moisture at the edges of my eyes. I blink it away and tears run down the side of my face. I know he's right. I can feel it. He's in control of my every action. Whatever he tells me to do, I'll do it.

"You will draw the spell web to you, and you will use it to create an earthquake all the way along the western coast of the US, starting below where we are in Portland. You will keep us safe here. You will make it deep in the earth, and it will rock the ground for at least ten minutes. Begin."

Without hesitation, I dive deep into my core and pull at the spell web. It's not completely healed from the previous session, but I'm under a compulsion I can't control, so I force it forward. It's sluggish but moves at my command.

I send out my consciousness along the lines of the spell grid, past the walls of the building and outward, heading for a place south of Portland as directed. I'm part of the spell web, a tiny blip on the glowing grid lines, my consciousness entwined with the spell itself. Part of me is screaming as I travel faster than I could in my physical form, trying to stop the impulse that's driving me. But it's too strong. There's nothing I can do to stop what's happening.

Starting low, near the ground, I let the spell web grid roll out in front of me, and draw on its power. I feel the dormant energy inside the earth, and I feed the magic of the spell web into it. And then I use the spell web's magic to slam deep into the earth, creating a rolling tide of movement underground. It rips and rolls, causing the earth's crust to tremble and move. Tiny cracks appear in the surface and I pull my consciousness high up into the air to get a better view of the destruction I just unleashed. I can see cars weaving unsteadily along roads, buildings shaking, and people screaming. There's destruction everywhere and I caused it.

After all this time, Vincent was right. I *am* bringing destruction and chaos into our world.

I don't want to watch, but I force myself to stay where I am, high in the air, looking down over the coastline as enormous fissures and cracks break open the earth, buildings become rubble and roads collapse—some of them splashing into the sea.

All I can do is stare down at the devastation, my insides crumbling, dull ache working through my soul.

When it finally ends, the carnage along the coastline is more than I could have imagined. I don't know why Lakas wanted me to do this, but it's the worst thing I've ever done. I move downward again, not sure what I'm planning to do, but thinking there must be a way to help. Maybe I can find someone—

"You will return to your body now," says Lakas, his voice strange and distant.

Immediately my mind travels back along the spell web grid, and I return to my physical form. The difference between flying through the air and being trapped back in my unmoving body is almost too much and I cry out.

And then the real pain starts.

The expected attack from the spell web floods my body. It feels worse this time, and I don't know if it's the simply the trauma from the harm I've just done, or if I'm really getting worse, and maybe this is the time the spell web finally kills me.

Maybe I deserve it.

I know I just killed innocent people in that earthquake, and I'm not sure I'll ever be able to forgive myself for that.

Lakas frowns down at me as I shudder on the bed. "I can't have you dying on me. You're too useful. I will return shortly with someone who will help keep you alive."

I close my eyes and let myself fall into the oblivion of unconsciousness. I hope fervently that this is it.

The time when the spell web finally takes what's left of my miserable life.

CHAPTER
FOURTEEN

When I wake, it's completely dark in the room. I feel a crawling disappointment, but I don't understand why.

The only light is a tiny glowing dot from the IV machine, which is attached to a line in my arm, pumping some anonymous liquid into me. The pain from my attack is mostly gone, but my brain feels foggy and disorientated. I wish I could reach over and pull the line out, stop them from whatever they're doing to me. But I can't even manage to lift my head, let alone move an arm. Yet again, I'm stuck inside this body, lying here like it doesn't even belong to me.

Without thinking, I close my eyes and will myself to leave my body. I rise up in the air and into the shadow realm. I rise up and up, out of the building, into the night air. Around me, everything is peaceful, the city mostly quiet. It must be the early hours of the morning.

"You've been gone a while," says a voice nearby, and if I'd been in my body I'd have jumped out of my skin. Aurelia is nothing more than a faint ball of light nearby.

"Aurelia," I say, a sob rising in my non-existent throat.

"What's the matter?" She reacts immediately to my distress, moving closer and peering at my face. *"What's happened?"*

"They made me use the spell web to hurt people." The words are ragged and uneven, and I wish they weren't true.

Aurelia's unformed shape glows extra bright for a second. *"I'm so sorry. What did they make you do?"*

"I sent an earthquake down the coast. People were hurt, maybe even killed."

Aurelia drifts further into focus near where I'm hovering. With no truck to cling to, I'm simply floating in the middle of the air. She peers at my face. *"You must be very powerful to do something like that."*

"I wish I wasn't," I reply miserably. "It's only ever bought me pain."

"How did they force you to do it?"

"A cursed piece of bone, and a spell." I glance down at my shoulder, but I've left the bone back with my physical body, thank the gods. I can't bring myself to tell Aurelia that it's a dragon bone, and that it's been stabbed into my body.

Aurelia growls. *"These people, they talk about how dragons are so violent, and yet the things they do are far worse. They believe they have the moral high ground, but they are just monsters."*

I think of Lakas and everything Hazel told me he did to her. About the people he killed at the rebellion headquarters. *The look on his face when he killed Liling.* "He's done some terrible things in the time I've known him, all in the name of revenge. What do you know of the Minokawa race from your time? Were they a violent people?"

"They kept to themselves. But felt anger with the force of a thousand suns."

"That's definitely how much Lakas hates me," I say. "I've never done anything to him, but I represent all dragon kind to him. He's determined to destroy me. Slowly."

"I'm sorry, Mei," says Aurelia, her eyes wide and sad. *"You're just a baby dragon, and you're receiving the full brunt of the punishment."* She shimmers in and out of visibility, as if her emotions are affecting her concentration.

"It's not your fault," I say. "Lakas is an evil man. When I get free of this spell, I'm going to rid the world of his presence, and I'll enjoy doing it." Visions of all the ways I would fight and kill Lakas fill my head, and for a moment I allow myself to wallow in the feelings of satisfaction it gives me. I try not to think about what might happen if I never get free.

"One person should never pay for the crimes of others."

I make a sound of agreement. It shouldn't happen, but it does. "Did the dragons you knew do the things they talk of? Fighting for territory with no care for the other supernaturals?"

Zane always talked about how his clan of dragons were peacekeepers, but they can't have all been like that.

Aurelia lets out a misty breath. *"Dragons are like any of the races. There were good dragons and bad dragons. Happy dragons and sad dragons. Dragons with immense power and dragons with very little power. It was simply that we had more power than anyone else, so if one of our kind chose to harm others, there was nothing their victims could do. Until they created their machines."*

It eases one of my old fears to hear her say that. "So not all dragons were intrinsically bad, like the Earthbound say?"

"No, of course not. But we were all punished the same way in the end."

"It's not always good to be powerful. It puts a target on your back." I feel the words particularly hard tonight.

"It also means you can help those who need it," says Aurelia softly. *"The earthquake was down the coast you say?"*

"Yes." I frown in the direction of the fault line that I created.

"Then perhaps you can do something to help?"

I blink. "Like what?"

"You seem to have mastered the art of whispering in the ear of those in the physical realm while you're in the shadow realm. And you're able to roam much further than I. Perhaps you could help with the recovery effort? Find lost people and whisper suggestions for where to find them? It would keep you distracted and perhaps mitigate some of what you have done."

For a moment, I stare at her. "You're right. I should be down there helping, not up here feeling sorry for myself." I feel stupid for not thinking of it before. I give her a quick bow, and then I'm gone, streaking off along the coast.

I'm going to help as many people as I can tonight, Lakas be damned.

CHAPTER
FIFTEEN

The next time I awaken inside my physical body, it's morning.

I know, because I'm no longer in my window-less room. I'm on a hospital gurney, being pushed across the concrete parking lot outside the building. The gurney is moving quickly, juddering over the uneven surface, and my head keeps hitting the plastic-covered mattress under my body. The medic pushing me seems to be in a big hurry.

I'm securely belted down, so I couldn't move even if my body was working properly. I peer around, disorientated, trying to figure out what's happening. My gaze hits the bone fragment still sticking out from my shoulder. I've been so busy in the shadow realm, I'd almost forgotten what they'd done to me. I tear my gaze away from the bone, determinedly searching for clues about where we're going.

There's an ambulance waiting in one corner of the parking lot. Lakas is talking to a burly man dressed in medic's clothing by the front of the vehicle. My heart lurches then hits a double beat. They're moving me.

Will I still be able to talk to Aurelia? What if they take

me somewhere that means I can't find her again? She's the only thing keeping me together. I can't lose her now.

Another man in a medic's uniform opens the back door of the ambulance, and I see a second gurney already in there, with someone lying under a sheet. The two men lift my gurney roughly onto the back of the ambulance, bashing it against the side of the one that's already in there. It only just fits the two beds, with a narrow aisle up the middle.

I recognize Blade next to me, even though he's unconscious and his face is covered in blue and purple bruises. There are rows of cuts that I'm fairly certain came from the sharp tips of Lakas's wings. I have a few of those myself.

Wherever we're going, they're taking both of us.

My eyelids close, as if weighed down by lead balloons. I'm too tired to worry any more. I've just spent several hours roaming up and down the coast of California in the shadow realm, whispering in the ears of people searching for survivors in the downed buildings. It was exhausting, but I helped them find several people who I'm pretty sure would otherwise have died. Aurelia was right. Helping those people was satisfying work.

It doesn't change the fact that I caused the earthquake, but it eases my heartache over it.

Someone climbs up into the back of the ambulance with me and Blade, and locks our gurneys into the floor of the ambulance. My eyes are still closed, but I hear them settle into the chair at the far end.

The engine of the ambulance roars to life, and then we're moving.

This might be my only chance to talk to Aurelia again. I let go and allow my consciousness to float up into the air above the ambulance. I reach out, searching for the other dragon. It doesn't take me long to find her. She's floating nearby—her presence nothing more than a glowing mass —watching what's happening.

"You're leaving," she says. A shimmer passes over her shape, and I know she's upset.

"Yes. I don't know where they're taking us," I say. "But once I get free, I'll come find you."

Her shape morphs into her familiar shadow realm presence. *"What if you can't find me?"* she asks, her eyes wide.

She looks so scared and fragile, I say the first thing that comes into my head. "I'll find you," I promise her. "I'll get you out of that volcano, and you'll be able to hang out in the real world again." I don't know how I'm going to rescue her when I haven't figured out how to rescue myself, but I can't leave her here without giving her some kind of hope.

"Don't die on me," she whispers, her voice cracking with emotion. *"Make sure you survive."*

For the first time, I wish I could touch her in the shadow realm, and give her a big comforting hug. I move closer. "I can't promise I'll be around forever, but I'm going to get you free. I promise I'll live long enough to get you free."

She nods, and then before either of us can say anything else, I'm being pulled back into my body. I concentrate on not fighting it, and the transition back is at least not as painful as it was the first couple of times I did it.

I lie there a moment, panting as I get used to being inside my body again. The ambulance lurches, and the man sitting in the back with us grunts as we're thrown about.

"Watch what you're doing," he grumbles to the driver.

"We're running late. We gotta get to the airport or the boss'll be pissed at us," he growls back.

Airport? They're taking us on a plane? All I can hope for is that wherever we're going will give me the chance I need to escape. This isn't just about rescuing my father and Blade anymore. I made a promise to Aurelia—rash but sincere—and I have every intention of keeping it.

~

THE PLANE MAKES a bumpy landing at a small tarmac in the middle of nowhere. The bone in my shoulder feels like it's burning a hole through to my back. I can't think properly through the pain. Blade didn't wake the whole time we've been in the air. I'm pretty sure they must have given him something to knock him out.

The medics wheel our gurneys off the plane, and stop beside an ambulance. There are cars as well, all waiting to take us to our destination.

Lakas comes over, a wisp of a smile on his long face. "I have another job for you, Mei," he says.

I shiver, and I know there's fear in my eyes. I can't hide it.

"You will use your control of the spell web to help us take back the Earthbound Compound from your friend Carrick, the self-appointed Mountain King. Our men are outside the compound now. You may begin."

I shake my head from side to side, and tears well. Even as I resist, I can feel my magic starting to swell, and the spell web emerging from deep inside me. The spell web carries me to the Earthbound Compound, and I see the trucks and cars of the SIG soldiers standing at the ready.

I try to stop myself, but I can't. On autopilot, I create a surge across all the spell web, across the whole of the country. I drag all the supernatural energy to me through the spell web, and I push it into the men and women waiting outside the gates, amping up their supernatural abilities.

I use the spell web's energy to blast open the gates, and then follow as the men rush in, overpowering the initial resistance. They shoot and kill several of the first mountain supers who arrive to defend the compound, but it's over very quickly after that. The supers inside the compound have all been drained of their powers, and the soldiers attacking have all been given access to more. It's a completely mismatched battle, and it's clear to everyone on both sides.

I notice Carrick, on one side of the main building, fighting against five SIG soldiers. Even as I watch, they overpower him, hitting him more often than they get hit. For a moment I think I could help him, maybe give him extra strength to help him fight. But when I try, I'm completely blocked, unable to move. My powers aren't my own any more, they're locked into the instructions that Lakas has given me.

Instead I hover inside the spell web, watching as Carrick is punched and beaten with the back end of a rifle, until he slumps to the ground. I'm scared they're going to kill him, but they stop once he's no longer conscious. Then, along with the remaining Mountain supers at the compound, he's dragged through the main doors and into the cells below. Only the fact that I can still feel his presence on the spell web tells me that he's alive.

As soon as the fight is over, my consciousness races back along the spell web grid lines and slams me back into my body. This time, when the terrible surge of pain arrives to take over, I welcome it. It's what I deserve for letting them hurt Carrick and the others like that.

The bone in my shoulder throbs in time to the blood pumping around my body and I wish for death.

CHAPTER
SIXTEEN

I wake a few hours later and still feel awful. My head is thumping, my whole body aches. I'm in another hospital bed, in another anonymous ward. I can only assume that I'm in the compound somewhere. The combined effects of using the spell web three times in such a short space of time and then spending the entire night helping rescue people from the shadow realm has left me exhausted and weak. It's like I've been hit by a truck and left for dead.

I don't know what they've done with Blade. We were separated once the ambulance arrived at the compound, but he hadn't woken the last time I saw him. I can only hope he's okay.

I was never sick enough to spend time in the hospital wing before now, so I don't actually know where it's located in the compound. But it doesn't matter, because I can't actually move. The dragon bone is still sticking out of my shoulder, a gruesome reminder that I'm not in control. Lakas loomed over me at one point and ordered me to stay in my bed, and now I couldn't move even if it was a matter of life or death. And if that didn't keep me in the bed, the discordant hum of an Earthbound machine is vibrating through the floor underneath me, keeping me weak and in my human form.

So instead of figuring out how I'm going to escape, I'm lying here, glued to this bed, wishing I knew how to make my brain work properly again. I need to figure out how to pull this god-forsaken bone out of my shoulder, but it seems beyond me right now.

Everything feels so out of my control, that I start to worry about Aurelia. I promised her that I'd come back and save her, but at this point, it looks unlikely. Lakas has me locked down too tightly. My shoulder throbs in time with my heartbeat, and it feels like a ticking clock, counting down my remaining hours.

My thoughts turn to Seth, my beautiful phoenix, and I wonder if he's still in his cave, destroyed by the idea that this is all his fault. I was angry with him when they kidnapped me, because of his forced marriage to the raven woman, but now I'm struggling to remember anything but my love for him. I'm glad I didn't stay and try to convince him that I was alive when I visited in the shadow realm.

He'd have been the one they captured, instead of my father, instead of Blade. It's bad enough that anyone at all was captured because of me, but after everything Seth has been through, the thought of him ending up in Lakas's hands... well, I'm happy he's out there, still in his cave, instead of here with me.

I'm happy, even though I'd like to see him right now, to touch his hand, to see that smile he saves just for me. His remaining hazel eye would bore into me, and he'd have a slight frown, like he was annoyed by my sorry state. And he'd definitely plot his revenge on Lakas like a military coup. Short and sharp, no nonsense, definite bloodshed. Once it was done, he'd smile down at me and tell me he loved me, and I'd know he meant it because it's the smile that is mine alone.

My vision of Seth is so clear, I'm convinced he's going to walk through the door of this hospital room any second. It's like it's a vision of my future, not a wish from my imagination. But it's only for a moment, and then reality hits me. There's a very real chance that I might never see Seth in person again. I manage to contain the sob in my chest, but my thoughts scatter in my head, like a herd of antelope that's just been attacked by a lion. I can't think like that. I can't allow the fear that maybe Lakas will win even enter my head.

I close my eyes, desperately wishing I knew what to do. How to fix this situation, save the people who are here because of me. Save myself.

Time passes—no idea how much—and I doze in and out of consciousness, until eventually I start to feel a little better. Like maybe I was only hit by a small car instead of a truck. I open my eyes again and look around the room, trying to find something that might be useful, or will jog an idea or a brain wave that will help me figure out how to get out of here. Lakas's instructions bind me to the bed and I struggle to even make a plan, let alone execute it.

If I didn't have the bone in my shoulder, maybe I could do something more?

I lift my hand tentatively, and reach out to touch it, half expecting some kind of spell to stop me from doing that as well. My hand inches closer and closer, and I'm tensed for the explosion of pain I'm sure is about to hit.

And then my hand touches the hard bone.

There's a zing of electricity, but nothing compared to

the pain I've been experiencing every time I use the spell web. I trace my fingers up the shaft of the bone, and over the leather ribbons that are wound around the top half. My brain stutters for a moment when I remember that it's the skin of some other dragon they killed. A golden dragon, dead before her time.

A surge of anger overwhelms me, filling my vision with a red haze. They're just as bad as the dragons they say they hate. Worse, even.

Without thinking, I grasp the bone in my hand. I know there will be more to removing it than the strength provided by my surge of anger, but I can't help myself. Fear and anger and desperation have all rolled up together into a fizzing ball inside my chest, and if I can't climb out of the bed, then this is the next best action.

Futile as it may be.

I yank hard on the bone. A blinding pain rips its way through my shoulder, but again, it's not as bad as the pain I've been experiencing. I pull harder, almost reveling in the pain, in the way it makes me feel alive and real. I feel the magic of the bone fighting against me, holding onto the flesh of my body, hooking into my skin and bone. I don't care. I keep pulling, my face scrunching into a tortured, silent howl as I focus on getting the bone out of me. The pain is intense, but I keep going. I'm not going to stop, and I don't care if this is the last thing I ever do. At least they won't be able to force me to do anything more to the people I love.

Or even to people I don't know. To strangers in the night, trapped inside buildings, screaming for help.

The thought makes me pull even harder. My hand feels raw, burned. But I won't give up. I'm getting this bone out of me. The agony in my shoulder is spreading through my body like a toxic wave. I'm shaking and sweating all over, but I keep pulling on the bone, fear, anger and desperation pushing me, forcing me to keep going.

There's a rushing sound in my ears, like I'm traveling through a tunnel, speeding faster than I can possibly handle....and then suddenly the bone is out of my shoulder.

I hold it in the air in one hand, my blood dripping down my arm and onto the sheet. I stare at the bone, incredulous. I can't believe I actually got it out. My head is spinning, my breathing ragged, and my whole body is trembling, but I did it. I let out a whoosh of breath. It feels like a weight has been lifted off me and I'm free again. *I did it.* I outsmarted Lakas and his terrible spell.

For the first time in a long while, I grin with pleasure, my triumph soaring inside me. The feeling of Lakas's compulsion to stay in the bed is gone.

I glance down at the wound. Blood is oozing out of the hole in my shoulder, and the edges of the hole are a violent red, with sections of pulsating green pus.

Okay. I don't think that's good.

But it doesn't matter. I'm free. Pushing my elbows into the bed, I wedge myself upward. This is my chance. I can escape, now that the bone is out of my shoulder. I try to push myself up properly so I'm sitting in the bed, and get my legs out from under the sheet.

Except I can't. No matter how much I push with my other arm, I'm too weak to even get myself to sitting. My whole body is like a dead weight, bound to the bed. I think maybe I have an infection from the wound. Tears of frustration well in the corners of my eyes, and I bang my head back on the pillow.

The door opens across the room, and Lakas appears. His

expression darkens when he notices the blood around my shoulder and on the white sheets, and the bone in my hand.

"You keep fighting, but you're too late. It's over. You've lost." His voice is smug and gravelly. It's the most hateful sound I've ever heard.

I don't say anything in return. There's nothing to say. I have this horrible feeling he's right.

"Your friend Hazel has agreed to give herself up to save her precious jaguar shifter," he continues. "We have your father and Carrick the so-called mountain king in a cell below us. Everyone who might have saved you has been neutralized." His voice is low and sneering, and I wish with every bone in my body that I could stand up and punch him in the face.

Instead, I close my eyes and block him out. I figure a dude like Lakas thrives on an audience. He likes people to know how smart he is and how well his plan is going. If I don't react, maybe I'll hurt him that way. I sure as hell can't hurt him any other way.

"I just came to tell you that I'm leaving, and you'll be in the capable hands of Connor for a couple of days. Try not to misbehave."

I keep ignoring him.

He walks closer until he's looming over the bed. His wheezing breath whistles over my skin as he bends down to gloat.

"I think I'll take this from you. I don't want you trying to stab anyone else with it." He pulls the dragon bone out of my tightly clenched fingers. I try to hold onto it, to fight him in this small way, but it's like he's taking candy from a baby. "It only works on other dragons, but there's no point giving you a knife to use against the guards or Connor."

My hands curl into fists on the bed beside me, and his small laugh is enough to let me know he's seen my reaction.

"Thank you for showing me that I need to give orders *not to take it out* to the next dragon. Maybe your friend Zane, the enormous black dragon? I think I'd like to have a pet like him."

I can't help my small outraged gasp. The thought of him having Zane—or any other dragon—under that kind of control is almost more than I can bear. The only thing that's helping me keep my eyes closed is the knowledge that he's trying to get a reaction out of me.

He sniffs the air around me. "You smell... old. Like you're decaying. I don't think you're going to last much longer." He leans in closer. "It's a pity, because there's so much more I would have liked to do to you. So many more pieces of vengeance I would have liked to eek from your bones."

He walks toward the exit, and I risk opening my eyes again. He stops, like he can tell I'm watching. Turning, he holds up the bone. "Perhaps I'll make another of these with *your* bones once you're dead. I think I understand the magic. It would be nice to keep you with me forever." He pauses, as if considering. "Maybe I won't even wait 'til you're dead to do it."

Bile rises up through my throat and I can't help the reflexive gag.

Lakas smiles, like that was exactly the reaction he was hoping for. "Yes, I think I'm going to enjoy spending time with you when I get back from New York, Mei." His voice drips with evil promise and I half expect him to start cackling as he walks out the door, closing it softly behind him.

CHAPTER
SEVENTEEN

For a long time after Lakas leaves, I lie in the bed, pressing a bunched-up section of my sheet on the oozing wound in my shoulder, wishing I knew what to do. I've always been able to find a way out of any situation.

Jeff and Si made sure I was a tactical thinker, an active part of any dangerous situation we found ourselves in. I've always been able to move fast, be strong, fight hard.

But I've never felt this weak before. This lost. For a moment, the temptation to wallow is so strong, I almost give in to it. Except I can't.

No matter what, you fight. *No matter what, Mei. I don't care if they've chopped both your legs off. You fight.* Jeff's words echo through my head, and I nod to myself. I can still picture him standing in front of me in his rumpled SIG suit, his slightly-longer-than-regulation hair and his scruffy beard taking away from the sharp agent look that my father always has.

Except Jeff was more of a father to me than my biological father was. He led me, taught me, trusted me. Made me trust him.

I can vividly remember his eyes, wise and warm, honorable. I trusted him, because I knew that I'd always survive if I just followed his rules.

Jeff was the first person to make me feel safe as a kid. I'd had so many near fatal attempts on my life by the time he arrived, I'd pretty much accepted I wasn't going to make it out of my teens. Big, straight-talking, with a healthy dislike for following the crowd, he gave me hope right from the start. He taught me how to be smart and strong. He didn't accept that I would die. He taught me to fight to the bitter end. Both physically and mentally. To never give up.

And so, even though it feels like there's no hope left, I can't stop fighting. I'd feel like I was letting Jeff down somehow.

And I refuse to let him down.

So that means I can't assume this is it.

There has to be a way to win against Lakas and the director.

And there's only one thing I can think of that I can still do with my physical body so close to death. I close my eyes again, and allow my consciousness to float up above my body and into the shadow realm. I can't do anything in this plane other than watch and maybe whisper in someone's ear, but at least I won't be stuck in this bed. It provides a feeling of freedom, no matter how false.

I hover uncertainly over the bed. Usually, I go upwards, but Lakas said he had Carrick and my father locked in the cells below. I'd like to see both of them right now. Perhaps I can help them.

So I head downward, my body ephemeral and light, no

more than a shadow. The stone walls and thick floors can't stop me as I search. I can feel the anti-magic of the Earthbound's machines buzzing through the walls in a way that's not possible in my physical body. There's an energy inside the shadow plane that's completely different to the spell web grid. The spell web feels powerful and flashy, bright and brilliant. The shadow realm is more subtle, on the edges. It's darker, less obvious, although just as powerful in its own way. As I float through the shadow realm, I soak up the energy, trying to understand it like I understand the spell web. It seems strange and transient, with understanding just out of reach.

The Earthbound Compound itself is a series of old buildings in the style of a South American hacienda, with high ceilings and thick concrete walls, and cold dark rooms the more you retreat underground. I pass the room where— the first time I was here—Viktor tried to prove I was a dragon by locking me in a furnace. At the time I thought he was a lunatic, but it turns out he was right. It would have been nice if he didn't feel the need to prove it to me so... vigorously.

It seems like a lifetime ago that I was here that first time, fighting for my life. I survived that time, surely I can do it again.

I hope.

I keep moving lower, and pass by the cells where they kept Seth on that same trip. My heart skips a beat at the thought of him in that cave in the mountains, all alone with his heartache. I want to make him feel better, to let him know that I'm still alive, still here for him. For a moment, the temptation to leave this place and travel to him is almost more than I can bear, and I actually turn around and start to move in his direction.

Then I stop. I wish I could go to him, I really do, but it

seems like a bad idea. What if I let him know that I'm alive, only to die on him again? Wouldn't that make his grief even worse?

Whereas my father and Carrick are locked in here somewhere, and maybe there's something I could do to help them. Maybe there's something they could do to help me as well.

And if I let Seth know I'm alive, he'll want to come save me. He'll end up trapped inside this compound like the rest of us. At least right now Seth's free, even if, because of me, he thinks he's hearing voices in his head up there in the mountain.

It's better to know he's safe and alive, than to rush to him so I can get the comfort I'm craving right now.

So, I force myself to keep going downward, until finally I find a dark hallway with a row of cells and heavy doors barring each of them. My shadow-self skims through the walls, and in the first three I find supers I don't know, people who've pissed someone off, and ended up here.

In the fourth room, I find my father and Carrick. My father is lying with his eyes closed on a hard wooden pallet, his face bruised and beaten. I wish I could use some healing energy on him, but given I can't even heal myself, it's a whimsical thought. Carrick is sitting on the wooden slat bed across from my father, his forearms resting on his knees and staring down at the floor beneath him. He looks defeated.

I hesitate, watching them both. My father already knows that I can travel the shadow realm, and he might react better to me whispering in his ear. But he looks like he's sleeping, possibly even unconscious. Carrick at least is awake. Hovering near him, I try to think of something to say that will let him know it's really me. Before I can speak, he looks up, directly into my face.

"Mei," he says calmly.

I float backward away from him, startled. "You can see me?"

Carrick nods slowly, his wise eyes like deep pools of power. "Your father said you told him where you were being held." He peers at me, as if trying to decipher a math equation. "Where are you? Is this part of your dragon magic?"

It's such a relief to see him and feel his calm strength, I can't help my grin. "I'm in the shadow realm."

Carrick's eyes widen slightly. "I've heard rumors of it, but I've never seen any evidence before today." He reaches out as if to touch my ghost-like form, then pulls his hand back.

"No one else has been able to see me," I say. How is it that Carrick has the ability? My brain can't quite answer that question yet.

"We've taken each other's wounds, so perhaps we've taken a little more from each other than we thought."

For someone who's locked in a prison cell, was pummeled by the SIG soldiers when they took over the compound, and looks like he hasn't bathed in weeks, Carrick seems remarkably calm. If nothing else, it makes me feel a little more real to have him talk to me and see my face. It doesn't matter why.

"Are you okay? How badly did they hurt you?" I ask anxiously.

Carrick gives a derisive snort. "It's difficult to hurt a mountain super, especially the Mountain King. I'm better off than Damien." He looks down at my father, thick brows furrowed. "They beat him up pretty good."

"It was Lakas. He...He made me use the spell web. Threatened to kill him."

Carrick nods, his face darkening. "Damien told me. Don't worry, we'll figure out a way to get him back for that."

I smile, absurdly pleased by his words. "Do you have a plan? A way to get everyone out of here?"

"Not yet. Damien said he thinks best when he's sleeping, so I'm hoping that when he wakes, he'll have something." Carrick looks at my dad's limp body dubiously, before turning back to me. "Are you okay? Where's your physical body?"

"In the hospital ward upstairs. Lakas said Hazel gave herself up, to save Blade. He tried to rescue me as well, and they caught him." I pause, staring down at my father. "They seem to have captured everyone."

Carrick's expression turns thoughtful. "If Hazel knows where we all are, perhaps the others will have formed a plan."

"The others?"

"Hazel, Mr. Fookes, Freddie. All the people on the west coast." He hesitates. "We haven't talked in a while."

I frown in confusion. "You're not working together?"

Carrick grimaces, and runs one hand over his face. "After you were kidnapped... There was a falling out. Damien and Seth wanted Hazel to use her third wish from the genie to find you, and she refused. She released Mr. Fookes instead of finding you."

My heart lurches at the thought of everyone fighting. "Hazel would have wanted to do what was right." I think about how close I was to maybe being saved, and my breath catches. Except... "She told me she promised Mr. Fookes she'd release him on the third wish. He would have disappeared otherwise, they wouldn't have been able to find him again."

Carrick looks away, staring at the stone walls of the cell as if they're fascinating. "Tensions were high. No one was thinking clearly. Everyone was worried about you. We didn't know where you were..." Carrick trails off, and I can see the pain on his face, and a bit of guilt.

"We all need to start working together again now if we're going to get out of this. I wonder if Hazel is here yet." I look around as if she's going to pop out of the wall. "I'm sure she wouldn't come by herself. Which means the others will be here too." My heart beats faster, unexpected hope filling my veins. "If that's the case, I'm sure we can set up a rescue party. I can help by telling them where everyone is, giving information."

Carrick sits up a little straighter. "If you come back here and tell me and Damien what's happening, maybe we can coordinate something. An ambush perhaps."

"How are you going to get out of the cell?"

Carrick smiles, his expression smug. "They didn't really think about holding a mountain super with an affinity for rocks when they designed these cells."

"You could have gotten out of here at any time since they attacked?"

Carrick shrugs. "They have Elena in another cell. And I wanted to be able to rescue everyone, not just sneak out by myself. I was just waiting for the right moment."

I nod, excitement thrumming through my shimmering body. "Hopefully this is it. I'll go see what I can find."

CHAPTER

EIGHTEEN

I swish through the wall, then up and up, until I'm above the Earthbound complex. I eagerly search the grounds to see if I can find anyone I recognize, but it's all just guards wearing the SIG uniform.

I don't know how I'm going to find the others, or if we're even right that they'll be here, but I'm determined to try. If I was going to bring people with me when I was giving myself up, where would they go? I search inside the compound and can't find them, so I move along the massive concrete wall at the edges, searching for possible ways to enter. I'm guessing they'll be close, but not too close. Not close enough to be found straight away, at least. But close enough they could try to enter later under cover of darkness.

I widen my search, and soon I can see a small village not far from the compound. I head into the town, and hunt for anyone I know. It's Zane I sense first. I guess I'm attuned to other dragons. He's sitting in a small black car with five others. Mr. Fookes I recognize, and the other three look vaguely familiar. All friends of Hazel's, I'm sure.

Hesitating, I hover in the air above the car, trying to decide what to do. But then the decision is made for me. Zane opens the door and climbs out, stretching his arms above his head. He looks up, and looks through me, like he can't see me. But I move closer, trying to find the best way to tell him I'm here and not freak him out.

In the end, I just say, "Zane, don't freak out. It's me, Mei."

Zane jerks and looks around quickly, arms out in a defensive position.

"I'm not really here, my body is back in the Earthbound Compound. I'm in the shadow realm."

Zane is still looking like he's wondering what the hell is going on. Maybe he doesn't know about the shadow realm?

"Ask me anything. Something only I would know. But hurry, because we don't have much time. Carrick and my father are locked in the prison cells in the basement, Hazel is in danger, and I don't know how we're going to save them all."

Zane lets out a breath. "Well that sounds like you, Mei. So answer this: What was it that attacked us when we went to my family home?"

"That's easy. It was the demon. The one that Hazel killed for me."

"How are you even doing this?" Zane is peering into the air around him, trying to locate where I am.

"I learned how when Lakas first kidnapped me. It was a way to escape for a while." Again, I don't tell him exactly what I was avoiding.

By the hardening of Zane's expression, he's guessed what I'm trying not to say. "I'm gonna kill that guy when I see him next," he growls.

I nod in complete agreement—except for who's going

to do the killing. "He's gone. He and the director left for New York on some urgent errand. Connor is in charge at the compound until they get back."

"They trust Connor to get things done?"

"I assume there are other people around," I say drily. Connor has a bit of a reputation; Hazel told me all about his crazy experiments on demons.

Mr. Fookes is looking out the window of the car, staring at Zane. He rolls down the window. "Are you talking to anyone in particular? Praying to the Gods that our plan works?"

Zane glances at Mr. Fookes and then at me.

"It's okay, tell him. Tell them all. I just want to help everyone escape."

Zane walks closer to Mr. Fookes's open window and puts one hand over the edge of the door. "Don't freak out when I tell you," he warns, unconsciously echoing my words to him. "But Mei is here with us, in the shadow realm."

Mr. Fookes peers over Zane's shoulder as if trying to spot me.

"You won't be able to see her. But I can hear her voice. I think we'll all be able to hear her."

Mr. Fookes climbs out of the car, followed by a woman wearing a bright pink knitted jersey, and Freddie, the guy who was with Blade at the medical centre.

"Is Blade okay?" asks Freddie as soon as he gets out of the car. "Have you seen him?" He looks a little worse for wear, although not as bad as Blade.

"He's alive, but they beat him up pretty bad. I haven't seen him since we arrived at the Compound. I-I... I was the one who helped them get in." I try not to think about

Carrick locked in a cell and the mountain supers who were killed because of me. "They captured my father."

The last two to exit the car are a tall, elegant black woman, and a short, red-headed woman with pale skin and a twitchy nose. They stare around them into the air, trying to pinpoint my direction.

"We figured," says Zane. "We realized Damien was missing. Seemed a good bet he was with you."

I nod, even though they can't see me. "That's why I have to help now. We need to find a way for you to get into the compound and rescue everyone."

"Where's your physical body? Can you let us in?" asks Zane.

I hesitate, not sure how to explain. "No, that's not possible," I say quickly, hoping Zane drops that line of questioning.

"You're being heavily guarded?" asks Mr. Fookes sharply, like he really wants that to be my answer.

"No idea." I clear my throat. "I...uh...just can't leave my bed right now. But I can talk to people while I'm in the shadow realm. Carrick and my dad are in the cells on the bottom level, and Carrick says he can break out at any time."

"We were waiting for a signal from Hazel," says the woman in the knitted jumper anxiously. "She and Blade decided to stay in there and try to rescue... well, you, Mei. She said she'd give us the signal when she needed us to come in and help. That was a little while ago, though. She's stopped transmission via her button. We don't know what that means."

Mr. Fookes puts an arm around her shoulders. "It's fine, Daphne. Hazel can take care of herself." He turns to me.

"But I do agree that we need to make a plan to get inside. Any ideas, Mei?"

I don't even hesitate. "There's a door on the far side, it's not guarded as much, and it has a latch that's fairly easy to break. I thought if you wanted to get in, that would be the place."

Zane and Mr. Fookes share a look.

"That's exactly the kind of information we need," says Zane. "What else have you got for us?"

I hesitate, thinking through what I'd do if I were planning this kind of a mission. "Not everyone should go in together. You need two teams. One to provide back up if required, and one to lead the charge and draw the fire, if any."

Zane nods again. "Makes sense."

"One team needs to free Hazel and Blade, and the other team needs to head for my father and Carrick and the people who are locked up."

"But what about the Earthbound machines?" asks Zane. "They have a large supply of them in there."

"I don't think they do. They've been farming them out to their allies, so I don't think there are many of them left."

"All they need is one," says Zane grimly. He's felt the effects of those machines, just like I have.

"Then maybe the team that's going to save my father and Carrick needs to do a side mission first, and get rid of the machine," I say.

"How about we break off into three teams of two," says Zane. "Me and Freddie can go after the machines, Mr. Fookes and Daphne can go down into the dungeons and cause some trouble there, and Iris and Poppy," he gestures to the two other women, "can go look for Hazel and Blade."

Everyone is nodding agreement. "I can be your eyes and

ears," I say, pleased to be able to lend a hand. "I can tell you if someone is coming. And I know where Hazel and Blade aren't, that might be helpful for Iris and Poppy."

"What about you, Mei? Who should come rescue you?" asks Zane. His expression is carefully bland.

"Me?" I'd forgotten about me, truth be told. I don't think there's much point trying to get me out of the Compound. "I, uh... I can get myself out," I say lamely. Zane is staring at me like he can see me, even though I know it's just because he's figured out where my voice is coming from.

"We don't leave anyone behind," he says. "Where are you?"

I hesitate, torn between telling them not to bother and letting them know the truth, and... well, lying to them. "I'm in the hospital wing," I say eventually. "It's at the back, ground floor." I don't have the heart to tell him I don't think I'm going to make it out of there.

CHAPTER
NINETEEN

"I'll meet you at the entrance to the compound," I say, as the others all climb back into the car. "Don't take too long."

They wave in my general direction and take off. My mode of transportation is a million times faster, and I'm back at the compound in seconds. I look nervously up and down the wall, trying to see if there will be any problems—like guards—by the entrance I've suggested. They don't seem particularly worried about security, which is weird, but perhaps they just haven't had a chance to settle into proper routines yet. There's definitely a general lack of security anywhere on the outside of the building. They seem to be concentrating on the front entrance, with a few guards on the roof to monitor the rest of the area. Perhaps they figure they've managed to capture all the people who'd attack them, so it doesn't matter?

I can't worry about it now, so I do the next best thing. I roam about on the other side of the wall, and plan the best route for each of the teams.

Freddie and Zane need to head to the main floors; I figure they'll have the machines out in the large hall where I first met and talked to Vincent, the previous leader of the Earthbound. Mr. Fookes and Daphne need to head down the side and through the back stairwell to get to the prison cells deep in the main building. I don't know where Hazel and Blade will be, maybe in the laboratories on the far side. It's the path that I'm least sure about, so I decide to go with that team at first to help them find their way.

I've scouted the area and returned by the time the others arrive. They leave the car a distance from the compound, and run at a low crouch to the door, trying to stay out of view of the SIG guards at the main entrance.

"I don't think they're monitoring this door," I say to Zane, making him jump. He growls and then glares in my general direction.

"Sorry, I forgot you can't see me."

"Are there guards on the other side?"

"No, they're all concentrated by the main entrance and buildings. There are some guards on the roof, but they're not really focusing on this side either."

"It's pretty desolate." Daphne looks around and over her shoulder. "Perhaps they think no one would bother entering from here?"

"Either that or they have some other way to monitor these entrances," says Mr. Fookes grimly.

"If they do, it just means you need to move fast," I say. "Get through, and separate to your different areas." I outline the paths I've found for each of the three teams. They all nod their understanding.

"Who's going to get us in?" asks Iris.

Everyone turns to look at Poppy.

"Who me? What makes you think—" She stops when

they all raise their eyebrows at her, almost as if they'd practiced doing it together previously. "Okay, sure, I can unlock this gate. But it's weird that you all just assume." She saunters over to the gate and pulls a couple of strange metal tools from the pocket of her black denim jacket. In less than two minutes, she has the door open and they're all hustling through.

I grin at Poppy; she's a useful person to have around. Hazel has managed to find some interesting friends. Loyal friends too, if they're willing to risk their lives to rescue everyone like this.

Mr. Fookes and Daphne nod at everyone and head off silently. Hazel told me that because he's a genie, Mr. Fookes could look any way he wanted, but he prefers the beer belly and thinning hair as a way to hide in plain sight. Daphne is a slightly overweight motherly looking woman who looks like butter wouldn't melt in her mouth—except for the faint hint of wildness in her eyes that makes me think she's more than she appears at first. They make a strangely graceful pair, despite how they look at first glance.

Zane glances overhead, like he thinks I'm floating somewhere in the sky. "Mei, once we've dealt with the machines, we'll come for you, okay?"

"Okay," I say, even though I'm starting to feel weaker now, and I'm not sure how much longer I have. My physical body is calling to me, but I'm determined to help for as long as I can. "Make sure you do your first task before you come get me."

"Aye, sir," says Zane mockingly, giving me a casual salute as he and Freddie head in the other direction from Mr. Fookes and Daphne. I watch them go, hoping they'll be okay.

"So where do we go?" asks Iris. She's bouncing one leg

to the other, like she's prepping herself for action. I immediately like her straight-forward attitude.

"I think they might be in the laboratories in the far corner of the compound. I'll show you the way, and keep you out of sight of the guards. If they're not there, we'll figure something else out."

They nod.

"Let's go. Run to the corner of that orange building."

They follow my instructions across the compound, and we don't meet any guards. We get to the building where I think the labs might be located, but when we search the first level, there's nothing there.

"We need to go down," says Poppy. "Be systematic. Mei, you go down two floors, and we'll go to the next one and search. Come back and let us know if you find anything."

"Okay," I say. "Good idea. I'll see you soon. Just take care. There are guards roaming all around this building." I take off, eager to find Hazel and Blade.

They're not in the next floor or the one after that. Even the one after that. I'm getting tired, and the pull of my physical body is getting stronger. I don't know how much longer I'll be able to help them, and I'm beginning to wonder if we're searching the wrong area of the complex.

But on the last level, the same basement floor as the prison cells, I finally strike it lucky. I find a series of labs made of the same cold stone as the cells. It's not exactly a friendly or warm environment, but when I move around I can tell that it's been used as a working lab up until very recently. There are books scattered over the metal bench tops and someone has left a jacket over the back of a chair.

At first, I think it's empty, that maybe they've taken Blade and Hazel somewhere else to lock them up. But then I realize there's someone through a second door on the far side of the lab, inside an enormous second room that's been carved out of natural underground stone. I move cautiously over to the second room, hesitating in the doorway, not sure if the person is alive or not.

I move closer, and immediately recognize Blade. I race over to his side, but he's not moving. I can't even touch him to see if he's breathing.

I race back up to the floor where Poppy and Iris are searching, my heart pounding in my ears. It's a strange feeling, given that my physical body is somewhere else. But I'm determined to get help for Blade, so I don't hesitate as I slam through the walls and along the corridors. I manage to curb the instinct to yell out their names—even if I'm not visible, they are, and I might give them away to any guards who might be patrolling around.

I eventually find them standing in the middle of an empty room that might once have been used as a meeting area, if the chairs stacked at the edges of the room is any indication.

I'm about to start talking at them, waving excitedly as if they can see my arms, when I realize they're not alone. They both have their hands in the air, and there's an SIG guard holding a machine gun on them.

He looks young, and a little nervous about what he's doing. Iris and Poppy are both doing their best to look young and innocent as well.

"Stay where you are," says the guard, his voice cracking in the middle. He's got lightly freckled skin and brown hair that's just long enough to stand up in a cowlick at the front. He looks like someone's younger brother rather than a guard for the SIG.

I can see Poppy eyeing him up, and I know she's considering rushing him. He's young enough that it might frighten him, and maybe he'll freeze up. It's a huge gamble, though. One I'm not prepared for them to take. I move closer to the guard. Maybe I should talk to him. But that seems like the kind of thing that would freak him out, and again, perhaps lead to accidentally setting off his gun.

Without thinking, I move even closer. I touch his skin with invisible fingers. I'm following my instinct. I want to try going inside him. Maybe I can confuse him enough to help the others to overpower him? It seems like it will be unpleasant, being inside another a person. But something is telling me to do it anyway.

I take a breath and move. I'm right. It's gross. There's too much moving around: blood pumping, mucus flowing, flesh clenching, organs beating. For a moment, it over-whelms me. All I can do is to shout inside my head: "Drop the gun. Lie down. Drop the gun. Lie down." I keep repeating the words, trying to block out the dripping and beating and flowing going on around me and through me.

It's only when he moves and I stay in the same place that I can tell it worked. He drops the gun and lies down on the ground, just like I was shouting. His face is confused and his skin looks a little green around the edges. I feel a little bit the same way.

Iris and Poppy glance at each other, and then both launch into action. Iris grabs his gun, and Poppy hauls him to the side of the room where she locks him to the door handle of the broom closet with zip ties that she finds in his pocket. She takes his handset and his mobile phone off him, as well as a small revolver that's attached to his belt.

He still looks like he's feeling unwell. Did I do that? What was it like for him to have me inside him? Will there be long lasting effects for him?

I shudder. I don't plan on doing again if I can help it.

"What happened?" Iris frowns down at the guard.

"Me," I say quietly. They both jump out of their skins.

"Jeez, a little warning, Mei," says Poppy, holding one hand to her heart like it's pumping faster than she'd like.

"Sorry. I keep forgetting," I say. "Although I don't quite know how I'm supposed to warn you that I'm here."

"You're starting to get hard to hear," says Iris. "Are you okay?"

"I'm fine," I say dismissively, even though I'm feeling much weaker after being inside the guard's body. "I've found the lab, and I found Blade. But I can't tell how he is. It's three flights down, in the basement."

I race ahead of them, telling them where to go as we get to junctions, and avoiding the guards. In no time at all, we're back in the lab with Blade.

Iris crouches down beside him, and pulls out a small bone. She starts waving it over him, and I can sense the powerful magic she's using to heal him through my connection to the spell web. After a minute, Blade opens his eyes. He looks at Iris and then over at Poppy.

"They have Hazel," he says, his voice croaking. He tries to push himself up.

Iris holds one hand firmly on his chest. "You need to give the magic time to work. You're not up to full strength yet."

He lies back. "They want her to create a new spell web using demons. It's Connor and her father, Gavan. They took her with them. I think they're doing it right *now*."

"We're going to get her out of here, don't worry," says Poppy.

I'm starting to feel weaker and weaker. My body is tugging me back. "Guys, I have to leave. I can't help any more. But good luck. Find the others. Carrick and my dad are in the prison cells on this floor. Help them all." My voice is getting weaker and I can't hold myself with them any longer.

"Wait, Mei! Hold on," says Poppy. "We need—"

But I'm gone before I can hear her request.

CHAPTER
TWENTY

I've been worried about the spell web slowly killing me ever since I found out that's what was happening every time I had one of my attacks. I was always secretly worried that I was about to die at any minute, and I wouldn't even know. Except for the excruciating pain of the attacks, I never felt any different.

But now I know what it's like to *feel* the spell web killing me.

When my body pulled me back forcibly, away from Iris and Poppy, I fought it. I wanted to help, I *needed* to help them.

But as soon as I slammed back inside my physical presence, the agony started.

Bolts of electricity are shooting up and down my arms and legs, like I'm being dissolved in a sea of lightning. The spell web is sucking out my soul, and it's getting smaller and smaller as I lie here, unable to fight back.

I can't catch a full breath, and every time I force myself to suck in a mouthful of air, it hurts so bad, it feels like my lungs are rejecting it, like my body doesn't want to breathe oxygen any more. And it's not just my lungs—everything inside me is aching. *Everything.* My muscles, my skin, my internal organs. I can feel the blood pumping through my veins, and it *hurts.*

I know I'm about to die. I know it, because everything is breaking down inside me. If I could cry, I would. If I could roll over and sob into my pillow, I'd probably do that too. I'm not too proud to admit it, even if it's only to myself.

But I can't move. I can't do anything.

I don't even jump in my bed when the doors of the ward slam open. My eyes are too heavy to open, and I can't move out of my body into the shadow realm any more. But I can hear Connor and another man arguing and the sound of the heavy booted footsteps that usually accompany one of the guards. They're dragging something into the room.

"She's the only one who can do it," says Connor, clearly annoyed.

"Just give me a little more time. I'm almost there," says the other voice. It's whiny, and a little slurred.

"You've had all the time you get. You saw how quickly she figured it out. She's the one. So you need to control her before she wakes up again and kills us all. That's your part in all this."

The other man grumbles something under his breath, but he seems to accept what Connor is saying. Who are they talking about? Is it Hazel? I have a terrible feeling it is, and that maybe they're dragging her body across the floor.

The darkness is dragging me downward. I try to stay awake, to listen to what they're saying, but I can't. My eyes are heavy, and so is my mind. I struggle to focus on what they're saying, then everything goes black.

WHEN I WAKE AGAIN, I feel a tiny bit stronger. I can still hear Connor talking, so hopefully not much time has passed. I have to find the others, tell them where Hazel is. I immediately try to going into the shadow realm, but I don't have the strength to lift my consciousness up out of my body any more. I'm stuck where I am. But it's okay, because when I force one eye open, I realize that everyone is already here in the room with us—under armed guard.

My heart sinks.

Mr. Fookes, Daphne, Zane and Freddie are standing near the door, all looking like they've just fought their captors and lost. Connor and the other man are standing next to a bed, and for the first time, I confirm that they've got Hazel tied up. She's awake and staring at them in horror.

"Now will you do what we want?" asks Connor.

"Don't do it," yells Daphne, suddenly starting to struggle against the guard holding her. He punches her in the stomach, and she folds over in pain. Without thinking, I try to do something, move even a tiny bit. But I just stay where I am, locked inside my dying body.

Mr. Fookes thrusts himself against his guard, trying to get to Daphne and the guard who just punched her. His guard slams him in the head with the butt of his gun, and Mr. Fookes slumps to the ground.

"Stop it," yells Hazel, her voice cracking. "Stop hurting them."

"It'll only get worse, if you don't help," says Connor, his voice smug.

I want to punch his stupid, arrogant face. Except my body is still aching, the spell web still stealing my vital essences.

Hazel looks between Connor and her friends. Her

expression is tortured. I know—before she even says anything—what her answer will be. Hazel loves her friends more than anything, she's not going to give them up, not when there's still a chance to save them.

Which means I need to do something quickly. If she agrees to their demands, we don't have much time. Once the spell web is in place and Connor has control of it, we're all dead. I force myself to concentrate. I peer at the people standing by the door, wondering if there's any way I can get back into the shadow realm and... I don't know what. How is me whispering in their ears going to help? I need to—

And then it hits me. Iris and Poppy are missing.

There's still a chance that they could get a rescue mission going. The thought sends a zing of energy through my veins. Suddenly I feel brighter. There's still something that we can do. And I'm determined to help.

"Okay," Hazel whispers. "I'll do it for you. But I want them with me while I work on it."

"Again with the demands, Hazel. You keep misinterpreting your position in all this," says Connor.

"I need help. They can be my helpers."

Connor shrugs. "Fine. If you cause problems or don't do what we ask, it'll be easier to kill one of them in front of you. You'll create the new spell web in the room where it was originally created," he continues calmly, as if he didn't just threaten to kill all her friends. "We'll all go there now. No time like the present to recreate history."

"I'll need the notebooks from the lab. Just to make sure I'm doing it right," says Hazel, her voice breathy. I'm hoping this is all part of some sneaky plan she's got going on in that brainiac head of hers. And if she's got a plan, then I need one too. It might use up the last of my strength faster than if I just stayed put, but I'm determined to do what I can.

I force myself back out into the shadow realm. It's harder than it's ever been, and I'm sluggish and slow, but I manage it. I feel a thrill of pride that I can still do *something*. I'm going to get everyone out of this shitstorm, if it kills me.

Which it probably will.

Before I can think anything else, I'm off. I have to find the others and help them save Hazel and stop her from giving Connor the power of the spell web.

It doesn't take me long to find Poppy and Iris. They're running down a hallway near the lab with Blade, who's now in a guard's uniform. His face doesn't look as beat up as last time I saw him. I think Iris must have used some of her magic on him.

"Hey, wait up," I say. I'm puffing, even though my consciousness doesn't breathe in the shadow realm. I don't have much time. I'll have to be fast if I'm going to help.

"Mei? You're here?" says Poppy, slowing down and peering into the air overhead. She's got a streak of dirt across her cheek, and her vibrant red hair is coming free from its hair ties.

"They've captured the others. Hazel has agreed to make the spell web," I say in a rush, trying to say the words quickly in case I get dragged back like last time. "I don't have long. But she's asked for her notebooks from the lab."

"Blade is going to infiltrate the guards," replies Poppy. "Maybe that's our chance?" She looks at Blade and they all stop running. "If you could be the one to take the notebooks to her, you'll be close enough to protect her, Blade. It's the perfect opportunity. Then we'll just need a distraction and a few more people to fight."

"And we need to know where it's all happening," says Iris.

"It's in the basement, where the old spell web was located. I can help with the extra people," I say quickly. "I'll go tell Carrick it's time to escape. There are people down there who would be happy to provide backup."

"Let's do it," says Blade, his expression dark and grim. "Tell Mr. Fookes as well. Everyone needs to be on the same page."

I nod, and then remember they can't see me. "Okay," I say. "Good luck." I disappear through the floor without waiting for their answer.

CHAPTER
TWENTY-ONE

I feel strange, wobbly. Like I'm shimmering in and out of existence. But I don't let it stop me. I have a mission, and we're running out of time.

Bursting in through the wall of Carrick's cell, I almost go right through the back of his head before I stop myself.

"Mei?" he says, looking around. He's sitting on the same hard bed pallet he was last time.

"It's me." I look around for my father, but instead Carrick is now sharing with Elena, the dragon priestess. She doesn't look as serene as she did last time I saw her. There are dark smudges under her eyes, patches of blood and dirt over her face and neck, and her hair is hanging limply around her face. She looks like she's been to hell and back. "Where's Dad?" I ask, suddenly scared. What have they done with him? Have they—? I can't even finish the thought.

Carrick smirks. "They moved him to a separate cell. They know how devious he is, and didn't like how much we were talking."

I let out a relieved breath.

"Do you have any news? Where are the others?" asks Carrick, leaning forward, looking me in the eyes. It's soothing to be with him again.

"You know how you said you could escape at any time?" I say in a burst of words. I feel my consciousness wobble unsteadily. I have to get this out fast, before it's too late.

Carrick nods. "Of course."

"Now's the time. Hazel has agreed to make a new spell web for Connor."

"It's happening now?" Carrick's face lights up, like this is the moment he's been waiting for. Beside him, Elena looks like she's ready to beat a few guards in the head as well. Given that she's always professed to be a pacifist dragon, it's the first time I've ever seen her like that.

I shake my head and focus on Carrick. "He's captured Mr. Fookes, Daphne, Zane and Freddie, but Blade, Poppy and Iris are still free. They're heading to the spell web room right now. Blade is dressed in a guard's uniform. He's planning to get into the room and disrupt things from inside. But they need help with their attack from outside the room." My energy is draining away. I don't have much time.

Carrick nods. "We can do that, can't we Elena?" He looks over at the dragon priestess.

"I'll rip their damned heads off," she growls, her eyes glowing with her glittering dragon colors of green and blue.

"What's the plan?" Carrick stands up, suddenly all business. He stretches his arms out, like he's prepping for a race.

I'm flickering in and out. I need to get the words out as fast as I can. "Once you're out, you need to set everyone else free from the cells as well. We need as many as possible to help overpower the guards. I have to go warn the others."

"Mei..." Carrick says my name and then stops, as if he wants to say something but can't.

"Yes?"

"It's good to talk to you again. I'm sorry... I'm sorry I couldn't find you when they kidnapped you. I tried, I really did." There are tears lurking in his eyes.

"Oh Jeez, Carrick," I say, feeling like I've got a lump in my throat, even though I'm just a ball of energy right now. "It's not your fault. It was Director Holden and Lakas. Connor even. Blame the people responsible. Not yourself."

"Even so. I'm sorry."

"It's okay. I'm fine—" I stop, thinking about Aurelia. I promised to save her. "But you can do something for me. There's a dragon named Aurelia. She's trapped in the lava inside a mountain near Portland. Mt. Hood I think. Can you save her? Just in case something happens to me?" I'm trying to pretend I'm only saying it as a backup, but I'm pretty sure I'm not going to be the one to save Aurelia.

"Nothing is going to happen to you, Mei," says Carrick quickly. "We've got this situation under control. You're going to be fine." He's trying to convince himself, as much as me.

"Just in case, Carrick. Will you promise me?"

Carrick opens his mouth as if to argue, but I catch Elena giving him a glare. He closes his mouth, and then nods. "Of course. I promise."

I hesitate, feeling faint but needing to get the words out. "Be careful, Carrick. And take care of my dad for me, will you?"

Carrick looks at me with narrowed eyes. "Where's your body right now?"

"Back up in the—" I hesitate, a strange rippling sensation moving over my consciousness. "Actually, I think they're bringing me down to the spell web room too," I say.

My physical presence is getting closer and closer. The movement is making me even more woozy.

"Well, you hold on too, Mei. I'm not ready to lose you yet," he says, looking directly at me and giving me his most stern expression. "I'm serious."

I nod, glad he can see me. He's the only one who can right now. It's already too late for me, so it's nice to know someone looked me in my eyes before I died. "You take care of yourself, too," I whisper. Then I disappear through the walls before he can say anything else.

I search the hallways and stairs for the main group. I find them not far from the cells in another hallway with the same stone walls and damp murky air. Connor is herding everyone into the spell web room, including my body on the hospital bed.

There's no time to waste. I can feel the spell web inside me, working its way up to another attack. It's weaker than it's ever been, and so am I. Mr. Fookes is waiting behind my bed at the door to the room, his hands tied together and his face looking even more bruised and battered in the dim light. They're struggling to get my hospital gurney through the entrance and everyone is being forced to wait.

"Mr. Fookes, it's Mei," I whisper near his ear. He jumps slightly, but doesn't let on otherwise. "Carrick is escaping as I speak. Blade is dressed as a guard, and will bring the notes Hazel requested. There will be backup. Be ready to move when they give the word. Just hold on until then." I say the words triumphantly, excited to be able to help in some small way.

Mr. Fookes doesn't look around, but gives a tiny nod.

I let out a breath that I don't need in the shadow realm, and relax. I did it. My job is done. I helped pull everyone together, and maybe it'll be enough to keep them all alive.

Immediately, my body pulls me the short distance back inside it.

If I could, I'd scream at the pain that stabs into me as soon as I'm there.

The spell web is dying and it's desperate to find a way to live. It's clawing at me, sucking at the last of my energy, using up every last piece of me that it can. My whole body is trying to fight it, right down to the very smallest cell, but I can't hold out forever. It's taking all my will to keep going with this battle for my life. I can't tell what's happening with everyone else, other than we've made it into the spell web room. But it doesn't matter. I'm fighting against my fate—I always will—but I'm also happy.

I managed to help with the final plan. They're all working together because of me. They have a chance to survive this situation.

Now that I'm back in my body, I can't move, I can't even open my eyes. I can't do anything but lie here fighting this battle inside my head. But I feel happy. Relieved. Like I did everything I could.

The air in the dark stone room feels damp and clammy on my heated skin. Muted talking echoes off the ancient masonry in waves. I still remember clearly the last time I was in this basement chamber with Vincent, when he killed Seth and I destroyed the original spell web in retaliation. It seems a lifetime ago. This time there's an abundance of demon energy buzzing around the room, ricocheting off the walls, bouncing and biting in the air around me. I wish I could absorb it like Hazel does. Her power has expanded out, I can taste the zing of it in the air. I hope it's enough that everyone is here working to help her. The thought of Connor or Director Holden controlling the spell web is more than I can bear.

I take tiny breaths, trying to just live long enough to make sure my friends survive this situation. Surely I've done enough. Blade is a powerful shifter, he'll fight with everything inside him to protect Hazel. I know he will. The others all understand how important it is that the spell web is protected too. Because even though it's killing me, even though I can't think for the pain, the spell web has always been more of a friend than a foe to me.

I'm slipping further and further from the room. The spell web inside me is growing faint and so am I. And that's when I finally allow myself to think about Seth again.

His familiar face, his one good eye flashing with the fire of his phoenix side. His strength and his kindness. His honor and his determination. I let his love surround me, hold me close. I wish I could have spoken to him one more time. Felt the strength as he wrapped his arms around me. I wish I could have told him how much I love him.

I'm slipping away. The image of Seth gazing at me with love in his eyes and his smile just for me, keeps me company as I die.

TWENTY-TWO

Without warning, a bright, buzzing piece of demon energy hits my body.

It's bright-blue and fizzing like a newly opened bottle of soda. It's also like being hit with a thousand volts of electricity, and suddenly I'm present again. My mind focuses, and I can hear some of what's happening in the room.

I know immediately who just helped me.

Hazel.

I want to let her know I'm okay, that she needs to concentrate on herself, but I can't even form the words. I used up everything I had talking to the others.

Her demon energy slides along my skin, making all the hairs rise, and then seeps inside, flowing through my veins, beating into my heart, and entering the deep core where my dragon side lies. It's been dormant so long—since Lakas made me create the earthquake—that tears form at the corner of my eyes.

The demon energy flows through my dragon magic,

empowering it with energy and vitality. It's like I'm properly alive again. I'm me again. I can't think for the joy of it.

I still can't move, and the spell web is pressing down on me like a vice, but at least I have my dragon magic to keep me company. It flows through me like a familiar friend, raw and sharp and fierce. I don't think it's enough to save me, but it feels like I've been given a precious gift.

Moments later, I hear chanting inside my head. The demon energy flares again, and I'm filled with blue light. The spell web expands, one last gasping breath. This is it. The spell web is going to die, and take me with it.

And then suddenly... it's gone.

The spell web that's been pushing down on me, suffocating me for so long, is gone.

And I'm still alive.

I try to open my eyes, but I'm weak as a kitten in my physical body.

At least I'm not dead.

I don't understand.

How am I not dead?

And then another soothing wash of blue demon energy flows over my body, and I know.

Hazel. Again.

She saved me.

She must have figured out how to separate me from the spell web. For a moment, I'm so incredibly proud of her and her abilities. She's so smart and so humble at the same time. No one else could have figured it out, no one else has her mix of super smarts and outside-the-box thinking.

And that's when it really hits me. *I'm going to live.*

At least until I find the next piece of trouble to get into.

I freeze. My whole body is rigid with tension, almost like I'm physically rejecting the idea of my survival. I've been steeling myself for my inevitable death for so long that this reprieve feels false, like it might be taken away at any minute. Maybe I'm wrong and the spell web isn't gone. Maybe I'm already dead and this is some kind of death dream? I take a gasping breath, trying to force the thoughts away. I know the spell web is gone. I can feel it. I'm just scared to fully believe it.

But as the demon energy continues to wash over me, and I start to feel stronger and stronger, it begins to feel more real. Like maybe I was right in the first place. *Hazel saved me.*

I know there's movement, and talking and people inter-acting on the other side of my bed, but for the moment, all I can do is wallow here inside my body. Emotion threatens to overwhelm me—fear, joy, anger, happiness, relief—all bundled up into a confusing ball inside me. I feel like I'm going to throw up.

It's too much. My future is now wide open in front of me. I don't know how to react or what to think. The blue demon light continues to wash over me, and I'm soothed by the feelings of calm from Hazel. I don't know why or how, but she's keeping an eye on me, despite whatever else is happening in the room.

I know there's fighting, and yelling and a scuffle happening right next to me, but I don't open my eyes. I can't. I have to accept that this fight is someone else's fight. It's against everything that I've ever been taught, against my natural instincts, which have always been to protect and defend, but I'm too weak. I gave everything to the project of saving everyone else. I was a whisker away from dying. I still can't believe I'm not dead.

And then suddenly an enormous burst of demon energy hits me, like a freight train thundering through the room.

My whole body jerks upward, my back arching before I suck in a deep breath of air.

Then everything goes black.

∼

WHEN I WAKE AGAIN, there's someone leaning over me, and I can feel some kind of healing magic flowing into me through my stomach. I crack open my eyes, and see Iris holding a strange artifact—I hope it's not another dragon bone—over me. Her eyes are closed and her face is a mask of concentration. As she works, I feel the soothing magic rolling through me, adding to the sizzling demon energy. I'm starting to feel like maybe I'll be okay.

I peer down at my shoulder—the grizzly open wound where the bone was sticking out is healed over, nothing more than a red and still-raw scar. I let out a ragged breath, trying to come to terms with the idea that I'm free again. That the spell web is gone. That the bone is no longer in my shoulder.

I turn my head and see my father hovering just behind Iris, his expression grim. He looks crumpled and creased and much older than before. There are bruises mottling his skin, and one of his eyes is bloodshot. I feel a wave of sadness. They tortured him because of me.

But as soon as he sees that my eyes are open, he smiles, and it lights up his face. His grimness is replaced by an elation that I struggle to associate with him and his feelings for me.

"Hey Dad," I croak.

"Mei," he whispers, his voice trembling. "You're alive."

I try for a grin, but I think it's only working on one side of my face. "Sort of."

He closes his eyes for a moment, then opens them and steps closer. "I thought you were dead."

"Almost," I whisper.

Between us, Iris nods once, sharply. "I've done all I can. The rest will just take time to heal," she says, looking down at me. "You need to rest. You've..." she hesitates, but then her eyes turn grim. "You've had a close call with death. It takes time to recover from that."

I nod. I can already feel my strength returning, the magic Iris was pushing into me added to my dragon ability to heal and it's already helping me return from the brink faster than I would have thought possible.

"Thank you," I say, wondering absently if Iris is speaking from her own experience. It kinda sounds like she is. "I appreciate everything you've done." I consider trying to lift a hand to touch her arm, but I don't think I'm strong enough yet.

She gives me another of her sharp nods, and stalks off toward her brother. I watch her for a moment longer, thinking she probably wouldn't have liked me touching her, even if it was only on her arm.

"What happened?" I try to lift my head, look around the room. There are no more guards, and there are two dead bodies up on the podium beside the new spell web. I think I missed a significant amount of the action while I was almost dying. "Who's..." I lay my head back down, finding that it's still too much to lift it for long.

But my father understands the question. "It's Gavan and Connor," he says quietly. "Hazel killed them when she...when she created the new spell web."

I close my eyes and let that soak in. Gavan was Hazel's father. He was a mean, angry drunk, who hated her, but still her father. Hazel must be heartbroken. "Is everyone else...?"

"Everyone else is...fine." My father swallows hard. I can tell he's keeping something from me, but I can't figure out what it is. "We overpowered the guards, got everyone away from them before Hazel created the new spell web."

"That's good," I murmur, my eyes half closing. I'm pleased that it all worked out. I feel like I helped make it happen, and there's a warm glow in my chest. This time yesterday, I could never have imagined anything other than my certain death.

I turn my attention back to my father. He moves forward, and clasps my hand. "I'm so glad you're alive, Mei." He looks up and down my broken body, and his expression hardens. "I'm so sorry for whatever they did to you. I'm going to—" He stops to wipe a tear that's escaping from the corner of his eye. He clears his throat. "I'm going to find Director Holden and I'm going to tear him apart, piece by piece. It's going to be painful, and it's going to take time. And I'm going to enjoy it." His voice is low and gravelly and I know he means every word.

I find that I don't mind at all.

I don't mention that Lakas was the one actually torturing me, not Director Holden. *I'm* going to be the one to find him. I don't know how, and I don't know when, but I'm going to hunt down Lakas and I'm going to make sure he can never do what he did to me to another person.

Maybe once upon a time he was a good person, maybe it was the deaths of his family at the claws of the dragons that made him who he is today... but I don't care. He's a monster, and I'm going to stop him.

Permanently.

CHAPTER
TWENTY-THREE

"She's still in there." Carrick's voice carries across the room, and I turn my head, curious.

Carrick moves closer to the large glowing ball of electricity in the center of the room. *The new spell web that Hazel created with demon energy.* I can feel it buzzing and crackling, but it's no longer inside me. *Thankfully.*

"What's he talking about?" I ask, confused. "Who's in there?"

My father sighs. "Hazel put herself into the center of the new spell web. It's how she saved us."

My chest tightens. "Is she going to be okay? Can she get out?"

Glancing at the middle of the room, my father's expression is somber. "She's still there, inside the spell web. But I don't know if she can get out. It seems unlikely."

My stomach churns unpleasantly and my throat clogs up. The others are talking across the room. I turn my body toward them, trying to hear what they're saying. Surely they can get her out again? Where's Blade? He'll make them do it.

I can't even imagine how he's feeling.

"Do you think it's possible?" Carrick is asking Mr. Fookes, his expression a mixture of hope and grief. "What do you know about the spell web?" Their faces are a mix of shadow and a reflection of the blue glowing light of the spell web.

"We both had the mountain clan memories placed inside us," Mr. Fookes says, his expression concerned. "I haven't been able to see all of them, but I do know that the original spell web was made by a long-ago chalice. And I'm pretty sure the chalice had to sacrifice himself when the time came to create it."

What? It takes a second, but then I make the connection. No. *No.* Hazel is a chalice, too. She must have figured out how the original supers did it, and sacrificed herself in the same way. A lump forms in my throat. Hazel worked so hard to save me. I can't bear the thought that she sacrificed herself. I blink and force myself to concentrate on what the others are saying.

"The original chalice was convinced it was the only way to create a spell web that would last," Mr. Fookes finishes with a sweep of his hand toward the glowing ball beside them.

"Do you think we can get her out?" asks Carrick. He's watching Mr. Fookes like he's worried that if he looks away he'll miss something.

My heart clenches inside me. I find myself nodding in agreement with Carrick. Surely there's a way?

"I don't think it's ever been done before," says Mr. Fookes carefully.

"That doesn't mean anything," I whisper softly, and Dad's hand tightens around mine, like he knows I'm up to something.

"Doesn't mean we can't do it," says Freddie, echoing my words and striding over to Carrick. His face is set. "She's done so much for us. She was prepared to die for us. We should do everything we can to save her." Freddie is glaring at Carrick, like he's waiting for the mountain super to disagree. He glances briefly behind him, and I finally see Blade, sitting on the steps off to one side of the glowing spell web, his upper body curled over and held completely rigid, like he's only just holding himself together. His hair is sticking up on end, as if he's been pulling on it, and I can hear a faint feral growl coming from his mouth. I've never seen him lose control like this before, and it's obvious that he's only holding on by a thread.

"I know how much she's done for us," says Carrick, also glancing worriedly at Blade. "She fought the demons in Newport News like it was her own backyard. She never once questioned why she should be helping."

"That's what she's always been like, even when she was trying to keep to herself," adds Mr. Fookes. "She used to fix all the appliances for everyone in our apartment building. Could never turn me down. Always willing to help people."

I find myself nodding. Hazel was always willing to help people, including me. If there's anything we can do to help her, we need to make sure we do it. I push myself to a sitting position, determined to participate in the conversation now that I'm not going to die.

The woman wearing the knitted jersey—Daphne—moves closer to the spell web, arm in arm with Poppy. "She got us out of Ravenwood. She let herself get captured when our escape went wrong, just so we could get out of there," she says.

There's a murmur from the room. They're almost at a decision point. All they need is one more person to show them how important Hazel is. I lift my legs over the edge of the bed.

"Mei, what are you doing? Stay where you are," says my father, like he's a mother hen protecting her chick.

"I need to tell them what Hazel has done for me," I growl. "I'm not going to rest until I do. So you can either help me get up, or move aside." I grit my teeth and push myself to standing.

I look up and see everyone staring at me. I swallow hard and force myself to take a step. It feels like I'm a hundred years old and I'm somehow walking through water.

No one moves or talks as I shuffle over to the podium at the far end of the room, helped by my father. I'd prefer that I was making a bit more of a dramatic entrance, rather than this slow turtle-like approach, but there's not much I can do to change it.

I clear my throat over the sudden frog in it. "Hazel saved my life. Today. Right here. She brought me back from the dead. She's actually saved my life more than once, and for that I'll always owe her." I pause to take a few ragged breaths. This is harder than I thought. My body is still so fragile. I hate being this weak, it makes me feel vulnerable, just like when I was a kid. And then suddenly there's this burst of energy inside me, blue and buzzing like the demon energy Hazel used to save me before. I jerk my head up and stare at the glowing ball of the spell web.

And I know. That wasn't an accident, or a random act from the spell web.

"She's in there," I whisper. "She really is. I can feel her." I stand a little taller, and give myself a shake. I already feel better. I step closer to the spell web, to Hazel, and hold up my hand, wishing I could touch her, to thank her for saving me yet again. Except there's too much electrical current on the outside of the orb, and I have to pull it away again.

Instead, I stare straight into the spell web, determined to tell her what's on my mind. "I never expected you to break your promise to Mr. Fookes, and I'm mad at my father, Carrick and Seth for ever asking it of you." My voice starts to tremble and I have to swallow hard before I can go on. "You're the bravest, strongest person I know, and if there's any way to get you out of the spell web, then I'm going to do it."

My dad clears his throat. "She's definitely still in there?" he says, looking uncomfortable.

So he should. What made him think I'd want Hazel to sacrifice Mr. Fookes for me? Or that creating a rift between the two main factions fighting against Director Holden was a good idea?

I give him a stern look. He should have known better than that. I'm definitely planning to have a few words with him when I'm feeling stronger. "Yes, she's in there. And we need to get her out," I say. "After everything she's done for us, you included. We can't give up without a fight."

Dad lets out a sigh. "You know you're in trouble when your daughter is smarter than you are," he says softly. He turns toward the glowing ball. "I'm sorry, Hazel. I'm sorry I ever asked you to find Mei. I'm sorry I was angry at you. I was just upset. We all were."

"Then let's make this happen. Let's get her out of there," says Freddie, rubbing his hands together like he's anticipating success already.

There's a general agreement from everyone else in the room to what Freddie is saying. I swallow over the lump that's still in my throat. We have to get her out of there. We don't have a choice. I glance over at Blade, and wish I hadn't. I can see his frantic energy through the spell web, even now it's no longer inside me, eating at my energy. He's so close to the edge, I don't think he's thinking properly. To have come so close to having her back, only to lose her again, must be devastating.

"How do we do it?" asks Mr. Fookes.

Carrick hesitates. "She's given me a connection to the spell web. Like a guardianship, I think."

I glance at Carrick then at the spell web. Hazel always was smarter than anyone else. My lips curl into a tiny smile.

"Instead of the Earthbound?" Freddie raises his eyebrows. I guess he figures they wouldn't give up without a fight, but ever since Vincent was killed, the Earthbound has been dormant. It's been Director Holden and his men who've been desperate to take power.

"Yes," says Carrick slowly. He seems a little over-whelmed at the idea of it, maybe even conflicted, but in all honesty, I think he's the perfect person to be looking after the spell web.

Freddie looks from Mr. Fookes to Carrick. "What about the power of three?"

I frown, no idea what they're talking about. But it doesn't matter. My strength is waning and I need to get back to the bed. I'm losing the ability to concentrate. At least we're all on the same page now, and working toward getting Hazel out of there.

"Can you help me back to the bed?" I ask my father, as the others keep discussing options. My head's spinning, and I know I've overdone it.

Immediately, he puts one arm around my waist. I put one heavy arm around his shoulders. I have to focus hard on not falling, and my brain feels like mush.

"I suppose there's no point in telling you that I told you to stay in bed."

I snort, amused at his light words. He knows he never had a show of telling me what to do.

"I think we should call a few people, ask for help," I hear Poppy saying to the group behind us. I want to nod in agreement, but it's more than I can manage.

I needn't have worried. There are murmurs of agreement from everyone else around the room and suddenly they're all moving into action.

I want to join them, but all I can focus on is getting back to the bed so I can rest my head for a bit.

CHAPTER
TWENTY-FOUR

When I wake again, there's a busy-ness and vibrancy to the people in the room that wasn't there before. The decision to save Hazel has given everyone a determination in their step. Carrick and Mr. Fookes are rushing about, ordering this and that be done, talking on the phone, making plans with people.

At first, when they suggest I should move my bed out of the spell web room, I resist. I don't know how much of Hazel's consciousness is still in there... but I don't want to leave her alone in this room. I'm getting my strength back, hour by hour, and I want to be there for her.

Except the spell web room is also the hub of activity. The place where everyone meets to discuss things and rushes to try things. And there's the constant buzzing energy of the spell web itself, which at the beginning was comforting, but is now just... keeping me awake.

So I don't resist when Carrick and my father sternly come in the next morning and push me out of the room. At first I assume they're taking me to the hospital, and my stomach flips at the idea, but instead I end up in a small room on the same level as the spell web.

"It's an old cell. But it's close to the spell web room so you'll be part of the action. We've spruced it up a bit. Everyone is mostly staying down here and on the next level up," says Carrick. He looks around the room apologetically, like he wishes it had wallpaper and plumbing or something.

"It's perfect," I say from my bed. I'm getting better all the time, but it's still a struggle to sit up, let alone get my feet onto the floor. "All I need. I just want to sleep."

I close my eyes, too tired to even say goodnight.

I'm still fast asleep when Hazel causes a commotion and starts speaking to people via the spell web grid. She calls Poppy into the room, and talks to Carrick. All while I'm snoring in my own little cell.

"She's in there, and she's still trying to fix everyone's problems," says my father later that day, shaking his head in amazement. "We're taking it in shifts to stay with her, so she doesn't feel alone." He's loitering next to my bed, his hair messed up and his suit rumpled. He looks healthier than he did when I first saw him, despite the fading bruises and myriad of cuts on his face and neck. I peer at him closely, wondering if there are wounds that I can't see. Being captured and tortured by Lakas doesn't seem to have slowed him down, not like it has for me. Then again, he's been an SIG agent his whole life. He's probably been through things like that before.

I'm sitting up, blankets pulled around my waist, and I almost feel close to normal. Maybe normal-adjacent. I roll my shoulders. They're stiff, but nothing I can't handle. There's definitely a benefit to being a dragon with powerful friends. "You want me to take a shift?"

"I'd *prefer* if you stayed in bed and tried to relax for a bit longer," he says with a mock frown. "But yes, we need you to take a shift. You're the only one who can do it at the moment. And it feels important not to leave her alone."

I nod. "I'll keep an eye on her." I make a crossing motion over my heart. "And I promise I won't overexert myself."

He gives me a stern look, but then ruins it by smiling. "I can't believe you're looking so much better. It's barely been twenty-four hours."

"Hazel and Iris both helped. And I have a dragon's constitution."

"I guess you do." He shakes his head in bemusement. "And I thought my chameleon healing powers were good."

"I'm still shaky, and I won't be leaping off tall buildings any time soon, but I'm alive. It's more than I was expecting."

His expression turns serious. "I'm glad you're still with us, Mei. The world is a better place with you in it." He leans down and wraps me in a tight hug.

Tears form in my eyes and I try not to sniff. "Thanks, Dad. I'm glad I'm still here too," I whisper.

He leans back and checks out my face, like he's searching for answers. He seems to find them, because he says, "Look, Mei, I have to go. Will you be okay? Do you need help getting to the spell web room before I leave?"

"No, I'm fine. I'll take it slowly," I reply. "You go." He's clearly itching to head off to whatever task he's been assigned.

He smiles and nods. "Take care of yourself, okay?" He pats my leg one last time, then heads out. He's just as eager as the others to get Hazel out of the spell web, and it's giving him a bounce in his step that I haven't seen in a while.

Pushing myself down onto the ground, I wince as one of my legs buckles painfully. I cling to my bed for a moment while I get my balance back. My breathing is ragged, and I haven't even taken a step. Maybe I should have gotten Dad's help.

I let out a huff.

Too late now.

I wrap the edges of my zippered hoodie across my front a little tighter, and take a determined step away from my bed. My feet are bare, and the cold stone of the floor sends a shiver up my body. I'm grateful for the baggy sweat pants that Carrick found for me earlier today. I keep shuffling along like an old grandmother, slowly heading toward the spell web chamber.

So much for being a powerful dragon shifter.

The only thing that keeps me going is the thought that it could have been so much worse. I would have died if it hadn't been for Hazel.

When I finally get to the chamber, I limp over to the spell web. The energy feels familiar, not just because I had a spell web inside me for all those months...it's because my whole life I've been entwined with the spell web, using the grid lines for my own purposes since I discovered I could do it when I was a kid.

All the other dragons I've met since then have been scared of the spell web, but I never was. I reach out, and get as close as I dare to the spitting demon energy that makes up the glowing ball in front of me. I'm in awe that Hazel could create something like this. Her power is beyond anything I've ever seen.

"You're amazing, you know that, Hazel?" I say quietly. I wonder if she's going to reply, but maybe she's asleep, because she doesn't say anything. I shrug and sit down, determined to make this time worthwhile. I'm planning to stretch out my legs and get them prepped for my return to being a strong, independent dragon. Someone who doesn't even think about Lakas.

For a second, I flash back to my prison cell on the truck, with Lakas leaning over me, his fetid breath brushing my face. The feeling of being completely at his mercy fills my senses and I can't move. My blood pounds in my head and I squeeze my eyes shut. I'm just as trapped as I was back then.

"It's going to be okay. You'll recover from this. And when the time comes, I'll help you kill him."

The words sift softly into my consciousness and break through my moment of frozen fear. I jerk back in surprise. I look around quickly, but I know who it is.

Hazel.

Talking inside my head.

TWENTY-FIVE

"Y ou'll help me get the son-of-a-bitch?" I say to her. "Are you sure you're not trying to get in on the action and just want to get him yourself?"

"We can do it together," Hazel promises with an amused edge to her voice.

I nod and sit down, content now she's spoken to me. She doesn't sound distressed. Instead she sounds... calm. But kind of distant, like she's not part of this world any more.

"We're going to get you out of there, you know," I say conversationally. "We've got the best of the best working on it."

"It's not possible," she whispers. *"I told Carrick. They know. But I can't convince them to stop."*

"We won't stop, not 'til we've tried every possible option," I vow. And I mean it. Hazel has always been the kind of person who helps others. Now we're going to help her.

I put my legs out in front of me, and start doing stretches, trying to convince my body that it's okay not to be sore any more. I have a feeling it's a wasted effort, but I'm determined to try.

I'm so focused on my stretches that when a shadowy figure stumbles into the doorway, I jump a mile, convinced it's Lakas back to finish the job. I only just manage to hold in the scream, and my heart thumps like a war hammer inside my chest.

But the figure stumbles further into the room and the light catches his face. His single haunted hazel eye stares at me like he's looking at a ghost. His face is lined, the patch over his bad eye is crooked, his clothes are dirty and he's just generally shaggy-looking—hair long, patchy stubble, wild eyes—but I recognize him straight away.

Seth.

My heart is still thumping, but it's for a different reason now.

I feel myself crumble into tiny pieces. I've been mostly okay up to this point, holding myself together because that's what everyone needs me to do. But now I realize what I've been waiting for.

I've been holding my breath, waiting to find out where he was.

Wanting to know what happened to him.

Wanting to know why he wasn't here.

"*Seth,*" I whisper.

He's standing there, staring like he doesn't believe it's really me. "Mei," he whispers painfully. "You're *alive.*"

I nod. I'm frozen in place, sitting on the ground, my legs out in front of me. I can only stare at Seth, my eyes hungrily taking him in, checking to see that everything I remember about him is still true. He has a wild edge to his gaze, and he looks like he's been through hell, but he's here. He's real.

We're both alive.

And then suddenly I scramble to my feet, almost falling on my face in my rush to reach him, and race across the room, faster than I would have thought I could move. I throw myself at Seth and he holds me tightly against him, like he never wants to let go.

I'm crying, gasping, sobbing tears that are dripping down my face. I'm broken and he's the only thing that can fix me.

Seth leans into me, his cheek against the top of my head, murmuring soft words that create a rumbling vibration against my skin. "I'm sorry. I'm sorry I couldn't find you. I tried. I tried so hard. It was like you'd disappeared. I couldn't sense you anywhere. I'm so sorry, Mei. I felt broken without you. I tried so hard to find you." He's muttering the words over and over, almost like a prayer.

"Shhhh," I say, when I can't bear it any longer. He's created a mountain of guilt for himself, and there's only so much of it I can take. I lean back and put my hands on either side of his face, forcing him to look me in the eyes. "It's not your fault, Seth. They had it all planned. They were driving me around in this enormous truck, protected by the Earthbound machines. It's not your fault."

"I couldn't find you," he repeats, his voice cracking. His eye is glassy with tears. "I searched everywhere, and then searched again. I thought I'd lost you, and the last time we spoke... You were angry with me. I needed to find you. To make it right. When I couldn't find you, it broke me." He hesitates, shadows in his eyes. "I didn't want to go on without you."

"It's okay, we're both okay now," I whisper gently, running my hand down the side of his face like I'm soothing a wild animal. "We're both okay."

He leans back and brings his hands up to cup my face

gently. "I love you more than anything in the world, Mei Walker. I never want to be parted from you ever again." He leans in and kisses me reverently on each cheek, then my eyes, as if he's trying to kiss away my tears. Then he leans down and puts his lips on mine, softly, gently, like he's worried I'm going to break. It feels like I've died and gone to heaven. I never thought I'd see him again, and I *for sure* never thought I'd feel his lips on mine again. Everything inside me is melting under the intensity of the joy I'm experiencing. The kiss is sedate, chaste even, but it's the most intimate kiss I've ever experienced. I touch his face reverently with my hands, and his warmth, his realness seeps into me. I shiver. All the fear, misery, and sadness we've both been experiencing rises up and swirls around us, dissipating under the onslaught of pleasure. It's the closest I've ever come to complete and utter bliss.

When the kiss reluctantly ends, I whisper against Seth's ear. "I love you too, Seth. I'm sorry I put you through this. It's not your fault. No one found me. Not 'til they brought me here, at least." Tears are running down my face, and I can't seem to stop them.

Seth looks down at me, and wipes away the tears from my face. "I love you," he says simply. Then he gazes around us, as if noticing the room and then the spell web for the first time. "This is the place where Vincent..." He trails off but I know what he means. This is the same room where Vincent killed him.

I nod shakily. "It isn't like it was back then. The spell web is Hazel. She removed the spell web from me, then put it back together, and killed Connor and Gavan."

Seth's wide-eyed gaze immediately returns to my face. "You don't have the spell web inside you anymore?"

I shake my head, and he pulls me tight against him

again, letting out a shuddering breath. "I can hardly believe this is happening," he says. "Pinch me. I must be dreaming. I'm going to wake in that terrible cave, cold and alone."

I pinch his side, and I feel him grin against my forehead.

"It's real," I say. "I can hardly believe it either. I thought..." I shudder. I thought I was going to die, but I don't want to say that aloud to Seth. "But Hazel did it. She saved us all."

Seth lifts his head again and stares over at the glowing ball of light. "Hazel's really inside the spell web? How is that possible?"

I shake my head. "To be honest, I don't really know. But she's in there. She's talked to me through the spell web."

Seth looks at the glowing spell web, his head tipped slightly to one side. "I think... I think maybe Hazel... I think she came for me," he says softly. "I heard a voice. She yelled at me. Didn't give up. Told me to come here." He laughs self-consciously.

"Sounds like something she'd do."

Seth puts one hand up to cup my face. He can't seem to stop touching me, staring at me, perhaps making sure I'm not going to disappear again. "I'm sorry Mei. I—"

"You need to stop saying sorry," I growl. "It wasn't your fault. No one could find me. *Everyone* thought I was dead."

"I can't stop saying it. I gave up on you. I gave up on everything." His voice is raw and painful, and I can tell he's still beating himself up.

"It's not your fault, Seth. I promise. It's not your fault." I tighten my arms around his body, and hold on, never wanting to let go. I'm so glad to be back with him that I promise myself I'll just keep reminding him that it wasn't his fault until he actually believes me.

I glance over my shoulder at Hazel. "Thank you," I whisper softly. She went and found him for me.

Which means I'm even more determined to get her out of that damned spell web. But for right now…. "I'm sorry, Hazel, I'm going to have to leave you alone for a while." I'm hoping she'll understand.

She's the one who brought Seth back to me after all. Then I grab Seth's hand tightly in mine, and pull him out of the room, planning to find somewhere more private.

CHAPTER
TWENTY-SIX

For lack of a better option, I lead Seth back to the little cell where I've been sleeping. We both sit down on the hospital bed—Seth helping me the whole way—and I lean my head on his shoulder. He's still clinging to my hand.

I don't want to let go of him either.

"What happened?" he asks quietly.

I shake my head. "I'll tell you. I will. Just... not yet. I'm not ready." I hesitate. "It really was me, you know. In the cave."

"What?" He looks down at me, his expression a picture of confusion.

"The voice you heard a few days ago. It upset you. You thought it was proof you were going crazy, so I left. I didn't want to hurt you even more. But it was me. I learned how to travel in the shadow realm."

"The shadow realm?" Seth's just repeating what I'm saying like I'm speaking a foreign language. I tighten my fingers around his hand and a take a deep breath, filling my senses with his familiar smoky scent.

"While they had me locked up, I discovered that I can leave my body and travel around in a shadowy place just behind this one. It's called the shadow realm and it kept me going. Gave me hope."

Seth looks around us. "It's here right now?"

I scrunch up my face, trying to think about how to explain it. "Most people can't see me while I'm in there. It's like you're here but not here. I can move around, but everything is shadowed. Like how I imagine it would be to be a ghost."

Seth's expression is grim, and he stares at the wall across from us. "How many times did you visit me?"

"Just once. I wanted to go back, but I was scared it would be too painful for you."

"There was more than one occasion when I thought I was hearing your voice, Mei. Over and over again, I kept hearing you. I kept thinking how the last thing we did was fight about me getting married, and how I didn't try hard enough to stop it from happening. How hurt you were. How maybe that was the last thing you'd think about as you died. That maybe you didn't realize how much I love you." Tears are silently running down his face, his eyes bloodshot and tortured.

I lift my head off his shoulder. In the pleasure of seeing him again, I'd forgotten about his marriage to one of the raven women just before the demon attack. "Are you still...?" I don't know how to finish the sentence.

Seth shakes his head quickly, looking at me in panic. "No. No. The ravens agreed to annul the marriage. It was clearly forced and nothing ever happened between us."

Grim satisfaction rolls about inside my stomach. I'd seen the way the raven woman had looked at Seth. She'd wanted something more, that was for damn sure. "And what happened when you battled the demons? Did anyone... get hurt?"

Seth shakes his head. "It was a trap, set by Hazel's father. Hazel figured it out." He pauses. "She kinda saved us all that time too."

"We have to help them get her out of there, Seth. Whatever it takes. She deserves more than this. Did you see Blade? He's devastated."

"I can empathize," says Seth, his voice rueful. "Except now I have you back. But there's no guarantee it'll be the same for Hazel and Blade."

I squeeze my eyes shut and pretend he didn't say that. I'm determined to believe that everything will work out. "If I can go from being on the doorstep of death to being here with you in less than twenty-four hours, then Hazel has a chance too," I say.

"Doorstep of death?" Seth's eyes widen, and a little of his panic returns.

I put my head on his shoulder and snuggle closer. "I'm fine now. Everything is okay." I take a breath and proceed to tell him a little more of what happened after I was kidnapped by Director Holden.

LATER THAT DAY, we gather with everyone else in the spell web room. Seth holds my hand, and helps me find a seat—I'm still pretty shaky when I'm walking and standing. But Carrick has a plan, and he needs our help, so I'm determined to be here.

There's a strange yet powerful mix of people in the

room with us, including, of course, Blade, Hazel's boyfriend, plus the mountain supers' First Elder and the High Council, a genie, a phoenix, multiple SIG agents, and several dragons. I even spot, strangely, the superstar musician Randy Crowe. How on earth does Hazel know *him*? I elbow Seth and point him out.

"What the hell—?" says Seth, just as surprised as I am.

Except it doesn't matter who's here. The one thing we all have in common is the burning desire to do everything we can to save Hazel. I watch Blade from across the room, and my heart lurches in my chest. He so close to the edge. He hasn't shaved in a long time, and the wildness in his eyes is making people give him a wide berth, despite the powerful supers crowded together. He keeps staring at the spell web as if he's trying to see inside it, maybe catch a glimpse of Hazel. I wonder if she's spoken to him, like she spoke to me? He only seems to be partly with us in the room, like he's not really concentrating on what's going on around him. I've never seen him like this before.

It's the mountain supers who have come up with a plan and they need all the help they can get. They're attempting a spell that's supposed to firstly get Carrick inside the spell web with Hazel, and then draw her back out with him. It all seems a little hazy, and no one seems sure that it's actually going to work, but it's better than leaving Hazel in there.

Carrick's up at the front of the room, talking to a couple of the other mountain supers. He looks determined, his craggy features set in serious lines. He's also glowing, just a little, from his connection to the spell web. He's head and shoulders taller than everyone else around him, which is saying something, given there are so many other mountain supers up there. He keeps glancing over at Blade, and I know he's worried about him, too.

Part of me is surprised that Carrick is willing to risk himself like this for Hazel. Except I've always known how courageous he is. He took my wound for me the first time he met me, and he knows Hazel far better than he knew me back then.

Because Carrick's connected to the spell web, he's more able to bond to all the supers in the room. I can feel his solid presence as he gathers the energy he needs, and it calms my shaky nerves. The whole room is buzzing, crowded with so many people who want to help Hazel.

"For someone who lived in hiding and barely tolerated friends until recently, she's sure found a whole bunch of supporters," says Seth quietly.

I just shake my head, and continue to allow as much energy as possible to flow up to Carrick and the other mountain supers.

Up the front of the room, they've built a stone wall around the glowing spell web orb. I can only see patches of the blue glow—the color of demons, and now this spell web.

The mountain supers have moved, so there's a solid circle of them standing shoulder to shoulder around it, with Carrick in the middle. Without meaning to, I glance to the far side of the room again, where Blade his hunched up by himself, his hands clenched tight, his neck stiff. I can sense his confusing mix of emotions from all the way over here. Hope, desperation, fear, frustration. He's trying not to hope for a positive outcome, despite it being exactly what he's desperately, fearfully wishing for.

I understand his frustration, too. Like him, I want to be the one up there saving Hazel. I wish I had the kind of magic that could save her from the spell web, just like she saved me. Instead, we've been forced to sit back and watch as the mountain supers use their mysterious magic to get her out of there.

Despite that frustration, I know that we're lucky we have the mountain supers here, and that they're willing to try an experimental spell to save Hazel. They wouldn't do it for just anyone. I can see the strain on their faces as they create the spell. Carrick has little beads of sweat running down the side of his face. There's a nervous tension in the air. It feels risky, and dangerous, and I'm not sure anyone really knows if this is going to work. But at least something is happening, at least we're *trying* to get her out. That's all we can do.

Seth and I sit together to the side of the room, close enough to see, but not interfere with the people at the front. I'm tucked up close to him, holding his hand, my head on his shoulder. Partially it's because I want to be close to him, to feel his warmth, to have his smoky scent surrounding me. We've hardly left each other since he arrived. I find it soothing to have him with me, and it makes me jump a little less at the shadows.

He seems content to be my guardian.

But it's also because I'm still weak, and being up for this long is taking it out of me. Not to mention having my magic used for Hazel's spell. I'm getting stronger every day, but it's going to take time... at least that's what I tell myself when I get frustrated at my lack of staying power.

I'm no longer the most powerful super in the room and I can admit to myself that it stings a little. Part of me enjoyed the feeling of having all that energy running through me. Now it's gone, and while I'm still healing and not yet back to full strength, without the spell web, I'm back to being an ordinary dragon. I'd probably only be somewhere in the middle of this crowd in terms of power.

If that.

I'm not even the last dragon any more. Zane is across the room—he gives me a nod when he sees me looking his way—and I know Elena is here somewhere too. Sergei isn't here—he marches to the beat of his own drum—but he's around as well. There are probably more dragons hidden away in the world.

It makes me think of Aurelia, stuck inside the lava of Mt Hood. She's been there, scared, lonely, waiting for someone to find her for more than three centuries. Did she have a lover? Someone like Seth in her life that she lost when the Earthbound set their machines on the dragons? I know she lost her family, everyone else she knew or cared about. She has no one now, no one except *me.*

In that moment, I vow that as soon as I can, I'm going to go rescue her. I won't let her molder inside that volcano for a moment longer than necessary. Seth draws me closer to him, tightening his grip on my hand, as if he can sense my agitated thoughts.

In the front of the room, Carrick suddenly slumps limply into the arms of two waiting—very muscular—mountain supers. There's a gasp from everyone who can see him, but it seems to be part of the plan. They're holding him up, their faces starting to turn red with the strain of keeping their enormous king upright. Everyone in the room is watching with bated breath, waiting to see what happens.

Will it work?

What if Carrick ends up stuck inside the spell web too?

What will we do then?

And then suddenly, the wall of stone cracks through the middle; bricks fall to the ground and at the feet of the mountain supers. A blurry figure bursts out of the spell web, and suddenly Carrick takes a gasping breath, now firmly back inside his body. He gives himself a full shake, like he's getting back into all the cracks and crevices of his body, then strides forward and grabs Hazel, pulling her out through the crack in the stone wall. She falls through the gap and lands on the ground, her body heaving.

There's an excited murmur across the whole room. Hazel's out. She's really out. Blade sprints toward her, practically climbing over people in his haste, his entire focus on Hazel. He pushes people out of the way, and everyone lets him. We all know who Hazel will want next to her when she opens her eyes.

The room is unnaturally silent. We all have a vested interest in making sure Hazel is okay. She's out of the spell web, but is she still alive? What has it done to her, being the center of such power?

I know precisely how much it can affect a person.

I stand up, dragging Seth with me, peering around the mountain supers, trying to see what's happening. Hazel is lying on the ground, held in Blade's arms. She lifts one hand up to touch his chin. He closes his eyes and says her name in such an anguished tone I wonder if maybe she's dying in front of him. My heart stalls in my chest. Surely that can't be the end to this?

But no, she's speaking to him, soft words that I can't make out. He crushes Hazel to him, murmuring something under his breath. A cheer erupts in the room, as everyone realizes that it worked.

We saved Hazel.

In many ways, we saved Blade too. His face is ravaged, and he looks completely overwhelmed by the emotions he's experiencing. But I don't know if he'd have survived if we hadn't managed to save her. He's still got a wild look in his eyes, but he's gazing down at Hazel like she's the only person in the world.

I turn away, pushing my face into Seth's chest, feeling like I'm intruding on a private moment.

CHAPTER
TWENTY-SEVEN

"We can't go. You're not ready," says Seth, a desperate edge to his voice. He's pacing in front of me, his eyes starting to turn the flaming orange of a phoenix. He looks much better than he did a week ago—less bedraggled—but his agitation is giving him a wild edge again. My dragon gives an internal purr.

I kind of like it.

We're in the front room at Freddie's strangely charismatic house on the clifftop, the sunlight draping itself over us like a warm and sparkly coat.

It's been two weeks since Hazel was released from the spell web. We had a massive party for her a few days ago, and she's doing great. The spell web, with Hazel's demon still inside it and under the guidance of Carrick, is working exactly as it should to keep supers hidden from the humans.

I've been recuperating at Freddie's place—doctor's orders, plus a promise I made to both my father and Seth—lazing around, reading books and doing nothing. Instead of feeling relaxed, I'm getting impatient to do something—*anything*—to ease my boredom.

"I'm more than ready," I say from my seat by the window. I put down the mystery novel I was trying to read, so I can concentrate on Seth's jittery reaction to my suggestion that we should rescue Aurelia from the bowels of Mt Hood. "I'm mostly back to full strength. All my wounds have healed, even the one on my shoulder." It pings uncomfortably as I gesture with it, but I manage to keep my face neutral. I'll never convince Seth to come with me if he thinks for one second that I'm in any pain.

"You're still limping, and you haven't gotten back to your proper weight. You'd fly away in a strong gust of wind." Seth gestures toward me with one arm.

"You know you shouldn't criticize a woman's weight, right?" I say severely, lifting an eyebrow at him. "I know I'm scrawnier than a scarecrow, but you don't need to point it out." I'm not really worried about my weight, I'll gain it back eventually, but I'm prepared to use whatever leverage I can to persuade Seth it's okay for me to head out into the world again.

His expression turns contrite and he hastens over to me, leaning down and pulling me close. "You know that I love you and you always look beautiful, right? And I'll always be here by your side, no matter what." His arms tighten. "It's just that I worry about you. It could be dangerous. We've already had so much danger, I wish we could have a little more...calm."

I shake my head, my nose moving against the warm skin of his neck. He smells how I imagine molten lava might smell. My dragon rumbles inside me, loving the scent, and I inhale a little deeper. Then I reluctantly lean back to look into his face. "I'm just rescuing a friend. It won't be dangerous. Aurelia's been stuck down there for more than three hundred *years*. I can't just leave her. I'm worried about her." I rub my hands down the outside of his arms, along the muscled forearms, trying to soothe his fears.

"What if Lakas is there?" he blurts, and then winces. Even he knows that argument is thin.

I frown at him, trying to understand why he's so worried. "Is there a good reason behind why you're so reluctant to do a simple rescue mission? Am I really so weak that I can't be trusted anymore?" I wince, hoping that's not true. "Or is it just because of what happened to me? Do you think I'm not strong enough?" I say the words before I can think too much about them. Irritation stirs in my chest. He's making me second-guess myself.

Seth leans down, gently placing his forehead on mine. "I'm scared, okay? I can't bear the thought of losing you again. You almost *died*."

My heart melts a little, and I push away my irritation. "I get it, I really do," I say, cupping his cheek. "Part of me wants to hide away here as well. But I can't. It's not in me to be like that. I have to get her out of there. I promised her I'd go get her as soon as I could." Aurelia's soft acceptance of me leaving, and her clear disbelief that I'd come back are part of the reason I'm so determined to rescue her.

Seth sighs and sits down next to me, his shoulder brushing against mine. "Waiting another week until you're properly healed isn't going to hurt her, Mei. She's already been locked up in that mountain for three hundred years. What's another week?"

I blink. He's right. Except... "You wouldn't say that if it was me locked up in the mountain." I take a breath, calming my ricocheting thoughts. I lean my head on his shoulder. "Seth, I get why you're worried. But it's not going to be dangerous. And you'll be with me the whole time to watch my back."

I haven't been coddled like this since I was a little kid, before Jeff came along. With Jeff and Si as my mentors I was expected to stand up, think for myself, and take action to defend us. I'm not used to someone questioning my decisions. Except... I almost died two weeks ago, and Seth lived through all of that. He thought I was dead. So I get why he's acting like this—I felt exactly the same way when I thought he'd died.

"I'm not exactly in top form either," he says, gesturing at his tall, thin body. He's right, he's lost weight too, and doesn't fill out his shirt the way he used to. He didn't take care of himself while I was kidnapped.

"We're not going to be fighting, or doing anything dangerous. We'll be rescuing someone who helped me escape from that monster. I *have* to go rescue her."

I sense Seth's resolve weaken. I think he's noticed the glint in my eyes.

"You're not going to let up about this, are you?" he says wearily.

I shake my head. "Nope. We saw Hazel and Blade at the party last week, Dad's gone off with Freddie to see what information they can gather about Director Holden. Even Iris has gone. Which leaves us free to find Aurelia." I take his hand, and cradle it in both of mine, rubbing my thumb against his.

"Has Zane heard of her?" he asks.

"No, he doesn't know her. But there were a lot of dragons in their time."

"You're sure she's okay? She wasn't locked in there on purpose? Setting her free won't start the next dragon Armageddon or something?"

I give Seth a severe look. "Aurelia helped me when I was trapped in the truck. She taught me how to get around in the shadow realm. She was good to me. I have to help her."

Seth sighs. "Okay, then let's go tomorrow. It's getting late." He looks outside at the early morning sunlight filtering into the room.

I shake my head, all determined purpose. "Today. I'm all packed. It won't take long for you to pack as well. I have Mr. Fookes on speed dial in case we need back up. Blade is lending us one of his pick-up trucks. I've found a motel we can stay at if we need to. I've thought of everything. There's nothing stopping us."

"A pick-up? We're not flying?" says Seth, his tone surprised. He rolls his shoulders like he's been wanting to stretch his wings.

"I don't know how... mobile... Aurelia will be when we find her. She might not be able to fly. We need to make sure we have some kind of vehicle just in case."

"Maybe we should wait, find a bigger vehicle?"

"Seth, this is important," I say, holding his hand tightly, willing him to agree. I need his backup for this plan to work.

Seth lets out a defeated sigh. He's not convinced, but he's given up on holding me back. "Okay, fine. Give me ten minutes and I'll be ready."

I lean forward and give him a tight hug. "It's going to be fine. It'll be like ripping a Band Aid off. It'll hurt at first, but better in the long run."

"I don't want it to hurt," says Seth into my hair.

"That was probably a bad analogy," I say with a wince. "It's not going to hurt. We're both professionals. We can both handle ourselves. This is going to be easy. No pain at all."

I hurry him along as he packs up his stuff, and no more than ten minutes later, we head out of the house. We're the last ones to leave—Dad and Freddie said their goodbyes to me last night before they headed out and Iris disappeared after the party on some secretive mission she wouldn't tell me about—so I lock the door carefully behind me, even though I don't think it needs it. No one would dare come into this house without permission. It can be menacing when it wants to be.

Seth is ahead of me on the path, looking like he's about to go on a holiday with his aviator sunglasses, and his bright blue T-shirt and grey board shorts. He doesn't notice when I shiver suddenly, despite the warm sun. I'm carrying my back pack, and I'm only wearing a light T-shirt with jeans shorts. But it's not that I'm cold. Even though I'm the one pushing for us to leave the house, I suddenly feel nervous. Like I'm going on my first mission ever, and it might be more than I can handle.

I growl under my breath and give myself a shake. There's no reason to feel nervous, and I know that. This sudden fear is the main reason I'm so keen to get back out into the world. I'm scared that being kidnapped has changed me. Made me worry about...everything.

And I refuse to let Lakas change me like that. In fact, I'm going to kill him for it.

So I grip the strap of my bag tightly in one hand and stride down to the road like I don't have a care in the world. Ahead of me, Seth jumps into the driver's seat of the large black RAM pick-up that Blade is letting us use. Seth grins when I open the passenger door and lift my eyebrows at him.

"It's a long drive, almost twelve hours. I'll take first shift," he says. "Don't worry, you can drive next."

I'm not going to tell him, but I'm actually happy not to drive. My shoulder is still giving me grief, little arrows of pain shooting through my muscles. "I get to choose the radio station," I say instead. I put my bag on the back seat and climb in next to him.

He rolls his eyes. "You better choose something decent."

We bicker like an old married couple over the music, until I find a classic rock station that's playing Randy Crowe music.

"Did you talk to him at the party?" asks Seth, even though I was right next to him while he chatted to the rock legend. His eyes were a little too wide the entire time, like he was trying to act cool, but was completely unable to act normal.

"Hmmm," I say, letting him go on about how amazing Randy Crowe is. How down to earth. How talented.

"What kind of super is he, do you think?"

I'm staring out the window, watching the scenery go by, and have to think for a bit before answering. "No idea. Something musical maybe. A siren?" It makes me think of Connor. I'm glad Hazel killed him, he'd been using his siren abilities to hurt people. I wonder if Randy has done the same thing in his lifetime. Is that why he's so famous?

"I had him pegged for some kind of shifter. Maybe a wolf shifter? He's definitely not a mountain super."

"No, nor a dragon." I turn to Seth, watching as he focuses on the road, his long tanned arms holding the steering wheel casually. He's thinner than he was when we first met, but he's still all lean muscle and quiet competence. He's got a few more lines around his eyes, and his hair is a shaggy mess. I give a tiny snort. He's starting to look a little more like Jeff every day.

Did Jeff start out like Seth? Was he a super-eager cadet,

with a buzz cut and an idealistic view of the world? I can't imagine Jeff when he was fresh from the SIG academy. It's hard to picture anything other than the cynical, rule-breaking agent I knew through my childhood. "Maybe he's only part super, like my dad," I say, then shrug. "Could be anything."

"You'd think we'd be able to tell somehow," Seth says.

"You'd think. Maybe we can ask Dad. It's the kind of thing he'd know."

We continue the discussion for the next hour or so, and then move on to other equally innocuous topics. Time passes quickly, we swap turns in the driver's seat, and my shoulder holds up okay. I even manage to catch a few naps along the way while Seth is driving. It's relaxed and soothing.

After being kidnapped and tortured, this time alone with Seth is like a balm to my soul. He's kind, careful, and, despite his new tendency to be overly worried about my state of health, there's no one else I'd rather be with. When I reach out my hand to touch his, he immediately takes it in one of his much larger hands, the warmth of his skin sooth-ing. My dragon side settles down immediately, and I close my eyes and smile.

About eight hours into our trip, we stop at the motel I found. A flashing sign outside announces that we've found the best motel in town, and the sleepy desk clerk barely even looks us in the eye as he hands over the key. As soon as we walk into the tiny room, we crash onto the bed, snuggle up close and go to sleep, both too exhausted to even think of anything more.

CHAPTER
TWENTY-EIGHT

"This is Mt. Hood?" I say incredulously, looking up at the mountain from the small village at the base where we've stopped. It's covered in snow, and there are people everywhere, skiing and snowboarding down the side of the mountain. I shiver, even though I found a warm jersey to put on before we climbed out of the pick-up.

"What did you expect?"

"I don't know. Something with fewer people on it."

Seth shrugs. "It's still ski season. Just."

"How are we going to get inside and find Aurelia with all these people around?"

"We fly," says Seth.

My dragon-self rises, excitement sizzling through my limbs. I haven't shifted since before I was kidnapped.

There's something in me that's almost scared to do it, like it's going to hurt. Logically I know it's going to be fine. But tension fills my limbs and sweat breaks out on the back of my neck anyway. When Director Holden forced me to change back to my human form while I was still injured from the missile launch, it was the most painful experienced of my life. Subconsciously, my body remembers that, and definitely doesn't want to do it again.

"What's the matter?" Seth looks at me with a frown. "Isn't that how you envisioned doing this?"

I nod jerkily, although I hadn't actually envisioned anything, I realize now. Or if I had, it had been a distant idea, not an immediate reality.

"I think we should wait 'til it's dark. Do a scouting mission first." I let out a breath and watch the mist blowing out in front of me. I say the words quickly and wonder if Seth is going to call me on it. I'm a little rattled, and can't seem to get my head thinking straight.

But he just gives me a look and nods. "Let's find somewhere to stay, and have some lunch. Maybe get a map of the area and try to figure out where she might be."

I nod. "I could go into the shadow realm, try to find her that way." It seems easier than shifting into my dragon shape and flying. "Do you remember when I almost killed you when I was first learning to fly?"

Seth raises his eyebrows at me. "How could I forget? But you're a pro at flying now, Mei. Is that what's wrong here? You're worried about flying?"

"I don't know what's wrong. I'm just freaking out about the change and it's pissing me off. I'm used to being the one who leaps into trouble with both feet. Why the hell am I so scared to shift?"

Maybe Seth was right, maybe this is a bad idea after all.

Seth steps closer and pulls me into a hug. "I don't know. Must be something to do with the kidnapping, maybe with everything that happened just before it, too? You were *hurt*, Mei, after you grabbed that missile. You almost *died*. And then Director Holden took advantage of that and kidnapped you. And you almost died *again*. It's surprising that you're managing to stay calm about any of this."

I wait for him to say 'I told you so' but he never does, and I tighten my hold on him. "You're awesome, Seth, you know that?"

"Of course," he says with a grin in his voice.

We wander around Mt. Hood Village, holding hands like teenagers, eventually coming to a small cafe with the smell of coffee and delicious baking wafting out onto the street. "Here seems good," I say, trying to push away the butterflies that are still crowding my stomach.

We walk inside, and I'm immediately charmed by the busy, bustling cafe. There's a queue that we join, loads of people chatting and laughing at the wooden tables scattered around the small space, and photos all over the wall of people, snow, and mountains.

"Maybe we'll be able to find some information in here," says Seth softly near my ear, his warm breath tickling my skin.

"Maybe."

Once we're settled in a seat, and a friendly waitress delivers our steaming coffee, Seth traps me with his intent gaze. "Are you afraid to change? Or is it the flying?"

I shake my head, allowing my long dark hair to flutter over my shoulders and partially block my face. "I don't know what it is. I swear I felt fine, right up until the moment I thought about shifting. It feels almost like it did before I shifted for the first time, like I don't know what I'm doing." My breathing becomes a little uneven and I shift my gaze up to Seth's. "But worse. I don't know what's happening to me. I've never felt like this before."

Seth reaches out and puts his warm hand over my forearm. "It's okay, Mei. You're safe. It sounds like a panic attack. I... I had them a few times after I woke in the volcano. After... I died."

My eyes widen, and I study his face like I'm looking for proof in his lack of laugh lines. He's never told me about his panic attacks before. "What happened? How did you get over it?"

Seth lets out a long breath. "I don't think it ever goes away completely, but I manage it now. I know that it's in my head, and I use a few...techniques...they taught me to calm myself down."

"Techniques?" I'm not sure about anything he was taught by those people he was with when he first woke. They sided with Vincent and tried to kill me. Not my favorite people.

"Breathing techniques. Mindfulness. That kind of thing."

"Si used to make me meditate with him," I say softly. "Said it was an important part of being a warrior, knowing how to stay calm."

"He's right. It helped me. What did he use?"

"Box breathing patterns. Deep breathing through the nose. That kind of thing."

"Maybe try one of those?"

I nod. "Okay," I say, and I realize I'm already feeling better. Even just talking to Seth is helping. Plus having an idea of something I can actually do to help myself. "Now how do we get Aurelia out of Mt. Hood?"

"We'll go in at night. Fewer people, and we've both got excellent night vision, so that won't be a problem. We can fly to the crater at the top, explore from there. Hopefully she's somewhere near the top. Maybe you can talk with her in the shadow realm beforehand so she's expecting us?"

I nod. "Good idea. But I need somewhere safe to go into the realm. My body is vulnerable when I'm not in it."

Seth looks out the window of the cafe as if he's thinking. "What if we book ourselves into a motel? We'd have the privacy we need, then we can have a sleep if we need it before our midnight excursion."

"Good idea." I nod. My mind is on the excursion into the volcano rather than the visit to the realm, but either way, a private room sounds awesome.

CHAPTER
TWENTY-NINE

S everal hours later, and I'm sitting on a plush bedspread in a fancy home on the outskirts of town. Apparently it's impossible to find a motel room at this time of year. The only place we could find was an empty vacation home that Seth broke into—apparently the ability to break into homes is a subject at SIG agent training.

I keep looking around me at the pristine furnishings and the photos on the wall, wondering what it would have been like to have a normal upbringing. To come to the mountains in winter to ski and go to the beach in summer to swim. To hang out with friends and not have a care beyond finding a guy I liked or maybe whether I should quit my job and travel the world.

I sigh and lie back on the bed. I long ago got over the childish need to be normal and fit in—I much prefer saving the world—so I know I'm not feeling quite right for that kind of thinking to edge its way into my consciousness. I move about, getting my head comfy on the pillows. They're extremely fluffy, and I have to take one off and put it on the floor.

Seth watches me from the corner of the room, amusement on his face at my struggle to get comfortable. "You'd prefer the floor?"

I make a face. "This bed is way too soft."

Seth glances toward the door of the room. "We could try one of the other bedrooms? There are six of them. One must have a decent bed."

"I don't think it's the bed. It's me. But I'm fine." I wriggle around a little more. "Remember, you need to stay here with my body." I swallow nervously at the idea of what could happen if someone discovered me while I was in the shadow realm. Someone thinking I was dead and ringing the police is the best possible option.

"Of course. I'm not going to leave your side." Seth comes over and grabs my hand. "I'm never leaving your side again, remember?" Flames surge in his eyes, and I know he means every word with the intensity of his phoenix side.

I nod. That's enough for me. I pull him down and kiss him, leaning into his warmth. His lips are soft, and he makes a groaning sound in the back of his throat when I take the kiss deeper. Eventually, I pull away. "I'll be back soon. Then maybe we can..." I trail off, hoping he understands that I'd like to do something more than sleep.

He smiles slowly, his eyes warming up. "I'll be here."

I lean back and close my eyes. My hand is still holding Seth's. I take a breath, trying to relax into the softness of the bed. I'm not actually sure how this is going to go, now that I don't have the spell web inside me. Was it the one thing allowing me to go into the realm? Maybe I can't go back anymore? I feel like slapping myself in the head. Why did that never occur to me before? I should have tested my ability to go back into the shadow realm before now.

It doesn't matter, I remind myself. *I can try now.*

I concentrate on breathing slowly and carefully, getting myself into the right frame of mind. Aurelia didn't have the spell web inside her, and she was inside the shadow realm. If she can do it, I can too. I focus on relaxing my whole body, bit by bit, and then focus on being there, in the other realm.

And then suddenly I'm moving up out of my body.

The room, Seth, everything, is all in dark shadows. *I did it.* I have to squint to see anything properly, but it doesn't matter, because I just float up through the ceiling and out into the world above the house.

Where do I go to find Aurelia?

My eyes catch on Mt. Hood looming in the distance. There's a good chance she's not with her body, but I guess it's as good a place as any to start. I zoom over the streets, high up in the air, not worrying about anything or anyone else. They can't see me down below, and I'm focused on how I'm going to find Aurelia. She liked to spend a lot of time in the shadow realm, traveling around. It's how she found me. I don't know what I'm going to find up on Mt. Hood. Maybe just her empty body?

Maybe she's not even there anymore? Maybe I'm too late?

Maybe—

I'm suddenly shoved to one side as an enormous presence smashes into me from the side, and a painful zing of electricity races through my body. I yelp, surprised, and try to right myself. For a moment, I'm tumbling head over heels through the air, and then I realize.

It doesn't actually matter in this realm, my body is

whatever I want it to be, and I can move it into being nothing more than a ball of shadow if I want to.

So I stop spinning and end up as a circle of darkness. I search around, trying to find my attacker. Part of me thinks it might be Aurelia, mad at me for taking so long.

But she was never violent. Not like that.

That's when I spot it. A dark, moving shape, like all the shadows came to rest in one place and then melded into each other, creating a black cloud so dense it almost hurts to look at it.

And it's heading back toward me.

I zip off in the other direction, frantically trying to figure out where else I could go.

I'm not as fast inside the shadow realm this time, and it's taking a minute to acclimatize. Not having the spell web inside me is making more of a difference than I thought it would. Or maybe it's just that I'm still recovering from my near-death experience. Either way, it doesn't matter. I just need to get out of here.

I look around, trying to figure out a plan for dealing with this shadow monster. But I hesitate for too long, and suddenly the shadow bashes into me again. I manage to drop down at the last minute and escape the worst of the hit. My breath—which I've established I don't need inside this realm—is coming thick and fast, like I'm hyperventilating...which I'm also pretty sure I can't do. I know it's all in my head, but it feels real. I look around, trying to sense where the shadow creature is now. I can't see it, but that doesn't mean it's gone. It's just better at being inside this realm than I am.

I need to get out of here.

Luckily, Aurelia taught me how to do that.

I close my eyes and focus on the top of Mt. Hood, and

then suddenly I'm there. The moon overhead makes it bright, but thin clouds swirl around me, and the falling snow adds another element to keep me hidden. Peering around, I look for signs that somehow the shadow creature followed me. My mind is racing, and my shadows are swirling, but I'm pretty sure I'm alone.

I hover over the mountain, wondering what I should do. I've never come across anything like that inside the shadow realm before. What was it? Another person? Some kind of monster from this realm? Aurelia said that you could be hurt in the shadow realm, that you could even be killed. I'm pretty sure that thing would have killed me if it had the chance.

What if it's hunting Aurelia?

Does she have to get past that creature whenever she leaves? She never mentioned it before, but it's possible. It would make it doubly impressive that she found me. But it might make it more difficult to find Aurelia in the shadow realm right now. What if she's hiding? Maybe she never even stays around here, and I'm wasting my time looking for her near her physical body.

Except I have no choice but to look for her, now that I'm here. I have to make sure I'm right about where she is. I head down into the dormant crater at the top of Mt. Hood. There are a few small caves leading out from the main crater, and I zip into one, my shadow body able to fit into the tiny space without a problem.

At first it's not just shadowy, but total darkness. I can't see a thing. But then as I go further into the cave tunnel, it starts to get lighter. There's a flame up ahead, that I follow, drawn to it like a dazzled moth.

As I get closer, it gets hotter and hotter, until I'm only fifty yards away and I recognize what it is: fresh lava.

I don't know how, and I don't know why, but there's fresh lava inside the mountain.

Surely it's supposed to be dormant down here? Where has the lava come from? Why are there people skiing on the mountain outside while it's flowing with lava so close to the surface?

I slow down, and cautiously move closer, searching for something that will tell me what the hell is going on down here. And then I hear it.

Voices.

I pull my shadow realm form into the tightest possible ball, and inch closer, not sure who it is and how much they can sense of me. I get to the end of the tunnel, and peer out into a larger cavern, where the lava is bubbling and spitting in a pool in the middle. It seems to be coming up from the ground; it's not oozing out from any other cracks or crevices inside the cave.

Two large men are standing to one side. Both mountain supers, one of them with his eyes closed and concentrating. The lava bubbles a bit more.

I think they're somehow controlling the lava. Maybe even making it?

I move closer, trying to hear what they're saying.

"...was very clear. If we don't sort this out, we're dead instead of her."

"It's not that easy, Rav. I can't just create lava from nothing. And it's all very well to tell me to suffocate her in lava, but she's not exactly in an accessible place."

"Just hurry. He said the other dragon's on her way."

Is he talking about Aurelia? And me?

They're trying to kill Aurelia.

And if we don't hurry, they might even succeed.

CHAPTER
THIRTY

I wake up in my body again with a gasp, sitting up so suddenly, Seth jerks back, almost falling to the ground.

"What's the matter?" he asks urgently, leaning forward again.

"They're trying to find Aurelia, and kill her," I blurt out, my hands clutching the bedspread.

"What? Who?" Seth's eyes are wide. I know he's expecting Lakas.

"Two mountain supers," I say quickly, trying to reassure him. "They're inside the mountain. One of them seems to be good with moving lava. They're trying to find her and kill her."

"But why? Who are they?"

I shake my head, just as bewildered as he is. "I don't know. But they were saying that whoever sent them would kill them if they didn't get it done. So I don't think it was anyone good." I put my hand to my head, my breathing shaky. I can't get past the thought that if we'd delayed it another week, thinking that we had all the time in the world, Aurelia would have been dead.

I don't even know for certain that she's not already dead.

"What should we do?" asks Seth. "Do we still have time to wait until it's completely dark?"

I shake my head vehemently. "No. We have to go now. I don't know how long it'll take them to find her, but we can't wait until after midnight. We'll just have to hope that the spell web takes care of masking our flight from the humans."

Seth nods. "Is it just two mountain supers? Or are there more of them?"

I hesitate, not sure whether to mention the dark shadow. Surely it was just in the shadow realm? Not something we have to worry about out here?

But Seth catches my hesitation. "Mei, tell me."

I explain what happened and he pales. "You don't even know what it was?" He shakes his head. "This isn't the simple rescue mission you said it would be."

"No, it's way worse. There are people trying to kill her. We have to hurry." I leap up out of bed, and start picking up my jacket and phone and other possessions that I've already managed to scatter around the room.

"But..." Seth moves over to where I'm shoving my jeans into my bag. "We need to think about this some more. We need—"

"I know, Seth. It's not ideal. I'm not at one hundred percent, and neither are you. But we can't leave her here like this, not when I know her life is in danger." I lean over and grab Seth's arm. "We have no choice."

"Then we need to get reinforcements. You ring Mr. Fookes. I'll see if there's anyone I know around this area."

"Mr. Fookes is on his way. But he won't be here for another twelve hours, no matter that he's a genie." I tuck my phone back in my pocket, and look expectantly at Seth.

"I found a raven colony in Seattle. They're going to try send some people out to meet us."

I shake my head. "That's more than three hours away. And we don't know them. We can't trust strangers for this kind of a mission. Even if we could, I don't think we have time to wait for them all to arrive. Those men were close to finding her."

Seth hesitates. "Maybe we can go in there and distract them? Keep them from achieving their goals until we have backup?"

I blink up at Seth. I know what it's costing him to suggest something like that. He's been worried about my safety ever since Hazel saved me, and he hasn't suddenly changed in the last hour or two. I step closer and wrap my arms around him in a tight hug, trying to convey everything I'm feeling right now.

He wraps his arms around me in return, and leans his cheek on the top of my head.

"Okay," I say against his chest. "Let's do it. We'll just be more... cautious... than usual."

Seth lets out a tiny huff of breath. "I don't think you have it in you to be cautious."

Fear prickles its way inside my chest. He's wrong, I'm more scared than I've ever been, and I don't think some deep breathing is going to be enough to calm me down. I overestimated my readiness for a mission like this, and I'm feeling shaky and uncertain.

But I have no choice. Aurelia saved me, and it's my responsibility to do what I can to help her in return.

"We'll shift out back, and then head to the crater."

I nod, and lead the way. "What will we need?" I ask. We left all our supplies in the pick-up, which is parked in the driveway.

"I don't want us to shift back into our human forms if we can help it. We'll be more vulnerable. Let's just do this in phoenix and dragon form." He hesitates. "But just in case, I'll take a bag with a change of clothes for each of us, and torches, and climbing gear."

I nod, and lead the way outside, although it's the last thing I want to do. The air is cold, and I can see my breath. I pull off my jacket and shirt, shivering in the mountain air. I was already nervous about shifting, but the cold is making it worse. Butterflies are flying about in my stomach and despite the cold, sweat is breaking out on my back as I take off my pants and boots and socks.

I just need to make it happen, fast.

I close my eyes and begin the shift into my dragon form. I've been doing it so easily and so quickly for such a long time, it's strange to have to think it through, like I'm a newbie dragon. There's something inside me that's resisting, despite the pleased dragon core that is aching to be set free.

I want to be in my dragon form again. I want to fly high above the clouds again, my wings outstretched.

I'm just scared. Terrified really.

I flick Seth a quick look, only to find he's watching me carefully, like he knows what I'm going through.

"I don't know if I can do it. And I don't know why." I growl out the last bit.

"The last time you flew, it was to save everyone from

the missile that the ravens had used on us all. Do you remember? You leaped into the air without any hesitation, and powered after that missile. You didn't even think twice, just leaped. You took it high into the air, without a thought for your own safety. And you almost died because of it. That's the last time you flew, Mei. *Of course* you're scared."

His words are like needles, poking into my skin. And he's right. I roll my shoulders, trying to relax my tense body.

Seth moves closer and takes my hand. "Your brain and body are trying to protect you from being hurt again. But you need to prove to yourself, and your brain, that it's okay. That being a dragon is safe. That you're up for this."

I take a deep breath and nod. "I can do it. It's going to be fine." I repeat the words over and over in my mind. Closing my eyes, I focus inward, toward my dragon self, hiding deep inside my core. My dragon roars inside me, itching to expand, to grow and grow until I'm no longer a puny human, but a magnificent dragon, scaled and strong, blood red and glittering gold, the strongest of all dragons.

And just like that I feel my body reshaping. Sizzling movement, flickering pain, energy bursting and breaking around me. The magic of it is overwhelming, and even though I'm still scared, I'm excited and euphoric too. I love being in my dragon form, it feels like nothing else.

Bones crack, skin stretches, scales form. My neck stretches up and out, reaching up into the sky, until I have a long nose and teeth larger than my hands in human form. I let out a puff of smoke and a growl emerges in an undertone. I look around, my head higher than the houses around me, and my gaze fixes on Mt. Hood in the distance. Snow is still swirling around the top of the mountain, and the lights of the ski field about half way down are bright against the snow. I can even see someone walking around the edge of one of the ski field buildings, doing a safety check. My vision is a million times better in this form, that's for sure.

A burning heat next to me demands my attention, and I turn my head. Seth is in his phoenix form, tall and majestic, with flames rolling across his body.

Shall we go? he asks.

Yes. I don't wait for anything more. I leap into the air, reveling in the strength of my dragon body. My wings pound the air, easily pulling me up and away over the houses in the small village, then up over the snowy landscape of the mountain.

Seth follows behind me, his body equally as graceful and powerful in the air. I love watching him fly, it's more like a wave of heat than a supernatural creature flying— power and energy rolled into one. I set off a burst of flames in appreciation and then push my wings faster and harder, until I'm flying up inside the clouds, hiding my form from any innocent humans watching below, but also anyone else who might be connected to the two men inside the mountain crater.

Now that the rush of adrenaline from the shift has worn off, I'm starting to think through the implications of everything that's going on. And it's not good.

The fact that there's someone in the mountain trying to kill Aurelia suggests two things to me. Someone else knows she's here, maybe even kept her trapped in the mountain on purpose. And they know that Aurelia and I know each other, and that I'm on my way to rescue her.

If she's a three hundred year old dragon, how would they know she's here? Who is old enough to remember that? Or did they find her body accidentally? That seems unlikely. The thoughts keep swirling around inside my head. Why would someone keep Aurelia inside the mountain on purpose? What kind of person would do that?

Seth's question about Aurelia bringing about the dragon Armageddon pops into my head. Was Aurelia locked in the mountain because she was going to do something terrible? Could setting her free be a big mistake?

The words create a sense of déjà vu inside me and a shudder runs along my scales. For a moment I struggle to understand why, and then I realize. It's what I've been accused of my whole life.

Why the Earthbound were hunting me. Why people have been trying to kill me.

They thought I was going to do something terrible, just because I was a dragon.

I refuse to believe the same thing of Aurelia. She helped me when I needed it most. I'm going to rescue her, and hope that my gut instincts are right.

We're just going to surprise them? Try overpowering them? asks Seth inside my head.

I take a breath, trying to figure out the best plan. *We need to find Aurelia first, even if we can't extract her right away. They said she's not in an easily accessible place, and that it might take a while to get the lava to her.*

What about distracting the men?

What if we could get her out of there before the men ever get to her? Wouldn't that be better than trying to meet them head on? I don't say it, but the thought that neither of us is up to a fight hangs in the air between us.

How are we going to do that? Seth gives me side eye as we fly next to each other, like he figured we'd end up changing the plans as soon as we were in the air, and isn't surprised by the suggestion.

I give a dragon grin, showing off my sharpened teeth. *You're a phoenix, I'm a dragon. I'm sure we'll think of something.* I'm aiming for the cockiness I used to feel, and it mostly works.

Seth gives me a look that says 'I told you so, you're crazy' and 'how do we get ourselves into situations like this all the time?', all rolled into one.

I don't think we'll get through the same cave system that I travelled through in the shadow realm, but there must be another way through. Surely we can use a bit of dragon fire to make a new entrance in the side?

A new entrance?

Dragon fire is very powerful, so is phoenix fire. Perhaps together they'll combine into something even stronger.

We're not the Transformers, says Seth, his voice so dry it could be the desert. His body undulates through the clouds ahead of me, almost like he's swimming rather than flying, and I have to concentrate to keep up with him.

We've never tried anything like that. It could work. I know it's a long shot, and I don't know why I'm arguing for it. It's mainly to cover my own increasing nerves, I think. Mt Hood looms in front of us, and I still have no idea how we're going to find Aurelia inside there.

Except... there's something about being up here in the sky, with the backdrop of the moon and the stars, accompanied by Seth in his glowing phoenix form. The flames burning across his body call to me like metal to a magnet. I feel more powerful around him, more able to be a dragon. I don't know if it's something to do with Seth being a phoenix, or if it's just a reflection of how I feel about him.

I fly beside him up to the top of the mountain, and we circle overhead.

There! I say, pointing with one taloned paw. *There's a*

darker section on the far side of the mountain. It looks like a cave site where perhaps we can create a wider entrance for our dragon and phoenix sized bodies.

Let's check it out. Seth dips down, and I follow him.

We land nearby, clinging to the rocks. The section where my back paw lands breaks off, and fragments tumble down the side of the mountain below me. I scramble about for another rock to hold onto, cursing to myself. It's not so bad when you've got wings, but it's still not ideal. Once I'm secure again, I turn to watch as Seth peers inside the cave.

He's the smaller super in this form, but he doesn't have the same long neck that I do, so when he pulls out his head and shrugs, I move closer. I want to check as well.

What can you see? I ask.

Not much. It's dark and small. We're going to have to find a way to make it bigger before either of us will be able to get inside.

My turn to look, I say.

He moves away from the tiny cave, and I move closer, pushing my head down through the opening. Inside it's dark and damp, water dripping somewhere in the distance. It's also hot and muggy, like a steam room.

I close my eyes and try to connect with the spell web grid. Now that it's not inside me anymore, it's much harder than it used to be. I let my senses roll along the grid lines, following the energy as it zips along the spell. I can't feel anything at first, but I'm not going to give up.

I'm determined to find Aurelia and keep her safe from the two mountain supers in the caves overhead.

CHAPTER
THIRTY-ONE

Find anything? Seth asks from where he's waiting outside.

I open my eyes again. *There's a wisp of something further down inside the mountain that might be Aurelia. If it's her, she's not doing great.* A strong sense of urgency is driving me now. We definitely don't have time to wait for backup.

Can we get to her through the cave? asks Seth.

I don't know. I look around the cave, wondering how we're even going to find her. *She's deep inside the mountain. I don't know if trying to access her from up here is the best option.*

Then let's try to find something lower down.

I pull my head and neck back out of the cave, and look around. Even now, having a completely different body takes some getting used to. Four legs and a long neck are helpful but disorientating if I haven't been in my dragon body for a long while. It's still light outside and I blink a few times, trying to let my senses adjust.

Seth takes off, and I follow, leaping into the air in a way that I'd find terrifying in my human form. We soar downward, both looking for another entrance, a new way inside that might prove more useful. I try to hold onto the tiny scrap of energy that indicated where Aurelia might be—although not confirmed—as we fly.

Up ahead, Seth lands, rocks flying out beneath him as he grasps onto a ledge. I swoop past, trying to see what he's found. There's another cave, this one hidden in the side of the mountain, under the ledge, but much larger.

This could work, I say.

He grins back at me, like he's excited about the prospect of going inside the mountain. He seems to have forgotten his initial reluctance—I just wish I was the same. Instead, I'm worrying about the two men I saw, and why they're here. Are they really our enemies? What if Carrick sent them? Or the mountain supers' First Elder?

Why are they trying to bury Aurelia for good?

But instead of voicing my fears, I smile at Seth as I land just below the opening, then crawl inside. I'm not worried about bears or other animals being inside the cave—for one thing it's too high—but I'm also the apex predator. Nothing is going to get me... at least not from the animal kingdom.

This cave is similar to the other one. Damp and dark, with dripping water somewhere in the distance. It's also much bigger and I manage to get my whole body inside the first section with room to spare.

It's larger in here, I say. There are a couple of smaller tunnels heading off to one side, both too small for my dragon body. *But not quite large enough.*

Seth squeezes inside, next to me. He looks around, and then suddenly there's sparking light and sizzling heat, and Seth stands in front of me naked.

I grin, enjoying the sight of his tall muscled body as he

bends over the bag he was carrying attached to one leg of his phoenix shape.

"We've changed the rest of the plan, why not change this bit?" he says dryly. "We can head down the tunnels much more easily in human form." He pulls out his clothes from the backpack and starts getting dressed.

My dragon side resists the idea of going back to my puny human body, but Seth's right. It's the easiest option. Hopefully we won't see the two mountain supers, and if we do, we can hopefully change back into our more powerful super shapes fast enough.

That's a lot of hoping in one sentence.

But we have to save Aurelia. I made a promise to her.

With a sigh, I close my eyes and allow the change to take over. Bones crack, magic sizzles, and suddenly I'm standing naked next to Seth. He grins and hands me my clothes. He pulls out a couple of energy bars from the bag, and, once I'm dressed, hands me one to eat. I open it gratefully, taking a huge bite. I'm so hungry it feels like there's a yawning pit inside my stomach.

Seth has wandered over to one of the tunnels, peering inside it, presumably for clues as to which way we should go.

"Any ideas?" I ask.

"This one has a breeze blowing out of it. Seems to indicate another external exit somewhere. The other one feels a little more stagnant and dark."

"As much as I hate to say this, I think the second one might be our best option," I say.

Seth nods. "Dank and dark it is. Can you feel her from here?"

I shake my head. "I can't feel as much in my human form. Even less now that I don't have the spell web inside me." I try to ignore the pang at the feeling of being less powerful. All that power from the spell web came at a cost —my life.

I'm grateful to Hazel for getting it out of me. *I am.*

"I remember when we first met, you could manipulate the spell web in your human form," says Seth.

I nod. "Yeah, I could. This is a new one, and I'm not as much of a natural at manipulating it. I just have to get used to it."

Seth nods, and turns back to the tunnel. "Then we just have to be very careful. No crazy stunts, and no unnecessary confrontations, okay?"

I nod. "Absolutely." I tie my second shoelace and stand up. "Let's get this done."

He grabs my hand as I walk by, and drags me back to him. I find myself in Seth's arms, being crushed to his chest. I lean back and look up at his face, then smile as he leans down to place a chaste kiss on my lips.

"Promise me you won't do anything stupid down here?" he says.

"As long as you promise me the same," I say.

He rolls his eyes. "I'm not the one who grabbed a missile and flew into the air with it."

I shake my head. "It's not like I had a choice. I was the only one who could have done it. And if I hadn't, most people in that room would be dead."

"You're right, as always. I know that. It's part of who you are. And with great power comes great responsibility, as they say. I just wish it wasn't always..."

"Me?"

Seth lets out a breath. "Yeah. I love you Mei, and I don't want to stop you from being you. But how I felt in that cave when I thought you were dead...? That was the worst thing that's ever happened to me." Seth closes his eyes. "If something ever happened to you again, I don't think I would survive a second time."

I reach up and touch his face. "I'll do my very best to stay safe," I say, not knowing what else to say. It's not like I'm the kind of person who can suddenly stop taking action.

Seth nods. "That's all I ask."

I hold him tightly for a moment longer, and then we both move apart. I focus down the tunnel, trying to figure out if I can feel that same little spark of energy I felt before. "I think you're right. This is the tunnel we should follow."

We turn on our flashlights, Seth hoists his backpack onto his shoulders and we trudge into the murky tunnel. There's moisture on the bottom of the tunnel, and it's so warm that I'm soon sweating through the jacket and T-shirt I'm wearing. I pull the jacket off and tie it around my waist.

Seth is moving ahead, and I hurry to catch up.

"You okay?" he asks softly.

"Just hot," I whisper.

We walk in silence for a while, both concentrating on not tripping over the uneven ground. We eventually come to a crossroads, two tunnels heading off in different directions. Seth looks over his shoulder at me, eyebrows raised.

I peer down both tunnels. They look exactly the same.

I close my eyes, trying to put feelers out along the spell web grid like I used to do when I was younger. This spell web feels unfamiliar, prickly, not the same as the one I grew up playing with. But it's the same kind of spell, which means I should be able to use it.

Next to me, Seth glows like a beacon, his full phoenix energy blasting my senses—I remember when I first met him as a new SIG agent, fresh from cadet training, and he looked patchy and broken on the spell web. Things have definitely changed since then.

I push past him, and out along the grid, trying to ignore the hooks and pricks that keep catching me as I let my senses flow out along the lines. In the distance, somewhere in the center of the mountain, I feel the same faint energy source as I felt higher up the mountain.

I open my eyes and look at the tunnel on the left. "That way. She's that way."

Seth doesn't question me, just turns and strides along the left hand tunnel.

I keep my senses open to the spell web as I walk this time, which means I'm more likely to stumble, but it gives me a sense of where we're heading, so that when we come to another cross section of the caves, I know exactly which way we should be going before Seth even asks.

We keep walking for at least an hour, going deeper and deeper into the cave systems inside the mountain. The tunnels are rough, broken stones littering the floor, and rugged piles of enormous rocks that we clamber over. It's a tunnel that's been carved by nature, but we're not the first people down here. I see several sets of footprints in the mud, and a few pieces of litter—lolly wrappers and a coke can—as we walk.

"Is this a popular place to walk, do you think?" I ask Seth. "Or is it our mountain super friends who came this way before us?"

"I don't know. But we need to keep an eye out. It's clearly a path that people have been using recently." He gazes down the tunnel in front of us. "It's getting narrower. If it keeps up like this, we're going to end up crawling. Are we close?"

I shut my eyes for a second, trying to pinpoint Aurelia's direction from where we are. "We're close. I can feel her. We just have to—"

Seth holds up one finger to his lips, and I fall silent.

There are voices further down the tunnel.

If they're coming this way, we're screwed. There's nowhere to hide.

CHAPTER
THIRTY-TWO

I glance behind us. Maybe we can run that way, keep ahead of them?

Except...

The voices aren't coming closer. If anything, they're moving away, getting softer.

Seth nods for us to keep moving forward, but he holds his finger over his lips for a moment longer to indicate we should stay silent.

We tiptoe down the tunnel, watching and listening even more carefully than before.

My heart is pounding, and I'm shaking slightly as I climb over a boulder in the middle of our path. I haven't felt like this about a mission since I was a kid. My confidence is shot, small noises are making me jump. If it wasn't for the thought of these men killing Aurelia, I'd tell Seth to turn around, and head home.

He was right, I'm not ready for this.

But Aurelia is stuck somewhere inside this volcano, and I can't bear the thought of leaving her to whatever fate those men have planned for her.

We have to at least *attempt* to save her.

So we keep going. The voices start getting louder again, and the light up ahead becomes brighter. We're approaching the entrance to another big cavern. It's like Swiss cheese in here. The light is flickering; it's either torches of some kind, or maybe more of the lava they were creating in the other cave. I turn off my flashlight, and ahead of me, Seth does the same.

Seth slows and creeps along the edge of the tunnel. He stops just before the edge, while he's still in shadow, and peers out. I wait, watching his reactions, trying to figure out what he can see, but he's too good at keeping his expression bland. He gestures for me to move forward and stand beside him.

We're up about four or five yards from the floor of the cave. There's another, much larger, tunnel at floor level just a bit further round from where we are. There's also a pool of lava in the center, just like in the cave where I saw them before.

Maybe this is even the same place? It's hard to know, sometimes my perceptions inside the shadow plane are different to when I'm here in the real world.

Across the room, the same two mountain supers are talking...arguing might be more accurate. They're gesturing and yelling, and standing so close to each other, it seems like they're about to start punching.

What I didn't see in the shadow realm is that there are five other men as well—all large, muscular mountain supers—standing around them, watching the fight with interest, like they've got a bet on the outcome. Not invested enough to intervene, but real curious about who's going to come out on top.

I close my eyes, using the spell web to figure out where

Aurelia is from where we are. She's close by, and I'm relieved to feel her a little stronger than I did before. The only problem is, I think we're going to have to go through the cavern to get to her.

"Can we sneak past them, do you think?" I ask quietly. I don't think I'm strong enough to take on seven mountain supers with just Seth as backup. My hand trembles against the rocks. This is so much more than I was expecting.

Seth is watching the men. "Maybe. They've been fighting for a while. They don't seem to be able to decide how to find her. Or who's in charge of the mission."

"Let's do this before they decide."

I'm grateful for the all-black outfits we're both wearing, as I slowly move toward the edge of the tunnel. I used to be able to use the spell web to hide from those around me, and I concentrate on the web, trying to connect in such a way that it blurs my movement to the men on the other side of the cavern.

It seems to work, and I make it down without a problem. There are enough boulders around the edge of the cave to make it easier to move once I'm down. I look back at Seth, trying to do the same thing for him, but he's too fast, and he's beside me before I even get much of a chance to blur him.

I move around the edge of the cave, going from boulder to shadow to boulder. I'm heading for a second smaller tunnel just down from the larger one they seem to have created with their lava. I'm like a mouse following the scent of cheese, stopping every few minutes to make sure I can still sense Aurelia along the grid.

Eventually, we make it to the hole in the wall that marks the tunnel I think we should follow. I can see why the other two ignored it. It's dark, and craggy, and water is dripping almost in a waterfall across the entrance. But I know this is the right way. I feel it through my connection with Aurelia.

Maybe that's why the mountain supers are arguing? They should have been able to find her before now, and haven't. They know they're not doing their job properly, and they're scared.

But scared of who?

I shake my head yet again, and push my way through the little waterfall into the darkness beyond. I switch to my dragon heat sensing vision, but it doesn't help. Everything down here is the same and not quite hot enough to show up. It's all just as black as it is in my normal vision.

Once we're inside the new tunnel, I let out a breath and keep moving forward, holding one hand to the rock wall to help me find my way. It's completely dark, with strange noises that I can't begin to catalogue. Are there other creatures down here? I've been so focused on the murderous mountain supers, I hadn't thought about that.

What if—

Something lands on my shoulder, and I jump, only just stifling a scream. But it's just Seth. He's moved closer, and I didn't even notice.

I was too busy panicking.

I'm starting to get really pissed off about how pathetic I'm being right now. Every little thing is startling me, my heart is racing and I'm trembling like a new-born fawn.

"We need to keep moving, fast. I don't know how long they're going to keep arguing, but their plan is to move the lava into the tunnel, and drown everything down here, along with your dragon friend."

I nod, trying to stay steady. That's what I'd figured too.

"You want me to go first?" asks Seth.

I hate the fact that he asked... and the fact that I *would* like him to go first. I hesitate over the idea of saying 'no', just for the sake of my pride. "Yes, please," I whisper, my chest constricted.

He tightens his hold on my shoulder for a moment, like he knows what's going on inside my head. Then he moves past me, his tread silent.

Behind us, the men are still arguing. The tunnel is dripping water and a drop lands on my face. I move forward, just as silent as Seth, desperately hoping we're going to find Aurelia in time.

We creep down the new tunnel, Aurelia's spark of life getting brighter as we go. We're so close I can almost hear her heartbeat with my normal senses. Up ahead of me, Seth pauses, glancing back at me. I move closer and peer around him.

There's a gap in the tunnel's path. A deep chasm separates the two sides, with a yawning twenty-yard void. The crevice is so deep it's impossible to see the bottom. My heart sinks. The tunnel isn't big enough for either of us to shift into our other forms, and it's a long way to jump. I narrow my gaze at the other side. I don't know if I can make it, not when I'm not even up to full strength. I close my eyes, looking along the spell web again for Aurelia, wondering how we're going to make it across—

Except she's not on the other side of the crack. She's down there, inside it.

We have to go *down*.

For a second, I desperately wish I hadn't insisted we do this. I wish we were back at Freddie's house, in the front room with the sunshine covering us, and the view of the sea sparkling in the background. I can almost smell the coffee and hear the comforting swish of the waves hitting the cliffs.

I open my eyes. Darkness prevails. I'm not there, and there's no point pretending I am. "She's not across the crack, she's down it." I peer into the gaping maw. "How good are you at rock climbing?"

Si used to make me practice with no safety ropes, but I haven't done it for a long time. I'm not feeling confident right now, and that's exactly when mistakes happen and you end up plummeting to the ground.

"I'm okay. Not my best talent," says Seth cautiously. He peers over the edge, with a thoughtful expression.

I crouch down to one side of the tunnel. "I think I need to go back into the shadow realm. See if I can find exactly where she is. Maybe even talk to her, if she's around."

Seth nods. "I'll stand guard. Let you know if anything happens."

I sit on the rough ground, wincing as a rock pokes into my butt cheek. Sweeping away the loose rocks with one hand, I get myself comfortable, then close my eyes. This time, I move into the shadow realm easily, almost leaping out of my body.

Can you hear me Seth? He'd heard me last time.

"I can. Just. You're faint."

I'll let you know as soon as I find her.

"Mei... Just be careful, okay?" Seth is standing in the middle of the tunnel, his hands clenched, looking down at my unmoving body.

I will.

I swish out and away, down the crevice, certain of where I'm going to find Aurelia's body now that I'm in the shadow realm. Except when I zoom down deep into the crevice, I can't find her. She's not here. I search around, zooming back and forth. I can't sense her on the spell web in this form, but I can move about in ways I can't in the real world.

All I have to do is use what I have here.

I move up the wall of the fissure, hunting for any sign of Aurelia. Where could she be? I've almost given up when I find a small crack in the wall, near the top. I slip through the narrow opening, and discover another cave about ten feet under the tunnel where Seth is waiting. I sweep through the gap, and into the pitch black space.

Aurelia's large dragon body is squeezed into the tight space, and she's partially covered by thick, ancient lava. Her scales are dried and cracking, her whole body is emaciated and her bones stick out everywhere that's not covered with lava. I want to gasp and cover my mouth with my hands, but I'm just a ball of energy inside the shadow realm.

Her eyes are closed, and I don't know how to wake her. Is she in the shadow realm? She always used to find me when I came back into the realm. How did she do it? Was she just waiting for me, or did she have some way of knowing?

Aurelia? Where are you? I call out through the shadow plane, trying to do it loudly enough for her to hear, but softly, in case anything else is around.

There's a rushing noise all around me and suddenly one of Aurelia's eyes opens. She opens her dragon jaw, as if to speak, but no sound comes out. I zoom in closer. *Aurelia? It's me, Mei. I'm here to rescue you.*

Except I don't know how I'm going to move this emaciated dragon body anywhere. I look around the cave where she's been locked away. There's an entrance on the far side that seems to be the source of the lava that's covering her and locking her in place.

Did someone do this to you on purpose? I ask.

She blinks, once. Her eyes are dark and rheumy, and I'm not even sure she can see out of them. When I accidentally woke Tarsal in Ireland, he woke up more vital than when he'd gone to sleep. Aurelia looks... like she's wasted away. Perhaps it's because she's spent so much time in the shadow realm?

I swallow hard at the idea. I don't want to end up like this. I vow to stop spending so much time in this realm.

We're just overhead. As soon as we figure out how to get to you, we'll rescue you.

She blinks again, although this time I sense disbelief in her expression. Her prison is completely blocked on all sides. She's been trapped here for centuries.

But she didn't have a phoenix helping her.

I zip back up to my body, thinking through how we're going to get down to her. It's going to involve a bit of... machination.

CHAPTER
THIRTY-THREE

"She's directly below us?" asks Seth, incredulous.

I nod, still trying to regain my equilibrium in the real world.

"How do we get to her?"

"Two options. One, climb down to the gap, and try to break open the rock. Maybe with dragon or phoenix fire."

Seth raises his eyebrows. "And option two?"

"We try to get in from up here."

"It's too thick from here," says Seth, although he's looking around, as if searching for somewhere that might be thinner and more permeable.

"Perhaps if we both shifted, and focused both our flames, maybe the combined force of dragon fire and phoenix fire might be enough?"

"That's a big 'if'." He runs one hand through his hair. "And there's barely enough room for one of us to shift, let alone two."

"What if we did both? What if you try to make a hole from up here, and I climb down and work on the hole down there?" I gesture toward the giant crack in the rocks.

Seth looks between me and the gap. "You'd be in your dragon form if you were down there?"

I nod.

"So no chance of falling?"

I peer over the edge again. "Not of falling." *Getting trapped because there's not enough room to fly, perhaps. But not of falling.*

My heart pounds and I wish I hadn't suggested it. But phoenix fire is more capable of carving a hole in the rock up here. We don't have a choice.

"Maybe we could swap after a while?" I say quietly. I'm not even sure how we're going to get Aurelia out of the lava. And then out of the mountain. She's clearly not capable of doing anything in her dragon form. What will she be like if she transforms into her human shape? I'm not even convinced she'll be able to shift.

"How long before our backup arrives?" I ask.

Seth glances at his watch. "Another hour and a half."

"Do you think...?"

He shakes his head. "No, I think they'll have sorted their differences before then. We need to get her out now."

"Then we try the fire?"

"We try the fire."

I stand up, and move to the edge of the crack. "I'm going to have to climb down a bit, until there's enough room for my dragon."

"Can you shift without letting go of the rocks?" asks Seth, his voice tense. He's probably regretting the day he let me convince him to come on this stupid rescue mission.

I definitely am.

Except if we hadn't, Aurelia would have been killed. At least this way we still have a chance of saving her.

"I think so," I say, peering over the edge. I'm totally not sure. I guess I just have to make sure I do it carefully.

"Okay, then let's get you sorted first. I have rope in the bag, enough to tie around your waist, and get you safely down to where you need to be." He starts unzipping the bag, and pulls out a thick rope.

I nod. "I'll have to untie it when I shift, though," I say. I swallow hard. I'm not confident that I'm strong enough to hold onto the rocks like I used to.

"You can use it like you're abseiling," he says. "Then once you're safely shifted, let go."

I nod, already pulling off my pants and T-shirt. I have to climb naked, so I don't lose any of my clothes in the shift. Seth ties the rope around my waist, all efficient energy, and I sit down at the edge, trying to ignore how cold and damp the rocks are. Flipping around, I lie with my stomach on the floor, and inch my legs out into nothing. The rough surface scratches at my sensitive skin, and I bite my lip to keep from crying out. As soon as my waist gets to the edge, I bend my body, and get my toes into footholds. Then I start to inch my way down.

It's difficult. My body isn't as tough as it used to be. The weeks of capture have affected my stamina and muscle power. But I'm determined and focused, and right now, that has to be enough. My fingers are white as I grasp the tiny outcroppings, and my feet are pinching across the base. I try not to look down. Every so often, pebbles fall, and I hear them clinking against the sides of the fissure as they tumble down.

It's a long way to the bottom.

I just have to keep breathing, ignore the voice in my head that's screaming for me to hurry, and move one arm or leg at a time. There's no other way to do it.

Eventually, I make it to the small weakening of the rock. I pull at the edges of the tiny crack I found, the weaker rock crumbling in my fingers, until there's a gap big enough to see Aurelia. I take a breath, try to calm my frantic heartbeat. So far, so good.

I can't stop, or let myself think too much about what I'm doing. I have a feeling that'll make it impossible to do the next step in this plan. Taking a breath to steady myself, I look down at the rope around my waist. This is it. The worst part of this plan.

I untie the rope, and lean back slightly, still clutching it in my hands, using it to hold me in place.

And then I shift.

Fizzing, crackling, heat. Bones cracking, skin stretching. A roar inside my body that's louder than anything outside it. My dragon emerges in a swish of magic and energy. I try to keep hold of the rope, but my hands bend and bones merge and suddenly it's gone from my paws.

The energy and momentum of the shift keeps me in the air while I'm changing into my dragon shape, but as soon as I'm fully dragon, I start to fall. There's not enough room for me to beat my wings, which means I can't fly.

In a panic, I reach out with my front and back legs. My claws dig into the rock, holding me tight against the cliff. My wings vibrate behind me, unable to properly maneuver in the tight space.

"You okay?" Seth calls down from above.

I growl. *Yes,* I say tersely into his head. *I'm fine.*

"I'm going to shift up here," says Seth. "Then I'll start making a hole in the floor of the tunnel. I'll try to keep it as direct downward as I can."

Okay. I'm peering at the rocks directly in front of me, wondering how I got myself into this mess. I have to figure out how to cling to this cliff face, while shooting a burst of flame at the hole in the rocks. I move myself around, until I'm in a position where I can actually see the hole, and have a good angle. I peer at it, wondering. The rock doesn't look that strong. I lift one paw, letting my claws extend fully, and scratch at the surrounding rock. Pieces of rock come away, and fall into the darkness below. The hole is bigger already. I punch at the rock with the back of my paw, and even more rocks fall away, this time into the cavern behind. I scrape around the edges, and it gets bigger and bigger. I might not even need my flames at this rate.

I'm just using my dragon strength to break apart the rocks. It's volcanic rock, so it's not that strong.

I've started using phoenix fire on the rocks up here. It's working, I'm burning a hole downwards. Seth sounds surprised.

Just be careful you don't accidentally burn Aurelia.

I hear Seth growl above me, but he doesn't answer. I'd laugh, but everything feels deadly serious right now. I don't think I have it in me.

Eventually the hole is big enough for me to get most of my head into the hole. I peer in, trying to see Aurelia.

She hasn't moved. She's small for a dragon, much smaller than me, but her scales are a pure golden sheen. They look ragged and faded for the most part, but a few pieces of her hide are glinting at me in the darkness. She must have been beautiful before she was trapped down here. She opens one weary eye, and peers at me, her dragon eye flaming dully.

Mei? she asks inside my head. *You really came for me?*

Her tone is so incredulous, I pull my head out, and start ripping at the rocks, doubly determined to get her out of here. *Yes, it's me. And my friend Seth. We're going to rescue you.*

The rocks come away easily in my large dragon claws,

and I wish the tunnels were big enough for me to stay in this form. It would be so much easier if I could just rip the rocks apart, pull Aurelia onto my back, and fly out of here.

I don't... I don't know... that you can. Aurelia's voice is wobbly and small inside my head.

I'm gonna damn well try, I say, even though I'm thinking the same thing.

I keep ripping at the rocks, my dragon claws scraping against the rough surface. It's starting to hurt, even through my thick hide. I take a breath, thinking.

Maybe it's time to use my dragon flames?

How are you going up there? I ask Seth.

Slow going, but I'm definitely getting through the rock.

I have a hole that one of us could get through in human form. But I think we're gonna need to be in our dragon and phoenix forms to get her out of here.

Then we keep working.

I inhale, filling my lungs with the sulfurous oxygen from the cave, and then breathe out a line of fire that slams into the rocks around the edges of the enlarged hole.

Normal fire probably wouldn't do a thing to the rocks, but since becoming a dragon I've learned that dragon fire is special. It's magical, made from something indefinable inside my body. I'm just hoping... I halt the fire, trying to see if it's done anything more than char the rocks. The hole seems a little larger. Maybe.

I blast it again with more flames, pushing everything I have into my dragon fire. Again, I stop. Peer into the darkness at the rock.

The rock has started to melt away. The gap is widening, rocks are falling and finally it feels like I'm getting somewhere.

I keep going, breathing in and then letting out a precise

stream of fire, trying not to get too close to where Aurelia is lying. I'm trying to figure out how we're going to get her out of the lava without burning her hide, especially as she's so weak and brittle. I don't think I'll be able to use my dragon fire.

The hole gets wider and wider, and soon I'm at the edge of a hole that's big enough to fit my dragon frame inside if I squeeze through. Above me, I can hear Seth working with his phoenix fire to make a second entrance down through the floor.

Seth, I'm inside the cave.

I'm almost there too, he replies.

A moment later, I see a burst of phoenix flames come through the roof of the cave, and half melted rocks fall to the ground inside. Moments later our bag tumbles through the large hole, and thumps down on the rocky floor. Seth's fiery phoenix form slides down after it into the space next to Aurelia, filling the cave with his glowing presence, throwing up billowing dust and pebbles everywhere. He's covered in rock dust and soot, and his flames are dulled from their usual brightness, but we're both here.

We did it, we found her.

Except as I look around the room, and out into the darkness of the fissure, I don't know how the hell we're going to get her out of here.

THIRTY-FOUR

S eth changes back into his human form with a flash of fire and feathers.

He pulls on his jeans, then walks around the cave. He's covered in soot and ash from the hole he created, his hair is sticking up at all sorts of crazy angles, and there seems to be blood dripping from a cut on his arm, but I can't help watching him greedily. There was a time when I thought I might never see him again, and I can't seem to get enough of him now that we're back together. Except now isn't the right time to be mooning over Seth. I huff out a breath of smoke and force myself to focus on our rescue mission.

The cavern is large, with an entrance on the far side that's been filled in with ancient lava, the same flow that's covering Aurelia. She's coated in the thick, black lumpy rock, except for her tail, one wing and flank, and her head.

As I watch, Seth moves closer to the lava rock, and taps it, as if testing how thick it is. He looks up at me. "It's going to be difficult to get this off without hurting her."

I don't care, says Aurelia in my head. She opens her eyes

again, looks behind her to Seth. *Do it. Get me out of here, even if it hurts.*

I pass on her words to Seth. We share a look. I don't even know if she'll survive us getting her out of the lava rock, let alone going through the tunnels.

But she'll definitely die if we leave her here. I move closer and lean down to sniff at the rock. It still smells like lava—a mix of sulphur and fire—even though it must be more than three hundred years old.

You were hibernating when this happened? I ask her, trying to distract her from what's coming.

Yes. By the time I woke, it was too late. I couldn't move. I couldn't even get my head around to blast it with fire.

I wince, realizing that wasn't the best memory to put into her head.

We're going to have to use anything we can to get you out of the lava rock, including our fire. We'll try to be gentle, but we might catch you with the flames. If we do, make as much noise as you can, to let us know that we need to stop.

She nods awkwardly. *Just do it.*

Seth takes off his pants again, packing them away into the bag, and moving it to one side of the cave. Then he shifts back into his phoenix form, which makes the cavern crowded again. We stand opposite each other, looking down at Aurelia.

We need to do this in a specific way. Where will have the most impact in terms of getting her out? Seth asks.

Her back legs. They'd be the most powerful part of her body, she might be able to help us by pushing with them?

And I think it would help to have her neck out, so she can turn and blast with her flames as well. So that's what we each work on.

We each move to the side of the body we've suggested. I

know I don't have to tell Seth to be careful, but I wince when he starts using his fire on the lava around her neck. What if he misses? What if he hurts her? Aurelia's body looks so weak and ravaged. We should have been more prepared, brought more equipment with us. More people even. If only we could leave and come back, or even wait for our reinforcements. More people would make this so much easier.

But we don't have the luxury of time. The men in the caves above us will be here soon. Once upon a time, I would have been able to take out that many supers on my own—I'm a dragon after all—but right now... I don't think I could put up much of a fight against a single water sprite. Yet more proof that Seth was right about this rescue.

I move closer to her hind legs, and breathe a stream of flames onto the lava rock. It's soft, like most of the rock around us, but my flames are too gentle, and don't do much. I'm going to have to use a stronger blast.

I hesitate, scared of hurting her. I try to break at the rock with my claws. A little comes off but not enough. It will be too slow, anyway. I glance over at Seth, who is already using his flames to break into the lava rock. I don't have a choice. I have to keep going.

I breathe out flames again, this time stronger and hotter. It hits the rock, and creates a dent in the thick rock over her back legs. I keep going, trying not to worry about hitting her scales when the time comes. In a normal healthy dragon, a bit of dragon fire wouldn't hurt, but a dragon who's been covered in lava rock for three centuries? I'm pretty sure her weak hide isn't going to be able to handle it.

But I keep going, trying not to let my fear of hurting Aurelia stop me from doing it properly. When I get close to where I think her flank will be, I stop, and decide to use my claws to break the thin layer of rock that's left in that spot.

I use the largest one on my paw, and tap on the rock, harder and harder, until it breaks. It's brittle, but it sticks to the scales in places, and Aurelia growls as I scrape away a particularly big piece of rock. I manage to remove most of the rock in that small area, revealing the dragon hide underneath. The golden scales have turned a white-gold color, but are still strangely beautiful in the flickering light. They're mesmerizing and I pause for a moment and stare down at her unusual coloring.

Mei, come on. We don't have time for breaks.

Sorry. I shake my head and snap out of it, returning to blasting my fire at the lava rock, trying to stop before I hit her skin, until I have one side of the rock mostly burned away. Then I pick at it with my dragon talons, peeling the last thin layer of the rock away, trying not to hurt Aurelia. Her scales shudder and I can feel her distress, but she doesn't say a word to stop us.

How are you going? I ask Seth. I'm starting to feel tired from all the dragon fire I'm using. I don't think I have much left to work with. I look up, and the first thing I see is Aurelia's head, turned to look at me. Her neck and shoulders are out of the lava.

I let out a relieved huff.

I can help, she says. *Between the three of us, I'll be out soon.*

The expression on her face, of hope mingled with fear, spurs me on. Does she know about the men in the mountain? Probably.

I use more of my flames and work twice as fast to break out the next section of Aurelia's body. Seth's focused on her middle section, while Aurelia is sending weak bursts of flame to the rock covering her front legs.

In the distance, I hear the sound of voices. I look up, and catch Seth's glance. He's heard it too. I work even faster. That mountain super who can control lava could mess up all the work we've just done here. I don't want to have a direct confrontation, especially not after having used up most of my flames getting Aurelia out of the lava.

I use my talons again, and soon the other side of her back leg is free of the lava rock. Her tail swishes experimentally. It's hard to know how mobile she'll be. She's been in hibernation for part of the time, and when Tarsal came out of hibernation, he was up to full speed almost immediately. But Tarsal hadn't been held down by layers of burning hot lava. His hibernation had been his choice.

And I know Aurelia has been awake for a while now. The thought makes me shudder.

The voices are getting closer. Soon they'll get to the tunnel and realize that Seth has created a hole there. Probably the perfect hole to pour lava into, and reseal Aurelia away. If they realize we're here with her, they'll probably try to seal us away too.

I turn my body awkwardly inside the confined space and start to work on the front part of Aurelia's body, alongside her flames. Soon her front legs are free. The voices are really close now, and I know Aurelia has heard them too.

We have to hurry, says Seth. *They're almost here.*

The mountain supers are getting louder. In fact, I hear the tone of their voices change, and then running feet. They've noticed the hole in the tunnel.

I open my mouth and let out another controlled blast of flames over Aurelia's middle section. The flames are patchy and sparse, and smoke puffs out as well. I'm close to running out. This has never happened before and I glance up, fear pinching at my chest. My heart does an uncontrolled thump, then takes off at a gallop. We have to get out of here. My flames are no longer able to help get Aurelia out of the lava rock. Except... she's almost completely out. *Aurelia, you need to push yourself the rest of the way. We don't have time to finish getting it off with the flames.*

I glance up as the sound of feet thumping echoes down through the tunnel in the rock that Seth made.

"What is it?" The voice is gravelly and low.

"Don't know. Do we tell the boss?"

"Nah. This just makes it easier for us to finish her off. She's below us, I can feel her inside the rocks. Damn golden dragon."

"But what if she's the one who made the hole?"

"She's weak and covered in lava rock. And if she somehow made the hole, she's not very bright. It's too small for a dragon to sneak through."

Our only exit option is the hole I made in the fissure, I say.

Seth nods.

But with the fissure getting narrower as it goes down, and not being quite big enough for a dragon to actually fly in, I don't know how we're going to get out through it.

Aurelia pushes up against the rock, her eyes scrunched shut, her jaw clenched, straining as hard as she can. I grab at the remaining lava rock with my talons, trying to pull it off her and get her out of there faster. I don't even know what we're going to do once we've freed her.

I just know that we need to remove the rock to have a chance.

Glancing up again at the tunnel Seth created, I notice the rocks around it starting to steam. They're already creating their lava flow. A drip of hot liquid falls down and plops to the floor, sizzling.

We need to leave here, right now. Those two supers are going to turn this whole cavern into lava and we don't want to be here when that happens, I say desperately to Seth. He gives me a grim nod.

Aurelia gives a big push, and suddenly the rock cracks, pieces fly out from her body. She stands up, takes a wobbly step, then stumbles. She's clearly weak. Her wings are folded down against her body, but I doubt she can use them. Her whole body is pale, her scales patchy and in some cases broken off. There are pieces of lava rock still stuck to her, making her look like some kind of golden stone dragon.

She looks back at me, and I swallow. I've never seen anyone cry in dragon form, but she's managing it, large wet drops forming in her golden dragon eyes.

We don't have time for tears right now, I say gently. *We have to finish this escape. Then you can break down.*

She opens and closes her jaw, and then nods once.

How do we get out of here then? she asks, looking expectantly between me and Seth like she thinks we have a plan.

I wish.

CHAPTER
THIRTY-FIVE

How well do you know your way around the mountain cave system? I ask, looking around as if an idea is going to pop up and hit me on the head. It doesn't.

Pretty well. That's why I chose to hibernate down here. I felt safe.

How did you get inside this cavern?

Aurelia looks over to a large entrance that's been filled by a lava flow, turned into rock. *It must have flowed down from the main volcano.*

Or someone made *it flow down,* says Seth.

I nod. That thought had occurred to me as well. Especially given the two men turning rock into lava above us.

For now, we have to get out of here before—

A big fat drop of lava splatters to the ground near Seth. He jerks back before it can hit his body.

We need to leave.

Seth nods as if that makes perfect sense without a plan or any idea how we're going to actually do that.

Aurelia, can you shift into your human form? I think our dragon bodies are too big to get through the tunnels.

Aurelia shakes her head, her eyes sad. *I tried in the beginning, when I first woke up and found myself trapped. But the lava was too hot for my human body. I would have died. Later... I was afraid. My scales were attached to the lava in places, and I worried that my skin would be stuck to the lava rock, and that it would kill me to shift.* Her scales shudder across her body, and then her tail swishes.

And now?

Now I'm just too scared, full stop.

Seth looks up at the tunnel he dug, which is drooling lava like some dog hungry for a bone. *Do you think they know we're here too?*

They don't seem to.

Which is good for us. We still have the element of surprise.

I'd rather try to get out of here without actually letting them know we're here. Or that Aurelia is out of her lava rock prison. If we can convince them that their lava has killed her, then she'll be safer.

I peer out the hole in the wall that I created. *Up or down?* I ask.

If we go up, we have to pass the supers. And we're trying to avoid them, right?

A large dollop of lava drips out of the hole and oozes to the ground. Aurelia hisses.

I climb out the hole in the wall I created, and use my dragon claws to hold onto the rocks of the fissure. The sound of lava being created is louder than I would have expected—rocks cracking in the heat, steam rising—and it covers the sound of me crawling out. A few rocks tumble to the ground, and I wince, but the sounds from above are loud enough that I don't think they hear me.

I hate to think what would happen if they saw us and started turning the rocks to lava around us.

I crawl down at bit, using both sides of the crack to hold myself steady. It's only five or six yards wide, and my body is cramped. I try to extend myself lengthways, letting my tail drop down as far as I can, and pushing out my wings to each side. I keep moving, trying to be silent.

It feels so different from my usual strategy of meeting people head on in a fight. But I don't think Aurelia is up for any kind of combat, any more than I am. Seth would just end up trying to defend us, instead of being able to fight himself.

No, it's definitely better this way.

Aurelia comes next. She's hesitant, and I can see she's worried, even in her dragon form. *I don't know if I'm strong enough to hold myself up,* she whispers.

That's okay. That's why I'm below you. If you fall, I can catch you. I hope.

She looks at me dubiously, like she's thinking the same thing.

Hopefully we won't have to go too far down, I say. *There might be another cave we can use. But if you stay there, you're definitely dead.*

Aurelia nods, and climbs out slowly, more like a rest home resident than a dragon. She's been trapped all this time, on her own, with no hope of escape. It's amazing that she's even still alive. She gets out of the hole and into the fissure, her legs shaking as she clings to the side of the rock face.

Seth crawls out last, his movements quick and efficient. He's bigger than Aurelia in his phoenix form, but he only has two legs and his wings, which makes it awkward. He's dulled his flames, but he's still burning and for a moment I worry he's going to alert the mountain supers that we're down inside the rock crevice.

Except there's more light coming from the tunnel overhead than anything Seth is putting out. The lava is taking all their attention, and it's giving off a bright light as well.

Maybe you should shift into your human form to climb down? I say to Seth, as I watch him awkwardly try to maneuver down the wall using his beak as a third hold.

In reply, he holds out his wings, and uses the claw at the top center to hook into the rocks. *I'm fine. Just get moving.*

Keeping a careful watch on Aurelia, I move slowly downward, making sure I have a safe claw-hold before moving the next one. I don't know how Seth is going to manage with only his feet and a couple of claws in his wings, but I'll be able to catch him if he falls.

I hope.

Aurelia follows me down, her movements far more cautious than mine. Pebbles shift and fall as she descends, some hitting me on the back and wings. She uses her tail as a fifth point of contact, and I notice a sharp little hook-like claw at the end that's helping hold her body in place.

The lava falling into Aurelia's cave is making the fissure hot and steamy, the heat making my body uncomfortable. I can't imagine what it was like for Aurelia to wake and find herself buried alive under the hot molten rock. I shudder and vow that we're going to make it out of here without finding out.

We keep inching lower and lower, stopping to take short breaks. Part of me wants to rush ahead, to try and find another opening that's going to set us free from this climb, but I'm too afraid of not being there to catch Aurelia or Seth.

There's lava dripping out of the hole into the fissure, says Seth. His voice sounds calm, but the words make my heart stutter in my chest.

Is it going to drop onto us? I ask, peering up into the light above. When I blink into my dragon heat sensing vision, I see a dribble of lava coming down the side of the rocks, far too close to Seth.

Soon. It's slow and clumping at the moment. But we need to move faster. The urgency in Seth's voice says more than his words.

Aurelia, do you know if there's a tunnel close to where we are now? Even if it's not directly feeding into the fissure?

I don't know. It's hard to get my bearings. I don't think this fissure was here when I used to roam the caves and tunnels. In the shadow realm it's different.

A few pebbles fall down as Aurelia moves above me. I duck my head to avoid getting anything in my eyes. *A guess would be enough. It's more than I have,* I say.

At a guess, I would say there should be a tunnel directly under us. I don't know if we'd all fit into it.

I look up past Aurelia and for the first time can see the large foot-wide drop of lava coming out of the hole in the cavern. It's getting close to Seth. We don't have time to waste.

I could use dragon fire to break through to it. Come on.

I climb a little faster down, urging the others on, trying to make Aurelia stronger through force of will alone.

There. Stop where you are now, and try on your left.

I look to the rocks on my left. It looks the same as everywhere else.

You sure? I don't want to put all the effort into creating a hole with my flames only to find out it was the wrong place. Especially as I don't have many flames left to use right now.

Not really. But do you have a better plan? Aurelia pokes her nose down between her front legs, her golden eyes glowing in the darkness. She blinks, and I nod. She's right.

I look down at the fissure below me. It's dark and I can't see the bottom. Even worse, it's getting narrower the further down we go. Soon, we're not going to even fit inside this section of the mountain.

I push myself to the right-hand side of the fissure, aim my head to the spot Aurelia indicated, and let out a rush of flames. They're weaker than usual, and smoke puffs out as well. Even worse, it's hard to tell if it's working. But I have no choice, I have to keep going.

My flames have only melted through a few inches of rock and already my muscles are straining, my legs shaking. I can't keep this up for much longer. I'm breathing like an eighty-year-old smoker who's been dragging on three packs a day since childhood.

I'm almost out of fire, I say, trying not to panic. There's no guarantee I'm even using my flames in the right place. The lava is crawling inexorably downward. *Am I close?*

There's plenty of dragon stone down this deep. You could use that to help your flames.

I frown up at her in confusion. *Dragon stone?*

Aurelia blinks. *You really have had a strange upbringing, haven't you?*

You have no idea, I say. *So what's dragon stone?*

It's a type of rock often found deep inside volcanoes. It amps up our flames, helps us last longer, and gives them more... omph.

Why don't the other dragons know about this? I ask, thinking of Zane. *Or use them to help their strength?*

It's not easy to get dragon stones out of a volcano. They're often deep down, in difficult to get places. Dangerous places. She winces as she looks around us, clearly realizing what that means for our current position. *In my time, dragon stones were a very expensive luxury.*

Which ones are dragon stones? I say, looking around me. It all looks the same to me.

Aurelia uses one claw to scratch at the wall next to her. I see a strange sparkle in the dark. *Open your mouth, and chew on this,* she says as the scraps of rock start to fall.

The rocks shower down on me, and I open my dragon jaws wide, capturing as many as possible. I crunch down on the tiny rocks, blinking as they fizz inside my mouth like sherbet candy.

Immediately I start to feel stronger. My muscles cease aching, and my throat eases. I open my mouth and push out flames that are stronger than the ones I started with before we freed Aurelia.

I can't believe there's a stone that can do this for a dragon. I push out the flames, eager to get through the rock and into another section of the mountain. I'm sick of feeling trapped down here.

I work quickly, until I feel my strength draining.

Is there any more, Aurelia?

She scratches more of the rock, and I open my mouth to accept the stones falling down to me. It's then I realize that Aurelia isn't taking any of the rock. *Is there a reason why you're not using it to give you strength, too?* I ask.

I can't, she says.

Can't?

I... I... had too much of it. I became... addicted. It's like a drug for dragons.

I stare up at her, incredulous. *You just gave me a dragon drug?*

No, no. You'll be fine. It takes much more than a few rocks on one occasion to become addicted.

Questions start to form inside my head. She said it was expensive stuff. How did she afford to have enough to get addicted? Who is she exactly? And what was she doing down in the mountain in the first place?

But I don't ask the questions. We don't have time. I don't want to waste the energy the rocks have given me. I focus back on the wall, pushing my flames into the rocks.

A yell above makes me stop, worried that Seth might have been hit by the lava. But it's the mountain supers. They've noticed that the lava is flowing out the side of the cavern.

Even worse, they've noticed that we're clinging to the rocks a couple of hundred yards down below them.

THIRTY-SIX

Q*uickly,* says Seth. *Keep going, Mei.*

More dragon stone. You need more, says Aurelia.

I give Aurelia a glare, but open my mouth for the dragon stones that she scrapes out of the wall for me. If it's a choice between dead and addicted, I know which one I'm going to take. Besides, she said I hadn't had enough for anything like that.

Now they know we're here, I don't bother to be quiet.

I blast a fully heated burst of flame into the rock. It practically melts under my flames, and I feel a rush of satisfaction. It feels good to be this powerful. We could just give up on getting out of here, and I could fly back up, blasting my flames at the men. I'd be able to roast them before they even blinked.

I shake my head. Those thoughts were... strange. Not like me at all. More aggressive, more violent.

And in that moment, I know what happens when you take too much dragon stone. I clench my paws tighter around the rocks where I'm clinging to the wall, and blast more flames at the other side of the fissure. For a moment there's nothing visible but flames, and then suddenly I'm through to the other side. It widens quickly as the stone melts away beneath the onslaught of my flames, and I push my head through, peering into the darkness.

It's another large cavern. I can see at least two exits already.

I pull my head back, and push out another blast of flames, moving my head around the edge of the hole I've created, making it wider and bigger.

Then I use my paws to grab the heated rocks at the edges, hissing as it burns into the softer pads on the underside. I ignore the pain and continue pulling it away from the wall, letting it drop below.

Shouts from above distract me for a millisecond, but I don't even take the time to look up. I push myself through the hole, forcing myself against the rocks that snag on my hide. I'm going to regret it later, but right now, we have to get inside the new cavern before the mountain supers start dropping lava on us.

With one last dragon roar, I push through, falling head over heels down onto the cavern floor, which is about ten feet down from where I was boring the hole.

Aurelia tumbles through after me, and then Seth.

I let out a gasping breath, then another, still lying on the floor. I feel exhausted, like I can't move another inch.

Like maybe the only thing that will make me feel better would be some more of that tasty rock. I growl, looking over to where Aurelia is crouched, her tail twitching. She gave me that rock, knowing what it could do to me. Without giving me a choice. She's staring at me like she knows exactly what I'm thinking.

It was the only way to get us out of there, she says. *You saved us all.*

We're not out of here yet, says Seth. *Which way?* He gestures to the three tunnels on the other side of our cavern.

I don't say anything, still watching Aurelia cautiously. I've discovered too many strange things about her since attempting this rescue. She's not the dragon I thought she was, and it has me worried.

My body shudders as I shake off the feeling. I can't waste energy on it right now. We have to get out of here. I take a sniff. There's cool fresh air inside here with us, so there must be some kind of exit somewhere.

Aurelia looks to the three options. *That one is too small for us to travel through in dragon form,* she says. *Of the other two, I don't know which would be better. Do we have time to test them?*

Seth peers out the hole I just made in the wall. *They're trying to climb down. If they make it down here, we don't have long.*

Perhaps we could... take them out? says Aurelia. She looks like she's been dragged through the shrubbery backwards —broken scales, rocks and dust covering her, ash and blood everywhere—including on her hesitant expression as she suggests it.

I shake my head. *We need to conserve our energy for our escape off the mountain. I don't want to waste it on the men chasing us.* I glare at Aurelia. *And I don't want to eat any more dragon stones.*

Then let's explore the other two options, says Seth. Between one breath and the next, he's shifting to his human form. He pulls his jeans and T-shirt from the bag and puts them on, before heading over to the tunnels.

"I'm gonna try this one first," he says. "I won't go far."

I nod, then walk over to the other tunnel. I consider shifting out of my dragon form, but I feel stronger in this skin, despite the fact that I don't think I have any flames left, and I'm a little wobbly as I walk. I'm not feeling confident about shifting either, even though I managed it with Seth in the garden before we came on this mission.

I poke my nose down the tunnel a short way. I can't see much further down, there's a turn about fifty feet along. I feel a faint breath of air on my face, and it gives me hope. If Seth's tunnel doesn't work, this one might be the one.

We wait for a few minutes, until finally Seth returns at a run. "This one's a dead end. We have to try the other one."

I can hear voices in the fissure behind us. *We just have to go, and hope for the best*, I say.

We both look at Aurelia. She's scared of shifting, but this tunnel should be big enough for her dragon body. At least at first. Who knows what's going to happen later?

But we have no choice. *Come on, let's go,* I say.

Seth leads the way in human form, the backpack on his back. I motion for Aurelia to go next, and then follow at the rear. I can hear the mountain supers behind us, getting closer inside the fissure. The tunnel—more of a zig zag of cracks and breaks in the rock—is dark, but we follow our noses.

We're not far enough ahead, and we need to get down the tunnel and around the corner before they enter the cavern. It's our best hope for disappearing without a confrontation. It doesn't take long for Seth to get to the corner, but Aurelia is puffing and wheezing ahead of me, her feet unsteady. She almost trips over a rock, and only just catches herself.

She's slow. *So slow.*

I have to wait for her, and I'm feeling more vulnerable by the second. My tail swishes behind me, and every time I hear a noise from the cavern, I jump, convinced it's the mountain supers. It would be so easy for them to fill this tunnel with lava. We're sitting ducks. Or dragons. *Whatever.*

Aurelia, you need to hurry, I say to her, even though I'm pretty sure she can't go any faster.

I'm doing my best, she replies, her voice distracted.

And I know she is. She's been trapped in lava for three hundred years. I just wish she'd hurry up.

She turns the corner of the tunnel just as I hear the men's voices echoing in the cavern behind me. They sound excited, like they think they're close. I can't tell if they've seen me, but I keep moving, trying to be as quiet as possible while also getting the hell around the corner and out of sight. My wing scrapes into a rock overhead, and I have to bite down on my growl of pain. My vision flicks into heat sensing, and I'm momentarily blinded. Panic slides around in my stomach and for a long second, I can't think, can't move, can't *do anything.*

Is this it? The moment when they see us and realize we've gotten ourselves trapped?

THIRTY-SEVEN

And then I hear a determined grunt as Aurelia fights her way through the tunnel ahead of me. If she can do it after being entombed in lava all these years, so can I. I take a deep breath, then another. I manage to blink my vision back to normal, and force myself to focus on crawling my way through the tunnel and away from our hunters.

Finally, eventually, what feels like eons later, I turn the corner, and let out a sigh of relief. My tail swishes around the edge, and I feel a little safer. They'll probably still check all the tunnels, but at least it will take them some time.

We have to hurry, I tell the others. *They're in the cavern.*

Aurelia looks like she'd rather lie down than continue on, but she grits her jaw and keeps going. This section of the tunnel seems narrower than the first part, and I'm starting to wonder if we've made a terrible decision. Are we trapped? Will they just send a flow of lava down after us?

I shake my head, and force the thoughts away. I can't think about it. I just have to focus on getting through this tunnel. Up ahead, Seth is clambering over a large rock formation—in his human form, he's much smaller, and it's easier for him to maneuver over and around the rugged rocks. Aurelia and I have to squeeze our much larger dragon bodies past those same outcroppings, our wings tucked in tight. I get more than a few scrapes on my sensitive wing edges, and even my tough dragon hide is complaining. I briefly consider shifting back into my human form, but I still feel safer as a dragon.

My heart pounds with every step, and every time I hear the mountain supers yell or call out to each other, my scales shudder. Ahead of me, Aurelia stumbles and gasps for breath like she's just run a marathon. She's unsteady on her feet, and what little golden color she had left seems to be fading as we walk. I can only hope she makes it out of the mountain and back to a healer in time.

Where does this go? I ask Aurelia as I pull my body through a particularly tight gap.

I don't know. I've never been this way before.

I try not to let her words freak me out too much. I'm sure it'll be fine. The air seems fresher here, and the breeze stronger. We're going to find an exit somewhere at the end of this tunnel. The only problem will be how big it is, and where it's situated. I've lost all sense of where we are on the mountain. We could be near the top, or at the bottom, and I wouldn't be surprised. We seem to be climbing up more than down. We often have to clamber up over boulders that are taller than Seth. If we're at the top, it'll be a problem. I'm fairly certain Aurelia won't be able to fly out of here. Her wings don't look strong enough, which means I'll have to carry her away from the mountain.

I'm just starting to think we're never going to find the exit, when I clamber over a particularly large boulder and see a faint glow in the distance. I let out a relieved breath.

Seth is still striding ahead, with Aurelia crawling between us, her wings lopsided.

The light ahead gets brighter and brighter, and my eyes have to adjust to the increasing glow. Aurelia's hide, covered in broken and damaged dragon scales, becomes more visible, and I have to swallow a couple of times over my dismay. Will she heal from that much damage? Is there a limit to what a dragon can endure?

And how are we going to carry her out of here without hurting her even more? Let alone without being attacked by the mountain supers. We need to be in the air, away from them, but Aurelia's body is so ravaged, I don't know how we'll do it.

Come on, there's an exit. And it's big enough for dragons, says Seth in my head. He's standing at the center of the glow, his form outlined by the light behind him.

I shuffle forward to join him, Aurelia stumbling just ahead of me. We crawl out onto a wide ledge that looks down the mountain, and I squint out at the early morning sun, just rising in the east. How is it possible that we've been inside the whole night? The darkness must have muffled the passing of time. I let out a long breath, glad to see the sky again.

How are we going to do this? I say to Seth.

I think I need to shift back, he replies. *We'll both help Aurelia fly off the mountain.*

Aurelia's not paying attention to us. She's holding one hand over her eyes, as if the light is too bright, and I guess after three centuries underground, that's probably true. She's breathing heavily, and blinking like she can't actually believe what's happening.

Out in the sunlight she looks even more ravaged—the scales across her back are a mix of broken, faded, and lava-rock-covered, and she's mostly skin and bone—I'm guessing she's barely eaten anything more than insects and rocks in a long time—and she's swaying where she stands.

We'll need to take her back to Freddie's place, I say.

Yeah, she'll need healing from Iris. And a lot of time to recuperate. Seth's face is grim.

I glance around us nervously, wondering if we're really free and clear. *We need to get her out of here, before we run into more trouble.*

Agreed. Seth pulls off his T-shirt and jeans, shoves them into the bag, and moments later, he's back in his glowing phoenix form. I can't help admire him every time he makes the shift, it's somehow more graceful and poetic than anything I manage when I do the same thing.

Giving my shoulders a shake, I turn my neck to face Aurelia, trying to assess how much help she's going to need in the air. I have a feeling those almost-transparent wings aren't going to get her anywhere. *Aurelia? We need to leave now. How are you feeling? Do you think you can fly?*

Aurelia turns to me, her eyes shining golden. *I don't know how I can ever thank you, Mei. You got me out of there,* she says, completely ignoring my questions.

We're not out of the woods yet. We have to fly back down to our car, and get you home. Can you fly?

She glances over her shoulder to where her wings are resting, held lightly against her side. She seems to be considering her answer, although I don't think will-power alone will get her into the air.

Suddenly, a dark shadow looms overhead. I blink, confused.

A high-pitched screech is the only other warning we get before an enormous black shape hurtles down toward us, slashing and kicking out with its back legs.

Black metallic wings hide the sun for a second, and Aurelia screams, the sound somewhere between fear, agony and anger. For a millisecond, I freeze. Shock locks me in place and I can't even emulate Aurelia's scream. I'd recognize those wings anywhere.

Lakas is here and he's attacking us.

How the hell did he even know—?

I'm standing in front of Aurelia, and there's no more time to question anything. I take the brunt of the attack and it's only instinct that causes me to react in time—ingrained into me during all those years of training with Si and Jeff— and I manage to lurch to the side and deflect the claws, giving him a shove with my hind leg as I do so.

He gets one arm close, but my thick dragon scales can take more than a scratch from his claws. He tumbles past us, swooping back up into the sky as we backtrack into the tunnel, me pushing the other two back in my haste to get out of his way.

Flashbacks to my time as his prisoner make my vision blur and my heart hammers like a builder who's behind schedule. My hide shudders uncomfortably and I can almost feel those sharp metal wings cutting into my human skin even now. Remembered fear shoots along my veins, making me wish I could curl up in a ball, and let someone else take care of everything. I'm not ready for this.

I'm not sure if I'll ever be ready for Lakas.

Is that Lakas? asks Seth in a stunned voice.

Yes, I say, shaking my head to get rid of my intrusive memories. My eyesight has automatically shifted to heat sensing vision, and I have to force it back to normal. What the hell is *Lakas* doing here? Surely it can't be—

He's here for me, says Aurelia, her voice like granite. *I would recognize that devil's spawn anywhere.*

242

CHAPTER
THIRTY-EIGHT

*Y*ou know Lakas? I ask incredulously.

I swivel my head to stare at Aurelia. My vision flicks to heat sensing and back again, and I blink a couple of times, still trying to clear my eyes.

*He's the one…*She hesitates. *He's the one who trapped me in the mountain.* She's hiding behind me, apparently just as scared of Lakas as I am.

My head feels like it's about to explode. This whole mission is turning out to be the opposite of what I expected. *I thought you ended up there accidentally? That you were hibernating?*

That's how it started out. When the mountain erupted, I was still in my hibernation state. I'd picked a terrible spot to take a rest. But I could have gotten out, except… Lakas figured out how to change the flow of the lava, so it covered me while I was hibernating. She peers through the cave entrance, out into the sky, searching for Lakas. *He waited until the lava had cooled into rock. Then he woke me up.*

He woke you up?

To punish me, like he was punishing you.

Why didn't you tell me that when we met? I don't understand why she kept it a secret all this time.

Aurelia looks away, and a puff of smoke comes out her nose as she breathes out. *I was suspicious at first. I thought maybe you were part of some new torture of Lakas's. He likes to taunt me, to let me think I'm about to escape, before taking it away again. He's done it before. Whenever he's bored, he comes back to the mountain, and finds new ways to make me pay for the deaths of his family. At first, I thought you were working for him.*

So you lied to me? Didn't tell me he was involved?

I was worried you wouldn't rescue me if you knew the truth. You were so scared of him.

I'm definitely wishing I hadn't, now I know you lied *to me,* I say angrily, peeking out into the sky above. Part of me acknowledges that she was right, I wouldn't have come to rescue her if I'd known Lakas might be here. But mostly I'm angry that she put me in this position. *I deserved to know.*

I'm sorry, whispers Aurelia.

I don't reply, just watch the patch of sky I can see through the entrance. Lakas has disappeared, but I'm sure he's out there, waiting for us to emerge again. How are we going to escape him? He's vicious and ruthless. He won't stop until he has me back in his control. My heart rate skyrockets, and a shudder runs along my scales. I can't go back to being under his control. I can't.

I'd rather die. This whole rescue has been a disaster from start to finish. I glance at Seth, and we share a worried frown. He was right, we should never have attempted this rescue.

Aurelia moves closer to me, her golden eyes filled with tears. *I'm so sorry, Mei. I know I was wrong. But I was scared.*

And just so, so tired. I thought if you knew, you might not rescue me. I know he did terrible things to you.

I stare over my shoulder at her. She's right, I wouldn't have come here and risked meeting up with Lakas again.

You lied to me, I say. *Now I can't trust anything you say.*

I couldn't risk telling you. She's watching me intently with her wide dragon eyes, like she's willing me to believe her. To stay on her side. I don't know if I can.

Look, says Seth, his voice stern even inside my head. *I know there's a lot to unpack between you both. But right now, we need to work together to figure out how to get out of this mountain. How can we beat Lakas?*

I let out a huff of smoke and turn back to the entrance. He's right. We all have bigger problems right now than worrying about whether we can believe any of the stories Aurelia has told us.

I don't think we'd win in a direct attack against Lakas. So what could we do to distract Lakas? Maybe we have to go back inside the mountain again, find another exit? I'm not keen on any of our options.

I have an idea, says Aurelia hesitantly. *But you probably won't like it.*

What is it? I ask, not even bothering to look back.

I collected extra dragon stones. Just in case.

I jerk my head around to glare back at her. She's holding out her paw, revealing several large pieces of the stone she fed me. I immediately feel the pull of attraction to the stone, like a rumbling series of butterflies in my stomach. Growling, I turn away again. *I'm not having any more of that stuff. It's dangerous.*

I'll do it, she says, like she's a soldier volunteering for an important mission. *I'll chase him away. Dragon fire with a boost of dragon stone will defeat Lakas, at least temporarily, so we can get away.*

I shake my head. *Your flames won't be strong enough. You're... not as strong as you once were.*

Her eyes darken and an intense look fills her face. *I used to be far more powerful than a mere minokawa. He didn't beat me because he was stronger, he beat me because I was already incapacitated. Even now, after three centuries... He wins by intimidation and trickery, not because he's more powerful. My flames plus the dragon stones will be enough to hurt him and give us time.*

I meet Seth's eyes over her head. He nods. What choice do we have? I know from first-hand experience that Lakas is powerful—despite what Aurelia believes—and he holds the superior position right now. He can win this stand-off, just by sitting and waiting outside this tunnel. I don't have any better ideas, and I'm definitely not going to have any more of those stones.

Okay. Eat the dragon stones, go out on the ledge, wait for him to attack and then blast him with dragon fire. Once he's incapacitated, Seth and I will carry you out of here.

She nods. *No time like the present,* she says.

I lean into the wall, and she squeezes past. She doesn't look like much right now, but I imagine when she was in her prime, with her golden scales and her regal bearing, she was probably impressive.

And for all that she said she was afraid to tell me the truth, she's certainly being brave right now.

Seth and I watch closely as Aurelia pauses at the lip of the cave. She puts the dragon stones in her mouth, chewing determinedly. Then she strides out on all four paws, her tail flicking defiantly behind her, and growls, looking around for Lakas.

Nothing happens at first, and my breath hitches. Where's he gone? What's happening?

And then a black shape dives down from the sky, a screech of triumph on his lips, like he thinks he's got his prey right where he wants her. Huh.

Aurelia turns to face him, her small frame frozen, and for a second I think she's literally frozen at the sight of Lakas and won't be able to actually push out the dragon-stone-laced flames she promised. I take a step forward, planning to defend her.

But I needn't have worried. Aurelia is just waiting until he's close enough to get him properly with the flames. As we watch, she opens her jaws and a stream of powerful flames pours out. Lakas tries unsuccessfully to move out of the way but he's committed to the sweeping dive. Her flames roar, and Lakas's scream of triumph turns into a gurgle of pain as he feels the brunt of her fire. He falls backwards over the ledge, one wing damaged and flapping uselessly.

She did it, says Seth. He sounds surprised.

Come on, we have to hurry, I say. I'm not convinced Lakas won't be able to come back and get us. He's worse than a cat with nine lives.

We emerge onto the ledge, and peer over, searching for Lakas. His body is lying prone on a ledge a few hundred feet below us. He's not moving.

Take me down there. I can finish him off, says Aurelia, excitement in her voice. She's peering over the edge, her whole body vibrating with excitement. Her wings are half unfolded, and if she was able to, she'd already be down there, trying to burn him up with her flames.

No. We get out of here, I say, determinedly. *We can't be sure this isn't another trick of his.*

She growls. *Take me down there.*

No. You lied to me from the start. I don't trust you anymore. You're going to do what I say, when I say it, if you ever want me to trust you again.

Aurelia opens her mouth as if to protest, and then closes it again. *Okay,* she says meekly.

I glance at Seth, not quite trusting her sudden meekness.

Let's get out of here, he says. *Before anything else goes wrong.*

CHAPTER
THIRTY-NINE

I t's not easy flying whilst holding another dragon. Especially one who's squirming.

Aurelia is between Seth and I, each of us holding her on one side by her front legs. It's the most awkward I've ever felt while flying, we're bobbing up and down as we try to stay together while carrying a *dragon* between us. Aurelia keeps trying to push out her wings, and they flap around in our faces when she manages it.

Stop that, I growl. *This is hard enough without you adding to it.*

We're almost back at the house where we left the truck. I keep glancing back over my shoulder. I'm expecting Lakas to find us at any second, or maybe for another henchman to attack us, while we're completely vulnerable. It's a calm morning, the sun is barely in the sky, and I see very few humans below us. Seth growls as Aurelia accidentally hits him with her wing. Again.

Sorry, she mutters, clearly frustrated with this form of transport.

When we land in the backyard, I let out the breath that

I've been subconsciously holding for the last five minutes—luckily dragons can hold their breath much longer than humans.

Aurelia slips heavily to the ground, her wings bumping my side as she goes.

How are we going to get her into the pick up? I say. *She's way too big for the back.* I don't know what I was thinking when I suggested the truck would help us bring her home.

Our only options are to find something bigger, or for her to shift, says Seth.

I'm still here, I can hear you, says Aurelia, frowning between us.

Do you think you can shift? asks Seth, unperturbed.

Aurelia takes a breath. *I feel better now that I'm away from Mt. Hood. The dragon stones gave me a bit of energy too.*

Maybe we need to get you something to eat, I suggest. *That would probably help too.*

A big bit of steak, perhaps, says Aurelia, her golden eyes lighting up.

Beside me, Seth shifts into his human form, pulling on his clothes without a word. He heads into the house. I'm assuming that he's gone to see if there's anything in the house suitable to feed a hungry dragon.

We can't hang around here too long, I say. *We need to prepare ourselves before coming up against Lakas again.*

He won't stay here, not now that I've burned him. He'll retreat back to his lair, and plot my downfall.

Aurelia is speaking like she knows Lakas well, and it chills me to the core. What have I done? I've let her out, and discovered she isn't the person I thought she was. Have I made a terrible mistake?

Is that what happened? I ask. *You bested him somehow?*

Aurelia shakes her head, the remaining golden scales on

her face glittering in the weak early morning sunlight. *He attacked me, blamed me for something I didn't do. When I overcame him, he decided to use a more subtle attack. He watched and waited. Used his spies to manipulate me into choosing Mt. Hood as a hibernation place. And it worked. He's been keeping me alive, barely, ever since.* Her eyes flash with hatred. *I should have killed him when I had the chance.*

He's the reason you're still alive?

He's been bringing me just enough sustenance to keep me alive all this time. And he would torture me just enough to give himself satisfaction, but not enough to kill me. He's been visiting me sporadically for a long time. Any time I managed to go into hibernation, he'd pull me out as soon as he realized.

This is even worse than I thought. *What does he think you did?*

He thinks I killed his family, his village.

That's what he's always accusing me of, I say indignantly. *Why has he been torturing me, when he had you, the actual dragon who he thinks did it?*

He says it's the fault of all dragon-kind. He hates all of us.

He's been punishing me for it the whole time I've known him. I narrow my eyes at Aurelia. *Did you kill his family?*

No. She takes a breath. *But I know who did it.*

Who did it? I say, prompting her when she hesitates.

My sister, Tatianna, and some of her friends. She looks enough like me that I understand his confusion.

I pause, but have to ask. *Why did she kill them?* I know it's not going to be a good story.

Aurelia hesitates again, glancing around like she's wishing she was somewhere else—anywhere else. *She... She was...high on dragon stones. My family, we were... wealthy...in my time. We had the gold to afford dragon stones any time we wanted. My father was an alpha dragon, high on pride and his own consequence. He didn't even notice anything wrong with Tatianna. But If you take dragon stones for too long, they affect your personality. She ended up addicted, took too many, and...she started doing terrible things.*

What kind of terrible things? I ask incredulously. Aurelia gave *me* dragon stones, knowing they were dangerous.

Aurelia seems to know exactly what I'm thinking. *It's okay, you have to take them for a long time before anything like that happens. At first, you only feel the positive effects. The strength. The power. It's only later the dark side emerges.*

I narrow my eyes suspiciously. *You seem to know an awful lot about the dragon stones.*

Aurelia looks away from my gaze, peering off into the distance, up toward Mt Hood. *I used to take them sometimes too. Nothing like my sister, but enough.*

What kind of terrible things did she do? I ask again.

Hurting people. Killing people. Nothing imaginative. Just awful things.

When we first met, that wasn't accidental, was it? You weren't just passing by. You were stalking Lakas.

Aurelia nods. *I've been watching him whenever I can. He knows how to travel in the shadow realm too, although his form in there is a little more aggressive than mine.*

I remember the black thing that attacked when I entered in the shadow realm. *I think I saw him when we first arrived, he attacked me in the shadow realm as I was looking for you. I should have known it was him.*

Seth comes back outside at that moment, holding a large frozen piece of meat that looks like it might be a side of lamb. "I hope you like your meat on the cold side," he says. "We don't have time to heat it up..."

I love meat popsicles, says Aurelia, delight on her face.

Seth looks to me for a reply. I'm the only dragon he can hear while he's in human form. *She says thank you.*

Oh yes, thank you, Seth, says Aurelia apologetically. She's already chewing on the piece of meat, holding the bone between two dragon claws.

I watch her closely, wondering if she'll be able to shift. It's as much a mental thing as a physical one. I consider shifting back into my human form, but Aurelia won't be able to communicate if I do that. Now that I know she's less trustworthy than I thought, I need to keep her on a short leash, and that means staying in dragon form.

Maybe we need to get some clothes for Aurelia from inside, I say to Seth, trying to sound calm, when my thoughts are rushing around inside me a mile a minute. Most of me is wishing I never attempted this mission. That I'd listened to Seth and stayed home like a normal dragon.

"There's not much in there. Maybe some ski clothes."

Just get what you can. Otherwise she's going to be wandering around naked.

"We should have thought to bring clothes with us," says Seth. "I'll see what else I can find inside."

It seems obvious now, I say, as he heads back into the house.

I turn to look at Aurelia. She made short work of the frozen side of lamb, and she's now using the bone like a toothpick.

Aurelia, do you want to try shifting? I ask. I'm feeling antsy, and keep glancing up to Mt. Hood, wondering if Lakas is already planning how he's going to get us back.

I need to try, she says. She looks concerned, but not overly so. She turns her neck so she can look at her back. *Maybe I should pick off some more of the lava rock first? I don't know what will happen to it when I shift.*

253

Best case scenario, the magic will burn it off. Worst case, it'll be stuck to you.

Yeah, I figured out those two possibilities on my own, she says drily.

Seth returns, carrying a brightly colored jacket and a pair of thermal pants. "This is all I could find that might work."

Better than nothing, I say. I move back, away from Aurelia's immediate area and closer to Seth. If anything happens, I intend to protect him first.

Not that he needs protecting.

"She's going to shift?" asks Seth, looking between me and Aurelia. He puts one hand on my side, his warmth radiating through me, even in my dragon form.

Yes.

Aurelia closes her eyes. Her body starts to shimmer, like she really is made of gold. Magic sizzles around her, powerful and intense. But also a little erratic. Tiny lines of electricity dart out, hitting objects nearby like a tree branch and the roof, leaving little black burned spots.

Maybe we should step back a little further, I say to Seth.

As we shuffle back, the energy around Aurelia gets even more intense, the air gets thicker, the magic crackling and sputtering.

Bones start to crack, skin moves, and Aurelia screams. I step forward, but then stop. There's nothing I can do. We have to let Aurelia manage the change herself.

Aurelia seems to be struggling somewhere in the middle, unable to move into her human form, but not able to shift back into her dragon form.

Come on, Aurelia. You can do it, I say inside her head, trying to make my tone upbeat and encouraging. *Concentrate. Think about your human form. Make it real. You can do it.*

I remember Zane saying it was bad for a dragon to remain in one form for a long time, and wonder if that's what's happened to Aurelia. But she was trapped inside that mountain, and in hibernation for some of it. She didn't have a choice. It doesn't seem fair.

Come on, Aurelia. You can do it. I repeat the words, really meaning it this time. We watch as she struggles, trapped between her two bodies. The magic sizzles, fighting itself, sending out sparks that burn the grass underfoot.

Scales mix with skin, arms and legs are blending in with claws and paws. Neither form seems to be dominant, and I suddenly imagine Aurelia's transformation ending with her in some terrifying mix of human and dragon. My heart leaps into my throat and I desperately try to think of some way to help her, to draw her through this process. All I can think of is to keep talking to her, encouraging her. *You can do it, Aurelia. Just focus on your human form. You can do it.*

Aurelia lets out another scream, this time mingled with a guttural growl that makes my scales shudder. Sparks fly from her horribly mangled half-shifted body. She's been stuck in this half shifted place for too long.

I don't think she's going to make it.

CHAPTER
FORTY

I step forward, a growl coming from deep inside my dragon core. *You can do this, Aurelia,* I say. Without thinking, I pulse out energy along the spell web grid, just like I used to do in the old days, before I knew I was a dragon, before I destroyed the first spell web.

This spell web is different, strange and uncomfortable, and I feel awkward in a way I never did when I was growing up. But this is important, and I push past my reluctance.

The pulse of energy surges along the grid lines, until it surrounds Aurelia. On the grid, she's like a sunburst, bright and powerful, but uncontrolled. I surround her, pulsing in soothing energy, trying to calm the supernova of wild, unchecked power.

At first there's resistance. It's like there's some kind of untamed energy inside the spell web that's attached to Aurelia and doesn't want to let go. I'm tempted to simply squash it, to coat Aurelia and her ball of light in my energy until it submits. But some buried instinct tells me that's not going to work. That maybe I'll hurt her even worse than she's already been hurt. So instead I tease out the lines of her energy ball, like someone pulling apart a ball of string that's been knotted up over time.

At first, it doesn't work, and I give a growl of frustration.

Easy, Mei. Take your time. Rushing will only get you mistakes.

It's been a while since one of Jeff's phrases of wisdom last popped into my head, but it makes me take a breath and calm down. I continue to pick at the ball of wild sparking light, teasing out the twisted strings of power, helping them settle back into smooth lines.

Slowly but surely, the power calms. I keep pulling, until eventually the glowing ball of power inside the spell web is still and serene, although crackling with energy. I let out a breath, feeling like I've just deactivated a bomb.

Focusing back on the physical world, I peer around. Seth is standing beside me, one hand still on my flank, looking concerned. Aurelia has finally started to shift on from the confusing mess of dragon and human. Slowly, carefully, her human form starts to dominate.

And then she's done.

She's shifted into her human body for the first time in three hundred years.

Part of me braces. I remember what Sergei was like. When we first found him, he was half-crazed from spending too much time in his dragon skin, all on his own. He'd also braved the nuclear tests of the humans in the area where he'd hibernated, so perhaps Aurelia's more settled hibernation will help?

She appears to be fine. She's standing in front of us calmly, not like she's planning to try and murder us, like Sergei did.

She's medium height, with long, golden hair falling down her back and striking eyes the color of fossilized amber. She's a much older dragon than me, but would maybe pass for a human in her mid-thirties. Her golden brown skin is coated in lava rock dust and blood from several scrapes. Despite everything, she's beautiful, and I can't help but gape at her for a few seconds before I catch myself. I let out a relieved breath when I realize that the transformation has broken down the lava rock rather than leaving it half sticking out of her skin as I'd feared.

"You did it," says Seth like a proud father—except he's looking up at me.

What did I do? I blink at him. Aurelia did all the hard work.

"Thank you, Mei," says Aurelia, tears welling in her eyes. "I wouldn't have been able to do it without you." She runs forward and slams into my side, her arms wide in a hug that I can't reciprocate in my dragon form.

"Thank you, thank you, thank you," she mutters the words over and over. "You have no idea how much this means to me. I..." She can't finish, she's so choked up.

I look over her head to Seth. *We need to get on the road,* I say for his ears only. Now that I know Aurelia is okay, all my fears about Lakas come crowding back inside my head.

He catches my eye and seems to understand my discomfort. "Aurelia, I have some clothes for you. Maybe you could go inside and change? And then we need to leave this place." He glances toward Mt. Hood. "Before anything else can happen."

Aurelia glances at Seth, and then back at me. "Why are you both so worried about Lakas?" she says, her voice smooth and velvety, despite her sneering words. "He's nothing more than a worm underfoot. The only reason he bested me was because he developed a cunning plan and used the mountain's natural resources. Not because he was more powerful."

Seth looks up at me, his eyes full of guilt and regret, then at Aurelia. "Lakas is more powerful, possibly more twisted, than he was in your time."

"Because he captured Mei?" She makes a 'pfft' sound. "He didn't even plan or execute that. He just took over once she was under his control. Don't make a worm out to be a dragon."

"He *tortured* her," Seth blurts like he can't help himself. "Mei's still recovering from that."

"He locked me in a mountain for three hundred years," says Aurelia. "I get it. I'm just saying don't make him out to be more than he is."

"How about we discuss this further when you're dressed, and we're in the truck on our way out of town," says Seth.

Aurelia rolls her eyes at him but takes the clothes he's holding out to her and moves to one side. She doesn't bother going inside the house, just pulls the thermal pants and jacket on without another word.

I hesitate for a moment, feeling more powerful in my dragon form, then give an internal shrug. Aurelia is right. Lakas is a worm. I need to get over this fear of him, and figure out a way to take him down. I close my eyes and shift back into my human form, letting the fizzing electricity of the magic energize me. When I open my eyes, Seth is standing in front of me, holding out my clothes. I smile and pull on my underwear and then jeans, T-shirt and jersey as fast as I can in the cold autumn air, wishing we weren't always in a hurry.

Seth rings his raven contacts and tells them to stand down. He also warns them about Lakas being in the vicinity. After that, it doesn't take long for us to get back on the road.

I ring Mr Fookes as we're driving out of Mt. Hood Village.

"We're already on our way, almost to Redding," he says. "I'm driving the van, so I can make the trip shorter for a couple of you."

"Who's 'we'?" I ask.

"Me and Daphne. And Poppy. And Hazel and Blade." Mr. Fookes sounds sheepish. "I was worried. I wanted to make sure I had enough back up."

I shake my head but don't say anything. It's actually nice that Mr. Fookes was so quick to put together a rescue party for us. "I thought Hazel was still recovering?"

"Yeah, but Blade won't go anywhere without her at the moment, so we had to bring both of them."

I hear an indignant voice in the background, possibly Hazel. Mr. Fookes answers in a low voice that I can't quite catch.

"Well, thanks for answering my call for help. We managed to finish the rescue, but we ran into another problem. Lakas was there."

"You found him? That's excellent news. No one else has been able to even catch a sighting."

I squeeze my eyes shut at the irony of that. "Let's meet in Klamath Falls. It's almost half way between us now. We can debrief there. Tell you what we found." Klamath Falls is also where Jeff had a safe house and left another lock box, which means supplies and a safe place to rest, even if it's only a few hours.

"See you then," says Mr. Fookes and ends the call.

"So that's where we're heading?" asks Aurelia from the back seat of the pick-up. "Klamath Falls?"

"For now." I nod. "I know somewhere safe. But we need to make a plan about Lakas." I glance at Seth. He's next to me, concentrating on the road, his strong hands settled on the steering wheel. "He needs to be taken down. Otherwise we won't be safe. No one will be safe."

"The plan has always been to get rid of Lakas and Director Holden," says Seth calmly. "They're dangerous, and they've already hurt too many people. That's what everyone is committed to doing now that Hazel is okay and we have a new spell web. They won't stop until we do."

I give a short nod. I've been planning to kill Lakas since I escaped his clutches, but it was a vague and distant notion. Now that I've seen him again, it has solidified inside me, and become more real. I'm scared, but there's a steely determination inside me as well. He's going to be stopped, and I'm going to be the one who stops him.

"Lakas isn't the kind of guy who gives up easily," says Aurelia. "I'm a testament to that."

"Then we'll be even more determined," I say. "He's made too many enemies. He's done too many evil things."

Aurelia shudders audibly in the back. "I have to say, I don't like the feeling of this spell web now that I'm in my human form. It's like having a blanket wrapped over you the whole time. It feels...heavy."

"You get used to it. It can actually be helpful," I say. "It's how I helped you finish shifting."

"I doubt I'll get used to it, but I can definitely see how it's helpful." Aurelia is silent for a while. "I don't suppose we can stop somewhere and get something to eat? A nice side of beef? A roasted lamb? Maybe some of that McDonalds everyone seems to be so keen on?"

"We can get take out and eat on the road," I say, turning to smile at her. "You can even choose what we get. But not for another hour or so. We need to put distance between us and Lakas, make sure he doesn't follow."

Aurelia gives a low growl. "He's not brave enough to follow us. It's not his style. He lets others do the hard work, and then reaps the benefits later."

"What makes you think you know him so well?" asks Seth, his voice grim. "You've been locked in a mountain for the last three centuries. You don't know what he's capable of."

"I've been watching him in the shadow plane for the last twenty years. I know what he's been doing, I know where he likes to hang out, and I know where his lair is," says Aurelia with relish. "I know exactly what he's like, and exactly how to take him down."

CHAPTER
FORTY-ONE

The small cabin on the outskirts of Klamath Falls is full of people.

Or at least, that's how it feels. When I've been here in the past, it was just me, Si, and Jeff. It was generally a quiet, serious space—except for Jeff's big laugh—where we trained and planned.

Now it's filled with me, Seth, Aurelia, Mr. Fookes, Daphne, Poppy, Hazel and Blade.

Too many people.

It also feels like a convention for those who want to kill Lakas.

I hugged Hazel when I saw her, because if I shouldn't be out and about, she really shouldn't be either. Being trapped inside a spell web isn't easy—I should know. But she gave me a lop-sided grin, and shrugged when I suggested she should have stayed at home. "Like you should have?" she said with a smirk.

She was probably right, so I left it at that.

Since then we've all eaten the snacks Mr. Fookes brought with him, we've had a coffee, and I even managed to find some spare clothes for Aurelia, so she no longer looks like some kind of snow-field hobo. The jeans and shoes are mine, and the shirt is an old one of Si's, and the baseball cap is Jeff's. But at least she's dressed semi-normally for the actual century we're in. Something about her makes me think she'd be more comfortable in some kind of long floating dress, maybe a circlet crown around her golden hair.

Shaking my head at my strange imaginings, I look around the room, trying to figure out the best way to handle our situation. Everyone is sitting in small groups, chatting like we're at some kind of a social gathering—maybe the Anti-Lakas Convention—and not about to start planning how to find and kill our mutual enemy. Aurelia seems certain she can predict what he's going to do, and where to find him. It's too much of an opportunity to miss.

Except...am I ready for all this? Are we foolish to be going ahead with these plans? I remember vividly how it felt to be in the crevice, feeling trapped and scared. Or when Lakas attacked from above without warning. He's devious like that. Always managing to tip the scales in his favor. I clench my right hand tight, then let it go and stretch my fingers out, trying to stop the trembling.

The aftereffects of facing Lakas again are still with me. He was so close, I could see the green flecks in the black feathers on his head, smell his fetid breath, taste his elation as he dragged his claws across my body. I tip my head to one side, stretching along the side where he scraped my dragon scales. It didn't leave much of a mark—nothing that my scales couldn't easily deflect—but I'm a little stiff none-theless. I could have gone a year—ten years—without seeing him again, and it wouldn't have been too long.

I spare a glance for Aurelia who's sitting in one corner,

talking to Poppy. She's already looking better, her skin not so gaunt and pale. In fact, she's almost glowing in the evening light. It doesn't seem possible that she could have healed so quickly. Not after three hundred years in darkness.

Is she shaky, like I am? Does she even feel nervous about going on a mission to find the man responsible for keeping her locked in her prison? Or is she just as excited and pleased as she appears?

An arm snakes around my waist, and a comforting scent of ash and fire fills my nose. I lean back against Seth and close my eyes, taking comfort in his closeness. He kisses my neck, his breath tickling my skin.

"What are you thinking?" he asks softly.

"That maybe we shouldn't be doing this," I admit in an undertone. I feel like I'm betraying myself by even suggesting it. I put my hands over his, trying to get comfort from his warmth.

His arm tightens. "We don't have to do anything right now. We can wait until everyone is feeling better."

"But will we still have this advantage? Lakas is hurt. Aurelia knows where to find him. With everyone here and ready to go, we have our best shot at getting him."

"And what do we do when we find him? What's the plan?"

"I—I don't know, exactly. Attacking him head on seems too dangerous." I tremble a little at the thought, and Seth tightens his arms around me.

"He's devious and smart," he says in agreement. "He probably has a hundred traps at his lair."

"Exactly. Which is why we should just watch his lair and follow him when he leaves. He'll be more vulnerable away from his territory."

"That could take a lot of time. Time we don't have. What if he decides to lie low for a while?"

I shake my head, my thoughts spinning. I can't tell if what I'm saying is a good idea, or just a symptom of my reluctance to confront Lakas. "I don't think he will. There's too much going on." I wish I could put my hand behind my back and cross my fingers like a kid. I'm not sure I'm even right about any of this. I'm just feeling overwhelmed by the rescue mission and everything that happened.

"I don't know," I whisper. "I just know he's a smart, cunning, conniving son-of-a-bitch. It won't be easy."

"None of this will be easy. But it's important. We need to stop Lakas and Director Holden for good. Your father is taking on Director Holden, and he'll do everything he can to succeed. Which leaves us with Lakas."

I shiver. He's right. My father—normally so calm and controlled—is raging angry whenever he talks about Director Holden and how he kidnapped me. How he let Lakas do whatever he wanted. He's not going to show mercy. Except... "He's not a dragon. He's an SIG legend. They'll accept his actions in that regard far more than they will mine."

"Then we don't do it. We wait."

I let out gusty sigh. "I don't think I can wait either." I settle my head on Seth's shoulder. "This used to be easier. I used to be able to leap into action, throw myself into danger without a second thought. Now I'm worrying about everything."

"You're growing up. Realizing that there's more at stake than just your own wants and desires."

"That sounds dangerously like a criticism of my past actions," I growl. But he's right. In the past, I had a tendency to leap before I looked. Thinking through the long term ramifications was never my strong suit. "It doesn't feel like I'm growing up. It feels like I'm scared," I whisper.

Seth rubs his hands up and down my arms. "Maybe it's the same thing?"

"Not helpful."

"No, I suppose not."

Mr. Fookes steps into the middle of the room. He holds up his hands, trying to get everyone's attention. "Okay, okay. Quiet down. We need to figure out our next move."

"We're finally going after Lakas, what's to know?" says Poppy, her eyes sparking with excitement. "Aurelia knows all about him. We can use her intel to corner him and take him out. Easy."

"He's smart," snaps Blade. "You can't just turn up and expect to overpower him. We need a plan."

"Well, what's our plan then?" says Poppy. Her red hair is tied up in a high pony tail, and she looks about twelve, but she seems the most bloodthirsty person here. Hazel once told me that she's a talented investigator, and it's the only reason I'm not seriously worried right now.

"We know he's hurt," says Blade. "That gives us an advantage."

"Not for long, minokawa heal even better than dragons," says Aurelia. Something flashes across her face. I'm pretty sure it's the residual resentment from our insistence that we leave instead of finishing Lakas off.

She's not thinking clearly. She doesn't understand what he's capable of, not like I do.

"Will he still be where you left him?" asks Daphne.

Aurelia shakes her head. "No. He was stunned I think, but it wasn't fatal. And he had henchmen with him. He's probably gone by now."

"Where to?"

"Back to his lair, to lick his wounds."

"Where's his lair?" asks Blade, his sharp eyes focused on Aurelia. He's tall and dark haired, with muscled arms that are so big it looks like they're trying to escape the shirt he's wearing. He's also not afraid to call a spade a spade. He'd tell me what he thinks of Aurelia.

I'm desperate to ask all the others what they think of Aurelia. Do they think she's for real? Do they believe her?

Should I?

"He's got more than one," says Aurelia, for once looking just as serious as Blade. "The one in the Philippines where he's from is his largest, but that would be too long a flight for him. I think the one he'll try for is the one in the US. It's nearby—at least for those of us who can fly." She glances around the rest of the room at the people gathered. Only Seth, me and Aurelia are flyers. I hope she's not going to say something obnoxious, like supers who can't fly are inferior. When it comes down to it, I know very little about her and her beliefs.

I let out a frustrated breath. Have I rescued someone I shouldn't have? She's the enemy of my enemy, so does that make her a friend? The fact that she lied to me is sitting in my chest, making me worry. Maybe Lakas did everyone a favor by keeping her locked up? I have no real way of knowing whether I've made a mistake by helping her escape.

"Where's his closest lair?" repeats Blade sharply. He's protective of Hazel, who was another victim of Lakas's delightful torture techniques, and he's not going to put up with Aurelia playing games.

Good. Because I'm not keen on it myself.

"I don't know the location's name," she says, then holds up her hands when there's a murmuring from several people in the room. "I've followed him there in the shadow plane, many times. I can find it, I just don't know what to call it."

"How far away is it?"

"I'm not sure. Maybe a few hours by car. It's in another mountain area. A cave system he discovered, and has taken great pains to keep hidden all these years. He created a myth around a monster in the area, and the locals avoid it."

"So what are we waiting for?" asks Poppy. "This isn't complicated. We outnumber him, we know where he'll be. Let's go."

"What are we going to do with him, when we find him?" asks Hazel carefully. She's looking at me. She has as much reason to hate Lakas as I do. He flew across country with her clutched in his claws, just to scare her. She vowed to destroy him for me when she saved me.

I blink carefully, trying to think through my answer. "I'd like to kill him, if I'm honest. But does that make us just as bad as he is?"

"If we don't get rid of him permanently, he'll just figure out a way to escape and then we'll be back to square one," says Poppy impatiently. "Of course this is about killing him."

"It's not like we have a handy supernatural prison to put him in. If we just capture him, what the hell are we going to do with him?" says Blade. "Poppy's right. He's evil."

"I know, I know," I say impatiently. "But I don't want to be a cold-blooded killer either."

"I'll do it," says Aurelia from the corner. "I have no problem killing him after what he's done to me." From the bloodthirsty expression on her face, I believe her.

Seth clears his throat from behind me. "I think perhaps

we need to check in with my father. He always has a good sense for what needs to be done and how to do it."

There's a murmur of agreement from everyone except Aurelia. "That's it? We're going to let this go because you want to get permission from Daddy?"

I growl at Aurelia, not liking her derisive tone. "There's more at stake here than you and your vendetta. There might be things in play that we don't know about. I don't want to mess up the situation by going in half-cocked and killing Lakas." Not like I did when I stormed into the Earthbound Compound and got Seth killed the first time and destroyed the spell web. Not exactly my finest hour.

I swallow over my fear. I hope Seth's right and I'm just growing up, not becoming too scared to take action. I'd hate to think I was losing my edge.

"What could possibly go wrong by us killing Lakas?" asks Aurelia, clearly frustrated.

"I don't know. I just know that he's as cunning as a badger, and we've all just been through something major, you included. Everyone is on edge and we need to make sure we're not making a mistake. Taking time to talk to my father tomorrow isn't going to hurt anyone."

"The only mistake you're making is not taking this opportunity by the horns," says Aurelia angrily, her amber eyes glowing.

Seth's arms tighten fractionally around my waist, and I know what he's thinking.

Aurelia is different to what either of us expected. Part of me is already wishing I'd never rescued her at all.

FORTY-TWO

"How's the hunt for Director Holden going?" I ask my father.

His voice at the other end of the cell phone is distant and filled with static. "He's not trying to hide. He's at the SIG offices in New York. He's shoring up his power base, talking to powerful people and trying to get them on his side. He was very careful to keep himself away from being implicated in the whole demon plague thing, and also in your kidnapping. He did the deed, sure, but he didn't participate after that. He's blaming Lakas, saying he went rogue."

"That's ridiculous. He was knee deep in all of it," I say, unable to keep the outrage out of my voice.

I'm sitting on the edge of the bed in one of the bedrooms at the safe house, Seth lying behind me still under the covers. It's dark outside, and the only illumination is the small bedside lamp. Aurelia is sleeping in one of the other bedrooms, and Hazel and Blade have taken the last one. Everyone else is staying out in Mr. Fookes' magical van, which has far more space than a van should.

"He's always been smart, I'll give him that," says Dad.

"What are you going to do?"

"I'm going to ask him politely to resign. And if he refuses, I'm going to tell him impolitely that he's going to die."

His answer makes me sit deeper into the bed. "You really think you'll be able to do that?" I ask quietly.

"I'm going to try, Mei. He's done so much harm to our world. He's lost his way, and I don't think he can find it again. He needs to pay for what he did to you." His voice is like steel on the last sentence, and for once he's not hiding his real feelings behind a bland exterior.

"We know where Lakas is," I say quietly.

His sharp inhalation is clear, even down our shaky phone line.

"Seth and I, we rescued the dragon who helped me in the shadow plane. Her name is Aurelia. And it turns out she's been watching Lakas inside the shadow plane for a long time."

"And she knows where to find him?"

"Yes."

"Why was she following Lakas?"

I let out sigh. He's always been able to find the relevant point in any conversation. "Lakas is the one who kept her locked in the mountain. She's got a vendetta against him, wants him dead."

"As do you," he says gently.

"As do I," I reply just as gently. "I'm just worried we're making a mistake, running off after him. And I feel...I feel... like I *can't*. Him attacking me, I'd do what I had to. But chasing him down? I don't know." I pause, thinking it through. "It's weird, Dad. Not that long ago, I'd have charged at him, wanting to destroy everything about him.

I'd have wanted to push him to the ground and watch him squirm in pain." Seth moves over and hugs me from behind, and I lean into the safety of his embrace. His warmth envelops me, the comforting scent of sulfur and ash at the edges of my consciousness. "But I'm hesitating. Wondering what I should be doing. I don't know what's wrong."

"You've been through a lot. And hunting someone down and killing them is different than killing in self-defence."

I nod, even though he can't see me. "So what do we do? Do we still hunt him down? Or do we wait?"

"We need to make a plan," he says carefully. "Are we staging a coup? If I kill Director Holden, what then? Who's in charge then?"

"You are," I say softly. "People would follow you. They'd know we were in good hands."

Now it's my father's turn to be silent. There's a long pause, and I think he's not going to answer. But then he does. "I don't know, Mei. I don't know if I'm up for that level of responsibility. And anyway, it's not just a matter of me killing Holden, so I get to take over. It's a position that's granted by the President of the United States. What's he going to see when he looks at me? The guy he's never heard of, who killed Director Holden. I doubt he'll give me the role."

"Director Holden is a scheming, two-faced monster who's been trying to kill me since I was a baby. You'd be doing the world a favor if you killed him. And I'll tell the president that." I'm trembling, and Seth tightens his arms around me, trying to give me comfort. I put my free hand along his arm, letting his warmth seep into me.

"Same goes for Lakas, Mei. He's pure evil. What he did to you and Hazel? That wasn't right. That wasn't for a greater cause or because it needed to be done. It was because he enjoyed it."

"So you think we should do it? Hunt him down?"

"I think we need to all meet up again. We need to know exactly what we're intending to do, and then do it. Does Lakas know you know where his lair is?"

"I don't think so."

"Then you won't lose the advantage of surprise. Come back to Freddie's place, and I'll do the same. We'll call in some of the others, and have a meeting. Discuss what needs to be done. As they say, no one is as smart as everyone."

"Okay," I say, more relieved than I expected to be. "I'll see you in a couple of days."

"Take care of yourself, Mei," he says, then hangs up abruptly.

I hold the phone, looking down at it absently.

Seth puts his chin on my shoulder, his arms still holding me close. "He doesn't think we should go racing off after Lakas?" he asks, his breath making the hair on my neck flutter.

"Not yet, at least," I say, snuggling up against his warm chest. "I'm relieved. Is that weird? I want him dead, I want my revenge, but I'm relieved we're not going to take him on. I don't understand."

Seth shifts about behind me, moving to one side so he can see my face. "A week ago, you were almost dead, Mei. From what you've told me, and speaking to Hazel and the others, it was a close run thing. *Of course* you're not feeling in top condition. *Of course* you're fearful. *Of course* you're relieved you don't have to face the man who's been plaguing you in your nightmares."

I glance up at him sharply. "You know about that?"

"Of course I know about that. We share a bed, Mei."

I close my eyes and rest against him, feeling the turmoil inside me as I try to regain my equilibrium. "I feel like I'm lost. Like he's taken away some vital piece of my personality, the piece that helped me take action, get things done."

"You'll get it back. Or maybe you'll get it back in a different way. I meant what I said earlier. Maybe this caution is a positive thing. Maybe it's about you gaining some perspective."

Right now, here inside his arms, I feel like maybe I can get back to being myself again. Perhaps even be able to make a decision, or feel like I might be able to take out Lakas.

But it's going to take time.

"Aurelia is going to hate having to wait," I say.

Seth gives a quiet half-laugh, half-snort. "Definitely."

"If she's at all interested in what's best for everyone, she needs to do it."

"I'm not sure Aurelia is interested in what's best for everyone," says Seth. "She's not exactly a group thinker."

"Dragons don't seem to be," I say wryly. "Zane, Sergei. Tarsal. All the other dragons I've ever met haven't been like that either."

"Elena was a priestess. She acted for the greater good, even if it was a little misguided."

"Hmmm." My eyes are closed, I'm warm and cozy up against Seth's chest, and I'm starting to find it difficult to concentrate on our conversation.

I don't object when I feel Seth moving me back onto the bed, and tucking me under the blankets. I snuggle up to him, and fall asleep, and dream about running through caves, chased by an angry bat shooting lava out its eyes.

CHAPTER
FORTY-THREE

"What do you mean, she's gone?" I ask Blade sharply. Maybe I didn't hear him right.

"Hazel went in to check on her this morning, offer her some coffee, and she wasn't there. The bed hadn't been slept in."

I pace up and down the small living room, trying to figure out what this means for us. It's still early morning and everyone is gathered in the living room in various states of undress. Blade woke us as soon as Hazel realized Aurelia was gone.

My brain can't seem to comprehend this new piece of information. "Why would she do that?" I ask, even though I know why.

"She's gone hunting on her own," says Seth grimly.

"She wasn't even at full capacity. She was still so weak. Why would she do that?"

"She was locked in that mountain for three hundred years at Lakas's mercy. Question is, why did she wait so long?" says Poppy as if it's obvious. Maybe it is.

"She's going to get herself killed," I say, as I keep pacing.

I'm annoyed, but it's not entirely with Aurelia. I'm also annoyed that I'm *not* the one who went haring off on a crazy plan to rid the world of Lakas. That I'm this meek dragon who waited and was willing to discuss the situation back in Stanford with everyone else.

I'm annoyed that I'm scared of Lakas.

"We have to go after her," I say, clenching and unclenching my hand, trying to let out the energy that feels like it's building inside my chest.

"To stop her or to help her?" asks Blade. "Because I for one vote that we let her kill Lakas."

"Everything we know about Lakas tells us he's smart. Conniving. He's not just going to let someone come into his own personal lair and kill him," I say, gesturing out into the wilderness behind the house. "He'll have traps, he'll have systems in place. He'll catch her like a spider in a web, and then he'll eat her alive. She's not ready to go after him alone."

"Ew. He won't really eat her will he?" says Poppy, her face screwed up.

I glare at Poppy, wondering how she could possibly be the amazing investigator that Hazel claims she is. "That was a figure of speech. But I wouldn't put it past him."

Seth's phone rings, and he turns away and goes down the hallway to answer it. I immediately miss his warm presence and the room seems a little... less.

"So if it's another rescue mission you're thinking of, how do we even know where she went?" says Hazel. "She couldn't explain it to us last night."

"I might be able to help with that," says Poppy with a shrug. "I put a bug on her. Figured she might try something, and that you'd all go batshit crazy about it."

"A bug?" I say. "How does that even work on a shifter?"

"It's a nano-bug. Designed by the lovely Hazel when I asked her to invent one." Poppy grins at Hazel, who looks like a kid caught with one hand in the cookie jar.

I shake my head, rejecting the idea. "As soon as she shifts, it'll disappear."

"Nope. We've tested it. Goes on like a cream, and stays on the skin through the shift. It'll tell us where she is, and we can follow her trail."

I look between Hazel and Poppy. "You just asked for it, and Hazel casually provided it?" I can't keep the amazement out of my voice.

Hazel blushes even harder, like she's embarrassed to be found out, but Poppy just shrugs. "Hazel's a freaking genius when it comes to inventing technology. I provide the ideas, she delivers the product."

I look between the two of them for a moment. Then let out a breath. I'm getting off track. "Dad's expecting us back at Freddie's place. We were supposed to discuss the plan, do things properly." I hesitate and take a big breath. "But I don't think we can leave Aurelia to face Lakas on her own. She might be confident she can take him, but I'm not." I look around at everyone else, and see nothing but agreement.

"So we're really going to do this?" says Hazel. She looks... serene. Like she's not actually that worried about taking on Lakas. That she's just checking in to make sure everyone is happy with the situation. Everyone else murmurs their agreement.

Am I the only one who's worried?

Mr. Fookes clears his throat. "Perhaps if we all go in the van initially, Daphne and I will take turns driving. That'll keep the rest of you fresh for your confrontation."

Hazel sees my confused expression. "Mr. Fookes's van is

magical in more ways than one. It's not just bigger inside than you'd expect. When you're sitting in the back, time passes way slower. You remember that rescue at the mental health facility where I was held? That's how we got all those people out."

I nod with understanding. I'm excited to see how the van works.

Seth comes back into the room at that moment. "That was Damien. Things have changed since last night. He's been working with some senior SIG agents who are equally unhappy with the way things have been going, trying to figure out a way to wrestle control of the SIG back from Director Holden. They called, told him he needs to get to New York asap. They're making a move, today. Damien's on a plane as we speak."

"That sounds dangerous," I say, suddenly nervous for my father. "What are they going to do?"

"Your father can take care of himself." Seth gives me a reassuring look. "I told him what's happening here, and he agreed that our best plan would be to save Aurelia—again —and then those of us who can fly should meet him in New York. He may need extra backup."

"Who's going with him?" I ask sharply. This whole morning is going completely pear-shaped.

"Freddie, Zane and Carrick will be there with him," he says soothingly. "As well as others. This might be moving fast, but your father has made sure he has the support of all the different super factions."

I put one hand up to my chest, trying to calm the bubble of unease that's floating inside me. "I know, I know. It's just..." I wish I could control the speed of my beating heart. It's too much, too stressful being scared all the time.

"It makes it more important that we follow Aurelia,

rescue her as quickly as possible, so we can head to New York to support Damien," says Hazel.

"Okay, ten minutes, and we're leaving," says Blade, all business. And just like that, everyone is moving quickly to gather up our gear. It's not like any of us have much with us. I head back to the bedroom with Seth, wanting a couple of moments alone with him before we're thrust into another group adventure.

"This isn't what I had planned," I say apologetically. "I thought we'd be back at Freddie's place by now, all tucked up in bed, rescue complete."

Seth bundles me up against his chest, gently putting his chin on my head. I curl into his neck, happy to have a moment of peace before we get going again.

"It is what it is," he says, his voice vibrating inside his chest, and making butterflies leap about in my stomach. "Everything is moving very suddenly. I don't think Damien was expecting this either."

"Did he sound okay?"

"He was happy as a pig in mud," says Seth drily. "You know what he's like. Organizing others and intrigue are his two favorite things."

I nod against his chest and the cool cotton of his shirt soothes my fears. "You're right. He's a natural born conniver."

"He did ask that we get to him as soon as we could, provide backup. Although he did tell me to delay getting you there 'til after the fighting was over."

I pull back, looking up at Seth. "He said that? He wanted backup?" Even if he didn't want me there for the initial confrontation, the fact that he asked for help is so unusual, I know he must be worried.

"Yep."

"Then we're going to rescue Aurelia and get to him asap."

CHAPTER
FORTY-FOUR

I t feels good to be flying.

Seth and I are the only ones in the air, the others are following in the van. Poppy's using a tracking app on her phone as they drive. We travelled together in the van for the first few hours—although it only seemed like a few minutes to those of us in the back—but when we crossed the state line into Idaho and started climbing into the mountains, I figured we were getting close. So Seth and I became lookouts rather than spectators.

You really think he's in his lair? says Seth.

I don't know. He was wounded. How quickly could he heal? Surely not this fast?

We don't know what he's capable of.

Except violence and pain. I swoop down to avoid the look of pity in Seth's face, setting my wings to speed me through the air currents. Up here it feels like there's magic in the world. Below, the mountains creak and crumble into each other, a constant battle for supremacy.

Are we close, do you think? I ask once I've regained my composure.

This seems like a good place for a lair, says Seth. *Remote, difficult to get to.* He glances below us at the white van struggling through the windy mountain pass.

I know what he's thinking. Lakas is an air supernatural. It's likely his lair is unreachable to the non-flying members of this team.

It could be just you and me, I say.

It's possible, he agrees reluctantly. *Unless we agree to carry one or more of our team.*

We fly on, and I try to ignore the fear that's clawing at my insides. I wasn't ready to see Lakas on Mt. Hood, and I'm definitely not ready to see him now, either. Especially if it's just me and Seth. Back at the safehouse, it felt like we had a strong team. Now, flying over the mountains, I realize the limitations of our team. *I can carry a couple of people,* I say.

Seth's phoenix body is covered in flames. No one can ride on his back, except another flame-based super. He once carried Carrick out in front, using his claws, but it was such a horrible way to travel, I don't think anyone would voluntarily do it.

I'm going to check in with the van, says Seth. He swoops down, flying next to the driver's side. Mr. Fookes is at the wheel, his body sagging after long hours of driving.

Aurelia is in the same place she's been for the last two hours. She's just up ahead somewhere. Seth glances at me, his amber eyes filled with an emotion I can't name.

I'm convinced Lakas has captured her. That she might even be dead. It's the only explanation for how still she's been. She's not exactly the kind of dragon who looks before she leaps. I want to freak out, to speed down there and tear his lair apart, looking for Aurelia. We rescued her. She was supposed to be safe.

We need a plan, I say instead. *So we don't get caught up in whatever she's gotten herself into.*

We go in slowly, the others as back up. We don't do this alone. That's our plan.

I huff out a breath, knowing he's right.

When the van stops a half hour later, Seth and I circle around overhead, and then land when Mr. Fookes gestures for us to come down.

"She's just up ahead," says Poppy, her phone in one hand, pointing up to a gap in the rocks with the other. "There's a cave entrance that's visible from here, but I'm thinking it must be some kind of distraction or trap. He wouldn't have something so easily visible as the entrance to his lair."

I nod, then flap my wings slowly, trying to communicate my belief that his entrance will only be accessible to wings.

"Mei is right. It'll be somewhere you need wings to get to," says Hazel, stepping forward.

I nod again, relieved that Hazel is so good at reading my signals.

I gesture toward my back with my snout.

"You can carry someone?" says Mr. Fookes sharply.

I nod.

I hold up two claws.

"Two people?"

I nod again, feeling like I'm playing charades.

"I really need to work on a way to translate dragon thoughts into human words," says Hazel, looking at me with narrowed, thoughtful eyes.

I give her a startled look back.

"Who's going to go up with them?" asks Mr. Fookes. He looks at Blade. "I think you might be one of the volunteers."

Blade nods grimly. He's the most experienced fighter, after me.

"I'll go," says Poppy. "I'm good with coming up with ideas on the fly."

"No," says Hazel, stepping forward. "I'm going." She holds her hand up when every other person in the group practically howls the negative.

Blade steps closer to her, glowering down at her. "I didn't bring you along so you could go into danger again," he says. "I can't protect you up there."

"I need to be there when you face him. It's important. And I'm not without my own resources," she says, her eyes glowing faintly.

"Did you eat a demon before we left?" he asks.

"I don't *eat* demons," she says. "I *destroy* them." She crosses her arms. "And I'm not taking no for an answer."

I'm proud of her and scared for her at the same time. I'd think she didn't understand how evil Lakas truly is—except she knows. I was one of the supers who rescued her from the prison cell where Lakas was holding her. I saw what he did to her.

Blade glances at Mr. Fookes over her head, who gives a small shrug. They're not in charge of Hazel, any more than I am.

"Okay, fine. It's me and Hazel on Mei's back. You guys stay here, and if we're not out in say..." Blade glances at his watch. "Twenty minutes, figure out a way to come save us."

I'd have preferred if he'd grinned to show he was joking about needing to be saved, but instead he looks grim.

"How will we do this?" asks Hazel. "Do we just storm in there and hope for the best?"

"No." Blade gives her a dark look. "And that question is exactly why you shouldn't be going in with us."

She grins, making it clear she was only messing with him. "What's the plan then?"

I can practically hear his growl. "We go up there, try to maintain a level of surprise, and be as stealthy as possible. And look out for traps."

Seth nods in agreement. *We need to be vigilant,* he says to me. *We will have a better viewpoint of the whole lair.*

Because we're bigger?

Because we have wings. I'm expecting it to be set up for a minokawa.

Blade gestures for Hazel to climb up ahead of him onto my back. Once they're settled between the ridges, I look over my shoulder to confirm they're both holding on tight, then leap into the air.

It only takes a few moments to get up to the cave entrance that Poppy indicated. Instead of stopping, we fly a little higher, looking for another entrance.

Over there, look. Seth's sharp phoenix gaze has spotted a new cave.

This one is a little more hidden, with no easy access without wings. As we cruise over the new entrance, I try to find evidence of a trap, or even that it's really his lair, but it looks like any other cave on the mountainside. Weeds cling to the sparse dirt on the tiny ledge and broken pieces of rock are scattered everywhere. There's nothing to indicate we're in the right place, but it's our best option. I land awkwardly on the ledge with my back legs, my front claws clinging to the rock on the far side. The entrance is big enough for my dragon form to fit inside, but not with Blade and Hazel on my back.

They manage to slide off my back and Blade pulls out a knife, holding it casually in one hand. He's just as competent with weapons as I am, and the knowledge is reassuring.

"Wait here. I'm going in to scout," says Blade. Hazel nods, crouching just inside the entrance, and very specifically looking away from the outside ledge where it drops into nothing. Seth is flying in circles overhead.

Blade walks silently into the cave, and is soon enveloped by the darkness. I can smell him, but it's not enough, so I switch to heat sensing vision, and there he is, walking carefully inside.

There's no other heat signatures. Maybe we've found the wrong place?

Maybe the tracker is wrong. Maybe Aurelia isn't here anymore. I let out an annoyed puff of smoke. I need to focus.

I shift against the rock, and tiny pieces break away and fall down the cliff face. Hazel swallows hard and moves a little further into the cave. If I could speak to her in my dragon form, I'd tell her it's okay, that I'll catch her if she falls.

Eventually Blade returns. "Come on, I need your help," he says with his usual grim expression. It's hard to tell if he's worried or everything is going to according plan.

Hazel stands up, and follows him in. I peer inside, trying to make sure I'll fit, before I commit to it, but it's a large cavern inside, easily big enough for a dragon.

We're going inside, I say to Seth.

I'll follow you in.

Hazel and I follow Blade deeper into the cave, down a short tunnel. When I catch up to them, Blade and Hazel are standing at the edge of a wider cavern that drops away to a rocky floor about thirty feet below us. There are several ledges around the cavern, and various tunnels leading off from the main area. At the bottom there's a large flat area that's set up like a laboratory.

"She's in a cage down there," says Blade in a whisper. "I can't see Lakas. I don't know if he's here."

I nod, to let Blade know I understand, and then reach out with my senses across the spell web grid. The only bright spots around me are Blade and Hazel, and Seth, who's just caught up to us, his phoenix glow eclipsing the other two. There's also a glow at the bottom of the cavern from Aurelia. There's nothing on my heat sensing vision either.

I don't think he's here, I say cautiously to Seth.

Let's assume he's hiding somewhere, and stay alert, he replies.

I shake my head at Blade, trying to tell him Lakas isn't here. He seems to understand.

"I need one of you to fly down there and see if we can get her out of her cage," says Blade. "We may need Poppy after all, she's the expert with picking locks."

Seth moves forward before I can even think about doing it, and coasts down to the floor. He stops in front of Aurelia's cage. She's in her dragon form, hasn't even bothered to change back again. I can tell they're talking to each other, but they keep the conversation between themselves. Seth touches the bar with both front claws, and the flames burning over his body increase in size, burning up into the air, sparks leaping out everywhere. The glow over his front claws gets brighter and brighter until it's almost painful to look at. It's so hot that the metal bars on the cage start to soften, and Seth pulls them apart. He does the same with the other bars on the cage, until there's a big enough gap for Aurelia to squeeze through.

"Is it really this easy?" asks Hazel, looking around nervously. "This seems too easy."

"Don't jinx it," says Blade, his sharp eyes watching the shadows for a possible new threat.

Hazel takes a step closer to the edge, and peers over. "If he's not here, where is he? And how did he trap Aurelia?"

"Could have been a trap set up to go off when he's not here," says Blade. "Just part of his security."

"Then wouldn't there be more?"

"Probably. Which is why we're gonna wait up here and see if Seth and Aurelia can just come back up here to us. So we don't have to go down there and get ourselves killed by some kind of ridiculous booby trap."

I nod my agreement, and don't take my eyes off Seth until he and Aurelia fly back up to the ledge, and land next to us. I let out the breath I've been holding.

This is familiar, I say to Aurelia. *Us rescuing you.*

Aurelia manages to look sheepish and defiant at the same time. *I was trying to save you the pain of having to make the decision to kill him.* Her expression hardens, her eyes glinting from the light of Seth's flames. *He held me trapped in that mountain for centuries, hurt me, tortured me. I have to be the one who kills him. It's the only way I'll be able to go on with life.*

You're not at full strength. I gesture toward her with one hand. *Look at you, half your dragon scales are still broken or bent. You could have been killed.*

Aurelia makes a face and looks back down over the ledge to the cage that held her. *He wasn't even here. I got caught by a trap.*

Where is he? I ask, but I don't hold out much expectation for her knowing where he might be. She never even saw him. Except, as always, Aurelia surprises me.

I looked for him on the shadow plane while I was in that cage. He's in New York.

I look at Seth, his eyes wide like mine. *That's where Dad and the others are heading. Is it a trap?*

Probably.

Then we need to get to New York and warn Dad.

FORTY-FIVE

"No, that's a terrible idea," says Mr. Fookes. "We need reinforcements, we need to get more people to help."

I take a step forward, my hands clenched at my sides. "No. We can't wait that long. Dad said to follow him to New York as soon as we rescued Aurelia. You can go get reinforcements, tell them Damien and the others are in trouble. But I need to get to my dad." I'm itching to leave, and having to explain myself to Mr. Fookes is making it worse.

I've shifted back into human form to talk to the others, and my jeans and T-shirt feel scratchy and uncomfortable, as if my body knows it's supposed to be in dragon form, flying toward New York. Seth and Aurelia are looming over us, still in their supernatural bodies. Seth's blazing phoenix feathers are creating strange lighting effects over everyone's faces, even in the afternoon sunlight.

"Damien is smart. He won't have gone into this without a plan. And a plan B."

"He doesn't know Lakas is there. He doesn't have all the

information." I don't know why I'm so convinced that we need to get there fast, but I am.

Mr. Fookes lets out a sigh. "I can see you're going, no matter what I say. We can follow in the van, be back-up to the back-up. I'll ring everyone I can think of, initiate a telephone tree. Who else went with Damien to New York?"

"He said Freddie, Zane and Carrick."

Mr. Fookes raises his eyebrows. "He was taking in the big guns, then."

"He knew there'd be trouble. I just don't know if he realizes how *much*. We need to leave now, so we can get there in time to be useful."

Aurelia shuffles next to us, and jerks her head toward the sky. *We need to leave.*

I turn back to Mr. Fookes and the others, who are all gathered around the side of the van, expressions ranging from concerned (Hazel and Daphne) to annoyed (Blade).

Poppy just looks like she wishes she could come with us.

"Do you want a ride to New York?" I ask her, just in case.

She shakes her head. "Hazel told me what it was like flying on the back of a dragon. I think I'll wait for the comfortable seats and the goggles before I go on anyone's back."

I laugh, despite the situation. "I'm still waiting for Hazel's dragon riding gear." I don't mention that there are very few people I'd ever allow to use it.

"I was too scared to create it," says Hazel with a smile. "I'm pretty sure you told me that you don't like people traveling on your back."

"Only select people. In desperate times." I give them all my serious face, trying to alleviate their concerns, except I'm just as concerned. I don't feel ready to face Lakas, let alone Director Holden and whatever else he's got going on at the SIG Headquarters in New York. "I have to do this. I can't let Dad go into this alone."

"And we can't just ring one of them?" says Blade. He looks frustrated by the situation. I think it's probably because he can't be one of the people flying off to help. Maybe I should have offered to have him on my back? Except I know that he's stuck to Hazel like glue at the moment, and I don't intend to put her into a dangerous situation like this right now.

"Dad told Seth he'd have his phone off for a while. That it was too dangerous. Freddie hates phones, so his is on silent all the time. I don't think Zane has a phone, and Carrick... I don't know about Carrick. Maybe you could try his number. But we have to go."

I give everyone a quick hug—they came out to help us without even questioning what was happening—and then shift into my dragon form on the other side of the van.

"Take care of yourself, okay?" says Hazel, her voice slightly shaky. "I didn't rescue you so you could go off and get yourself killed."

I nod, a sharpness in my throat making me want to belch flames to get rid of it.

"We'll meet you in New York," says Mr. Fookes. "As soon as we can." He looks worried, like there's something he's forgetting but he doesn't know what.

I nod to show I've understood. *Let's go, before they change their minds and try to stop us.*

How could they possibly stop us? We're dragons, says Aurelia with such confusion, I get a sense of what it was like to be a dragon all those years ago.

Not by force, I say. *By caring.* Then I leap into the air, dust and rocks swooshing out below me as my wings push out. I don't look back until the others are just dots against the mountain.

We fly in silence for a few miles, each of us getting used to the feeling of being in the air again. Aurelia is starting to look stronger, despite everything she's been through. I'm not sure how, but she's healing faster than I'd have thought possible, even for a dragon.

Is gold a common color for a dragon? I ask.

No, it's a very uncommon color, she replies, smugly. She glances over at my red and gold coloring. *You're more uncommon than you realize.*

Does it signify something I should know about?

No. Nothing that means anything in these times. It's just not a common color.

I feel like she's not telling me something, and I glance over at Seth, wondering if he's feeling the same way. Aurelia seems to be pretty casual with the truth. It's hard to know what's real and what's not.

Except I believe her about Lakas being in New York. She wants to kill him so bad, I don't think she'd lead us on a wild goose chase. Not again, at least.

What's our plan? I ask. We're flying high above the earth, at top speed. We're all eager to get there and make sure Lakas doesn't have some kind of trick up his sleeve.

Aurelia looks over at me in surprise. *We kill him.*

I shake my head. *It's no wonder he managed to trap you in that mountain. You're so convinced that no one can defeat a dragon, you don't allow for smart people. I'd have thought you'd be the first to realize it's not always about brute strength.*

She flicks me an annoyed look, and then dives down and back up again, like she needs to shake off her emotions.

Am I wrong? I ask Seth, who's flying serenely next to me. *You're not wrong. She's just headstrong and strangely convinced she's invulnerable—especially given she just spent three hundred years trapped in a mountain.*

She might be more of a hindrance than a help in this mission.

I'd like to see you try to convince her to leave this to you. Seth gives me an amused glance over his wing.

I make a face back at him. *I'm not sure I want anyone to 'leave this to me'.*

Then let's just keep going, and hope that all we have to do is warn them.

I don't say it, but we're both thinking the same thing. There's no way we're going to get out of a fight that easily.

Aurelia comes back up to fly next to us again, and we form a V, just like migrating ducks, our internal direction focused on New York. It's almost early evening, and getting darker the more east we get.

Do we fly through the night? asks Seth.

I hesitate. I know why he's asked me that question. I'm starting to feel like I've just been used as a punching bag at my local gym and I'm sure I look just as ragged. Aurelia isn't much better.

Being a dragon usually means that I'm at the top of the food chain, the biggest predator around. Except right now, I'm not.

Right now, I'm much lower down that food chain, and definitely not up to fighting a whole bunch of Director Holden's minions. Or facing off against Lakas.

But the thought of my father—and Freddie, Carrick and Zane—going into a situation that might just be a whole lot more dangerous than they're expecting... that's what is spurring me on.

We need to keep going, I say. *Time is of the essence.*

He nods, as if he was expecting that answer, and faces

forward again. His glow is enough to keep us lit up in the few yards around us, but it soon becomes too dark to see much ahead. I switch to heat sensing vision, and use my internal dragon senses to make sure we're heading in the right direction.

Four hours into our flight, I admit to myself that I need to stop. I'm exhausted, and I need something to eat. Aurelia seems to be going on adrenaline alone, but Seth's fiery flames have dimmed as well.

We need to stop for a break, I say. *We all need rest and food. We won't be any help at all if we arrive half dead.*

Aurelia looks like she wants to argue, but a stray wind current knocks her off balance and by the time she rights herself, her expression is more resigned. We're all exhausted and no amount of will power is going to change that.

We're flying high over a large section of national forest, so we dive low over the trees, looking for a clearing to rest in. My stomach growls. I need food as well, although I'm not sure what we'll find this far out, in the middle of nowhere.

Seth points to a large swathe of grass below us and we glide down, landing with a thump.

We should stay in our supernatural forms, I say. *That way we'll heal faster.*

Aurelia looks around. *I can smell fire rock around here somewhere. We should be able to use it to fill our stomachs, for now at least.*

Fire rock? Is that like the dragon rock you fed me in the mountain? I glare at her with remembered indignation.

Aurelia shakes her head. *Sometimes I'm shocked by how little you know about being a dragon.*

I was the only dragon I knew for a while there, I say defensively. *I did the best I could.* I glance at Seth. He was there when I was trying to figure out how to shift for the first time, and then how to eat, fly and even just walk in my dragon form. I'm still surprised I made it through those early days. I was a hot mess.

I also nearly killed Seth—if he hadn't been a phoenix, I probably *would* have killed him.

Aurelia shakes her head, her golden scales glinting in the low light from Seth's flames. *I can't believe you managed to do the shift on your own,* she says. *In my day, we had a team of dragon nurses and mountain supers ready to help us through and teach us what we needed to know.*

I didn't even know I was a dragon until just before I shifted, I say.

How could you not know you were one of the most powerful shifters in the world? Surely you must have had an inkling?

Aurelia's incredulous expression stings a little, but I manage to give a casual dragon shrug, my scales shivering across my body. *All I knew was that I had an affinity for water. I didn't really spend a huge amount of time with any other shifters except my mentor, Si. It just never occurred to me that I was significantly more powerful than anyone else. Si and Jeff used to beat me in fights all the time. That's how I know that a sneaky human or super can win out over a powerful dragon.*

The world is a different place for dragons now, says Aurelia, suddenly subdued. *I wouldn't have imagined it could ever be this way.*

What was it like in your time?

Aurelia closes her eyes as if she's envisioning how it used to be. *It was...beautiful and terrible at the same time. There were dragons everywhere, and it was getting worse. Fights would break out over nothing. But...it wasn't always like that. Dragons are stubborn and prideful, but also loving and protec-*

tive. My family... They loved me. They searched for me right up until they were killed by the Earthbound and their machines.

I swallow against the lump in my throat. She must have watched in the shadow plane as it happened. She saw her family killed.

I'm so sorry, I say, feeling inadequate.

Lakas was there. He was part of it. My sister killed his family and he was determined to kill every single dragon he could. He killed many of my people.

And now you want to kill him?

Yes, she says, her eyes blazing. *I don't have the same qualms that you do. I don't care what people think of me, or if it's the right thing to do. I have been breaking down slowly inside that mountain for the last three hundred years and the only thing that kept me going was dreaming of killing Lakas.*

For the first time, I know for sure that Aurelia is telling the truth.

CHAPTER
FORTY-SIX

We're all exhausted when the lights of New York appear on the horizon. And it's another two and a half hours before we even make it to the outskirts of the city.

What's the plan? asks Seth as he soars beside me. His gaze lands on Aurelia. *Other than killing Lakas.*

We need to find the others. We have to head to SIG Head-quarters. I'm gazing ahead, trying to spot something I recognize.

It won't be easy to just get in. We can't exactly walk in the front door, says Seth.

He's right, I know he's right. I take another few beats of my wings before I answer. *What about the roof? Can we walk in from the roof?*

SIG agents tend to be half or quarter supers, which means they aren't as powerful as full supers, especially ones like us who can fly. Some of them are just humans who have a higher affinity for the supernatural than normal, like Jeff did. I've always suspected that he had an ancestor who was a super, but officially he was simply an extraordinarily perceptive human.

So it stands to reason that maybe they wouldn't protect the roof like they should, because they just wouldn't think it about it from that perspective.

Maybe.

Except Lakas can fly. Perhaps he's made changes to protect the roof since we were there last time, running for our lives?

But the other option—going in through the front door —doesn't appeal to me either. At least the roof has a chance of being stealthy, if we're careful and don't set off any of their alarms.

Aurelia doesn't say anything. Her golden body is almost glowing in the darkness. I don't think she's worried about getting in quietly. Or even avoiding others. Her whole focus is trained on Lakas and how she's going to kill him.

I try to feel something about that. Anger that she's stealing my thunder by wanting to be the one who kills him. Worried that she's so single-focused. Fear that maybe killing him is the wrong thing to do.

Instead, I watch what's happening as if I'm looking through a window. From a distance. Like I'm not involved, and have no skin in the game.

It doesn't seem healthy. It seems... I don't know. Like maybe I haven't properly dealt with everything that happened to me while I was in Lakas's power.

Which, of course, I haven't.

Now's not the time to fall apart. You'll have time for that later.

Jeff's voice pops into my head, and I know he's right. Or that he was right on one of those occasions where he said exactly that to me as I was growing up. Now's not the time. We're on a mission and I need to focus.

Except it's less than two weeks since I almost died because of Lakas.

And now I feel fear. It snakes its way up through my body from my stomach, reaching out to grasp my throat and choke the breath from my body. For a second, I forget about flying, forget where I am and who I am, and just fall into the fear. I dip down, and my stomach dips too, and it feels good. Better than the fear.

So I break formation and swoop away from the other two, twisting and twirling in the sky, trying to get rid of the fear that's choking me. I duck and dive, the air blustering against my scales, making me feel alive.

Mei, says Seth sharply inside my head. *We don't have time for games. You need to save your energy for what's coming.*

Except I'm not playing games. I'm deadly serious. But I do as he asks and return up to the formation that he and Aurelia have kept together, feeling slightly out of breath, but also not as fearful.

My heart is still pounding inside my dragon body. I can practically feel the blood pumping through my veins. I'm more alive than I was expecting to be when I was lying in that hospital bed at the Compound. That's enough for now.

Seth gives me an intense look, but doesn't say anything, for which I'm relieved. I couldn't explain what I was doing anyway. We continue flying toward the center of the city where the SIG Headquarters is located, each of us lost in our own thoughts.

By silent agreement we land softly on a rooftop a few buildings away from the SIG property. The SIG Headquarters is an old brownstone that looks like it wouldn't hurt a fly. But over the years, it's been secretly renovated by various SIG Directors and it now has several subterranean levels—like the lab where Hazel worked when she was employed here—plus hidden connections between the floors, secret passageways inside the walls, and magical protection that only affects supers.

In summary, it might not be that easy to get inside.

Except from this viewpoint, the rooftop looks empty. Unassuming. Like maybe they forgot about it in their rush to focus on keeping other supers out the front door.

How was your father planning to get inside? asks Aurelia.

I don't know.

I look at Seth, but he shakes his head. *He didn't tell me, either. Just said they had an opportunity to take out the director.*

He would have to destroy the magical protection somehow, I say.

We all look back to the rooftop, and I'm sure we're all thinking different thoughts. I'm remembering the last time, when we only just managed to escape with help from Hazel, and Seth is looking at it like he's planning our route. Aurelia is watching the rooftop with such intensity and anticipation, I can't help feeling worried. She's like a gun, loaded and ready to fire, but held by someone who's blindfolded.

We don't even know if they're in there yet, I say. *What if they were delayed? Or something happened? If we go storming in there to save them and they're still waiting outside for the right moment, we'll be making the situation worse, not better.* I'm trying to convince myself that I'm saying all this because it's the situation. But I kind of hate myself for being the one who's urging the others to be more cautious.

Seth is watching me, and I'm pretty sure he understands the conflict that's happening inside my head right now. He ruffles his flaming wings, and sparks fly into the night. *We go in silently, don't set off any alarms and just try to figure out what's happening inside the building,* he says. *We can do that by going in through the roof in our human forms. We assess the situation, and make a move from there. Okay?* Seth specifically looks over at Aurelia. He's just as worried about her as I am.

She nods. *Okay.*

Can we trust her word? I don't know.

The aim is to help Damien and the others, I say. *Our primary mission isn't to kill Lakas. That's a secondary goal, that might be provided by circumstances. But this isn't about him, this is about the wider goal of getting rid of Director Holden.* I frown at Aurelia, trying to make sure she understands the importance of what I'm saying.

Okay, okay, I got it the first time. Aurelia's starting to look like a sullen teenager. Her amber dragon eyes glow in the darkness.

One at a time, I'll go first. No big movements, no loud noises. We keep this in stealth-mode, says Seth.

Aurelia and I nod in synch this time. Seth is in full agent mode right now, and I love it. Maybe I should be doing the same thing—I've realized that Si and Jeff were basically training me to be an agent all those years—but right now, I'm just happy to be keeping it together and not lying curled up in a corner, sobbing like a baby. Which totally feels like an option. I take a shaky breath, pushing away the image of me losing my cool.

I just have to focus on the here and now. Which means that Seth can take over this mission all he wants. As long as it keeps me safe and not in that damned corner.

I'm going first, says Seth. *Follow me one at a time.* He moves to stand close to me, and I feel his warmth. He pushes his head close to mine, and for a second, I bathe in his heat, feeling calm and protected. And then he takes his warmth away and leaps into the air.

I swallow hard, watching as he lands on the SIG rooftop, heart in my mouth. There could easily be traps over there that we haven't spotted. Seth could be flying into his death.

He just gave the signal, says Aurelia. *Who's next, you or me?*

You go. I just need a moment more, I say, wondering if I need more than that. I think I need another hour. Maybe a week.

Aurelia takes off without hesitation. I wonder if she's ever felt doubt or fear. She was just locked away for three hundred years and all it seems to have done is given her a burning need for revenge. I suppose that's not exactly healthy either, but at least she's moving.

Before my fear can bubble up inside me again, I leap into the air. It's only a short flight to the building, and I land lightly on the ground. The other two are already changing into their clothes. Seth's bag is lying on the ground next to him.

I sniff the air, and look around in both normal and heat sensing, then along the spell web grid. The only supers I can sense nearby are Seth and Aurelia. There doesn't seem to be any kind of magical spell protecting the building. Seth is watching with amusement as I double-check his assessment.

I'm just making sure, I say.

Bones cracking, skin shifting, magic surging I shift out of my dragon form. And then I'm naked on the roof next to the others, the zing of magic in the air and a metallic taste on my tongue. I grab my clothes, not wasting time as I pull my jeans and T-shirt on, then shove my arms into my jacket. It's cold in New York.

The roof door is locked, but there's a lock to pick, and Seth makes short work of it. We creep slowly in through the entrance, unsure what to expect. The stairs down to the next level are dark, and there's no sound.

In fact, it's weirdly silent. No hum of lights or the ventilation system. No clunking of the elevator.

"Has the electricity been turned off?" I whisper to the others.

"Yeah, I think so. Something's definitely happening," says Seth. "I think they've made their move."

"And how do we tell who's winning?" I ask.

"I think we just have to go down the stairs. One level at a time, until we find someone."

"Then what?"

"We do what we can to help. We're three powerful shifters. We're useful." Seth shrugs, as if it's common knowledge. I try to remind myself I'm a dragon, and that of course he's right. But the raging dread inside me is making it difficult to believe.

Who am I if I'm not the one leading the charge into danger?

I glance at Aurelia, but she's nodding enthusiastically, not at all worried about her less-than-perfect health, or potentially coming face-to-face with Lakas.

I'm not so confident, but Seth has no other answers to give, and I know we can't stand around worrying about what might be down those stairs. We're here to help my father.

Seth goes first, and even though part of me is antsy about the fact that I'm not leading the charge, a new, more fearful part of me is happy to follow. I take a couple of breaths, forcing myself to stay calm. I can always shift into my dragon form and fly away. Even as I think that, I rebel. Is this who I am now? Too scared to meet my enemies head on? It feels like Lakas has taken away an integral part of my personality.

I refuse to let him win.

My dad needs me.

I can be the powerful, forceful dragon I'm supposed to be. I can be like that again.

I keep repeating the words to myself as we creep down the stairway to the next level, and then the next. Everything is dark, except for the low generator lighting in the stairwell, the kind that comes on when the main electricity has gone out—or been taken out.

It feels like something my father would do, getting rid of the power. Or maybe even the director.

Keep them off balance, unable to escape via the elevators, or maybe even get through doors powered by electrical locks.

It's an environment that benefits stealth and hiding in the shadows, both things that my father is an expert at.

I just hope he's better at it than Director Holden.

CHAPTER
FORTY-SEVEN

I t's not until we've gone four levels down that we hear the first hint of noise. A warning siren of some kind is going off on a level below us.

"We need to speed this up," says Aurelia urgently. "The action's happening and we're not there."

And as much as I want to argue against her impatience, she's right. "If we don't get there soon, there will be no one to save," I say.

Seth nods, and moves faster down the stairs, using a military-style double time, rather than the creeping stealth we'd been using. It takes it out of me much faster, and I hear Aurelia in front of me puffing breathlessly as well.

Seth is managing it just fine. Dammit. I'm used to being the one who effortlessly eclipses everyone else, even in human form. Almost dying is not fun, in so many ways.

Ahead of me, Aurelia is bouncing down the stairs like she's never learned a thing about stealth or conserving energy. I don't think Aurelia has ever relied on her human strength. I get the impression that in her time they just turned up in dragon form and everyone let them have their way.

We get another two stories down and start to smell smoke. It's coming through one of the doors on this level, and as we get closer, we hear the sound of hand-to-hand fighting. Seth pauses by the door, clearly planning to enter this level. I'm panting hard, and I motion for Seth to wait. I need a moment to catch my breath... and maybe steel myself for what's to come. I'm ready for it, I want to help. I want to go storming in there like nothing is wrong.

But I'm also battling myself, the clawing feeling inside my gut telling me that Lakas might be in there, and he's stronger than me, that he's gonna... I push the thought firmly away. He doesn't hold the power.

I do.

I'm more powerful than he is.

I just wish my brain would remember that.

I give a quick nod to Seth, letting him know that I'm ready—as I'll ever be—and he opens the door, his body down low, and creeps inside. Aurelia follows next, and I'm last. I close the door quietly behind me.

I hear voices and orders being shouted. The smoke is from a homemade smoke bomb—I've made enough of those in my time to be able to tell—and makes me think we've found the others. It's the kind of trick my father would use to get an advantage in this kind of situation. He's obviously been preparing for this.

The thought makes me relax ever so slightly. If my father is prepared, maybe this will turn out okay. Maybe we're not throwing ourselves into a suicide mission.

This floor seems to be some kind of training area, with padded mats placed out on the gym floor. The alarm siren is blaring louder on this floor, and I wish I could hold my hands over my ears. Near the door there's a bucket with various weapons including short fighting sticks with bulbous ends and metallic nun chucks. Seth grabs a fighting stick from the bin, as do I. Aurelia sniffs at them, but shakes her head. I don't think she knows what to do with the weapons. I'm pretty sure she's just planning to shift back into her dragon form as soon as we get into heavy fighting, maybe bite the heads off a few people. Only problem with that idea is if we're in a room that's too small for her dragon-sized body.

There's not much to hide behind, so we race along the edges of the room, hidden by the smoke. I hear a couple of shouts and then the sound of fighting.

Seth moves faster, and we all follow.

Suddenly, two figures burst out of the smoke, grappling against each other, each trying to get supremacy. One I recognize—it's Zane in his human form—the other is a large muscled guard in SIG uniform. I can't tell who's winning, but it doesn't matter. Seth goes up to the fighting men, and slams the bulbous end of the fighting stick down on the back of the SIG guard's head.

He slumps to the ground.

Zane looks up, ready to attack Seth, then recognizes who it is.

"How'd you get here?" he says, then shakes his head. "Doesn't matter. I'm glad to see you. He was big."

I step forward, alongside Seth, and Aurelia follows behind me. "We're here to help," I say. "Lakas is here with the director, and we figured it might be a trap."

Zane glances at me and nods, and then his glance flicks to Aurelia. His eyes widen, and he takes a step back. "Your majesty, what are you doing—?" He bows, lowering his eyes to the ground.

I've never seen Zane bow to anyone.

I glare at Aurelia. "Your *majesty*?"

She sighs. "It's okay, dragon. I think my royal status is defunct. We're all equals now."

My eyes are now practically bursting out of my head. "You're *royalty*?"

Zane straightens his spine, as if he's trying to look tidier in front of Aurelia. "I don't think that's how it works, your majesty. You can't change your royal status just like that." He glances at me and Seth. "But what are you doing here? How did you find her?"

Seth frowns between Zane and Aurelia, trying to untangle the conversation, just like I am. "We rescued Aurelia from a volcano. Lakas has been keeping her trapped. And now she wants revenge."

"Perhaps you should wait in a safe location, your majesty, until the fighting is over," says Zane.

I blink. He looks completely sincere. I've never seen the badass older dragon look more deferential.

"No, I'd prefer to stay here, in the middle of the fighting." Her eyes are glowing and I've never seen anyone look more bloodthirsty in my life.

"What kind of royalty are you?" I ask, not expecting a reply, since she ignored all my other questions.

"She's the Crown Princess, second in line to the throne, after her sister," says Zane. Then he checks himself. "At least she was. I suppose the Crown Princess Serena is no longer alive."

Aurelia nods jerkily. "My parents were also killed. But given that we live in a strange new world, where the surviving dragons can be counted on two hands, I believe we can cease with the whole royalty thing. All I want to do right now is kill the man who imprisoned and tortured me."

"Well, come with me, and I'm sure you'll get your wish, your majesty," says Zane with another small bow.

I roll my eyes and follow Zane. This whole day has taken yet another unexpected turn.

CHAPTER
FORTY-EIGHT

Zane looks to me and Seth. "We need to meet up with Damien and Carrick, tell them you're here, and see if we need to change the plan. I was just sweeping this floor with a couple of the others, and making sure it was empty when that guard jumped me."

"Where is everyone else?" I ask.

"They're sweeping the lower floors, ferreting out stray guards, just like we are."

"And who's with you?" asks Seth.

"A couple of mountain supers who came along with Carrick. We're working our way down to the director's level. He seems to have retreated there when we cut the electricity."

"Sounds like it's all under control," says Seth.

Zane gives him a dubious frown. "I doubt it. Director Holden's too smart not to have a counter-attack planned."

I just nod. He's right.

"Come on then, let's move," says Zane, then seems to remember Aurelia, and bows. "Your majesty."

I raise my eyebrows at Aurelia and she shrugs, before

stepping in behind Zane. We follow him in a single line—like ducklings following their mama—out of the training area and into the hallway beyond.

The alarm is blaring even louder out here, almost painfully so. I see Aurelia up ahead of me wincing, and even Seth looks uncomfortable. The smoke in here is less thick, but it smells stronger, making my nose twitch.

Up ahead I spot two large figures emerging out of the smoke. Mountain supers. Their eyes widen in surprise when they see Zane leading us, but both of them just nod quickly when we meet in the middle of the hallway and Zane explains who we are.

"We need to find Damien."

"They should be finished sweeping their floors by now. If we go to the meeting place, we should find them," says one of the mountain supers. His craggy face reminds me of Carrick.

"Everything else clear on this floor?" asks Zane.

"Yes. All guards neutralized."

We head to the other side of the building to a second entrance and a separate stairwell, then go down to the next floor. Zane pushes open the door and we're in an open plan area that's clearly office space with desks and ergonomic chairs, and papers stashed in filing trays.

"It's all a bit mundane," I whisper to Seth. "I can't imagine agents just sitting at these desks doing paperwork."

"There are some desk-bound SIG agents," he says. "They do analysis and computer hacking, that kind of thing. Can't all be field agents."

"Guess not. Seems like they got the short end of that straw," I say.

"Some people prefer working without the constant danger," says Seth with an amused smile.

"I guess," I say dubiously. Is that me, now? Looking at the desks, I try to imagine working in here all day and staying out of danger. "It seems more like a prison sentence."

Zane glares back at us and we shut up. For a second, I forgot that we were on an important mission. This office just doesn't look like somewhere that should be in the middle of a coup.

We follow Zane at a jog, across the office area and through a door on the far side. We're in another hallway and Zane turns left without hesitation.

"How does he know where to go?" I ask.

"Damien has been studying the layout of the SIG building. I guess he had the others do the same," says Seth.

"Where are we going?" I ask.

"This is the main analyst level. Director Holden's office is two floors down," Seth whispers.

"Isn't the top floor usually reserved for the big boss? The penthouse suite?"

"The middle floor is the most protected in the building. There's essentially a steel box surrounding the whole floor. Impossible to break in or out when all the shields are up."

Zane glares back at us again, and I shut up. This is way past the gathering intel stage, even though it's empty up here.

Except...

"Where are all the analysts?" I whisper.

"As soon as the alarm went off, they would have scattered for the emergency meeting points outside."

"And why are we sure Director Holden and Lakas didn't just do the same thing?"

"I don't know. Maybe they know it's Damien, and figure they can beat him," replies Seth.

I wince. "If they're so sure of that, why are we so sure we can win?"

Zane halts at the front of our group. "We aren't," he says. "Damien doesn't work in absolutes. He works with off-chances, hopefullys, and the maybe-magic of being the underdog."

I open my mouth to argue his assessment of my father, and then close it. He's actually kind of right. My father does operate like that.

And yet he always seems to come out on top. Or at least most of the time. Maybe he's part leprechaun?

"Now, can we do the rest of this in silence? We really do need to be quiet." Zane's expression is just like a school teacher who's tired of dealing with the naughty kids.

Everyone nods briskly, including me, looking sheepish. I should know better than to chat during an operation.

Zane turns around and jogs off, the rest of us following. When he comes to the end of the hallway, he opens the door at the end, peering inside to make sure it's clear. Then he widens the door and we all traipse inside.

It's a large office space, with a window view of the city outside where the morning is in full swing. Inside, the desk has been swept clear, and my father and Carrick are leaning over the map, talking quietly. There are six others in the room, including Freddie.

Everyone looks up as we crowd into the cramped space. There's a variety of reactions, none of them exactly pleased.

My dad is at first surprised to see us, then he frowns. But he strides over and grabs me in a hug. "What the hell are you doing here so soon? You're not ready for combat yet," he says gruffly. "I meant for you to get here once the fighting was done."

Carrick follows just behind him, and frowns down at me, looking me over like he's trying to make sure I don't have any wounds he needs to heal.

I ignore him, and focus on my father. "We rescued Aurelia...again," I nod toward her. "And then... she figured out that Lakas had flown to New York so we decided to come warn—"

"Lakas captured Aurelia *again*?" My father barks the words out. "You had to rescue her a *second* time? I hope you didn't go in alone."

I glance at Aurelia. I definitely wouldn't have gone into Lakas's lair if I'd had a choice. "Not precisely. We had others with us. Mr. Fookes, Daphne, Blade and Hazel, Poppy."

My dad glares at Seth, his expression somewhere in the vicinity of *'Why the hell didn't you stop her?'*

All Seth can do is give him an apologetic shrug. "Sorry, sir. It all just got out of hand." He glances at Aurelia. "Would you like to meet the dragon we saved? Queen Aurelia, of the royal line of dragons."

My father's eyes bug out a little at this announcement. Aurelia is shaking her head, scowling at Seth.

"I told you, I don't think there's any point in having dragon royalty when there are so few of us. You don't have to call me that," says Aurelia, looking more embarrassed this time.

"There are royal dragons?" asks Dad, as if she didn't speak.

"But the main point..."—I draw my father's attention back to me—"is that we found out that Lakas came back to SIG Headquarters. He wasn't in his lair. So we came to warn you. We think it's a trap. They're waiting for you."

"We already knew they'd be waiting for us," says my father impatiently. "Director Holden has had the SIG on high alert for the last week. They're operating on tenterhooks, stretched too tight and freaked out by the changes to the power structure in the supernatural world. We're here to send them over the edge."

"You're trying to send someone like Director Holden over the edge, *on purpose*?" I say incredulously. "He's like a rabid raccoon. If you corner him, he'll come out fighting."

"Rabid raccoon? That's a new one," says my father with the ghost of a grin.

"You know what I mean," I say. "This is too dangerous. What were you thinking?"

"I was *thinking*, that my daughter—who almost died only a week and a half ago—would be safe at home while the rest of us—who are at full strength and have been planning this for a long time—could go execute my very smart, very strategic plan." My father is standing in front of me, and Carrick is still looming at his back, like the pair of them think they can intimidate me into backing down.

They should know better. "Pfft. You wing it half the time, Dad. Zane is right about that one."

My father looks offended. "I don't *wing it*. I always have a plan. And I just happen to be really good at pivoting when a plan goes wrong, as they often do."

"So you admit your original plans are never very good?"

My father glares at me. "It doesn't matter. What matters is the outcome, and that's always positive."

"Sir," interrupts one of the mountain supers who was in the room when we arrived. He appears to be monitoring something from a tablet. "They're making a move downstairs. I think they're going to attack."

"Then let's stop them before they can."

CHAPTER
FORTY-NINE

"You stay here, monitor the screens. Keep me up to date on what's happening via the walkie talkie," says my father.

"Are you kidding me? I'm not doing that." I put my hands on my hips and give him an outraged look. "I can help. I'm a *dragon*, Dad."

"You're a wounded dragon," he says stubbornly. "You almost died. I'm not going to risk you on a mission like this. Not this soon."

I look to Seth who shrugs. "I agree with him."

I shake my head. "Well I don't agree. I'm not going to wait around here while you go off and do all the work."

"Mei, this isn't a democracy. I'm in charge, and you're staying here." My father is using his agent voice, and is glaring at me like he's my superior officer.

Except he's forgetting that I was raised by Jeff and Si. I'm not afraid of him glaring at me, and I'm not about to sit here like a baby and wait for the rest of them to complete the mission. Even if I *am* scared of Lakas. "I'm not an agent. And you're not my superior officer. I'm going out there and

I'm helping you take over this building, and you can make me part of the mission, or I can do it by myself."

I cross my arms over my chest, and glare at him and Seth.

"You're more of a firecracker than I realized," says Aurelia, grinning. I glare at her too, for good measure.

"Fine," says my father tersely. "You're with Bravo Team. You'll be clearing the subterranean floors, making sure there's no one hiding down there who can come back to bite us on the ass later. Zane is in charge of that team. All three of you can go with him."

From the surprised expression on Zane's face, I doubt there was a Bravo Team until two seconds ago. But I'm not going to argue. Those floors need to be cleared. And I know for sure that Lakas isn't going to be in the thick of it, fighting. That's not what he does. He'll be lurking around the edges, waiting for the result. There's a chance he'll be down there.

"Okay," I say. I glance at Seth, but he seems okay with that mission too. Aurelia is looking mutinous, like she thinks she's being made to play with the little kids, but she keeps quiet. For now.

"Right. So everyone knows what they're doing?" Dad looks around the room, and everyone is nodding. "We stay alert, we each do what we've been assigned to do, and then we meet back at the ground level." He checks his watch. "We have one hour. Make it count."

"One hour 'til what?" I ask.

"'Til the other leaders of the SIG arrive for their meeting with Director Holden. Our inside sources said he was making plans to execute all of them. This is us stopping that from happening."

"Oh shit," I say.

"Exactly. We need to stop him in his tracks. Everyone. This is it. Go time."

He nods to Carrick, who leads the first team out of the room, which consists of the two mountain supers who had been with Zane, and another smaller super who looks like he might be a water elemental. Carrick gives me a look that might be annoyance, or it might be 'good luck'. I'm going to assume it's the latter.

I nod at him, silently wishing him the same.

Freddie's team is next. He has another mountain super, an efficient looking man who I think I've seen before but I can't quite place, and a woman who might be a chameleon. Freddie nods in our direction, and then leads his team out, weapons bristling from every possible place.

That leaves two mountain supers, one of whom is on the tablet that seems to have the camera feed for the entire building, my father, plus our newly established Bravo Team.

"Fallan, you're here with the tablet. Let me know if anything changes on the feeds. Sharlo, you're with Zane and the Bravo Team."

"What about you, Dad?" I ask, confused.

"I'm on an individual mission to start with. I'll meet up with Carrick's team shortly."

"Isn't that dangerous? Being on your own?" I catch a look that goes between my father and Zane. "Was Zane supposed to go with you?"

"It won't be for long. I'll be fine." He gives me a tight hug, and then turns to Zane. "Keep them safe. Sweep the area, same as up here."

Zane nods. "Will do." He turns to the rest of us. "Okay team, you heard him, let's go."

"Take care of yourself," my father calls softly after us.

"You too, Dad."

Zane leads us back down the same hallway, through the office area, back to the stairs we originally came down. Without a word, he heads down the stairs, as quietly as possible. We're soon passing the ground level, and then we're down in the subterranean levels.

"How far down does it go?" I whisper to Seth.

"Five levels. This is where they have the labs, and the library," says Seth.

"It must be where Hazel had her lab," I say.

"Exactly."

Zane looks back over his shoulder at us. "We're going to start at the very bottom, and then move our way up," he says. "No more talking."

We all nod obediently.

When we step out of the stairwell at the fifth sub level, there's a flickering glow, as if the lights want to be on, but are battling whatever my father's team did to them upstairs.

"That light, it's coming from that room," says Seth, pointing.

He's right. It's not the main lighting system, it's coming from a small window set into the door across from us.

Zane points to Seth and me. "You two, take that way, we'll sweep the rest of the floor."

We both nod, and the two teams split up. Zane and Sharlo walk away with Aurelia in between them—almost like they're guarding her. I think Zane is planning to be Aurelia's royal guard, at least for the duration of this attack.

Seth and I move toward the door, and I peer through the window. "There are big tanks of some kind in there."

Seth is looking over my shoulder. "Storage tanks. What the hell is inside them? It's glowing."

"I don't know. But I guess we have to find out."

I push down on the handle, but it doesn't turn. "Locked," I mutter.

Seth pulls out his lock pick, and gets to work. I tap one finger nervously on my leg while I wait for him to get us in. He finally opens the door, and goes through first, peering around to make sure we're not about to be jumped by a guard.

I follow him in. As soon as I do, I feel like I've been enveloped by an enormous static-charged blanket. The whole room feels wired up, electric.

And it's because of the two large glowing tanks in front of us.

"What's in there?" I ask Seth, although I think I know.

"Looks like demons," says Seth, confirming my theory. "Lots and lots of demons."

I shiver. "That's awful." Now that I know—because of Hazel—that demons are just the tortured souls of super-naturals who were trying to fix something before they passed over to the other side, the thought of all those people trapped in there makes me queasy.

Not that I'm planning to let them out. Demons aren't exactly friendly to most supers. "We'll have to tell Hazel it's here, so she can deal with it," I whisper.

Seth nods.

We creep around the room, looking around the tanks, making sure the room is empty.

"Maybe we should have guns," I say. "Or at least something to defend ourselves from attack."

"I thought Jeff and Si taught you to fight and defend yourself without resorting to guns?"

"They did. I'm just not quite up to a fight right now." I make a face. I don't like admitting it to Seth, because I practically forced him to come with me on this whole debacle of a mission by telling him I was fine, when I wasn't really.

Seth nods. "Next guard we meet, we'll steal his gun," he says. "Especially for you."

CHAPTER
FIFTY

We head back into the hallway, and it's a relief to shut the door and get rid of the buzzing feeling on the back of my neck. There's not much else down at this level—we search a cleaning cupboard and a small meeting room that I doubt ever gets used, because it buzzes with the residual energy of the demons.

We meet the others back at the stairwell, and go up a level.

This time it's a little busier.

"You search the labs on this side, we'll do the other side. Meet at the end," says Zane.

Seth and I nod efficiently. Aurelia is looking shifty, like she's considering something she shouldn't. Maybe even trying to disappear and go find Lakas on her own. I give her a look, meant to indicate she stays put. "Don't do anything stupid," I say in an undertone to her.

She glares back at me, but it's enough to distract her, and she seems to forget about whatever she was planning.

Seth leads the way into the first of the labs, and initially it seems empty. I'm about to declare it, when three SIG guards leap up from where they were hiding at the back of the room behind an old desk. They're all armed, and it's only luck that Seth and I manage to dive out of the way before they start shooting, the sound of bullets whizzing overhead making me shudder.

"How did I miss *three* guards?" I say, pissed off.

"We've found them now, that's the important thing," says Seth grimly, peering around the edge of the enormous stainless steel counter we're hiding behind. "How do we overpower three armed guards with no weapons of our own?"

"Ambush?" I suggest. "Or one of us could shift?"

Seth immediately drags his T-shirt over his head, and pulls off his jeans. "I wish you'd stop trying to find sneaky ways to get me naked," he says with a grin. "All you have to do is ask."

I roll my eyes, because he's asking for it. But at the same time, I peek out of the corner of my eyes. He's tall and tanned and muscled in all the right places, and there's just something about him that makes me want to reach out and touch. If it wasn't a completely inappropriate time, I'd totally do just that, run my hands over his arms, down his chest, just to get closer to him and his phoenix heat.

Instead, I give my body a quick shake, and force myself to get back in the game. It's completely the wrong time to get distracted. I allow myself to watch as he shifts, a strangely graceful and beautiful transition involving sparks of light and beautiful flames. As his phoenix emerges, the lab suddenly seems much smaller and the smell of sulphur and fire becomes overwhelming. Seth lets out an enormous screech, and I put my hands over my ears to stop it hurting. Small little fires break out in a couple of places where Seth's fiery wings have touched flammable objects. I can hear the panicked shouts of the guards on the other side of the room. Seth screeches again, and this time, one of the men makes a desperate run for the door. Seth sweeps around, his flames whooshing through the air, and whacks him over the head with the hard bony upper section of his wing. The guard drops to the ground. Using the cover of the stainless steel counter top, I run to where the guard is lying unconscious and grab his gun and taser. Immediately I feel safer. And also see Si's judgmental glare like he's actually here with me.

Gunshots ring out and I risk poking my head up over the bench top to make sure Seth is okay. But nothing so mundane as bullets is going to break through the magical fires of a phoenix's body.

The guard pokes his head and shoulder out, and leaves himself open to my eagle eye. I aim and fire a shot, hitting him in the shoulder. He cries out and falls backward, slumping behind the desk.

There's silence for a few moments. I wait it out, catching my breath and counting to five before inching out of hiding. I'm just about to move further into the room, when a sound behind me makes me flinch. I turn in time to see another guard looming over me—I don't even know how he got there—but before I can raise my hand to shoot, Seth's clawed wing sweeps around again and knocks him off his feet. He's unconscious before he hits the ground. I let out a breath, my heart hammering.

"That was close," I mutter, a little unnerved by how close I came to being knocked out. I would never have let that happen in the past. I used to be like a ghost. Now I'm more like Scooby Doo.

I stay low and run along the counters to the end of the room where the other guard was hiding.

"All clear," I say to Seth. He nods, and peers around on his side of the room before changing back into human form. I gather the weapons from the other guards, then find a cloth for the guard I shot to hold over his wound, and tie him up with his hand tightly bound to it. He moans, but doesn't try to fight it. The other two guards are easier, because they're still knocked out.

"That was unexpected," I say, puffing from the exertion of tying up the last guard. I'm crouched down next to him, securing his hands behind his back with his own zip ties. He's unconscious, but I don't want him waking up and deciding to come after us again.

"You're just not in top fitness right now, Mei. Don't make it mean anything it doesn't," says Seth, coming to crouch down next to me, so he can look me in the eyes.

"It was too close," I whisper. "If I can't even take out a random guard, how am I going to go up against Lakas? Or the director? Or anyone else for that matter? Dad was right."

"Good news is that you don't have to do it alone," says Seth with a tiny half-smile. "If at all. If Aurelia meets Lakas first, she's gonna take care of him for you."

I shake my head slightly, my hair slipping over my shoulder. I feel... frazzled. Like it's all too much. "I don't think she can take him on by herself either."

"You might be surprised. Zane was telling me that she's not just from the royal line. Royal dragons—the gold ones —they all have special powers. He couldn't remember what Aurelia's is, there were several other royal princes and princesses, but he said they're all deadly."

I stand up. "I hope that's true. Because if Lakas has

something up his sleeve—and I'm pretty sure he will—then he's going to be difficult to kill."

Seth stands up too. He wraps one hand around my shoulders in a quick hug. Then he's all action, pulling the two unconscious guards—and one wounded guard—into the storage room at the back of the research lab. I'm now holding a gun, but it doesn't make me feel better. If anything, I feel worse, because I'm doing what Si always told me not to do: relying on a weapon to make me feel safe.

But I'll take having a gun—and the taser that's in my pocket—over feeling completely vulnerable.

Before we leave, I walk around the lab, looking for anything that might be useful. I don't know what precisely, but I'll know it if I see it. Except there's nothing here, other than the guns and taser, that I think we'll need.

"Come on, Mei. Let's go," says Seth, waiting by the door. We head back out into the hallway, and meet the others coming from the east wing.

"All clear down this way," says Zane.

"All clear our way," says Seth. "Now that we've tied up the guards."

"Next level?" I say.

"Let's go," says Zane with a nod.

The next level is the third, where Hazel had her lab. There was a guard at the elevators the last time we visited, but there's no one there now as we creep past. This level has several labs, a large lunch room, and the security station. I'm expecting to find a larger number of guards, but it's strangely empty here as well.

We split up again, Seth and I taking half the floor, Aurelia, flanked by her two guards, on the other. She looks determined, and I wonder if Zane really thinks he's going to be able to save her from whatever she's planning to do when she meets up with Lakas.

If she meets him.

Except I'm still convinced he's more likely to be hiding down here somewhere than up on the director's level where the others are attempting to get in.

I stand guard in the hall while Seth unlocks one of the labs, peering around me, determined to see any guards before they see us, when there's a scream from the other end of the floor.

It sounds strangely familiar.

"Aurelia," I say. I take off, Seth right behind me.

FIFTY-ONE

W hen we reach them, Zane and Aurelia are hiding behind a turned over table in the lunchroom, near the door. I can see the body of Sharlo splayed, unconscious, on the cold tiles further into the room.

Two guards are shooting at us from inside the kitchen area. There's a door into the kitchen, and an open servery.

"They came out of nowhere," says Zane, slightly panicked. "Didn't even have time to pull back. I think Sharlo is dead."

I peer through the doorway of the room, and a shot sounds, the bullet whooshing past my head. I pull back. "I don't think I can get a shot off," I say. "Not one that's going to actually hit anything."

"You're a better shot than me," says Seth. "How about I provide cover, and you get inside and see what you can do? Take cover behind a table, like the other two."

I nod. His plan is solid. And doesn't require me using my non-existent strength. "Okay. On three." I count off, then race into the room, crouched low, as Seth lets off a barrage of bullets from the other gun we took from the guards. I make it to a dining table along the side wall, and flip it over. I'm not convinced that the metal and laminate material is going to protect me from an actual bullet, but at least it keeps me out of sight. I keep moving, tipping tables, using the action to confuse the enemy.

I keep moving along the outside of the room, hiding behind tables and keeping my head down. Seth occasionally shoots in the direction of the kitchen to keep them from focusing on me. It works until I get about halfway down the room, and then suddenly a barrage of bullets hits the wall behind me, bouncing off the metal of the table I'm hiding behind. I curl up into a small ball, and hope the table offers more protection than I'm expecting.

Seth shoots from the doorway, and they hide back down behind the kitchen counter. I peer out, holding my gun steady with two hands. I wait for the next time one of them peers out, then fire.

The SIG agent falls to the ground.

"We don't want to kill anyone!" Seth calls from the doorway. "You guys get to choose whether you live or die."

The agents reply with a barrage of bullets.

I shoot the agent who's firing at Seth. Blood splatters onto the wall at the back of the kitchen. Just because he didn't like guns, didn't mean Jeff neglected my education.

I wait to see if there are any more agents hiding inside the kitchen. No one moves. I creep closer, focused on keeping everyone safe, ignoring the fluttering of fear in my stomach. This is what I've done a million times before. Scouted out a dangerous situation. Doing what I have to do to survive.

I make it to the kitchen, my gun held ready in front of me. I peer around the corner, and when a third agent leaps out at me, I shoot. He falls limply to the ground, the shot killing him instantly. I'm not messing around right now.

Someone comes to stand behind me and I glance back, expecting it to be Seth. Instead I see Aurelia peering around me to look at the blood and carnage inside the kitchen.

"Can I have one of those?" she asks.

"No," I say. "They're harder to handle than they look. I'll teach you how to use it, once we're out of this situation."

She gives me mulish look, and I think she's going to argue.

"It took me years to learn to shoot like that, Aurelia. And once you've shot someone, you can't take it back."

Something in my face must convince her to keep her mouth shut. She nods. "Okay, when we make it out of here, then. I definitely want to learn how to use that gun."

I shake my head and wonder if I've said the right thing. She's turning out to be bloodthirsty, that's for sure.

"Let's go, we have more floors to clear," says Zane.

"What about Sharlo?" I ask.

Zane looks over at the mountain super, sadness streaking across his face before it hardens again. "We leave him here for now. We'll come back when we can."

I nod. There's not much else we can do. We can't carry a dead body around with us.

We jog silently out of the floor, and into the stairwell. It's starting to feel like this whole mission might be a terrible idea. Did we really need to sweep through these levels? Or am I right and my father just made up this mission to keep me out of the worst of the danger?

Did Sharlo just die because of a misguided attempt to keep me safe?

I let out a huff and remind myself—yet again—to focus

back on the here and now. I can break down once we're out of this stupid building.

"This is level two," says Seth, like we should know how important that is.

"What does that mean?" I say.

"It's the Records and Relics floor," he says.

"That's where Hazel spent so much time," I say, my eyes widening. "She told me all about the cats."

"Yeah. Which means this level is going to be tricky," says Seth. "We may not even be able to get in."

"Maybe we should just leave it?" says Zane. "If we can't get in, no one else will either."

Seth shakes his head. "Any agents who've been granted access to this level could be hiding out in there. We have to clear it, like all the other levels. Otherwise our job isn't done."

"We just have to be careful. It's basically coated in magic in there," I say. "Based on what Hazel told me."

Zane opens the door to the stairwell, and we end up in another little foyer. There's nothing to show that there might be a magical library on the other side of the small internal room. It's mostly white paint and boring linoleum. The door to the library is large and wooden, with a tiny key hole next to the handle. Seth tries the door. It's locked.

He pulls out his pick and kneels down, getting to work. The other doors he's opened today have fallen apart within seconds. This one stays stubbornly locked.

"It's not working," says Seth after about five minutes of trying. He looks back at the rest of us.

"Keep trying," I say. "There must be a way inside."

We all watch nervously over his shoulder as he tries again. Eventually he pushes the lock pick too hard, and we all hear the snap as it breaks inside the mechanism.

"Shit," says Seth. "I've never had that happen before."

"Does that mean we can't get in?" says Aurelia. She's got this weird intensity about her, like she's so focused on finding Lakas that it's hard to concentrate on anything else. She seems pleased that we can't get into the Records and Relics Room.

Maybe she figures Lakas wouldn't hide in a library. I have no idea whether that's true, but I don't like the idea of not being able to get inside. Who knows what's hiding on the other side of this door? It could be the one thing that topples my father's attempt to take over here today. I'm positive he sent us down here as a soft mission to keep us occupied while he and his other teams do the real work, but I'm determined to do it properly. These floors are going to be clear, and there's no way I'm leaving the Records and Relics floor out of our sweep. I look around, trying to find another way in. Maybe there's a vent—

The door to the stairwell scrapes open behind us, and we all swivel, holding our guns on whoever is sneaking up behind us.

Except no one is there.

The door opens and then closes. My heart beats double time. What the hell is happening?

"Meow."

We all look down and see a small black cat sitting calmly beside the now-closed door.

"It's a cat," I say stupidly.

"Not just any cat," says Seth quietly. "I think it's a library cat."

Aurelia moves forward with a small squeak of pleasure and reaches out one hand. I wince, half expecting the cat to bite her and somehow morph into some sort of scary swamp monster. But it allows her to pat it, even leaning into her hand with a definite cat smooch.

"It likes me," she says with a smile.

It's the first time I've seen her genuinely happy since we rescued her.

Huh. A dragon who loves cats.

"Ask it to let us into the Records and Relics level," I say. I'm *not* a dragon who loves cats. I've been bitten one too many times by the wild cat who lives at Si's safe house in Colorado.

The cat looks up at me with a certain kind of stare that cats everywhere have perfected. A kind of superior look that's a mix of judgement and annoyance—as if they couldn't be bothered to glare, because you're not actually worth a real glare.

I scowl back.

It returns its attention to Aurelia, leaning into her continuing pats, and almost—no, surely not?—*smiling* at her. Cats don't smile. After another couple of smooches, the cat steps out of Aurelia's reach and glares over at me. Then it walks up to the door Seth was just trying to open.

We all move cautiously out of its way—everyone except Aurelia who seems determined to be allowed to pat it again and follows closely behind—and watch as the cat half jumps up so both its front paws are on the door. It grabs the door handle in its mouth, and pulls it down.

And in some way that I don't completely understand, the door handle turns on its axis, and the door opens—as if it wasn't locked after all, and we were just messing around.

The cat gives me another glare—I'm not even sure why it's so angry at me in particular—and then walks through the door into the Records and Relics floor beyond.

CHAPTER
FIFTY-TWO

"Quick, get the door!" I say in a rush. I wouldn't put it past that cat to lock the door after it. It seems vindictive. Seth leaps forward and grabs the door before it slams shut.

"I guess we can sweep this floor after all," says Zane softly. He looks as dazed as I feel.

"Here kitty," says Aurelia softly as she follows the black cat into the SIG library.

Inside the door, there are book shelves everywhere, floor to ceiling. There are only dim overhead lights, and the shadows cover more than they reveal. The musty smell of old books makes my nose twitch.

Hazel always spoke of this place with reverence, but I don't get the appeal. It's dark, dank and smells of books. I peer into the shadows ahead of us, and something small moves gracefully along the gap between the shelves.

Cats.

The library is filled with cats.

I shudder. I didn't know I had such a strong aversion to

cats, but apparently I do. Or maybe it's just these cats? Something feels off inside this place.

"Come on, let's get this over with," says Zane. "We'll pair up and each take a row, make sure it's clear, then meet at the other end. Any problems, give a yell, and we'll be there to help. Aurelia is with me. Mei and Seth, you're team two."

"Got it," I say, holding my gun at the ready. I'm not going to let anything leap out at me unexpectedly in here. Especially not the cats.

Aurelia takes the lead, heading down into the first row of shelves after the black cat, not really paying attention to what Zane just said.

"I guess we're doing that row first." Zane's eyebrows dip into a deep scowl as he stalks after the royal princess.

"We'll be right next to you," says Seth. He gives me a look. I think he's conveying that Aurelia is a loose unit, and asking why we ever rescued her in the first place.

I'm beginning to wonder that myself.

We walk quickly down the aisle, only stopping when we see movement, which happens fairly often, because *cats*.

They're everywhere. It's like they're stalking us. I keep seeing flashes of their eyes on the shelves, down on the ground, above us on top of the bookcases. And they're watching us.

"Okay, seriously. Have you nothing better to do?" I whisper fiercely to the closest one, a fluffy calico cat that is watching me with an intensity that's unnerving. "Couldn't you help us at least? Aren't you supposed to be guardians of the library?"

The cat glares at me, then stands up leisurely and gives a stretch, before jumping off the shelf, and running down the row ahead of us, its tail waving in the air like a flag.

"Well done. You scared the cat off. You're a real badass," says Seth softly, with an amused glance at me.

"It was staring at me. I feel like it was a win," I say, unrepentant. I try to reach out along the spell web for Lakas, but something about the library is making the web short circuit, and the grid lines are all shaky and weird.

I hear Aurelia calling to the black cat through the shelves.

"Is she really that oblivious?" I say. "It feels like she turned into a different person as soon as she saw that cat."

"I don't think it's a good idea to underestimate her," says Seth. "She may be acting all cat crazy, but there's more to her than that."

I nod. He's right. We've seen some of her other sides in the short time since we let her out of the lava rock.

We continue down the aisle, me trying to ignore the other cats that we keep seeing, Seth managing to focus much better than me.

Eventually we get to a break in the middle of the aisle where one set of shelves becomes another. "Where are the others?" I ask, peering down into the row next to us. I can't see either Aurelia or Zane in any direction.

"Not down this one either," says Seth from the next shelf over. I search down another couple of rows. Nothing.

"Where could they have gone?" I ask, starting to panic. We can't lose any more people. This was supposed to be the easy task, the place my father was sending us to keep me safe. "Where the hell are they?"

"Meow." The sound is soft but authoritative. If it had been from a human mouth, I imagine the person would have been telling me to pull myself together.

I look down and see the calico cat.

I frown. "What do you want?"

"Meow," it says again, and this time I know it wants us to follow it.

I have no idea how I know.

I glance at Seth and he's looking down at the cat like he wishes it wasn't there. Which means he probably understood what it meant as well.

"You want us to follow you?" I ask, just to make sure.

The cat doesn't even deign to reply, just turns around and sashays—I kid you not—up an aisle a bit further over from us.

"I think we have to follow it," I say to Seth. He doesn't reply in words, just nods, holding his gun out in front of him, like he's ready for anything.

The cat is way ahead of us by the time we turn into the row, and we have to jog quietly to catch up. It doesn't turn back to make sure we're watching, but suddenly darts into another gap between the rows.

I race to follow it, worried that we might lose the cat. It's our only lead right now, and the fact we've lost Zane and Aurelia is making me nervy.

The cat is just up ahead, sitting on a shelf half way up, licking its paws.

Like it's just a normal cat, and not a clue to helping us find the others, and maybe even Lakas. Dammit. Am I reading too much into the cat?

Does it just want me to feed it a tin of tuna?

We catch up to the calico cat, and then it turns again, looking through a gap in the shelves. I peer through after it. On the other side, there's an open space with a table and chairs, presumably for someone who might want to study in the library.

Currently it's taken up by three guards, all sitting and leaning back in the chairs like they haven't a concern in the world. One of them is playing cards by himself, like he's trying to mark the time on a really boring assignment.

What the hell? Don't they know what's happening upstairs?

The calico cat turns and gives me a significant look. Like it's telling me, 'See? I can be useful if I choose.'

I put one hesitant hand out, and it allows me to stroke my fingers down its back. Once. And then it jumps down and leads the way along the row again.

I glance at Seth and shrug. We should follow. We can't actually access those guards right now, they're on the other side of the thick bookshelf, and there's no gap coming up.

We keep going after the cat. We'll have to come back and overpower those guards later. But right now, I think the cat is actually leading us somewhere even better.

We're going deeper into the Records and Relics floor. It's so dark down here it feels oppressive. It's only my excellent dragon eyesight that is allowing me to keep going. The carpet underfoot is starting to feel threadbare, and the books on either side of us are crackling with energy.

I can't help my shudder. This place is creeping me the hell out.

The cat stops up ahead. Even in the darkness, I can see a glimpse of white from her long furry-white patches. She sits down. Then lies down on the ground, and starts purring. Like she's proud of what she's done, and has to take a moment to rest.

When we catch up, I hear voices on the other side of the shelf. I peer through the books and my breath catches.

Lakas. He's partially shifted, his enormous metallic wings flaring up behind his cadaverous human form. The power needed to do that is immense. He looks even more monstrous than usual in the flickering candlelight, the shadows catching the sharp lines of his face. There are a few other cats sitting around him on the shelves, their eyes glinting, and he has a small candle burning on a table in the clearing where he's standing.

Even worse, he has Aurelia and Zane. Aurelia is standing with her hands tied behind her back, a guard holding her in place. Zane in lying on the ground, unconscious.

At least I hope he's unconscious.

Seth puts one finger to his lips, but he needn't have bothered. I'm not going to say anything, not this close to my most hated enemy.

Lakas is holding something in his hands. He opens it up, and I see dragon stones, like the ones Aurelia fed me inside Mt Hood.

"Did you really think you'd be able to overpower me with dragon stones a second time, Aurelia?"

She just growls back at him.

"The answer is that no, I don't fall for the same trick twice. I learn. It's how I've survived all these years. I don't have the same raw power that dragons wield, but I have something else." He moves closer and grabs Aurelia by the chin. His wings curl over his head, almost completely enveloping them both. "I have something much more powerful. I have a burning desire for revenge. And I have the capacity to learn and change and grow. Unlike dragons."

"You're a monster," spits Aurelia. She has a cut down one side of her face. Lakas has been using his feathers on her.

"No more than you," he replies calmly. He looks around. "So where are the others? I know there were more of you when you first arrived."

"They're dead. We got into a gun fight with some guards down a level. They were taken out."

"Nice try. Now tell me where they are." He squeezes her chin, and Aurelia cries out. "You're not as strong as you used to be, little princess. In fact, you're just a pathetic shadow of the dragon you once were. Tell me what I want to know, and I might even spare you. Maybe I'll lock you up for another three hundred years?"

Aurelia struggles against him, her breathing ragged. He just tightens his grip.

"Answer me," he says, his fingers digging into her skin.

"We split up. They could be anywhere," she says finally, her voice almost inaudible.

"They're here in the library?" he says, glancing around.

She nods. He lets go of her chin, and her head drops, hanging limply.

Seth points up the row we're in. He wants to move, to go round and rescue them. I shake my head frantically. How can we take on Lakas just the two of us? He said he's more powerful than a dragon, and I believe him. Panic flares in my stomach, and only my deeply ingrained sense of self-preservation keeps me from screaming or running off down the row of books. My body is trembling, my hand gripping the bookshelf like it's my only lifeline.

We need back up. I can't do this.

Seth moves closer, his expression concerned.

Through all the fear and panic, I feel something by my ankles. If I wasn't frozen in place, I'd probably have jerked away. But it's only the calico cat, smooching against my legs, acting like I'm its favorite sofa. A strange sense of calm swirls through me, pushing away the fear, filling the spaces with a brilliant white light. The cat doesn't make a sound, but I know it's the one helping me fight my panic attack. I take a deep breath, then another. The fear recedes and I can think again. The cat continues to weave itself through my legs, letting me get my breath back. It looks up at me, its eyes flashing in the darkness.

It's telling me that we're not alone. That the cats of the library will help us as well.

Great, so the cats can read minds too. Awesome.

Eventually the cat moves away, toward Seth. It looks back at me impatiently, and I can tell it's asking what I'm waiting for.

The answer is that I'm scared of Lakas. I'm not waiting, I'm fighting the urge to run in the other direction. I'm not strong enough yet, and I'm still terrified of him. I keep flashing back to being in his power, to his metallic wings digging into me, cutting my skin and trying to break me.

The calico cat just sits and stares at me like that's not a good enough reason. Not when I have to save Aurelia and Zane.

I curl my hands into fists and stride toward Seth.

I'm not going to let myself be dictated to by fear.

Damn cats.

CHAPTER
FIFTY-THREE

There are two guards and Lakas, says Seth inside my head, and I look up sharply. It's not something we do often, because it takes a lot of concentration to talk inside each other's heads in human form. It's not exactly natural—in fact it's exhausting—but I understand why he's doing it.

I nod. *You have a plan?* I'm hoping for a really good plan that doesn't involve us directly. Maybe the cats could swarm over them all?

You take out the guards, I'll take on Lakas, says Seth.

I should—I stop. What was I going to say? That I should be the one to fight Lakas? Everything inside me rebels at the idea. I put one hand to my stomach to alleviate my sudden queasiness.

Just let me take him on, says Seth like he knows exactly what I'm thinking.

I hesitate. Now that we're this close, I can say with crystal clear certainty that I have no desire to take on Lakas. It hurts, it makes me feel vulnerable, it makes me feel like I'm not the same person I was before I was kidnapped. But it's there. It's how I feel. I'm scared of him, and that fear has changed me. I can't go rushing into situations like I used to. I can't forget the fear. It's crippling me...and it makes me feel broken.

The calico cat smooches against my ankles again, and more of its calming magic flows through me. I nod. *Okay, you take Lakas, I'll take the guards.* I'm just glad that we can talk to each other in our heads while we're in human form. I've never heard of anyone else being able to do it.

There's shuffling nearby, and I look up. Surrounding us are the glowing eyes of cats. They're on top of the shelves, and threaded through the books. Some are on the floor. And they're all waiting for the order to go.

What are the cats going to do? I ask Seth.

Hell if I know. Hopefully help us.

On your mark, I say.

Three, two, one, go, says Seth, then runs down the aisle, gun out in front. He lets off a couple of shots, high into the air so he doesn't accidentally hit Aurelia or Zane. We sprint to the middle of the row, where we just saw Lakas and the others.

Except they're not there.

"He knew we were coming," says Seth out loud.

"Come on, we have to find them," I say urgently.

"Meow."

The calico cat's meow is a demand. It's sitting on the other side of the small area where Lakas had just been.

"I think it wants us to follow it," says Seth.

"I think so," I say.

The cat takes off at a run, and we follow, trying to be as quiet as possible. The cat leads us deeper into the Records and Relics level, and the books start to feel even darker and more dangerous. A discordant buzzing sets me on edge, and goosebumps raise up over my skin as we run after the cat, along shelf after shelf.

We'd be lost without the cats leading the way.

All around is a sea of cats, running along the top of the shelves, on the floor next to us, and even weaving their way through the books on the shelves, following the calico cat too. They don't make a sound, and the only way I know they're with us is the swish of a tail or the flash of their glowing eyes when one of them glances down at us from their position high on the shelves.

We end up in an area of the library where the shelves are no longer metal. They're made of ancient wood, and each book has been chained to the shelf. I don't think it's to prevent stealing. I can feel dark and dirty magic emanating from the books, worming its way over my skin and making it tingle. I can't help my shudder.

Where are we? says Seth.

Dark magic book section, I'd guess.

One book catches my eye. It's made of leather, and looks kind of like alligator skin. Except... "Oh fuck. I think that book is made of dragon skin," I say out loud, horrified. My breath gets stuck in my throat.

Seth pushes me forward, away from the book, and I let him.

The calico cat is still moving, so we follow her again. Up ahead there's a glowing light, and we move faster, sensing the finale of our chase.

We get to the end of the row and peer around the edge.

It's a much larger seating area, with tables and wooden chairs and even a couple of sofas. The tables have been pushed to the sides, and in the middle of the area, Aurelia and Zane are each sitting on a wooden chair, tied up, back to back. A tall lamp is glowing nearby, spreading a dim light over the area. All around, dark magic books are buzzing with discordant energy.

Zane still looks dazed, like he doesn't know who he is, let alone where he is.

Aurelia is struggling and pushing against the ropes holding her in place.

"Did you really think you'd be able to best me, Aurelia? Poor deluded little dragon. So full of your own importance." Lakas is standing in front of them, his wings curled around his arms like a cloak. Every time he moves, they glint. The light from the lamp is creating shadows across the half of his face that's closest to me and Seth. He looks like a devil.

"You're a monster, and you need to be put down," snarls Aurelia. She doesn't seem entirely rational. She's fighting the bonds, but they're not even moving.

"It's pointless to even try to escape the ropes, my dear. They've been painted in dragon blood, and spelled to keep you secure."

I shudder. I wish Lakas would stop using dragon body parts in his magic. I don't want to know where he got the dragon blood from.

The calico cat is still walking serenely toward Lakas, keeping to the shadows, avoiding notice.

"That's far enough," snaps Lakas suddenly, and turns his whole attention to the calico cat. He points a gun directly at the cat. "I know what you're doing, and you should stop now, while you still can. I know the secret of the library, your friend Dorothy Adler told me. I know how to destroy you."

The calico cat stops, the tip of its tail twitches, and then it sits down.

What secret? I ask.

Seth shrugs. *No idea.*

"Speaking of Dorothy, do you have them yet?" asks Lakas, his voice raised.

"I do," says a voice behind Seth and I.

I jerk around. Behind us, holding a gun pointed in our direction, is Dorothy Adler, the woman who gave Lakas the dragon bone they used to force me to hurt people. I snarl at her and my shoulder twinges as if it remembers her too.

At first glance, she looks like a sweet old lady wearing tweed. Or at least she would if she didn't have such a nasty expression on her face. Overhead I hear cats hissing. They hate her too.

She glances up at the cats, and I see pure hatred on her face. Her mouth twists into a sneer, and her eyes glint in the low light. Her struggle is visible on her face. She really wants to shoot one of the cats, but manages to keep the gun trained on us.

"Throw your weapons to the ground," she says, jerking toward the floor with her gun.

I swap a loaded glance with Si. But there's no choice, she's got the upper hand. I throw my gun, like she asked. Seth does the same.

My thoughts are running in circles, and I'm trying not to panic. Si trained me to survive without a gun. He always said that guns were like a security blanket, and he was right. I have to keep reminding myself that I'm capable of fighting Lakas and his guards without it. I just need to start thinking strategically, instead of letting my fear rule my brain.

"Hands in the air. Move out into the open," says Dorothy.

I'm really starting to dislike her.

Seth and I reluctantly put our hands into the air and walk out into the open research area.

"So nice to see you again, Mei," says Lakas. "I was devastated when I realized I'd lost you."

"Fuck you," I spit out. I'm visibly shaking, despite my brave words. The metallic feathers that make up his wings clink together as he turns in our direction, and I have to fight the instinct to cringe away from him.

I stop walking, and a black and white cat winds its way around my legs. Calm fills my body, and I manage to stop trembling. I could get used to whatever calming magic they're using on me. It's definitely keeping me focused.

"So eloquent," says Lakas with an arrogant smile. "I assume I have you to blame for setting my pet dragon free?" He smiles down at Aurelia.

"I'm not your *pet*," seethes Aurelia. She barely even looks at me and Seth. Being captured by Lakas again has sent her over the edge. She's not going to be any use in this situation.

Another cat winds its way between my legs. I focus on standing still, and not tripping up over their malleable bodies. The cats might be useful...and Dorothy's hatred of them. That seems like the kind of distraction that might work. If I could just figure out a plan.

I move forward again, like I'm moving closer to Lakas, but I angle myself along the closest bookshelf, to where a large number of cats are sitting and watching the unfolding scene.

If I can get Dorothy to follow me, perhaps the cats could distract her long enough for us to take her down?

"That's far enough in that direction," snaps Lakas.

I stop. I'm not quite close enough. Dammit.

"The cats won't attack Dorothy, if that was your plan, Mei. They can't."

"What do you mean?" I ask, startled into blurting out the words.

"Dorothy is protected by a spell. As the librarian, she's connected to the cats. They can't harm her in any way."

Almost as one, all the cats in the vicinity hiss and yowl. They're not happy about it, but they're confirming his words.

"Stupid animals," snarls Dorothy. "I've always hated cats. This job has just made it worse. I'll be glad to get out of this God-forsaken place."

"We knew you'd come after me," says Lakas, ignoring Dorothy's outburst. "Both of you. You're pathetically predictable."

I barely manage to hold in my denial. I didn't want to go chasing after him. It's the last thing on my to-do list right now. But it's not exactly a good look to admit it, given my reputation for leaping before I look.

I feel my eye twitching, and I curl my hands into fists. I'm a fucking bundle of nerves right now, and it's all his fault. If only I could channel some of this anger in his direction. Instead, it's all been turned into immobilizing, roiling, gut-churning *fear*.

"What happens when they overpower the director up above?" asks Seth casually, like we're not being held at gunpoint.

Lakas snorts. "Director Holden is smarter than the dragon's father. He knew what Damien was planning, and prepared accordingly. They're not going to overpower him from his fortress, any more than you're going to overpower me down here."

"You think the library is your domain?" I ask. It seems the extreme of arrogance to think that he could be in charge in this place.

"I think the library is *Dorothy's* domain," Lakas corrects me softly. "But thankfully she has been kind enough to join forces with me."

"He'll betray you," I say to Dorothy. "You can't trust what he says."

Lakas shakes his head sadly, his sunken eyes glinting on his cadaverous face. "Dorothy knows better. We have an understanding."

"It doesn't matter. You're going to lose." My words are a stab in the dark, an attempt to rattle him and make him think we have a plan.

Which, to be clear, we don't.

"I have you under my control, Mei. You won't attack, not while I could kill your friends if you do. You are just as trapped as the cats. I control this situation, not you."

"How on earth can you control *cats*?" I say. "They're ridiculous animals. They do whatever the hell they want." I apologize in my head to the cats around me. They seem to understand and don't hiss at me.

"I know their secret," says Lakas, his expression smug. He steps to one side and for the first time I see a large cage with about ten cats in it. They're all sleek and black, with green eyes, and they're all staring intently at Lakas.

CHAPTER
FIFTY-FOUR

I take a step toward the cage. "What does that achieve? There are hundreds more of them around us outside of the cage."

"One of those cats is the Mother Cat. The queen who controls the hive," says Lakas, his voice smug. The cats all hiss again, and I can feel their bristling anger like another presence in the room.

"Hive?" I say.

"The cats have a hive mind. One knows something, they all know something," says Dorothy, like it's the worst kind of habit. I suppose it must feel like that, if she's been trying to help Lakas and the director take over the SIG. "They're all interconnected."

"You have her in there?" I peer at the cage, wishing I could figure out a way to save everyone that Lakas has captured.

"I know she's a black cat with green eyes. So with some help from Dorothy we rounded up all the black cats. Now we control the cats. They won't make a move while we have their Mother Cat."

"Are you sure it's not a calico cat?" I say, glancing at the cat who's been helping us. She seems pretty smart.

"It's the black cat that's always getting in the way, turning up just when you don't want it to, telling the others what's going on. And it's the one that always has the kittens," says Dorothy as if that clinches it. "It's definitely the hive leader."

"Enough with the information gathering. Mei, if you would please move a little closer, I'd like to make sure you don't do anything stupid."

I move forward, Seth in step beside me. His solid strength grounds me, and allows me to take a breath. How the hell are we going to get out of this mess?

I catch movement on a shelf above Lakas's head. A black cat with green eyes, that's almost twice the size of the calico cat we've been following. As our eyes meet and for a split second, I feel the sizzling pressure of immense power. I glance away, desperate not to let Lakas know what I've just seen. She has to be the Mother Cat, still out and very much not in that cage. It's a relief to know he doesn't hold *all* the cards.

Except, what if the big black cat attacks, and Lakas kills her? Will that kill all these other cats too? The thought is horrifying and I don't want to find out the answer. I take another small step toward Lakas. I need to take him on before the black cat—the Mother Cat—decides to protect her family. If a dragon is worried about attacking Lakas, then what the hell can a damn cat do? I don't want to be witness to the destruction of all the cats in the library. They're kind of growing on me.

We need to take him out, I say to Seth. *Fast. Before anything else happens.*

But how? All he has to do is put a knife to Aurelia's throat and we're done.

I'm going to shift into my dragon form.

You can't. It'll take too long. And you're vulnerable during the shift. He could kill you before you even become a dragon.

I hesitate. Seth's right. I should have changed into my dragon form about half an hour ago. But then I wouldn't have been able to wander up and down the aisles.

We need a distraction of some kind. Something that will allow us to disarm Dorothy, and untie the others. Maybe if he didn't have Aurelia and Zane as pawns, we could take him out more easily.

Something catches my eye moving along behind Lakas, out of his line of sight. It's a cat, dragging something. I hope it's not a mouse. It's crawling under the shelves, but I catch the glint of metal. It's dragging a small dagger in its mouth.

The calico cat moves away, closer to the side of the shelf where the cat is working its way to us. If I could get that knife, it would give us a chance to overpower Dorothy so we can distract Lakas and save Aurelia and Zane, and the cage full of cats.

You need to get that knife, I say to Seth. *I'll distract him.*

What knife?

Over there, under the shelf. The cat is bringing it to us.

I move another step toward Lakas. I really don't want to get close enough to smell his fetid breath. "What has Director Holden promised you, if you help? He's a liar too," I say. "He'll kick you to the curb as soon as you're no longer useful." I sense rather than see Seth moving slowly toward the cats and the knife, inch by inch. I strain to keep all my attention trained on Lakas and not give Seth away.

"Spoken like a true dragon," sneers Lakas. "Just because

that's what you would do, doesn't mean it's what others do."

"I would never betray anyone. I'm just telling you what Director Holden has done to others."

Lakas tips back his head and laughs. "I have no fear of the director. He'll do what he promised, or suffer the consequences."

"You're just one person. All he has to do is set his SIG agents on you, and you'll be toast by dinner."

I take another step in his direction.

"Stop right there," he snaps. "That's far enough. Dorothy, keep your gun trained on her. She's the one who'll cause trouble, not the other one."

Just goes to show how little he knows of Seth. I don't take my eyes off Lakas, don't let him see how wrong he is. "What's going to happen here? What are you going to do with us?"

"I'm going to put you back in your cages," says Lakas, almost licking his lips with anticipation. "I enjoyed having you both locked up. It showed me that power doesn't have to be something you're born with. It can be *earned*."

"You didn't *earn* power. You're a weak, pitiful mino-baby who needs to hurt others to feel powerful," snarls Aurelia. It snaps Lakas's attention back to her, and he growls in her direction, his eyes darkening in anger.

Seth takes the opportunity to move. He grabs the knife the cats have pushed out in front of the shelf. I turn, meaning to help Seth, but find Dorothy's gun trained on my chest.

"Shoot her," yells Lakas.

Dorothy hesitates, and I watch—like it's happening in slow motion—as her finger pulls the trigger.

Then I'm shoved roughly aside as Seth crashes into me.

355

I hear the sound of the gunshot, and a scream—maybe mine?—then bodies thudding to the ground. It all happens so fast, I don't know the order in which it happened, but I know it's bad. I'm on the ground, and next to me, Seth is bleeding. I scramble to my knees beside him, searching frantically for the source of the blood. There's a circle of blood spreading across his chest, and his eyes are starting to glaze over.

"Seth," I cry out. "No, Seth."

He gasps in pain. "Meet me. You know where." His words are choppy, his breathing ragged. "Survive this... find me."

I shake my head, tears gushing down my face. "No. You're not going to die. You're going to be fine." I grab his hand, holding on tight, forgetting where we are, eyes only for Seth.

"Focus, Mei. You have to...kill Lakas." His words are almost inaudible. I lean closer, my ear by his mouth. "You'll all die...if you don't.... You...can do...it." He closes his eyes and lets out a breath.

And doesn't take another one.

"No!" I cry. It feels like my heart has been wrenched out of my chest through my throat. I clutch his hand, pressing it to my cheek, trying to force him back to life.

Laughter cackles behind me, harsh and quick. Whipping around, I face Lakas, anger blazing out of every pore. I crawl to my feet, Seth's blood dripping from my fingers. Lakas is laughing so hard, he's almost crying.

"Shut up," I snarl, my whole body vibrating with grief and anger. "Don't you dare laugh."

"But it's all so exquisite. You got rid of Dorothy, as well as the one person who isn't a dragon and could have untied your friends. You did my job for me, and I didn't even have to raise a finger." He's pointing behind me, and I turn, confused.

Dorothy's lifeless body is splayed out beside the bookshelves, a knife sticking out of her chest. Several cats, including our calico cat, are weaving around her, sniffing her body and cautiously touching her unmoving limbs. I take a raw, painful breath. Seth must have thrown the knife just as she pulled the trigger.

"You know what's even more amusing?" says Lakas, drawing my attention back to him. "You've lost any leverage you had. Your friends will stay tied up until I decide to kill them both."

Aurelia and Zane both snarl, and I swallow over the lump that's forming in my throat. I have to do what Seth said, I have to save us all, so I can go find him again.

I have to.

I swallow, frantically thinking. "I thought you were going to keep us as pets."

Lakas stops laughing abruptly. "I've decided it's too dangerous to keep pets that bite." He lifts his hand and points a gun at my chest. "You're a menace, Mei, and I'll be congratulated for killing you." His expression is almost dreamy, like he's already imagining the kudos he's going to get, the hands he's going to shake.

I, on the other hand, can't think of anything else but Seth's body beside me, the blood pooling at his back, his blank eyes staring up.

Lakas is going to pay for this.

I clench my fists, and my body tenses, ready for action. I feel out along the spell web—it's still unfamiliar to me, but I sense Lakas, shining bright on the grid. Perhaps I can use it to confuse or fluster him somehow?

Except before I can make a move, a large black shape

leaps for Lakas's head from the bookshelf behind him. The black Mother Cat lands with all four paws wrapped around his face, claws digging deep into his pale, wrinkled skin. She's growling and hissing, the sound echoing around the library.

Lakas screams, dropping the gun as he desperately grabs at the enormous cat wrapping his head in her deadly embrace. He stumbles back as the cat bites his head, scratching deep into his face. I run forward, grabbing the gun from the floor, and then scramble back again.

"Shoot him," screeches Aurelia.

I hold the gun, my finger cocked over the trigger...except Lakas is moving too much, desperately trying to remove the cat attached to his face, while his metallic wings swoop down around him, protecting him from any bullets I could fire.

I have no choice. I drop the gun on the nearest table, and move closer. Lakas has both hands on the cat, stumbling around as he yanks at her paws. He isn't expecting the first rage-filled kick I aim at his stomach and he stumbles backward with a screech, his wings flicking out to the side to keep his balance. He makes a sound that comes from deep in his chest, and finally manages to yank the cat off his face, the skin ripping as he drags her claws free. She yowls as he throws her away from him, but she somehow manages to land on her feet.

Lakas turns his entire attention to me. Blood is dripping from deep cuts in his face and one eye is closed and puffing up. His wings expand out on either side of him, and he looks like a fallen angel, foul and beautiful at the same time.

I'm too filled with rage and agony to appreciate his glory, but there's also no room for fear. I roar, a sound torn from deep inside my dragon soul. My flames are closer to the surface than they've ever been, and everything around me lights up under my heat sensing vision. I'm not in control, but I don't care.

I know from experience that his next move will be to flick the outer feathers around to stab whatever part of my body he can reach. So I move in close, crowding him until the smell of his rank sweat fills my nostrils, and I struggle not to gag. But he can't attack with his metallic feathers at this range.

He seems confused by my move. Most people run as far and as fast from him as possible. Stepping into his personal space probably isn't a normal reaction. But I was trained by two men who believed in disruption and discombobulation as the primary tools in a fight.

So I don't give Lakas a chance to acclimatize. I slam my fist into his chin, and knee him in the balls.

He grunts but doesn't go over. I land another punch to his stomach and stomp on his toes. I keep hitting him with everything I have, my fists, my elbows, and my knees. I'm fighting tight and dirty, aiming to cause as much confusion as I can. Other than holding up his arms to protect himself, he's not fighting back, and I realize it's because he doesn't know how—not at such close range.

Aurelia is right. Lakas isn't used to fighting, not like this, at least. He uses intimidation to keep people in line, not hand-to-hand combat. If he indulges in a fight, it's only ever with someone he knows he can outmatch. He prefers his prisoners to be completely under his control before he toys with them.

The thought of how he tortured me makes my anger spike again, and I land a punch to his face, just under his mouth. I might not be full strength, but I know how to punch for maximum effect and Lakas stumbles backward, tripping over his feet. Arms wide, wings flapping, Lakas lands on his butt, looking indignant.

I'm panting, my arms held at the ready for the next round. I'm no longer afraid, just angry and determined to wreak havoc. Before he can catch his bearings, I bring up my leg and kick him in the face, stunning him. I do it again. He falls back, hands up over his face, screeching. He begins the transformation into his minokawa form, but it's sluggish. I step forward, planning to knock him out before he can turn and fly away.

Before I can make another move, I feel something pushing past me, swarming around my legs. I look down and see cats everywhere, forcing their way past me, leaping overhead from the shelves. Most of them land somewhere on Lakas, scratching and biting at his most vulnerable places—the veins that will produce the most blood. Neck, wrists, groin, wings.

Lakas manages to hit out at a few of them, knocking them back, but with so many covering his whole body, he can't do anything more than scream and defend himself blindly. More and more cats swarm over him, coating his whole body in a moving, fur-covered death machine.

The cats are also attacking the two guards in the same way, hissing and spitting as they do it. I look around for the Mother Cat, and she's sitting on top of Dorothy Adler's body, licking her paws clean of Lakas's blood. Something about the way she's sitting makes me think she's extremely satisfied with how things are going.

Behind her, one of the guards manages to escape his attackers, and runs screaming down the aisles, hissing cats chasing him.

I struggle to figure out what's happening. Lakas said the

cats were held in check by Dorothy. Perhaps her death set them free? I don't know how Lakas missed that loophole, but he probably didn't believe the cats were a force to be reckoned with. I turn back to the moving swarm of cats covering his body. He paid for that mistake.

I notice the cage filled with cats on the table behind where Lakas was just standing. I creep around behind him and open the cage, letting out the black cats trapped inside. They immediately run to join the carnage.

And then I just stand there, stunned, as the cats rip and bite and scratch at Lakas, until he's no longer moving. My arms are hanging limply by my side, and I feel like I've aged a hundred years since arriving in the library.

Eventually the cats—almost as one—stop their frantic attacks, and walk away from the two mangled bodies. I've never seen anything like it. There's blood everywhere, including all over their fur. I spot the calico cat next to a bookshelf, licking blood off her previously pristine white fur with a satisfied expression. I think I would have been more horrified by all this if Seth wasn't lying beside me, pale and still. I let out a sob, and crouch back down beside him. I touch his face, a lump forming in my throat. He took a bullet for me. He killed Dorothy. He trusted me to save the others and then come for him.

The only thing that makes this okay is that I know where to find him.

I just hope I get there in time.

CHAPTER

FIFTY-FIVE

"Can you please untie us?" asks Aurelia, her voice sounding strangled.

I look up, startled. I'd almost forgotten Aurelia and Zane were even here. I stand up reluctantly, and shuffle over to where she and Zane are still tied up. They're both looking at the mangled body of Lakas, their faces pale. I feel like a ghost as well, so I guess it's not surprising.

"I didn't get to kill him," whispers Aurelia like it's the worst thing about what just happened. She's visibly shaking, and her eyes are unnaturally wide.

"You were here," I say, my voice breaking in the middle. "You got to witness it." I try not to think of Seth's body behind me.

One of the cats comes over and smooches against my legs, and calmness floods my veins. I bend down and pick up the fluffy ginger cat, and it smooches at my chin.

"I wanted to be the one who did it," says Aurelia, her words high-pitched and verging on hysterical. I exchange a worried glance with Zane. A black cat—maybe the same one who let us into the library—pads over to her and starts winding its way around her legs. She stops trembling, and lets out a breath, immediately looking more settled.

"The ropes," growls Zane so suddenly, I jump. It's a reminder that we still have work to do. This isn't over yet, Lakas was just a cog in a wider wheel.

I find the place where the ropes were tied together on one side, and start trying to pick at them. It's like they've been bound in steel, not rope, even with my dragon strength.

"Get the knife," growls Zane. He's sounding increasingly desperate.

I look over my shoulder at the knife sticking out of Dorothy Adler's chest. "Do you think—"

"*Yes.*" Zane grits out the word.

I crouch in front of Dorothy's body, wondering if I really can pull out this knife. But then I hear Zane's ragged breathing behind me and I know I don't have a choice. If I don't at least try, it's going to send him over the edge. So I put one hand on the silver handle and pull. It's easier than I was expecting, and the knife slides out like a hot knife through butter. Blood drips from the blade, but I ignore it. There's so much blood in here right now, it's not even the worst thing in my general vicinity. I can't help glancing over at Seth's body, to the blood that's blossomed on his chest, and is pooling underneath him. His face looks so wrong—all still and empty—that I forget what I'm doing, and lose myself in the injustice of it all. A cat presses up against my legs, and it's like a switch is flicked back on. I move again, away from Seth, and back to Aurelia and Zane.

I find a spot on the rope that I can hold easily, and try to cut the ropes with the ornate knife. It doesn't work. It doesn't even make a mark.

"He said something about dragons not being able to

untie the ropes, didn't he?" I say, glaring down at the rope, then looking up at Zane. "I think that might be the case for anything I do. I'm going to have to find someone else."

Zane growls, but then stops. There are three cats smoothing themselves against his legs. He looks a little stunned, but otherwise okay. He's lost his panicked edge, and I let out a breath of relief. The cats will take care of him while I figure this out.

"Thank you," I whisper to the cats.

I look around, but there's no one else down here, except the cats, but I doubt their paws could manage the knots. They're smart, but they can't change their biology. I step away from Aurelia and Zane. "Sit tight. I'll send someone down here to get you free."

"Wait, what? Where are you going?" says Aurelia in confusion.

"I have to find Seth," I say. His absence feels like a hole in my chest. The only thing keeping me from hysterics is the knowledge that he's coming back to me. I just have to go get him in time, and make sure he's okay.

Aurelia looks down at Seth's body. Then up at me. "Are you having some kind of psychotic break?"

"It would take too long to explain," I say, backing away from them. "But I'll send someone to get you untied, I promise." Then I turn and run. I notice the large black cat running alongside me. "Thank you," I say to the cat. "We couldn't have done that without you."

The cat just glances back up at me, and then takes the lead, guiding me down the aisles, until we're out at another entrance, this one with a front desk and elevators.

The cat walks over to the elevators, stands up on its hind legs and presses the button for up. I stand beside the doors. This has been the weirdest day. I can't believe Lakas is dead.

I can't believe Seth is dead—again—and I'm not falling apart.

"Thank you," I say to the cat again.

Send the demon researcher to us.

The words are clear inside my head. I blink.

"You've been able to do that the whole time?" I ask.

I've had a few years to learn to speak human. I just don't talk to everyone.

I nod. "Fair enough." I say, although I want to yell at the contrary creature. Everything would have been so much easier if we'd known we could talk to the Mother Cat. "You mean Hazel? You want to speak to Hazel?"

Yes, Hazel. Send her to us.

"I will. But right now..."

You must save your pack. We know.

I stop suddenly. "I forgot. There were three more guards in another clearing. We need to sort them out."

The black cat's eyes flash. *We have already taken care of them.*

Another cat—a smaller black and green-eyed one— comes running from a row of books on the other side of the library. In its mouth is a strange flat circular metal disk with ancient markings engraved over it. It drops the object at my feet. The disk doesn't even make a thud on the carpet.

Take that with you. You'll need it when you get upstairs.

"What for?" I say, as I bend to pick up the disk. It hums in my hand.

It will be obvious when you get there. Now go. You must hurry or it will all be in vain.

"In vain?" I feel like I'm missing something. Like the cats have been planning this all along, and I'm just one of the tools at their disposal. Maybe that *is* the way it works around here...

The doors ding open, and I turn to stare at them. "I thought the power was out?"

I used magic from the library. It will take you where you need to go, says the black Mother Cat.

I walk inside, shell shocked. It's not every day that you talk to cats. Or find out they can use the magic of the library. I peer out the closing doors, and the cat is still sitting there, watching me with its brilliant green eyes.

The doors close, and I hesitate over which button to press. In the end, I go to the director's level. There's really no choice.

When the elevator doors ding open, I'm expecting smoke, gun shots, running people, or some kind of indication that there was a battle taking place.

Instead, all is quiet. Deathly quiet.

Have they lost already? Did the director overpower my father and Carrick and the others, and take back the building? For a moment, all my fears come rushing back, and I have a disorientating moment of confusion.

Only the thought of Seth waking up on the side of a volcano by himself, maybe hurt like he was last time, spurs me on. I focus all my energy on the moment. I know how to survive situations like this. I'm just as good at this as any SIG agent. And something about punching Lakas and getting him to the ground—where he was killed by a deadly swarm of cats—has given me back some of my confidence.

Clutching the metal disk in one hand, I crouch low, and run from the elevator to the nearest doorway. Peering inside, I make sure it's empty, then move further down the hallway, to the next door. I reach out along the spell web, trying to see what's happening. There's no one around. Where are all the people?

All of a sudden, gunfire rings out, echoing around the hallways. I wince, hoping against hope that everyone on this level is okay.

I creep along the hallway, following the sound of the gunfire. It doesn't take long to find them.

Halfway down, two large metal doors have been opened out into the hallway, and Carrick and the others are crouched down behind them. There's a small circular indentation in the center of one of the doors. I'm pretty sure it's the same size as the disk the Mother Cat gave me. I race toward them. A barrage of gunfire erupts from inside the room, and I stumble to a halt just outside the door.

Carrick is carefully reloading his gun, Freddie and the others are all taking turns at shooting into the room. My father is pacing nearby, like he knows he needs a better plan, but isn't sure what it is just yet. Maybe he's been talking to the cats as well.

"Dad," I say quickly. "I think—"

"Shush," he says quickly, gesturing with his hands. "The director has a feed out here. He can see and hear everything." He strides over to me, and wraps me in a hug. I don't know if he can tell something bad has happened just by the look on my face, but I lean into the warmth of his arms.

"Where's everyone else?" he asks.

I swallow hard, trying not to let myself get overwhelmed by the question. "Aurelia and Zane are in the library, but they're tied up with dragon spelled ropes that I can't get undone. Seth..." I swallow again. "Seth is dead. And Sharlo."

My father's sharp inhale is all the reaction I get, but I know that's a big one for him. "Is Seth...?"

I nod shakily. "He'll be resurrected in the volcano, same as last time. But I have to get to him, make sure he's okay." The urgency to go to him is rising inside me, and I struggle to stay focused on the conversation with my father.

"What happened?"

"We met Lakas. And Dorothy Adler. They were working together."

My father's expression is horrified, and it's all the confirmation I need to know that he sent us down to those levels to keep me out of danger. "Where's Lakas now? Did he escape?" He looks at me with his sharp eyes, searching my expression. "Are they still alive?"

I shake my head. "No. Both dead."

He lets out a bigger sigh this time. "Good. So we just need to finish off this part of the plan, and we're almost home free."

"What's the plan?"

"There are too many of them inside Director Holden's office." A barrage of bullets from inside the room emphasise what Dad's saying.

"If they're locked in there, don't we hold the advantage?"

"We would if we had more people, or more weapons," says Carrick, coming up from behind. "We didn't expect them to have the numbers they have."

I pull out the disk, holding it up for them both to see. "I think I have something that might help. The library cats gave it to me. It looks like it goes on the door."

Dad looks at me, and then down at the disk. "The library cats?" he says quietly. He shares a glance with Carrick then immediately starts barking orders for everyone to be ready for the next phase of the operation. He reaches out to take the disk, but I pull away.

"No, it was given to me, and I'd like to be the one to place it," I say. "I don't want to be on the front line, but I do want to do this." I look down at the disk. "Whatever it is."

He nods once, his expression grim. "Okay. Do it. I trust the library cats."

Dad and Carrick are either side of me. Freddie and the mountain supers are on the same side of the doors, the water elemental and a couple of others on the right.

I take a breath, and step up to the closest door, and stand directly in front of the circular indentation. For a moment, I hesitate, wondering if this is really going to tip things in our favor. Except what other option is there? All we can do is hope the cats know what they're doing. I put the disk into the gap in the door.

As soon as it's placed into the space, the disk starts to glow. The doors start to move inwards, inexorably moving back into a closed position.

"Dammit, it took us ages to get those doors open," growls Carrick. But he doesn't try to stop them. Like my father, he seems to know about the cats. We all watch silently, weapons at the ready, until the doors slam shut with a boom that reverberates through the hallway. I don't look at my father or Carrick. I hope I haven't just messed up their attack.

Smoke starts to waft out from the disk and I cough. The smoke is sweet and thick. It makes me feel woozy, and I sway on my feet. That's not what I was expecting.

I step back, away from the disk. If we're knocked out, it'll be an easy kill for the director and his men. Were the cats on the side of the director after all? I stagger away from the door, holding one hand to my face.

But then, just as suddenly as it appeared, the smoke is sucked under the doors and into the room beyond. There's scuffling and the sound of people whispering urgently.

Then we hear bodies hitting the ground.

Thud. Thud. Thud.

"What the hell...?" says Carrick.

"I think it's knocking them out," I whisper.

Dad shakes his head. "We can't be sure of that. It could be a trick."

Suddenly the doors open outward again. I have to skip backward a couple of steps to avoid being hit as they swing apart. I peer around the edge of the door closest to me. The scene is beyond anything I was expecting.

The walls, ceiling and floors of the large chamber are all made of metal. Soundproof, bulletproof, everything-proof. It's an impenetrable fortress, just like Lakas said.

Except because it's effectively a box that can't be breached, it's also an enclosed space where an airborne drug can affect every single person. There are more than a hundred guards squeezed into the chamber, but they're all on the floor, inert and lifeless.

Hardly breathing, I walk forward and place two fingers on the neck of the first guard I come to. "He's still alive. It must have just knocked them out." I look around at the other men. "I hope so, anyway." I don't think I'd be able to live with killing a room full of people, even if they're SIG guards loyal to Director Holden.

At the back of the room there's a sofa and chairs, filled with more sleeping men. These men are all SIG agents, rather than guards. Director Holden's body is lying prone on the larger sofa, his head leaning back over the headrest. At my father's order, Carrick and Freddie stride over to tie him and his buddies up and make sure they can't get away.

My father turns and hugs me again. "Well done," he says, his voice raw. He pushes me back, still holding onto my arms like maybe he's not quite ready to let me go. "How did you know what would happen?"

I clear my throat, trying to focus. Adrenaline has been flowing through my body, but now it's starting to recede. All I can think about is that I need to go to Seth. "The uh... um... I didn't know. I just hoped the cat knew what it was doing..."

Dad leans forward and touches my scalp. "Did you get hit on the head?" There's blood on his hand when he pulls it back.

I don't think it's my blood.

"No. I'm fine." I shake my head impatiently. I don't want to think about whose blood it might be. "What do we do now?" I ask with a nod toward the room filled with unconscious guards.

"We'll need to talk to the other SIG leaders, figure out what to do with Director Holden." He shakes his head. "I guess he's not really the director anymore, huh?"

"It's going to be very different around here," I mutter. "Maybe the SIG will finally be able to take me off their "Most Wanted" posters?"

Dad grins, and puts his arm around my shoulders. "Now where did you say Zane and Aurelia are?"

"Oh shit," I say, glancing back behind me. "You need to send someone down to the Records and Relics level to untie them. The cats will show you where they are. I have somewhere else to be."

FIFTY-SIX

The wind is freezing, like needles blowing across my scales, hitting in some places like it's frozen solid. But I don't stop. Not when I'm so close.

I've just flown over Greenland, a giant icy expanse that does nothing to earn the name, and I'm so close to Iceland I can practically taste it. But even in my dragon form, the weather is frozen and difficult. I'm chilled to the bone, my wings feel like they might snap off at any second, and when I switch to heat vision it's so cold, it's like I'm blind. I've been hit by sleet, hail, snow and angry clouds. And if you don't know what an angry cloud is... it's not something you want to know about. It hurts.

I have to make it to the Fagradalsfjall volcano before anything bad happens to Seth. Last time he was hurt, the spell web had just been destroyed because of me, and the humans could see supers...and Seth ended up hating me. I don't want the same thing to happen again. I'm going to protect him, and make sure he's okay, even if he doesn't remember me. Again. Something wrenches in my stomach. Fear that he won't remember me. That maybe this time he won't like me. That maybe everything I had will be lost after all.

Except it doesn't matter, not really. This is more about Seth than me. I'm going to make sure he's okay. I'm going to protect him. Whatever else happens is...mostly irrelevant. As much as it breaks my heart to think that.

Back at SIG headquarters my father is working with the other heads of SIG to put everything back how it should be. Having a power-hungry megalomaniac in charge has been a problem for the smooth running of the SIG for the last decade or so. Things that were supposed to be done were ignored. Monitoring, managing, recording, caretaking. All these things were put aside. Instead it had all become an effort to control the spell web. He'd been intent on overpowering first me, and then Hazel, and lately Carrick and the mountain supers. Gaining ultimate power and the rest be damned.

Suffice it to say, it'll take some time to untangle the mess.

They've already had a call with the President, who was grateful to say the least. Being a super in a world where the SIG has gone rogue wasn't easy for anyone, but it's even worse when you're the President of the United States and have to pretend it doesn't exist. She's only an eighth super, but it's a powerful eighth, and she's an honorable person, so she did her best.

But yeah. She's relieved.

I'm flying over an expanse of water, the cold temperatures making my dragon breath puff out white, before disappearing behind me. Up ahead I see a small island that becomes a larger island the closer I get.

Iceland. It's a beautiful place, strangely green and mountainous, glaciers and rivers everywhere. Rocky cliffs and crooked fjords are the first things I see up close. Except I'm not here for the sightseeing. I focus on the line of mountains and head straight for them.

The largest volcano on the island is smoking, and I dip one wing and soar into a turn. The smell of sulphur hits me, and I take a deep breath, loving the scent. It's warmer here, the first pleasantly heated moment I've had in a while.

I fly over the volcano, once and then again. I have no idea where to find Seth. I imagine it's going to be somewhere in the lava at the tip of the cone, but I'm not entirely sure. I dive down, trying not to get too close to the rumbling core of the mountain, just in case.

As I fly over the tip of the volcano again, I see it. A smidge of pale skin against the darker black and grey of the volcanic rock. My heart leaps and swoops.

Seth.

Diving down with no thought to myself or what a newly awakened Seth might think of me, I only just manage to land nearby without rolling end over end and breaking every bone in my body. Shale sprays around me as I skid along the mountain tip.

Seth doesn't even wake.

Is that bad? Normal? I don't know.

On the ground, it's harder to be graceful as a dragon, especially when I'm so desperate to get to Seth. The mountain tip is steep and not entirely stable—shale slips out beneath my dragon paws and makes me slide as I scramble over the shaky surface. The wind is blowing hard up here, and the billowing smoke is filled with sulphur. Air is definitely my element, not this harsh mountainside. But I manage to amble over to Seth without hurting him or myself. He's completely naked, his tall frame curled up into a ball and smudged with ash and pieces of rock, like he just crawled out of the lava. Maybe he did.

I sit down, pulling off the dragon bag that I packed with clothes for both of us and other essentials we'll need while he recovers. Then I curl up around him, nestling next to his body, keeping him warm and protecting him from the elements.

And then I wait.

He sleeps for another hour, maybe two. It feels like forever, and at the same time, no time at all. I don't know what I'll say to him, or even if he'll be able to hear and understand me in my dragon form anymore. Will he be scared of me? Will he know me?

The wait is excruciating.

And then he blinks. Opens his eyes. Looks around. And then up.

He squints at me, like he's trying to figure out what his reaction should be. I can't do anything but wait.

"Where am I?" he asks, his voice deep and rumbling. "What's happening?"

You're on a volcano in Iceland. You died, and then came back from the ashes. You're a phoenix. I say the words inside his head, hoping it doesn't freak him out. Will it still work even if he doesn't know me?

He blinks. Nods cautiously. "Okay. And who are you?"

I can't help it. A pair of dragon-sized tears roll out of my eyes, sizzling their way down the sides of my face. *I'm Mei.*

"And you're a dragon?"

I'm a dragon, yes. And your... friend.

Seth nods again. "I don't suppose you have any clothes?"

CHAPTER
FIFTY-SEVEN

The noise from the party is deafening.

Everyone who is anyone in the supernatural community is here. A royal dragon coronation is apparently the event of the season.

We're up on the roof top of the SIG building, which has been decorated with fairy lights and glowing Japanese lanterns for the evening's event. Tables and chairs surround an enormous dais where Aurelia is sitting with Carrick, Freddie and my father, as the leaders of three of the most important organizations in the super world.

Aurelia is resplendent in a long golden dress that brings out the natural golden highlights in her hair. Her amber eyes sparkle and there's a flush on her cheeks as she looks out over the crowd, and listens to something Carrick is saying to her.

Carrick glances into the audience as well, and I see him lock eyes with Elena. He's finally come out and admitted they're in love, and planning a marriage ceremony in the not too distant future. The responsibility of not only being the Mountain Super King, but also in charge of the spell web sits comfortably on him, like he was meant for it. His large muscled body almost looks like it's glowing.

Freddie is here representing the magical human community—people who don't shift, but are still on the supernatural spectrum with their powers. He looks as debonair as usual, his handsome face and physique perfectly set off in an expensive suit. He's like a supernatural James Bond. He's getting interested looks from more than one woman in the audience.

My father is a little less obvious. He's wearing a black suit with a crisp white shirt, and is a good head and shoulders shorter than Carrick. But he still has a presence about him, a charisma that will carry him in his new role as director of the SIG.

I honestly don't think he intended to end up in that position. I know he thought long and hard before deciding to accept the offer from the President. Turns out there's much to be done to bring the organization back to its former glory, after years of machinations by Director Holden.

Warm arms circle me from behind, and I lean back into Seth's body, a warm hum vibrating in my chest.

"Enjoying the party?" he asks softly next to my ear, his warm breath moving stray strands of my hair ever so slightly.

I shiver. In the months since I found him on the volcano, we've been learning each other again. His memories are starting to return, but there's a chance some of them will never come back. The only thing I care about is that he remembers me, and how much he loves me.

"More so, now that you're finally here," I say, turning to face him, putting my arms up to circle his neck. He's been at his desk, finishing off paper work on a particularly gnarly case.

He gives me a tight hug, his crisp SIG agent suit brushing against my bare arms, making me shiver.

"Sorry, an urgent call came in just as I was about to head up." He kisses my forehead, and then pulls back. "You look stunning, by the way," he says, gazing admiringly down at the glittering sheath dress I'm wearing.

I make a face. "This is the first time you've ever seen me in a dress, I think." I glance down at the tight confines of the dress. "And it might be the last."

"You prefer your SIG agent uniform?"

"At least it's comfortable. This feels constricting. What if something happens? What if I need to run, or leap off the building?" I still can't quite believe my father convinced me to become an SIG agent, but I have to admit he was right—I do enjoy it, and I'm really good at it.

He's widened the scope, and anyone can apply to be an agent now, not just people with only a fraction of supernatural blood in them. I think supers are a little surprised when a dragon turns up to sort out their issues, but it certainly helps us keep the peace. Carrick and Dad work closely together to ensure our lives are all much calmer these days.

Seth grins down at me. "I'm sure someone else could save the world for five minutes while we watch the coronation of Aurelia, Queen of the Dragons."

I shake my head. "I can't believe they're actually going to give her that title."

"She's earned it with all the negotiating she's done in the last few months. She's managed to bring the supernatural community together like never before."

"I think they're just afraid of her. She's unpredictable.

One of the ravens told me they kept expecting her to rise up and flame them all in their meetings. That's why they agreed to work with us."

"Whatever their reasoning, they signed the treaty. Everyone did."

"Everyone we could find," I say, unable to keep my scepticism to myself.

"They're almost one hundred percent sure that Lakas was the last minokawa, Mei. We sent teams out to search, and nothing was ever found."

I nod, resigned. "It just feels like..."

"I know. A missing thread. But there's no point worrying about it until a problem actually turns up. We have enough on our plates right now."

"Have you seen Si?" I ask, reminded of my other concern right now.

"He texted to say he was running late. He'll be arriving shortly."

I nod, looking around the room. Zane and Sergei are with Elena at a table near the front, laughing and looking relaxed for the first time in ages—if ever. It's the first time we've been celebrated as dragons in this modern era. Even Sergei is on his best behavior. Aurelia has brought dragons back into fashion with her golden scales and her royal bearing, and always managing to say the right thing with just a hint of a cheeky smile. Turns out her power was never as strong as her sister's, so she learned to rely on her persuasive skills when she was younger. It works for us. When she's not demented with rage and grief over being locked up for a few centuries, she's actually an excellent negotiator.

Let's just say that I don't get as many suspicious looks these days, even in my dragon form.

"Quit canoodling, you ridiculous love birds," says a voice behind me, and I turn quickly, searching the crowd for Hazel. She squeezes past a large mountain super loitering nearby, and appears beside me in a gorgeous red-velvet halter neck dress that I'm pretty sure Mr. Fookes magicked up for her. Her hair is pulled back off her face in a sleek updo and her make up is subtle but striking. She looks amazing.

I give her a tight hug. "You made it," I say, almost squealing in my delight at seeing her again.

She looks stronger, like our ordeal of five months ago is finally forgotten. Or at least not at the surface all the time.

"Of course I made it. I wouldn't miss Aurelia's coronation for the world." Her tone is dry, and I'm pretty sure it's because Aurelia has been talking her ear off about it, the same way she has to me.

"She's very excited. I think more about the dress than her royal status being acknowledged."

"It's definitely the dress," agrees Hazel with a grin. "Carrick told me that the mountain supers made it for her, and Mr. Fookes put the finishing touches on it, to make it sparkle as she moves."

Blade comes up behind Hazel, two champagne glasses in his hands. "Mei. Seth," he says with a brisk nod in our direction. He hands one of the glasses to Hazel, who takes a sip.

"Oh, this is so good," she says with a sigh.

"Are you allowed to drink?" I say dubiously.

"It's non-alcoholic," she says with a secret smile at Blade. She only just told me they're expecting their first child last week and I'm still shell shocked over the news. Apparently the cats in the Records and Relics Room knew before she did.

"How's the library? Did it survive without you?" I ask.

When the Mother Cat told me to send Hazel to them all those months ago, I didn't think much about it. After I returned with Seth, I dutifully let Hazel know they were asking for her. Two days after the death of Dorothy Adler, Hazel went to the Records and Relics room to visit the Mother Cat, and the title of Head Librarian was bestowed on her. I'm not sure what would have happened if she hadn't wanted the job, but luckily she agreed.

With a few caveats that they're still working out, mostly regarding her role as a Chalice, and saving the souls of supernaturals before they turn into demons.

"The cats were upset with me. They didn't feel it was part of our bargain for me to leave for stretches of time like that. I just reminded them that their insistence on the librarian living in the library full-time had turned Dorothy into a monster."

"Are they okay with the idea of you having a baby?"

"As far as they're concerned, the baby will be theirs to raise as part of the litter," says Hazel with a cheeky glance at Blade. He doesn't look amused.

"They're trying to take over," he says in a growl. "Damn cats." Luckily he's a big cat himself, so perhaps he'll be able to negotiate better terms.

"Where are the others?" I ask, looking around.

Hazel gestures toward a table in the corner. "Poppy insisted on choosing the table, mostly for ease of escape in case something happens during the ceremony. She's not entirely convinced that no one will attack or otherwise attempt to mess with the proceedings."

"But didn't you finish your protection bubble invention?" I squint out into the darkness beyond the rooftop. I can't see anything, but I know it was Hazel's plan to have a

381

magical bubble in place in time for the party, so anyone who didn't have an invitation would be stuck outside.

"Of course she did," says Blade. "But that doesn't stop Poppy from being overly dramatic."

Hazel gives him a look. "She's just trying to protect me and the baby." She glances back over her shoulder. "Luckily Mr. Fookes and Daphne are distracting her so Blade and I can actually mingle without her insisting on ID from everyone I talk to." She smiles, and it lights up her entire face. It's clear that she's happy to put up with Poppy's sudden overprotectiveness.

I give her another hug. "You're amazing."

"So are you," she whispers.

Movement catches the corner of my eye—Carrick is waving us over to their table. It looks like the official part of the night is about to begin. "I think we have to go to our seats," I say, as I pull away from Hazel. "Poppy will probably be looking for you."

"Are you with your father and Carrick?" asks Hazel.

I wince. "Yep. I'm at the diplomats table. They'll be arguing about the best way to ensure the continued peace and security of the supernatural community the whole time. Awesome."

Hazel laughs, and kisses my cheek. "You love it," she says, before taking Blade's hand and following him toward the table where Poppy is staring around at everyone suspiciously.

"Come on, let's get this over with," says Seth.

He grabs my hand and we weave our way through the crowd, waving to various people we know along the way. When I reach the table, Dad stands up and gives me a hug.

"I feel like it might be inappropriate for the Director of the SIG to hug one of his lowly agents," I say with a grin.

"Stuff the rules, no one is going to stop me from hugging my gorgeous daughter." His voice sounds a little croaky and I pull back to search his face. Does he have a cold?

Except he looks fine... just a little red around the eyes, and... wait, are those tears in his eyes?

"Dad, what's the matter? Are you okay?" I ask, worried. This is my father, who never shows emotion and likes being hidden in plain sight at all times.

"Nothing. Si just turned up, and he reminded me of something Jeff told him, years ago."

I look around, and sure enough, there's Si chatting to Carrick, his tall, lean Protector's build like a doll's next to Carrick's sturdy mountain super bulk.

"What did he say?"

"Jeff apparently always said that you were a chip off the old block. He never doubted that you were the dragon. He saw that inside you from the very first moment he met you, saw that fiery spark in your soul, and always believed in you. I never had that certainty. I tried to be a good father, but I never believed in you back then." He wipes away a tear. "I'm sorry for that. I'm sorry for not being a better father while you were growing up."

I'm holding his arms and drag him back in for another hug. "That's ancient history, Dad," I say. "We all make mistakes. I've moved on, and you should too." I say the words easily, but I suddenly realize they're actually true. I don't resent my father any more for leaving me with Jeff and Si to raise. I am who I am today because of the way I was raised. My father isn't a bad person, and he did what he thought was best at the time. That just makes him human.

"Am I interrupting a family moment," says a deep voice

next to me. I look up into Si's stony face, his eyes the only place where he's sparkling. "Or can anyone join in?"

I pull away from my father, and lean in to hug Si. "It's so good to see you! I can't believe you made it all this way for the coronation."

"I had to. I've been protecting Aurelia on her tours of the various supernatural factions, and she insisted I come to see her in her 'beautiful gown'."

I roll my eyes. "She's been telling everyone about it."

"Hey, I can hear you," says Aurelia from behind Si. She moves to one side, and looks me up and down. "You don't scrub up too badly, Mei Walker."

"You scrub up okay as well, Aurelia, Queen of the Dragons."

She does an excited little scream, and then moves forward and hugs me tightly. She's wound up tighter than a spring. "I can't believe this is happening. I never asked for them to make me queen. It's a bit silly really. I'll have fewer than ten subjects."

I shrug. "It's more for the outfit at special occasions," I say with a grin.

An officious-looking woman with a clipboard comes up behind Aurelia and taps her on the shoulder. She looks like a raven. "My queen, the ceremony is about to start," she says softly. "You're needed on the stage."

Aurelia looks behind her, and then draws me in closer. "None of this would have been possible without you, Mei. You're the reason we're all here tonight. You saved me, and I will forever be in your debt. I will never be able to do enough for you to repay that."

"You saved me, too, Aurelia. The only reason I escaped from Lakas was because of you. I'm proud to call you my friend."

Aurelia nods once.

"Now get up there on that stage and get that gorgeous crown," I say in a mock growling voice.

As Aurelia walks up to the stage, and is helped up the stairs by Carrick, I look around the room. It's hard to believe that I've gone from a lonely young girl, forever hiding and running, to being here, out in the open at the crowning of the new Queen of the Dragons.

It's a whole new world out there, and for the first time, I feel like dragons can be part of it, instead of the destroyers.

~

THANK YOU!

I'm so pleased you read Warrior Dragon!

It's the final book in the Dragon Rising series... which is such a sad feeling for me as an author. I can't believe it's finished. I've loved spending time with these characters, and I hope you have too!

But don't worry, it doesn't have to be the end! There are more books set in the same universe, and you'll recognize some of the characters from Dragon Rising.

Turn the page to find out more about the **Demon Hunter in Hiding series**, which features Hazel and Blade, and all their demon hunting friends from the Sanctus Apartments!

New series linked to the Dragon Rising series!

To look at me, you wouldn't think my whole life is a lie.

By day, I'm a nerdy researcher who likes to create inventions. At night, I hunt monsters.

Yep. I said it. Monsters. They're real, and they're out there.

Except it turns out I'm not the only one with secrets. My parents—before they were killed—were keeping something from me.

Something that's going to change my life forever.

So now I have to hunt down the truth, piece by piece, while avoiding all the people—and monsters—who want me dead.

My secrets and lies are about to catch up with me. Fast.

Hi! My name's Trudi Jaye and I've got a secret.

A secret society, that is.

Especially designed for people like you who love reading my books, the Trudi Jaye Secret Society is a place filled with magic and laughter, and most of all... free stories.

Everyone who joins the society is given access to an ancient tome full of the stories, novellas, bonus epilogues, and deleted scenes from all the different Trudi Jaye series.

Called **The Shadow Archives,** you can access it by clicking the link below, and joining the secret society...

Join my secret society... if you dare!

www.trudijayewrites.com/shadow-archives

Other Books by Trudi Jaye

Dragon Rising Series

Lost Dragon (Prequel Novella available via the Trudi Jaye Secret Society)

Hidden Dragon

Searching Dragon

Fighting Dragon

Cursed Dragon

Warrior Dragon

Demon Hunter in Hiding Series

Dreams & Demons (Prequel Novella available via the Trudi Jaye Secret Society)

Secrets & Demons

Agents & Demons

Magic & Demons

Dragons & Demons

Spells & Demons

Elemental Witch Series (With Tania Hutley)

The Trouble with Magic

The Problem with Witches

The Danger with Demons

Firecaller Series

Salt (Prequel Novella available via the Trudi Jaye Secret Society)

Subtle Knife (Prequel Novella available via the Trudi Jaye Secret Society)

Fire Mage

Royal Mage (coming soon)

Dark Carnival Series

The First Ever Wish (Prequel Novella available via the Trudi Jaye Secret Society)

If Magic Were Wishes

The Gift

Magic for Lost Souls (available via the Trudi Jaye Secret Society)

High Flyer

Hidden Magic

The Shadow Prophecy

Hi, I'm Trudi Jaye! I live in New Zealand on a beautiful rural property surrounded by horses and cows (not mine!) with my lovely husband and my cheeky tween daughter.

I've been writing since I was a kid, and for ten years I worked as a magazine writer and editor, on topics ranging from hardware and electronics to holidays, recipes and university-level research projects.

Now I write novels full time.

I enjoy yoga, although I'm not very bendy, and karate, although I don't like the idea of hitting anyone.

www.trudijayewrites.com